Dream Lake

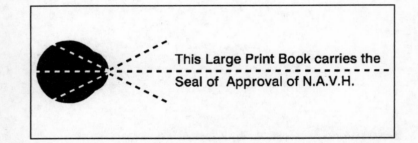

DREAM LAKE

LISA KLEYPAS

THORNDIKE PRESS
A part of Gale, Cengage Learning

Detroit • New York • San Francisco • New Haven, Conn • Waterville, Maine • London

GALE
CENGAGE Learning

Copyright © 2012 by Lisa Kleypas.
A Friday Harbor Novel Series #2.
Thorndike Press, a part of Gale, Cengage Learning.

Thorndike Press® Large Print Core.
The text of this Large Print edition is unabridged.
Other aspects of the book may vary from the original edition.
Set in 16 pt. Plantin.

LIBRARY OF CONGRESS CATALOGING-IN-PUBLICATION DATA

Kleypas, Lisa.
    Dream lake / by Lisa Kleypas. — Large print ed.
      p. cm. — (A Friday Harbor novel series; #2) (Thorndike
Press large print core)
    ISBN-13: 978-1-4104-4723-4 (hardcover)
    ISBN-10: 1-4104-4723-5 (hardcover)
    1. Hotelkeepers—Fiction. 2. San Juan Island (Wash.)—Fiction. 3. Large
type books. I. Title.
PS3561.L456D74 2012
813'.547mdash;dc23   2012022958

Published in 2012 by arrangement with St. Martin's Press, LLC.

Printed in the United States of America
1 2 3 4 5 6 7 16 15 14 13 12

To Tonia Boze,

For inspiring me with your strength, optimism, and compassion, and for giving me the courage to try things I never thought I could do.

Love always,
L.K.

ONE

The ghost had tried many times to leave the house, but it was impossible. Whenever he approached the front threshold or leaned through a window, he disappeared, the sum of him dispersing like mist in the air. He worried that one day he might not be able to take shape again. He wondered if being trapped here was a punishment for the past he couldn't remember . . . and if so, how long would it last?

The Victorian house stood at the end of Rainshadow Road, overlooking the circular shoreline of False Bay like a wallflower waiting alone at a dance. Its painted clapboard siding had been corroded from sea air, its interior ruined by a succession of careless tenants. Original hardwood floors had been covered with shag carpeting, rooms divided by thin chipboard walls, wood trim coated with a dozen layers of cheap paint.

From the windows, the ghost had watched

shorebirds: sandpipers, yellowlegs, plovers, whimbrels, plucking at the abundant food in tidepools on straw-colored mornings. At night he stared at stars and comets and the cloud-hazed moon, and sometimes he saw northern lights dance across the horizon.

The ghost wasn't certain how long he had been at the house. Without a heartbeat to measure the passing seconds, time was timeless. He had found himself there one day with no name, no physical appearance, and no certainty of who he was. He didn't know how he'd died, or where, or why. But a few memories danced at the edge of his awareness. He felt sure that he had lived on San Juan Island for part of his life. He thought he might have been a boatman or a fisherman. When he looked out at False Bay, he remembered things about the water beyond it . . . the channels between the San Juan Islands, the narrow straits around Vancouver. He knew the splintered shape of Puget Sound, the way its dragon-teeth inlets cut across Olympia.

The ghost also knew many songs, all the verses and lyrics, even the preludes. When the silence was too much to stand, he sang to himself as he moved through the empty rooms.

He craved interaction with any kind of

creature. He went unnoticed even by the insects that scuttled across the floor. He hungered to know anything about anyone, to remember people he had once known. But those memories had been locked away until the mysterious day when his fate would finally be revealed.

One morning, visitors came to the house.

Electrified, the ghost watched a car approach, its wheels ironing flat channels in the heavy growth of weeds along the unpaved drive. The car stopped and two people emerged, a young man with dark hair, and an older woman dressed in jeans and flat shoes and a pink jacket.

". . . couldn't believe it was left to me," she was saying. "My cousin bought it back in the seventies with the idea of fixing it up and selling it, but he never got around to it. The value of this property is in the land — you'd have to tear the house down, no question."

"Have you gotten an estimate?" the man asked.

"On the lot?"

"No, on restoring the house."

"Heavens, no. There's structural damage — *everything* would have to be redone."

He stared at the house with open fascination. "I'd like to have a look inside."

A frown pulled the woman's forehead into crinkles, like a lettuce leaf. "Oh, Sam, I'm sure it's not safe."

"I'll be careful."

"I wouldn't want to be responsible for you getting hurt. You could fall right through the floor, or a beam could drop on you. And there's no telling what kind of vermin —"

"Nothing's going to happen." His tone was coaxing. "Give me five minutes. I just want a quick look."

"I really shouldn't let you do this."

Sam flashed her a grin of renegade charm. "But you will. Because you just can't resist me."

She tried to look stern, but a reluctant smile emerged.

I used to be like that, the ghost thought with surprise. Elusive memories flickered, of past flirtations and long-ago evenings spent on front porches. He had known how to charm women young and old, how to make them laugh. He had kissed girls with sweet tea on their breaths, their necks and shoulders dusted with scented powder.

The big-framed young man bounded to the front porch and shouldered the door open when it stuck. As he stepped into the entrance hall, he turned wary, as if he expected something to jump out at him.

10

Each footstep broke through a scurf of dust, raising ashy plumes from the floor and making him sneeze.

Such a human sound. The ghost had forgotten about sneezing.

Sam's gaze moved across the dilapidated walls. His eyes were blue even in the shadows, whisks of laugh lines at the outer corners. He wasn't handsome, but he was good-looking, his features strong and blunt-edged. He'd been out in the sun a lot, the tan going several layers deep. Looking at him, the ghost could almost remember the feel of sunlight, the hot slight weight of it on his skin.

The woman had crept to the front doorway, her hair surrounding her head in a silver nimbus as she peered inside the entranceway. She gripped one side of the door frame as if it were a support pole on a lurching subway train. "It's so dark in there. I really don't think —"

"I'm going to need more than five minutes," Sam said, pulling a small flashlight from his key chain and clicking it on. "You might want to go out for coffee and come back in, say . . . half an hour?"

"And leave you here all alone?"

"I won't cause any damage."

The woman snorted. "I'm not worried

about the *house,* Sam."

"I've got my cell phone," he said, patting his back pocket. "I'll call if there's a problem." The smile lines at the corners of his eyes deepened. "You can come rescue me."

She let out a dramatic sigh. "What exactly do you think you're going to find in this wreckage?"

His gaze had already left hers, his attention recaptured by his surroundings. "A home, maybe."

"This place was a home once," she said. "But I can't imagine it could ever be one again."

The ghost was relieved when the woman left.

Directing the flashlight in slow arcs, Sam began to explore in earnest, while the ghost followed him room by room. Dust lay over fireplace mantels and broken furniture like gauze veils.

Seeing a torn section of shag carpeting, Sam lowered to his heels, pulled at the rug, and shone the light on the hardwood flooring beneath. "Mahogany?" he murmured, examining the dark, gluey surface. "Oak?"

Black walnut, the ghost thought, looking over his shoulder. Another discovery . . . he knew about flooring, how to sand and hand-scrape and tack-clean it, how to apply stain

12

with a wad of wool fleece.

They went to the kitchen, with its alcove designed for a cast-iron stove, a few scales of broken tiles still clinging to the walls. Sam directed the beam of light to the high trussed ceilings, the cabinets hanging askew. He focused on an abandoned bird's nest, let his gaze fall to the ancient splatters of droppings beneath, and shook his head. "I must be crazy," he muttered.

Sam left the kitchen and went to the staircase, pausing to rub his thumb over the balustrade. A streak of scarred wood shone ruddily through the grime. Placing his feet carefully to avoid perforations of rot on the steps, he made his way to the second floor. At intervals he made a face and let out a puff of breath, as if at some noxious odor. "She's right," he said ruefully, as he reached the second-floor landing. "This place is nothing but a teardown."

That sent a jolt of worry through the ghost. What would happen to him if someone razed the house to the ground? It might extinguish him for good. The ghost couldn't conceive that he had been trapped alone here only to be snuffed out for no apparent reason. He circled around Sam, studying him, wanting to communicate but afraid it might send the man screaming from the place.

Sam walked right through him and stopped at the window overlooking the front drive. Ancient grime coated the glass, blunting the daylight in soft gloom. A sigh escaped him. "You've been waiting a long time, haven't you?" Sam asked quietly.

The question startled the ghost. But as Sam continued, the ghost realized he was talking to the house. "I bet you were something to see, a hundred years ago. It would be a shame not to give you a chance. But damn, you're going to take some serious cash. And it's going to take just about everything I've got to get the vineyard going. Hell, I don't know . . ."

As the ghost accompanied Sam through the dusty rooms, he sensed the man's growing attachment to the ramshackle house, his desire to make it whole and beautiful again. Only an idealist or a fool, Sam figured aloud, would take on such a project. The ghost agreed.

Eventually Sam heard the woman's car horn, and he went outside. The ghost tried to accompany him, but he felt the same dizzying, shattering, flying-apart sensation that always happened when he tried to leave. He went to watch from a broken window as

Sam opened the car's passenger door.

Pausing for a last glance, Sam contemplated the house slumped in the meadow, its rickety lines softened by swaths of arrowgrass and clustered pickleweed, and the bristled tangles of chairmaker's rush. The flat blue of False Bay retreated in the distance, shimmers of tidepools beginning at the edge of fecund brown silt.

Sam gave a short nod, as if he'd decided on his course.

And the ghost made yet another discovery . . . he was capable of hope.

Before Sam made an offer for the property, he brought someone else to look at it — a man who looked to be about his age, thirty or thereabouts. Maybe a little younger. His gaze was cold with a cynicism that should have taken lifetimes to acquire.

They had to be brothers — they had the same heavy brown-black hair and wide mouth, the same strapping build. But whereas Sam's eyes were tropical blue, his brother's were the color of glacial ice. His face was expressionless, except for the bitter set of his mouth within deeply carved brackets. And in contrast to Sam's roughcast good looks, the other man possessed a near prodigal handsomeness, his features blade-

15

like and perfect. This was a man who liked to dress well and live well, who shelled out for expensive haircuts and foreign-made shoes.

The incongruous note in all that impeccable grooming was the fact that the man's hands were work-roughened and capable. The ghost had seen hands like that before . . . maybe his own? . . . He looked down at his invisible self, wishing for a shape, a form. A voice. Why was he here with these two men, able only to observe, never to speak or interact? What was he supposed to learn?

In fewer than ten minutes, the ghost perceived that Alex, as Sam called him, knew a hell of a lot about construction. He started by circling the exterior, noting cracks in the substrate, gaps in the trim, the sagging front porch with its decaying joists and beams. Once inside, Alex went to the exact places that the ghost would have shown him to demonstrate the house's condition — uneven sections of flooring, doors that wouldn't close properly, blooms of mold where faulty plumbing had leaked.

"The inspector said the structural damage was repairable," Sam commented.

"Who'd you get to do it?" Alex lowered to his haunches to examine the collapsed parlor fireplace, the fractures in the exposed chimney.

"Ben Rawley." Sam looked defensive as he saw Alex's expression. "Yeah, I know he's a little old —"

"He's a fossil."

"— but he still knows his stuff. And he did it for free, as a favor."

"I wouldn't take his word. You need to get an engineer in here for a realistic assessment." Alex had a distinctive way of talking, every syllable as measured and flat as unspooling contractor's tape, with the hint of a rasp. "The only plus in this whole scenario is that with a structurally unsound house on the property, it's worth *less* than vacant land. So you might be able to argue for a break on the price, considering the expense of demolition and haul-off."

The ghost was wrenched with anxiety. Destroying the house might be the end of him. It might send him to oblivion.

"I'm not going to tear it down," Sam said. "I'm going to save it."

"Good luck."

"I know." Sam dragged a hand through his hair with a scrubbing motion, causing the short, dark strands to stand up in wild dishevelment. He let out a heavy sigh. "The land is perfect for the vineyard — I know I

17

should settle for that and count myself lucky. But this house . . . there's something I just . . ." He shook his head, looking baffled and concerned and determined all at once.

Both the ghost and Sam expected Alex to mock him. Instead, Alex stood and wandered across the parlor, going to a boarded-up window. He pulled at the ancient sheet of plywood. It came off easily, offering only a creak of protest. Light flooded the room along with a rush of clean air, knee-high eddies of dust motes glinting in the newly admitted sun.

"I have a thing about lost causes, too." A faint, wry note edged Alex's voice. "Not to mention Victorian houses."

"Really?"

"Of course. High-maintenance, energy-inefficient design, toxic materials . . . what's not to love?"

Sam smiled. "So if you were me, how would you go about this?"

"I'd run as fast as possible in the opposite direction. But since you're obviously going to buy the place . . . don't waste your time with a regulated lender. You're going to need a hard-money guy. And the rates are going to suck."

"Do you know anyone?"

"I might. Before we start talking about that, though, you need to face reality. You're looking at 250K of repairs, minimum. And don't expect to lean on me for free supplies and labor — I'm going ahead with the Dream Lake site, so I'll be as busy as a cat burying shit."

"Believe me, Al, I never expect to lean on you for anything." Sam's voice turned arid. "I know better."

Tension laced the air, a mingling of affection and hostility that could only have come from a troubled family history. The ghost was perplexed by an unfamiliar sensation, a raw chill that would have caused him to shiver if he'd had a human form. It was a depth of despair that even the ghost, in his bleak solitude, had never experienced — and it radiated from Alex Nolan.

The ghost moved away instinctively, but there was no escaping the feeling. "Is that how it feels to be you?" he asked, pitying the man. He was startled to see Alex cast a glance over his shoulder in his direction. "Can you hear me?" the ghost continued in wonder, circling around him. "Did you just hear my voice?"

Alex made no response, only gave a brief shake of his head as if to clear away a daydream. "I'll send an engineer over here," he eventually said. "No charge. You're going to be spending more than enough on this place. I don't think you have a clue about what you're getting into."

Almost two years passed before the ghost saw Alex Nolan again. During that time, Sam had become the lens through which the ghost could view the outside world. Although he still couldn't leave the house, there were visitors: Sam's friends, his vineyard crew, subcontractors who worked on the electricity and plumbing.

Sam's older brother, Mark, appeared about once a month to help with smaller weekend projects. One day they leveled a section of flooring, and another they sand-blasted and reglazed an antique clawfoot bathtub. All the while, they talked and exchanged good-natured insults. The ghost enjoyed those visits immensely.

More and more, he was recalling things about his former life, gathering memories like scattered beads from the floor. He came to remember that he liked big band jazz and comic book heroes and airplanes. He had liked listening to radio shows: Jack Benny, George and Gracie, Edgar Bergen. He hadn't yet recovered enough of his past to have any sense of the whole, but he thought he would in time. Like those paintings in which points of color, when viewed from a distance, would form a complete image.

Mark Nolan was easygoing and dependable, the kind of man the ghost would have liked to have as a friend. Since he owned a coffee-roasting business, Mark always brought bags of whole beans and began each visit by brewing coffee — he drank it by the potful. As Mark meticulously ground the beans and measured them out, the ghost remembered coffee, its bittersweet, earthy scent, the way a spoonful of cane sugar and a dollop of cream turned it into liquid velvet.

The ghost gleaned from the Nolans' conversations that their parents had both been alcoholics. The scars they had left on their children — three sons and a daughter named Victoria — were invisible but bone-deep. Now, even though their parents were long gone, the Nolans had little to do with each other. They were survivors of a family that no one wanted to remember.

It was ironic that Alex, with his bulletproof reserve, was the only one of the four who had married so far. He and his wife, Darcy, lived near Roche Harbor. The only sister, Victoria, was a single mother, living in Seattle with her young daughter. As for Sam

21

and Mark, they were determined to stay bachelors. Sam was unequivocal in his opinion that no woman would ever be worth the risk of marriage. Whenever he sensed that a relationship was becoming too close, he ended it and never looked back.

After Sam confided to Mark about his latest breakup, with a woman who had wanted to move their relationship to the next level, Mark asked, "What's the next level?"

"I don't know. I broke up with her before I found out." The two were sitting on the porch, applying paint remover to a row of salvaged antique balusters that would eventually be used for the front railings. "I'm a one-level guy," Sam continued. "Sex, dinners out, the occasional impersonal gift, and no talking about the future, ever. It's a relief now that it's over. She's great, but I couldn't handle all the emotion salad."

"What's emotion salad?" Mark asked, amused.

"You know that thing women do. The happy-crying thing. Or the sad-mad thing. I don't get how anyone can have more than one feeling at a time. It's like trying to simultaneously watch TVs on different channels."

"I've seen you have more than one feeling at a time."

"When?"

"At Alex's wedding ceremony. When he and Darcy were exchanging vows. You were smiling, but your eyes got kind of watery."

"Oh. At that point I was thinking about the scene in *One Flew Over the Cuckoo's Nest,* when Jack Nicholson got the lobotomy and his friends smothered him with a pillow out of mercy."

"Most of the time I wouldn't mind smothering Alex with a pillow," Mark said.

Sam grinned, but sobered quickly as he continued. "Someone should put him out of his misery. That Darcy is a piece of work. Remember at the rehearsal dinner when she referred to Alex as her first husband?"

"He is her first husband."

"Yeah, but calling him the 'first' implies there's going to be a second. Husbands are like cars to Darcy — she's going to keep trading up. And what I don't get is that Alex knew it, but he went ahead and married her anyway. I mean, if you *have* to get married, at least pick someone nice."

"She's not that bad."

"Then why do I get the feeling when I talk to her that I'd be better off viewing her reflection from a mirrored shield?"

"Darcy's not my type," Mark said, "but a lot of guys would say she's hot."

"Not a good reason to marry someone."

"In your opinion, Sam, is there *any* good reason to get married?"

Sam shook his head. "I'd rather have a painful accident with a power tool."

"Having seen the way you handle a compound miter saw," Mark said, "I'd say that's entirely likely."

A few days later, Alex came to the house at Rainshadow Road for an unexpected visit. Since the ghost had last seen him, Alex had lost weight he hadn't needed to lose. His cheekbones were as prominent as guard rails, the ice-colored eyes undermounted by deep shadows.

"Darcy wants to separate," Alex said without preamble, as Sam welcomed him inside.

Sam shot him a glance of concern. "Why?"

"I don't know."

"She wouldn't tell you?"

"I didn't ask."

Sam's eyes widened. "Jesus, Al. Don't you want to know why your wife's leaving you?"

"Not particularly."

Sam's tone turned gently arid. "Do you think that might be part of the problem? Like maybe she needs a husband who's interested in her feelings?"

"One of the reasons I liked Darcy in the first place is that she and I never had to have those conversations." Alex wandered into the parlor, his hands shoved deep in his pockets. He surveyed the door casing that Sam had been hammering into place. "You're going to split the wood. You need to predrill the holes."

Sam surveyed him for a moment. "Want to lend a hand?"

"Sure." Alex went to the worktable in the center of the room and picked up a cordless power drill. He checked the settings and the tightness of the chuck, and pressed the trigger experimentally. A metallic squeal tore through the air.

"Bearings are dried up," Sam said apologetically. "I've been meaning to repack them with grease, but I haven't had time."

"It's better to replace them completely. I'll take care of it later. Meantime, I've got a good drill in the car. Four-pole motor, four hundred fifty pounds of torque."

"Sweet."

In the way of men, they dealt with the issue of Alex's broken marriage by not talking about it at all, instead working together in companionable silence. Alex installed the door casings with precision and care, measuring and marking, hand-chiseling a thin edge of the plastered wall to ensure that the vertical casing was perfectly plumb.

The ghost loved good carpentry, the way it made sense of everything. Edges were neatly joined and finished, imperfections were sanded and painted, everything was level. He watched Alex's work approvingly. Although Sam had acquitted himself well as an amateur, there had been plenty of mistakes and do-overs. Alex knew what he was doing, and it showed.

"Hot damn," Sam said in admiration as he saw how Alex had hand-cut plinth blocks to use as decorative bases for the casing. "Well, you're going to have to do the other door in here. Because there's no way in hell I could make it look like that."

"No problem."

Sam went outside to confer with his vineyard crew, who were busy pruning and shaping the young vines in preparation for the coming flush of growth in April. Alex continued to work in the parlor. The ghost wandered around the room, singing during the lulls between hammering and sawing.

As Alex filled nail holes with wood putty and caulked around the casing edges, he began a soft, nearly inaudible humming. Gradually a melody emerged, and the realization hit like a thunderbolt: Alex was humming along to his song.

On some level, Alex could sense his presence.

Watching him intently, the ghost continued to sing.

Alex set aside the caulk gun, remaining in a kneeling position. He braced his hands on his thighs, humming absently.

The ghost broke off the song and drew closer. "Alex," he said cautiously. When there was no response, he said in a burst of impatient hope and eagerness, "Alex, *I'm here.*"

Alex blinked like a man who'd just come from a dark room into blinding daylight. He looked directly at the ghost, his eyes dilating into black circles rimmed with ice.

"You can see me?" the ghost asked in astonishment.

Scrambling backward, Alex landed on his rump. In the same momentum, he grabbed the closest tool at hand, a hammer. Drawing it back as if he meant to hurl it at the ghost, he growled, "Who the hell are you?"

Two

The stranger looked down at Alex with an expression of surprise that seemed to rival his own.

"Who are you?" Alex demanded again.

"I don't know," the man said slowly, staring at him without blinking.

He was about to say something else, but then he *flickered* . . . like an image on a cable channel with bad reception . . . and disappeared.

The room was quiet. A bee landed on one of the screen windows and walked in repeated circles.

Alex set aside the hammer and let out a taut breath. He used his thumb and forefinger to pinch the corners of his eyes, which were sore and puffy from the previous night's drinking. Hallucination, he thought. Garbage from a wasted brain.

The craving for alcohol was so intense that he briefly considered going to the kitchen and rummaging through the pantry. But Sam rarely kept hard liquor; there would be nothing but wine.

And it wasn't yet noon. He never let himself drink before noon.

"Hey." Sam's voice came from the doorway. He gave Alex an odd look. "You need something? I thought I heard you."

Alex's temples were throbbing painfully in time to his heartbeat. He felt vaguely nauseous. "The guys on your vineyard crew . . . does one of them have short black hair, wears a retro flight jacket?"

"Brian's got dark hair, but it's kind of longish. And I've never seen him in that kind of jacket. Why?"

Alex rose to his feet and went to the window. He flicked at the mesh with a snap of his fingers, jolting the bee off the screen. It flew away with a sullen buzz.

"You okay?" he heard Sam ask.

"I'm fine."

"Because if there's anything you want to talk about —"

"No."

"Okay," Sam said with a careful blandness that annoyed him. Darcy often used the same tone. Like she had to walk on eggshells around him.

"I'm going to finish up here and take off

in a few minutes." Alex went to the work-table and began to measure a length of trim.

"Right." But Sam lingered at the doorway. "Al . . . you been drinking lately?"

"Not enough," he said with vicious sincerity.

"Do you think —"

"Don't give me shit right now, Sam."

"Got it."

Sam stared at him without bothering to disguise his concern. Alex knew he shouldn't have been chafed by the signs that his brother actually cared for him. But any sign of warmth or affection had always caused him to react differently from most people — it provoked an instinct to turn away, close up. People could either deal with it or get lost. It was who he was.

He kept his face expressionless and his mouth shut. For all that he and Sam were brothers, they knew practically nothing about each other. Alex preferred to keep it that way.

After Sam left the parlor, the ghost turned his attention back to Alex.

At the moment when he and Alex had been able to look at each other, the ghost had been shocked by an awareness, a connection opening, so that he could perceive everything the man felt . . . bitterness, a desire for numb oblivion, a seething lonely need that nothing could satisfy. It wasn't that the ghost felt all these things himself . . . it was more an ability to browse through them, like titles in a bookstore. Nonetheless, the intensity of the perception had startled the ghost, and he had backed off.

And apparently he had become invisible again.

Dark-haired, wearing a flight jacket . . . *Is that what I look like?* What else had Alex seen? *Do I look like someone you know? Maybe someone in an old photograph? Help me find out who I am.*

Thrumming with frustration, the ghost watched Alex install the rest of the door casings. Each strike of the hammer reverberated through the air. He hovered near Alex, the connection between them fragile but palpable. He had a sense of the slow corrosion of a soul that had never stood a chance, never enough caring, never enough hope or kindness or any of the things necessary to build a decent foundation for a human being. Although Alex was certainly not someone he would have chosen to be attached to — put more plainly, to *haunt* — the ghost didn't see an alternative.

Alex organized Sam's tools and picked up

the power drill that needed to be repaired. As he left, the ghost accompanied him to the threshold of the front door.

Alex walked out to the front porch. The ghost hesitated. On impulse, he moved forward. This time there was no disintegration, no fragmenting of consciousness. Instead, he was able to follow Alex.

Outside.

Walking to the drive where his car was parked, Alex felt an itchy, stinging impatience that had no identifiable source. His senses were uncomfortably heightened, the sun too strong for his eyes. The smell of cut grass and violets was nauseatingly sweet in his nostrils. Letting his gaze drop to the path in front of him, he noticed something odd. By some trick of the light, two shadows extended from his feet. Motionless, he watched the two silhouettes on the path. Was it possible that one of them had moved slightly while the other stayed still?

He forced himself to walk. Giving in to delusions, talking aloud to apparitions, was going to land his ass in lockdown rehab. Darcy would have seized on any excuse to shut him away. So would his brothers, for that matter.

Deliberately he turned his mind to the

prospect of going home. Darcy had left to go apartment-hunting in Seattle, which meant the house was empty. He would be able to get loaded in peace. It sounded good. So good, in fact, that the car keys shook a little in his hand.

As Alex got into the BMW, the shadow slipped inside with him, and settled across the passenger seat like an empty pillowcase. And together they went home.

THREE

This was the irony: after years of longing to escape the house at Rainshadow Road, a few weeks spent in Alex Nolan's company had been enough to make the ghost want to go back. But there was only so far that the ghost could drift before he encountered the parameters of yet another invisible prison. He was stuck with Alex. He could occupy another room, or glide several yards away, but that was it. When Alex left his ultramodern house at Roche Harbor, the ghost found himself being towed along like a balloon on a string . . . or more aptly, a helpless fish caught on the end of a line.

Women often approached him, drawn by the dark glamour of his good looks. But Alex was a distant and unsentimental man. His sexual needs were occasionally satisfied by Darcy, who was now living in Seattle but sometimes came to visit even though they had agreed to a legal separation as a prelude to divorce. They had conversations in which words nicked like razor blades, followed by sex, the one form of connection they had ever managed. Darcy had told Alex that all the things that made him a terrible husband were also the things that made him great in bed. Whenever they started going at it, the ghost prudently removed himself to the farthest room in the house and tried to ignore Darcy's ecstatic screams.

Darcy was greyhound-lean and beautiful, her hair black and straight. She radiated a diamond-hard confidence that would have made it impossible to pity her, except that the ghost had noticed signs of vulnerability . . . feathery sleepless lines around her mouth and eyes, brittle fractures in her laughter, all caused from the knowledge that her marriage had become less than the sum of its parts.

The ghost accompanied Alex around his on-spec residential development in Roche Harbor — something the ghost had heard him refer to as a pocket neighborhood. A grouping of well-tended houses, arranged around a green lawn commons and a cluster of mailboxes. People didn't necessarily like Alex, but they respected his work. He was known for running a tight operation and finishing a project on schedule, even in a place where subcontractors tended to work on island time.

It was obvious to everyone on the island, however, that Alex drank too much and slept too little, and eventually it was all going to catch up with him. Before long his health would deteriorate just like his marriage. The ghost fervently hoped that he wasn't going to have to watch the erosion of this man's life.

Trapped in Alex's sphere, the ghost was impatient to visit Rainshadow Road, where big changes were happening to the rest of the Nolan family.

A few days after the ghost had left Rainshadow Road, the phone had rung at an unusually late hour. The ghost, who never slept, had gone into Alex's room as the bedside lamp was turned on.

Rubbing his eyes, Alex had said in a sleep-thickened tone, "Sam. What is it?"

As Alex listened, his expression hadn't changed, but his face went skull-white. He had to swallow twice before asking, "Are they sure?"

As the conversation had continued, the ghost gathered that the Nolans' sister, Victoria, had been involved in a car wreck. She had died on the scene. Since Victoria had never married, nor had she ever revealed the father of her child, her six-year-old daughter, Holly, had just been orphaned.

Alex had hung up the phone and stared blindly at the bare wall, his eyes dry.

The ghost had felt a mixture of shock and sorrow, even though he had never met Victoria. She had died young — the cruelty of that, the unfairness of such loss, struck a chord of compassion. The ghost had wished for the luxury of tears, the relief of them. But as a soul without a body, he didn't have the ability to cry.

Apparently neither did Alex Nolan.

Out of the tragedy of Victoria Nolan's death, something remarkable had happened: Mark was granted custody of her daughter, Holly, and the two of them moved in with Sam. The three of them were now living together at the house on Rainshadow Road.

Prior to Holly's arrival, the atmosphere in the house had resembled nothing so much as a football locker room. Laundry was done only when all other clothing options had been exhausted. Mealtimes were scattershot and hasty, and there was rarely anything in the fridge beyond half-empty bottles of condiments, a six-pack of beer, and the occasional leftover pizza in a grease-spotted box. Doctor's visits were something that happened only if you needed stitches or a defibrillator.

But somehow Mark and Sam had managed to make room in their lives for a six-year-old girl, and that act of compassion had changed everything. The junk-food-loving bachelors had started to read nutrition labels as if it were a matter of life or death. If they couldn't pronounce an ingredient, it was banned. They learned new words like "rickets" and "rotavirus," and the names of at least a half-dozen Disney princesses, and how to use peanut butter to remove a wad of gum from long hair.

Before long, the brothers discovered that when you opened your heart to a child, it also left you open to other people. In the year after Holly had first come to live with them, Mark fell in love with a red-haired young widow named Maggie, and all his long-held prejudices against the idea of marriage collapsed like wet toast. After the August wedding, Mark, Maggie, and Holly would live in their own house on the island, and Sam would have Rainshadow Road back to himself again.

It seemed only a matter of time before Sam, too, would decide to take a chance on love. His fears were understandable — the Nolan parents, Jessica and Alan, had demonstrated to their four children that the seeds of failure and destruction were sown at the beginning of every relationship. If you loved someone, sooner or later you would reap a bitter harvest.

After a nasty legal battle, Alex and Darcy had agreed on terms that would allow their legal separation to be converted to a divorce. She cleaned him out financially, winning most of their assets, including the house. At the same time, the economy took a downturn and the real estate market plummeted. The bank had foreclosed on Alex's Roche Harbor development, and put his plans for developing property at Dream Lake on indefinite hold.

Alex drank until he had acquired the young-old look of someone burning out too early. He wanted numbness. Oblivion. The ghost could only surmise that as the youngest child of alcoholic parents, Alex's survival had depended on detachment. If you never felt anything or trusted anyone, if you denied every need or weakness, you couldn't be hurt.

Every day eroded Alex a little more. How much longer, the ghost wondered, before there was nothing left of him?

With his Roche Harbor project gone and

his other development at a standstill, Alex spent most of his time working on the vineyard house at Rainshadow Road. Some of the rooms had been so damaged by water leaks that he'd had to gut and rebuild them, starting with new subflooring. Recently he'd installed silk-screened reproduction wallpaper in the living room, after hand-cutting the panels and border from a master roll. Although Sam had tried to pay Alex for the work, Alex had refused. He knew his brothers didn't understand why he'd taken such an interest in the place. Mostly it was to assuage his conscience — or what was left of it — over not having volunteered in the past to help raise Holly. There was no way in hell Alex was going to have anything to do with taking care of a child. However, making the house safe and comfortable while she lived there was something he could do, something he was good at.

It was midsummer, and the crew at Rainshadow vineyard was busy tending the vines and pruning leaves to expose more of the ripening grapes to the sun. Alex arrived in the morning to do some work in the attic. Before heading upstairs, he went to the kitchen with Sam for some coffee.

Scents of the previous evening's meal — chicken soup flavored with sage — lingered in the air, subtle but comforting. An antique glass bell jar covered a pale wedge of cheese on the counter.

"Al, why don't you let me fry you a couple of eggs before you start working?" Sam asked.

Alex shook his head. "Not hungry. Just want coffee."

"Okay. By the way . . . I'd appreciate it if you'd keep the noise level down today. I've got a friend staying here, and she needs rest."

Alex scowled. "Tell her to take her hangover somewhere else. I have some trim work to do."

"Do it later," Sam said. "And it's not a hangover. She was in an accident yesterday."

Before Alex could reply, the doorbell rang. It was one of those old-fashioned rotary mechanical bells that worked with a turnkey.

"That's probably one of her friends," Sam muttered. "Try not to be a dick, Alex."

In a couple of minutes, Sam brought a woman into the kitchen.

Alex understood in a flash that he was in trouble, a kind he'd never experienced before. One look into a pair of round blue eyes, and it was a knockout punch, an instant defeat. Alarm and desire froze him where he stood. "Zoë Hoffman, this is my brother Alex," he heard Sam say.

He couldn't look away, could only respond with a surly nod when she said hello. He made no move to shake hands — it would have been a mistake to touch her.

She was like something out of a vintage magazine ad, a blond pinup girl with hair bouncing in every-which-way curls. Nature had been spendthrift with her, bestowing more beauty than one person was meant to have. But she stood with the vaguely apologetic posture of a woman who'd always received the wrong kind of attention from men.

Zoë turned to Sam. "Do you happen to have a cake plate I could set these muffins on?" Her voice was soft and breathy, as if she'd woken up late after a long night of sex.

"It's in one of those cabinets near the Sub-Zero. Alex, would you help her out while I go upstairs to get Lucy?" Sam glanced at Zoë. "I'll find out if she wants to sit in the living room down here, or visit with you upstairs."

"Of course," Zoë said, and went to the cabinets.

The prospect of being alone with Zoë Hoffman for any length of time, even a minute, gave Alex the alarmed impetus to move. He reached the doorway just as Sam did. He lowered his voice just a shade. "I've got stuff to do. I don't have time to spend chitchatting with Betty Boop."

Zoë's shoulders stiffened.

"Al," Sam muttered, "just help her find the damn plate."

After Sam left, Alex approached Zoë, who was straining to reach a glass-domed plate on a cabinet shelf. Standing behind her, he caught the fragrance of female skin dusted with talcum. A wave of longing came over him, raw and visceral. Wordlessly he got the plate for her and set it on the granite countertop, his movements dreamlike in their discipline. If he relinquished his control for even one second, he was afraid of what he might do or say.

Zoë began to transfer the muffins from the pan. Alex stayed beside her, his hand braced on the counter.

"You can go now," Zoë murmured, her chin angled down. "You don't have to stay and chitchat."

Hearing the reproachful echo of his earlier words, Alex knew that he should apologize. The thought evaporated as he watched the way her fingers shaped around each muffin, gently lifting them from the pan.

Saliva spiked in his mouth.

"What did you put in those?" he managed to ask.

"Blueberries," Zoë said. "Help yourself, if you'd like one."

Alex shook his head and reached blindly for his coffee. His hand wasn't quite steady.

Without looking at him, Zoë took a muffin and set it on Alex's empty saucer.

Alex was still and silent, while Zoë continued to arrange the plate. Before he could stop himself, he reached for the offering, his fingers denting the soft shape in its unbleached parchment liner, and he left the kitchen.

Alone on the front porch, Alex looked down at the muffin. It wasn't the kind of food that usually appealed to him. Baked goods usually reminded him of drywall.

The first bite was light and tender, a crisp dissolve of streusel on pillowy cake. His tongue encountered the tang of orange zest and the dark liquid zing of blueberries. Each bite brought a new shock of sweetness. He forced himself to eat with restraint, to keep from wolfing it down. How long had it been since he'd really tasted anything?

After he'd finished, he sat quietly, letting the sensation of warmth take hold. He let himself think about the woman in the kitchen. The blue eyes, the light curls, the face as feminine and rosy as an old-fashioned valentine. He resented his reaction to her, the contact high that lingered unforgivably.

She wasn't the kind of woman he had ever wanted before. No one took a woman like that seriously.

Zoë.

You couldn't say her name without making the shape of a kiss.

His thoughts collected into a fantasy, one in which he went back to Zoë, apologized for his rudeness, charmed her into going out with him. They would go on a picnic on his property near Dream Lake . . . he would spread a blanket beneath the cover of wild apple trees, and the sun would filter through the leaves and dapple her skin with brightness.

He imagined himself undressing her slowly, revealing extravagant pale curves. He would nuzzle into the arc of her neck and tease shivers from her body . . . taste her blushes with his tongue . . .

Alex cleared the thoughts with a rough shake of his head. He took a deep breath, and another.

He didn't go back to the kitchen. He slunk upstairs to work in the attic, taking care to avoid another encounter with Zoë Hoffman. Every step was an act of will. He wouldn't allow himself weakness of any kind.

Although he hadn't been able to read Alex's thoughts as he had sat on the front porch, the ghost had felt them. Finally, here was something Alex wanted, so much that his desire had thickened the air like boiling sugar. It was the most human reaction the ghost had ever seen from him.

But at the moment Alex decided to walk away from Zoë precisely *because* he wanted her, the ghost had had enough. He'd been patient for an eternity, and it wasn't doing anyone any good. Not himself, not Alex. They were getting nowhere. For all that the ghost *didn't* know about his predicament — about how and why he'd become the constant companion of an alcoholic engaged in slow suicide — it was pretty obvious that he'd been stuck with Alex for a reason.

If he were ever going to be free of the bastard, he would have to do something.

The attic was a large space with slanted ceilings and dormer windows. At some point knee walls had been installed in an attempt to make the space livable, but they were poorly built and drafty. Alex was in the process of fitting rigid foam insulation over the floor joists and caulking it.

Sitting on his heels, he began to replace the silicone cartridge of the caulking gun. He went still as he saw something on the wall . . . the dark hieroglyph of a shadow rising from a heap of debris and broken furniture.

The shadow had been with him for weeks now. Alex had tried to ignore it, tried to drink it away, sleep it away, but there was no escaping its watchful presence. Lately he'd begun to feel a sense of animosity coming from it. Which meant he was either crazy . . . or haunted.

As the shadow drew closer to him, Alex felt the cold sear of adrenaline in every vein. Purely by instinct, he moved to defend himself. In an explosive motion, he threw the caulk gun. The tube split, white silicone splattering over the wall.

The dark shape promptly disappeared.

Alex still felt the hostile presence nearby, waiting and watching. "I know you're there," he said, his voice guttural. "Tell me what you want." A mist of sweat broke out on his face and collected beneath his T-shirt. His heartbeat was fast and ragged. "And then tell me how to fucking get rid of you."

More silence.

Dust motes salted the air in a slow descent.

The shadow returned. Quietly it assumed the form of a man. A vivid, three-dimensional being.

"I've been wondering the same thing," the stranger said. "How to get rid of you, that is."

Alex felt his color drain. He moved to sit fully on the floor, to keep from toppling over like a domino.

My God, I have gone crazy.

He didn't realize he'd said it aloud until the stranger replied.

"No, you haven't. I'm real."

The man was tall, lanky, dressed in a scuffed leather flight jacket and khakis. His black hair was military-short and parted on the side, his features decisively formed, the eyes dark and assessing. He looked like some supporting character in a John Wayne movie, the rebellious hotshot who had to learn to follow orders.

"Hiya," the stranger said casually.

Slowly Alex got to his feet, his balance shoddy. He had never been a spiritual man. He trusted only in concrete things, the evidence of his senses. Everything on earth was made of elements that had originally been produced from exploding stars, which meant humans were basically sapient stardust.

And when you died, you disappeared forever.

So . . . what was this?

A delusion of some kind. Moving forward, Alex reached out in a tentative gesture. His hand went right through the man's chest. For a moment all Alex could see was his own wrist embedded in the region of a stranger's solar plexus.

"Jesus!" Alex snatched his hand back quickly and examined it, palm up, palm down.

"You can't hurt me," the man said in a matter-of-fact voice. "You've walked right through me about a hundred times before."

Experimentally Alex extended his hand and swiped it through the man's arm and shoulder. "What are you?" he managed to ask. "An angel? A ghost?"

"Do you see any wings?" the man asked sardonically.

"No."

"Didn't think so. I'd say I was a ghost."

"Why are you here? Why have you been following me?"

The dark gaze met his directly. "I don't know."

"You don't have some kind of message for

49

me? Some unfinished business I'm supposed to help you with?"

"Nope."

Alex wanted very much to believe it was a dream. But it felt too real, the stale warmth of the attic air, the dusty lemon-colored light coming through the windows, the caulking chemicals that always smelled a little like bananas. "What about leaving me the hell alone?" he eventually asked. "Is that an option?"

The ghost gave him a glance of purest exasperation. "I wish I could," he said feelingly. "It's not my idea of entertainment to watch you get sloppy on a fifth of Jack Daniel's every night. I've been bored out of my gourd for months. I can't believe I'm saying this, but I was happier living here with Sam."

"You . . ." Alex made his way to a nearby stack of flooring planks and sat heavily. He kept his gaze on the ghost. "Does Sam —"

"No. So far, you're the only one who can see or hear me."

"Why?" Alex demanded in outrage. "Why me?"

"Wasn't my choice. I was trapped here for a long time. Even after Sam bought the house, I couldn't leave, no matter how I tried. Then back in April, I found out I could follow you outside, so I did. At first it was a relief. I was glad to get out of here, even if it meant I had to tag along with you. The problem is, I'm shackled to you. I go where you go."

"There's got to be a way to get rid of you," Alex muttered, rubbing his face with his hands. "Therapy. Medication. An exorcist. A lobotomy."

"What I think —" the ghost began, but stopped at the sound of footsteps coming up the stairs.

"Al?" came Sam's muffled voice. His head appeared as he approached the top of the staircase, his scowl arrowing through the cream-painted spindles of the balustrade. Pausing at the top, he rested a hand over the top newel and asked curtly, "What's going on?"

Glancing from his brother to the ghost, who was standing only a few feet away from him, Alex was tempted to ask Sam if he could see him. The ghost was human and solid and so absolutely *there* that it seemed impossible for Sam not to notice him.

"I wouldn't," the ghost said, as if reading his thoughts. "Because Sam can't see me, and you're going to look crazy. And I'm not all that keen on the idea of sharing a padded cell with you."

51

Alex dragged his gaze back to Sam. "Nothing," he said in answer to Sam's question. "Why are you up here?"

"Because I heard you." An irritable pause. "I asked you to keep it down, remember? My friend Lucy is resting. What were you shouting for?"

"I was talking on the cell phone."

"Well, you should probably go. Lucy needs peace and quiet."

"I'm right in the middle of fixing your damn attic for free, Sam. Why don't you ask your girlfriend to postpone her nap until I'm finished?"

Sam gave him a hard warning glance. "She was sideswiped by a car while she was riding her bike yesterday. Even you should have a little sympathy for that. So while an injured woman is trying to heal up in my house —"

"Okay. Keep your shirt on. I'm leaving." Alex's eyes narrowed as he stared at his brother. Sam never lost his cool over a woman. And come to think of it, Sam never allowed any of his girlfriends to stay at the house overnight. Something unusual was going on with this one.

"Yes, he's falling for her," the ghost said from behind him.

Alex glanced over his shoulder. Before he thought about it, he asked, "Can you read my mind?"

"What?" Sam asked in bewilderment.

Alex felt his face heat with embarrassment. "Nothing."

"The answer is no," Sam said. "And I'm glad. Because it would probably scare me to know your thoughts."

Alex turned to start packing away his tools. "You have no idea," he said gruffly.

Sam began to descend the stairs, then paused. "One more thing — why is there caulk splattered all over the wall?"

"It's a new application method," Alex snapped.

"Right," Sam said with a little snort, and left.

Alex turned to the ghost, who was watching him with a smart-alecky smile.

"I can't read your mind," the ghost said. "But it's not tough to guess what you're thinking. Most of the time." His gaze turned speculative. "There are times you don't make any sense. Like today, the way you acted around that cute little blonde —"

"That's my business."

"Yes, but I have to watch anyway, and it's irritating. You liked her. Why not talk to her? What's the matter with —"

"I liked it better when you were invisible," Alex said, turning away from him. "Conversation's over."

"What if I want to keep talking?"

"Talk your head off. I'm going home, where I'm going to drink until you disappear."

The ghost shrugged and leaned nonchalantly against the wall. "Maybe you'll be the one to disappear," he said, and watched as Alex went to scrape off the caulk splatters.

FOUR

"Justine," Zoë said severely, "don't eat any more of those. I need at least two hundred for the cupcake tower."

"I'm helping you," Justine said around a mouthful of pink velvet cake with Chambord buttercream frosting. With her dark hair pulled into a high ponytail, and her slim form clad in a T-shirt, jeans, and sneakers, she looked more like a college student than a successful businesswoman.

Zoë glanced quizzically into her cousin's brown-velvet eyes. "How exactly are you helping?"

"Quality control. I need to make sure these are good enough for the wedding guests."

Smiling wryly, Zoë rolled out a yard of ice-pink fondant with an aluminum rolling pin. "Well, are they?"

"They're terrible. Can I have one more? Please?"

"No."

"Okay, then I'll tell you the truth. Given the choice between eating this cupcake or watching Ryan Gosling and Jon Hamm wrestle each other for the privilege of having sex with me, I'd choose the cupcake."

"I'm not even finished yet," Zoë said. "I'm going to cover each one with fondant and top it with pink roses, green leaves, and clear sugar dewdrops."

"You are the baking genius of our time."

"I know," Zoë said cheerfully. When the fondant was an eighth of an inch thick, she began to cover each cupcake in a smooth, perfect casing, trimming the excess with a spatula. She had worked at Justine's bed-and-breakfast for more than two years, handling the cooking, grocery shopping, and food orders, while Justine managed the business side. Immediately after the failure of Zoë's brief but disastrous marriage, Justine had approached her with an offer that included a share in the business. Zoë, still shell-shocked by the dissolution of her marriage, had hesitated at first.

"Say yes and you'll never regret it," Justine had said. "It's everything you like to do, all the cooking and menu planning, without all the business stuff."

Zoë had regarded her uncertainly. "After

what I've just been through, I'm afraid to make a commitment to *anything.* Even an offer that sounds as nice as this one."

"But you'd be making a commitment to *me,*" Justine had enthused. "Your favorite cousin."

Zoë forbore to reply that technically they were only second cousins, and furthermore, out of all the Hoffman cousins Justine hadn't necessarily been her favorite. In early childhood Zoë had been intimidated by Justine, who was a year younger but infinitely more daring and confident.

One of the things Zoë and Justine had in common was that they were only children being raised by single parents . . . Justine was being raised by her mother, and Zoë by a father.

"Did your daddy run away from home?" Zoë had asked Justine.

"No, silly. Parents don't run away from home."

"My mother did," Zoë had said, glad to finally have some bit of superior knowledge over her cousin. "I don't even remember her. My daddy says she left one day after dropping me off and never came back."

"Maybe she got lost," Justine had suggested.

"No, she left a good-bye letter. Where did

your daddy go?"

"He's in heaven. He's an angel and he has big silver wings."

"My grandmother doesn't think angels have wings."

"Of course they do," Justine had said impatiently. "They *have* to have wings or they'd fall out of the sky. There's no floor up there."

In third grade, Zoë's father had moved her to Everett, where her grandmother lived, and it had been years before she had seen Justine again. They had stayed loosely in touch by exchanging birthday and holiday cards. After graduating from culinary school, Zoë had married Chris Kelly, her best friend since high school. At that point, Zoë was busy with her job as a sous-chef at a Seattle restaurant, and Justine was trying to make a success of Artist's Point, and they had completely lost touch. Approximately a year later, however, when Zoë and Chris had filed for divorce, Justine had been an unexpected source of comfort and support, and had offered her the chance to make a new start in Friday Harbor. Tempting as the prospect was, Zoë had been more than a little apprehensive about the idea of working with her headstrong cousin. Thankfully the arrangement had worked out beautifully, playing to each of their strengths. They argued rarely, and when they did, Zoë's quiet stubbornness usually won out over Justine's bluster.

Artist's Point was just a two-minute walk away from downtown Friday Harbor and the ferry landing. A previous owner had converted an old hilltop mansion into a bed-and-breakfast, but the business had never taken off, and eventually Justine had been able to buy it at a rock-bottom price. She had renamed and redecorated the inn. Each of the twelve rooms in the main house had been turned into a homage to a different artist. The Van Gogh room was painted with rich colors and furnished in a French provincial style with a sunflower bedspread. The Jackson Pollock room was decorated with modern furniture and prints of drip paintings, and over the bathtub, Justine had hung a clear plastic shower curtain that she had covered with splatters of acrylic paint.

Justine and Zoë shared a two-bedroom cottage in the back of the main building, a scant seven hundred square feet with one bathroom and a cupboard kitchen. The arrangement worked because they spent most of their time in the bed-and-breakfast, with its spacious kitchen and common areas. To Justine's chagrin, Zoë had brought a companion to live with them: her white Persian, Byron. Admittedly, Byron was a little spoiled, but he was an affectionate and well-mannered cat. His only flaw was that he didn't like men — they seemed to make him nervous. Zoë understood exactly how he felt.

In the past couple of years, the bed-and-breakfast had become popular with both tourists and locals. Justine and Zoë held monthly events including cooking classes and a "silent reading" party, and they also hosted weddings and receptions. The event that would take place tomorrow, on Saturday, was what Justine privately referred to as the wedding-from-hell, in which the bride's mother was an even bigger bridezilla than the bride. "And then you've got a whole collection of bridesmaidzillas, and the groomzilla and the dadzilla," Justine had complained. "This is the most dysfunctional wedding I've ever seen. I think they should invite a psychiatrist to the rehearsal dinner tonight, and turn it into one big group therapy session."

"They'll probably end up throwing the cupcakes at each other at the reception," Zoë said.

"My God, I hope so. I'll just stand in the middle with my mouth open." Justine licked the last of the raspberry buttercream off her fingertip. "You saw Lucy this morning, right? How's she doing?"

"Pretty well, all things considered. She's on pain medication, but Sam seems to be taking good care of her."

"I knew he would," Justine said in satisfaction.

Their friend Lucy, a local glass artist, had been staying at Artist's Point for the past couple of months, ever since her boyfriend had broken up with her. After Lucy's bike accident yesterday, Justine had realized that in light of Lucy's leg injuries, and the wedding taking place that weekend, there was no way she and Zoë could take care of her. So she had talked Sam into letting Lucy recuperate at his house.

"I told Sam how much we appreciate it," Zoë said. "It's incredibly nice of him, especially since he and Lucy have only gone out a couple of times before."

"They're already in love with each other. They just don't know it yet."

Zoë paused in the middle of trimming the fondant from another cupcake. "How do you know it, if they don't?"

"You should have seen Sam at the clinic yesterday. He was so worried about her, and she was so glad to see him, and for a few seconds, you could tell they were the only two people in the world."

As Zoë worked with the cupcakes, she pondered what she remembered of Sam Nolan from elementary school. He had been geeky and skinny. No one would have guessed that he would have grown up into the robust, good-looking man she had seen earlier that morning. Sam had a roguish quality tempered with quiet strength . . . he might be exactly what Lucy needed, after her boyfriend had treated her so terribly.

"So now that Lucy's got someone," Justine said, "we have to find a guy for you."

"No we don't," Zoë countered evenly. "I keep telling you, I'm not ready to start that kind of relationship."

"You've been divorced for a couple of years now, and you've been a nun. Sex is good for you, you know. Relieves stress and improves cardiovascular health, and lowers the risk of prostate cancer, and besides —"

"I don't have a prostate. Men have prostates."

"I know, but think of how much you'll be helping some poor guy out."

A reluctant grin spread across Zoë's face.

There could have been no better antidote for Zoë's shyness and occasional self-doubt than Justine. She was like a cool, brisk

September breeze that blew away the sultry heat of summer and made you think of apples and wool sweaters and planting tulip bulbs.

Before rolling out the next sheet of fondant, Zoë poured some coffee, and told Justine about a phone call she'd received that morning. The previous day, her grandmother Emma, who was living in a senior apartment at an independent living community in Everett, had been taken to a nearby medical facility. She had complained of numbness in her left arm and leg, and had seemed disoriented. It had turned out to be a ministroke, but the doctor believed that with physical therapy, she would regain most of the use of the affected limbs.

"But when they did a brain scan," Zoë said, "they found that she'd already had a few ministrokes. It's a condition called — oh, right now I can't remember the word — but it basically boils down to a diagnosis of vascular dementia."

"Oh, Zoë." Justine reached out to put her hand on Zoë's back, and kept it there for a moment. "I'm sorry. Is that a kind of Alzheimer's?"

"No, but it's similar. With vascular dementia, it's a stair-step process . . . one of these ministrokes takes away some of your ability, and then you plateau for a while, and then you have another episode —" Zoë broke off and blinked against tears. "Eventually she'll have a major stroke, and that's that."

Justine frowned. "When Emma came out to visit over Christmas, she was in great shape. Didn't seem at all her age. What is she now, like, ninety?"

"Eighty-seven."

"Do you need to go to her?" Justine asked quietly.

"Yes, I thought tomorrow after the wedding reception —"

"No, I mean right now."

"I have a hundred and seventy-two cupcakes to cover with fondant."

"Show me how to do it. I'll take over."

"You've got too many other things to do." Zoë felt a rush of fond gratitude for her cousin, who could always be counted on in times of trouble. "And this isn't as easy as it looks. You'd end up with a pile of big pink balls."

"Then I'd put 'em on the groom's table," Justine said.

Zoë chuckled, and sighed. "No, I'll stay until after the wedding, and then I'll go to Everett." She hesitated before continuing. "I'll be meeting with Emma's elder-care consultant — she helps with insurance care facilities, and knows all the options for what my grandmother will need. So I'll be gone for a couple of days."

"Whatever it takes." Justine slid her a concerned glance. "You think your dad will come up from Arizona to see her?"

"I hope not." Although Zoë hadn't seen her father in years, they exchanged occasional brief e-mails and phone calls. And from what she knew of his relationship with Emma, it had been even more distant than that. "It would be really awkward. And he wouldn't be any help at all."

"Poor Zoë. I wonder if you've ever had a man in your life you could really count on."

"Right now," Zoë said, "a man is the last thing I need. Except for Byron, of course. Which reminds me . . . would you look after him while I'm gone?"

"Oh, jeez." Justine scowled. "I'll give him food and water, but that's it. No treats, no combing, no baths or special outfits, and no cat massage."

"It's just a light rubdown at the end of the day," Zoë protested. "It helps him relax."

"Zoë, I don't even do that for my boyfriend. Your big fat fluffball of a cat is going to have to deal with his hypertension on his own."

FIVE

Darcy's tense voice filtered through the answering machine as she left a message at nine in the morning. Hearing it, Alex dragged himself out of bed, pulled on a pair of sweatpants, and staggered toward the kitchen.

". . . don't know if you've found another place to live yet," Darcy was saying, "but time's running out. I'm going to start showing the house next week, so you have to be out of there. I want it sold by Labor Day. If you want to buy it from me, you can talk to the Realtor —"

"I'm not going to pay for the same damn house twice," Alex muttered, ignoring the rest of the message. He pressed a button on the automatic espresso machine and waited for it to heat. Through slitted eyes, he saw the ghost standing at the kitchen island with his forearms braced on the granite counter.

The ghost met his gaze. "Hiya."

Alex didn't reply.

Last night, he had turned on the TV and sat on the sofa with a bottle of Jack Daniel's. The ghost had sat in a nearby chair, asking sardonically, "You're not bothering with a glass now?"

Lifting the bottle to his lips, Alex had ignored him and kept his gaze glued on the television screen. The ghost had fallen obligingly silent . . . but he had stayed until Alex had passed out.

And this morning he was still here.

Seeing that the espresso machine was ready, Alex pressed the start button. The metallic squall of the automatic grinder filled the air. The machine clicked, clacked, pumped out a double shot of espresso, and emptied the grounds into a hidden plastic receptacle. Alex drank the coffee straight and set the empty cup in the sink.

He turned to face the ghost with grim resignation. It was pointless to keep ignoring him, since he didn't appear to be going anywhere. And in that weird secondhand way, Alex could sense the ghost's mood, the weary patience of a man who'd been alone for a long time. Although Alex had never been accused of having an excess of compassion, he couldn't help feeling a flicker of sympathy.

67

"You got a name?" Alex eventually asked.

"I did, once. But I can't remember it."

"What's with the flight jacket?"

"I don't know," the ghost said. "Are there squadron patches on it? A name tag?"

Alex shook his head. "Looks like an old A-2 with cargo pockets. You can't see it?"

"I'm visible only to you."

"Lucky me." Alex viewed him dourly. "Listen . . . I can't function with you following me everywhere. So you need to get invisible again."

"I don't want to be invisible. I want to be free."

"That makes two of us."

"Maybe if you help me figure out who I am . . . who I *was* . . . it might show me a way out. I might be able to break away from you then."

" 'Maybe' and 'might' aren't good enough."

"It's all I've got." The ghost began to pace in abbreviated strides. "Sometimes I remember things. Bits and pieces of my life." He stopped at the kitchen window to stare out at the beckoning blue flat of Roche Harbor. "When I first . . . had awareness, I guess you'd say . . . I was in the house at Rainshadow. I think in my former life I had a connection to that place. There's still a lot of old junk there, especially in the attic. It may be worth poking around for clues."

"Why haven't you done it?"

"Because I'd need a physical form to do that," the ghost said, every word drenched in sarcasm. "I can't open a door or move a piece of furniture. I don't have 'powers.' " He accompanied the word with a mystical waggling of all his fingers. "All I can do is watch while other people screw up their lives." He paused. "You're going to have to clear all that crap out of the attic eventually, anyway."

"Sam will. It's his house."

"I can't talk to Sam. And he might miss something important. I need you to do it."

"I'm not your cleaning lady." Alex left the kitchen, and the ghost followed. "There's enough stuff in that attic to fill a ten-yard Dumpster," Alex continued. "It would take me days to go through it alone. Maybe weeks."

"But you will?" the ghost asked eagerly.

"I'll think about it. In the meantime, I'm going to take a shower." Alex stopped and shot him a glare. "And while I'm in there, stay the hell away from me."

"Relax," the ghost said acidly. "Not interested."

■ ■ ■ ■

By the beginning of third grade, Zoë's father had told her that he was getting a new job in Arizona, and she would have to live with her grandmother until he sent for her. "I just have to get the house ready for you," he had said. "What color do you want me to paint your room?"

"Blue," Zoë had said eagerly. "Like a robin's egg. Oh, and Daddy, can I get a kitten when I move to our new house?"

"Sure you can. As long as you take care of it."

"Oh, I will! Thank you, Daddy." For months Zoë had painted pictures of what her new room and her new kitten would look like, and had told all her friends she was going to live in Arizona.

Her father had never sent for her. He had come to visit a few times, and he had answered the phone when Zoë had called, but whenever she had dared to ask if the house was ready for her, if he had made a space in his life for her, he was evasive and irritable. She would have to be patient. There were things he had to take care of first.

At the beginning of her freshman year at

high school, Zoë had called to tell her father about her classes and her new teachers. An unfamiliar voice had answered her father's phone — a woman — who had sounded very kind and said that she would love to meet Zoë someday. They had talked for a few minutes. And that was how Zoë had learned that her father had asked a woman with a twelve year-old daughter to live with him. They were his new family. Zoë was nothing but an unwanted reminder of a failed marriage and a woman who had left him.

She had gone to her grandmother, of course, and had cried bitter tears while laying her head on Emma's lap. "Why doesn't he want me?" she had sobbed. "Am I too much trouble?"

"It has nothing to do with you." Emma's voice had been quiet and kind, her face drawn with regret as she bent over Zoë's tousled blond head. "You are the best, smartest, most wonderful girl in the world. Any man would be proud to have you as his daughter."

"Then wh-why isn't he?"

"He's broken, sweetheart, in a way that I'm afraid no one can fix. Your mother . . . well, the way she left him . . . it did something to him. He's been different ever since.

If you'd known him before then, you would hardly recognize him. He was always in good spirits. Everything went his way. But he fell in love with your mother so deeply . . . it was like falling down a well with no way to climb back up. And every time he looks at you, he can't help thinking about her."

Zoë had listened carefully, trying to understand the secrets tucked between the spare revelations. She needed to know why she had been abandoned, in turn, by both of her parents. There had been only one answer: the fault lay somewhere in herself.

Her grandmother's gentle hand had smoothed her hair as she continued. "No one would blame you, Zoë, for being angry and bitter. But you need to focus on what's good in your life, and think about all the people who love you. Don't let this turn you all sour inside."

"I won't, Upsie," Zoë whispered. It was the name she'd called her grandmother ever since she could remember. "But I feel . . . I feel as if I don't belong anywhere."

"You belong with me."

Looking up into Emma's face, softly etched with lines carved by all the humor, sadness, and reflection of seven well-lived decades, Zoë had reflected that her grandmother had always been the one constant in her life.

Afterward they had gone into the kitchen to cook.

Three times a week Emma had made extra meals to carry to some of the older neighbors on their street. Zoë, who loved to work in the kitchen, had always helped her.

Zoë had chopped bars of dark chocolate until the cutting board was piled with fragrant coarse powder. While the oven preheated, she melted the chocolate, along with two sticks of butter, in a glass bowl set on a saucepan of simmering water. After separating eight eggs, she whipped the deep gold yolks and a tablespoon of vanilla extract into the melted chocolate, and added brown sugar.

Tenderly she had folded shiny ribbons of chocolate emulsion into a cloud of beaten egg whites. The rich froth of batter was spooned into individual teacups, which were set into a water bath and placed in the oven. When the cakes were done, Zoë had let them chill before topping each with a heavy swirl of whipped cream.

Emma came to survey the rows of flour-less chocolate cakes baked in teacups. A smile spread across her face. "Charming," she said. "And they smell divine."

"Try one," Zoë said, handing her a spoon.

Emma had taken a bite, and her reaction was all Zoë could have hoped for. She made a little hum of pleasure, closing her eyes to better concentrate on the rich flavor. But when her grandmother opened her eyes, Zoë was astonished to see the glint of tears in them. "What is it, Upsie?"

Emma had smiled. "This tastes like love you've had to let go . . . but the sweetness is still there."

Zoë walked slowly along the clinic corridors, her rubber-soled flats squeaking on the shiny green floor. Her mind was occupied with the information the doctor had just given her — facts about cerebrovascular disease, infarction caused by stroke, the possibility that Emma might have "mixed dementia," a combination of both vascular dementia and Alzheimer's. Too soon to tell.

Amid all the questions and problems, one thing was clear: Emma's independence was gone. She would no longer be able to stay at the assisted living community. From now on she would need more care and supervision than they could provide. Daily physical therapy for her left arm and leg. Safety improvements to her living environment, such as shower rails and a toilet seat riser with side handles. And as her condition inevitably deteriorated, she would need even more help.

Zoë felt overwhelmed. There were no relatives she could turn to: her father had declined to involve himself in her life long ago. And although the Hoffman family was large, the ties between them were negligible. "Solitary as skunks," Justine had once quipped about their unsociable relatives, and it was true, there was some kind of relentless introverted streak in the Hoffmans that had always made the prospect of family gatherings impossible.

None of that mattered, however. Emma had taken in Zoë when no one else, including her own father, had wanted her. There was no question in Zoë's mind that she would take care of Emma now.

The clinic room was quiet except for the muted beeps of the heart monitor and the occasional distant murmur of a nurse's voice farther along the corridor. Cautiously Zoë went to the window and opened the louvered blinds a fraction, letting in a spill of soft gray light.

Standing at the bedside, Zoë looked down at Emma's waxen complexion, the petal-like fragility of her closed eyelids, the silvery-gold tangle of her hair. Zoë wanted to brush and pin it back for her.

Emma's eyes flickered open. Her dry lips twitched with a smile as she focused on Zoë.

Zoë's throat went tight as she leaned over to kiss her grandmother. "Hi, Upsie." Emma usually smelled like L'Heure Bleue, the powdery, flowery perfume she had worn for decades. Now her scent was jarringly medicinal, antiseptic.

Sitting at the bedside, Zoë reached through the metal rails to hold Emma's hand, the fingers a cool, loose bundle in hers. At the sight of her grandmother's grimace, Zoë let go instantly, remembering too late that her left arm had been affected by the stroke. "I'm sorry. Your arm hurts?"

"Yes." Emma crossed her right arm over her midriff, and Zoë reached to hold that hand instead, careful not to dislodge the IV needle. Emma's blue eyes were weary but warm as she stared at Zoë. "Have you talked to the doctors?"

Zoë nodded.

Never one to shirk an issue, Emma informed her flatly, "They said I'm losing my marbles."

Zoë gave her a skeptical glance. "I'm sure that's not how they put it."

"It's what they meant." Their hands tightened. "I've had a long life," she said after a moment. "I don't mind going. But this isn't how I wanted it to happen."

"How, then?"

Her grandmother pondered the question. "I would like to slip away in my sleep. In the middle of a dream."

Zoë pressed her palm over the cool back of her grandmother's hand, covering the pattern of veins that crisscrossed like delicate lace. "What kind of dream?"

"I suppose . . . I'd be dancing in the arms of a handsome man . . . and my favorite song would be playing."

"Who is the man?" Zoë asked. "Grandpa Gus?" He'd been Emma's first and only husband, who had died from lung cancer years before Zoë had been born.

A glimmer of Emma's familiar humor appeared. "The man, and the song, are none of your business."

After Zoë left the clinic, she went to the office of Colette Lin, Emma's elder-care consultant. Colette was kind but matter-of-fact as she gave Zoë a pile of pamphlets, forms, and books to help her understand the scope of the situation Emma was facing.

"Vascular dementia isn't nearly as predictable as Alzheimer's," Colette said. "It can come on suddenly or gradually, and it affects different parts of the body at random. And there's always the possibility that a major stroke will happen without warning." Colette paused before adding, "If Emma has mixed dementia, as the doctors suspect, you're going to see some repetitive cycles of behavior . . . she'll forget things that happened recently, but she'll retain memories from long ago. Those are located deeper in the brain — they're more protected."

"What does she need right now?" Zoë asked. "What is the best situation for her?"

"She'll need a stable and healthy living environment. Good quality food, exercise, rest, a consistent schedule for her medication. Unfortunately she won't be able to go back to her apartment — they can't provide the level of care she needs now."

Zoë's mind was buzzing unpleasantly. "I'll have to do something with her furniture . . . all her things . . ."

Emma was a pack rat. A lifetime of memories would have to be put in boxes and stored somewhere. Antiques, dishes, a mountain of books, clothes from every decade since Truman had been in office.

"I can suggest a good moving company," Colette said, "and a local storage facility."

"Thank you." Zoë reached up and tucked

her hair behind her ears. Her mouth had gone dry, and she took a sip of water from a plastic cup. Too many decisions that had to be made too fast. Her life was about to change as drastically as Emma's had. "How long do we have?" she asked. "Before my grandmother has to leave the hospital clinic."

"I can make a guess . . . probably three weeks, maybe four. Her supplemental insurance will pay for a week in acute rehab, then she'll be admitted to a skilled nursing facility. Usually Medicare covers that for only a brief time. If you want her to stay longer, you'll have to assume the cost of custodial care — having someone help to bathe and dress and feed her — on your own. That's when it starts to get expensive."

"If my grandmother comes to live with me," Zoë asked, "would the insurance cover having someone come to the house every day to help me take care of her?"

"If it's only for custodial care, you'll have to pay for it. Sooner or later" — Colette handed her yet another brochure — "your grandmother will need to be checked into a lockdown facility where they have constant supervision, and assistance with daily living needs. I can definitely recommend this one. It's a very nice place, with a common room, piano music, even afternoon teas."

"Lockdown," Zoë repeated faintly, staring at the brochure, the photographs all tinted with warm amber and rose hues. "I don't think I could put Emma there. I'm sure she would want me close by, and since I live in Friday Harbor, I'd only be able to visit every —"

"Zoë . . ." Colette interrupted, her dark, tip-tilted eyes soft with sympathy. "By then she probably won't remember you."

Six

Zoë returned to the island after three days of feverish activity. She had sorted through Emma's clothes and personal items, and had hired a professional packing company to help wrap breakable items and put everything into boxes. Stacks of old photographs and memory books had been placed in specially marked containers — Zoë wasn't certain whether her grandmother would want to look through them or not.

As soon as she reached the inn, Justine gave her an assessing glance and said, "Go take a nap. You look totally beat."

"I am." Gratefully Zoë had gone to the cottage and slept for most of the afternoon. She awoke as low-slanting sunlight pierced the cream-painted plantation shutters of her bedroom and crossed her pink-flowered bedspread in brilliant stripes. A dressmaker's cloth mannequin stood in the corner, glittering with Zoë's collection of antique

81

brooches.

Byron lay nearby, watching her with golden-green eyes. As Zoë smiled and reached out to pet him, he began to purr loudly.

"Justine did comb you," Zoë murmured, running her fingers through his silky white fur. "I bet she gave you a cat massage, too, didn't she?"

Footsteps approached the doorway. "Only to shut him up," came Justine's voice. "He kept yowling for you." She ducked her head inside the doorway. "How are you doing? Can I come in?"

"Yes, I feel much better."

"You still have raccoon eyes." Justine sat on the edge of the bed and regarded her with patent concern.

"Even with the professional packers helping," Zoë said, "it took two full days just to go through Emma's apartment. Closets full of stuff. I lost count of how many sets of dishes she has. And so much old junk — a turntable record player, a leather-case radio, a porcelain toaster from the thirties — I felt like I was in an episode of *Hoarders*."

"I sense an eBay seller's account in your future."

Zoë groaned and sat up, scrubbing her fingers through her wild blond curls. "I have a lot to talk to you about," she said.

"Want to walk over to the big kitchen and make a decent pot of coffee?"

"Could we have wine instead?"

"Now you're talking."

As they ambled to the main house, with Byron following closely, Zoë told her cousin everything she had discussed with the elder-care consultant. They entered the kitchen, large and cheerful, the walls covered in retro wallpaper adorned with clusters of cherries. While Justine opened a bottle of wine, Zoë glanced at a glass-domed cake plate filled with pastries. In her absence, Justine had relied on a local bakery to provide breakfast for the guests.

"They were okay," Justine said in answer to Zoë's unspoken question, "but nothing close to your stuff. The first-time guests didn't know any better, so they were happy, but you should've heard the regulars bitching. 'Where's Zoë?' and 'I was looking forward to this breakfast so much and *this* is what we get?' I'm not kidding, Zo: this place isn't the same without you."

Zoë smiled. "Oh, stop."

"It's true." Justine handed her a glass of wine, and they sat at the kitchen table. Byron leaped into Zoë's lap and settled in a purring heap of white fur.

"What happens next?" Justine asked quietly. "Although I think I already know."

"Emma needs me," Zoë said simply. "She's going to come live with me."

Justine frowned in concern. "You can't take care of her all by yourself."

"No, I'll find a home-care aide who'll help with the basics and watch over Emma while I go to work."

"How long will that last? I mean, before Emma . . ." Justine paused uncomfortably.

"Before she becomes too impaired to live with me anymore?" Zoë finished for her. "I don't know. It could be fast or slow. But when it happens, I'll take her to a place in Everett — it's called a memory-care community. I went there yesterday and talked to the head gerontologist, who was incredibly nice. And I felt a little less guilty afterward, because I realized that when my grandmother can't walk or wash herself anymore, they'll be able to keep her more comfortable, and way more safe, than I could."

"Do you want to move her into the cottage out back? The two of you can stay there, and I'll take one of the rooms in the main house."

Zoë was touched by her generosity. "That's so sweet of you. But that place is too small for what we'll need. Emma has a lake cottage on the island. It's about twelve hundred square feet, and it's got two bedrooms and a kitchen. I think we're going to try living there."

"Emma has a lake cottage? How come I didn't know about it?"

"Well, it came from her side of the family — the Stewarts — and I think she used to spend a lot of time there when she was still pretty young. But she hasn't gone there in thirty years, and it's been closed up. Every now and then a property management company checks on it and does some maintenance." Zoë hesitated. "I think the cottage holds a lot of memories for Emma. I asked why she hadn't sold it by now, but she didn't want to explain. Or maybe she was just tired."

"You think she really wants to stay there now?"

"Yes, she was the one who suggested it."

"Where exactly is this place?"

"Dream Lake Road."

"I'll bet it's pretty rustic."

"Yes," Zoë said ruefully. "I've driven by it a time or two, but I haven't been inside yet. I'm sure I'll have to put money into it. Handrails in the bathroom, a handheld showerhead, and a ramp at the front steps in case Emma needs a wheelchair. Things

like that. I've got a list of home improvement suggestions from the elder-care
consultant."

Justine shook her head slowly. "You're going to need a lot of cash."

A forelock of hair had slipped loose from
her ponytail. Justine tugged on it absently,
as she often did while deep in thought.
"What if I buy the cottage at a fair price,
and let you stay there rent-free? You can use
the money to take care of Emma. I'll even
pay for the remodel."

Zoë's eyes widened. "I couldn't let you do
that."

"Why not?"

"It wouldn't be fair to you."

"I'll make the money back later by renting
it out after Emma . . . well, after the two of
you don't need it anymore."

"You haven't even seen the place."

"I want to help any way I can. I'm responsible for Emma, too."

"Not really. She's not a blood relation,
she's your great-great-aunt by marriage."

"Her last name's Hoffman. That's good
enough for me."

Zoë smiled, reflecting that beneath her
cousin's cheerful audacity, there was an
underpinning of compassion. Justine was a
kind person. People didn't always realize

how deeply it went, or how vulnerable it made her.

"I really love you, Justine."

"I know, I know . . ." Uncomfortable as always with displays of affection, Justine waved her hand dismissively in the air. "We'll need to find someone to start fixing up the house right away. Any contractor who does decent work is going to be booked up, and even the good ones are as slow as a wet weekend." She paused. "Except . . . maybe . . . well, I don't know . . ."

"You have someone in mind?"

"Sam Nolan's brother Alex. He's built some houses out at Roche — he does great work, and in the past he was known for being reliable. But he went through a divorce, and one of his real estate development deals fell through, and rumors are that he's turned into a boozer. So I don't know what the story is with him. I haven't seen him in a while. I'll get the lowdown from Sam."

Zoë dropped her gaze to the cat in her lap and stroked his lavish fur. Byron wriggled and curled into a doughnut shape. "I . . . I met him, actually." She took care to keep her voice casual. "When I went to Rain-shadow Road to visit Lucy. He was doing some work on the house."

"You didn't mention it." Justine's brows

lifted. "What did you think of him?"

Zoë shrugged uncomfortably. "We talked for all of ten seconds. I didn't really have a chance to get an impression."

A slow grin spread across Justine's face. "You are the worst liar ever. Tell me."

Zoë struggled to reply, her thoughts refusing to shape themselves into words. How could she explain her reaction to Alex Nolan? Striking, unsettling, his features austerely perfect, his eyes bright as if lit with the last spare voltage of his humanity. He looked thoroughly disillusioned, everything that had been tender and hopeful in him now crushed into diamond hardness. Thankfully he'd paid little attention to her, dismissing her as beneath his notice. That was just fine with Zoë.

From her early teens onward, men had always made certain assumptions about her, with the result that nice men stayed away and left the field open for the not-so-nice ones. She had always been approached by the kind of man who viewed hunting and seducing an attractive woman as a sport. If he got a woman into bed, he won the game. Zoë didn't want to be a notch on some guy's belt, and she didn't want to be used.

She had thought that in marrying Chris,

she had finally found someone who would value her for who she was. He was a caring and sensitive man who had always listened to her and treated her with respect and honesty. That had made it all the more devastating when Chris had told her a year after their wedding that he was in love with another man. The betrayal had been a cruel and ironic surprise, coming from someone who had always bolstered Zoë's self-esteem. Since then, she had gone two years without any kind of romantic involvement. She didn't trust her instincts where men were concerned. And a man like Alex Nolan was obviously beyond her ability to handle.

"I thought he was handsome," Zoë finally managed to say, thinking of Alex. "But not very approachable."

"I get the feeling he doesn't like women."

"You mean he's —"

"No, I don't mean it that way — he's straight by all accounts. He has sex with women, but I don't think he *likes* them." Justine paused and shrugged. "Of course, that doesn't have anything to do with remodeling the cottage. So if I call Sam and he says Alex is still on his game, what do you think? Would you have any problem with him doing the work?"

"Not at all," Zoë said, although her stomach did a little flip at the thought of seeing him again.

"No," Alex said flatly, when Sam told him about Justine's call. "I'm too busy."

"I'm asking as a personal favor," Sam said. "She's Lucy's friend. Besides, you need the work."

The ghost lounged nearby as the two brothers applied a resin medallion to the ceiling of the second-floor landing. "He's right," the ghost told Alex, who sent him a scowl.

"I don't give a shit," Alex muttered. He was on a stepladder, pressing the adhesive-covered back of the medallion to the dry-wall above, while Sam stood below with a makeshift padded wooden support.

"Take it easy, Blowtorch," Sam said mildly. "It wouldn't hurt you to earn some money."

Alex struggled to contain his exaspera-tion. He was still getting used to the idea that just because he could see and hear the ghost didn't mean anyone else could. "Tell her to get someone else to do it."

"There is no one else. Every other contrac-tor on the island is booked up for the sum-mer, except you. And Justine was trying to ask me with her usual sledgehammer subtlety if you were even capable of handling the job."

"Remodeling a lake cottage?" Alex was indignant. "Why couldn't I handle that?"

"I don't know, Al. Maybe it has something to do with the impression people have gotten lately . . . that if your life was graphed in a pie chart, half of it would be 'shitfaced' and the other half would be 'hungover.' Yeah, you can give me the evil eye, but it doesn't change the fact that someday soon, you're going to be too drunk to work and too broke to drink."

"He's right about that, too," the ghost commented.

"Screw you," Alex said to both of them. "I've never missed one damn day of work for any reason."

Sam wedged the padded support beneath the medallion, while Alex checked the pencil marks on the ceiling to make certain the resin hadn't moved.

"I believe that," Sam said quietly. "But you're going to have to go out there and prove it to everyone else, Al. From what I can tell, your 401(k) is now a 501(k)."

"What does that mean?"

"Your net worth is now located in the pocket of your Levi's."

"I still have the Dream Lake development. I just need to find new backers."

"Great. In the meantime, this little cottage of Zoë's is right on Dream Lake Road. You've probably driven past it a hundred times. So you can take a couple of weeks to fix up her place, and —"

"Zoë?" Alex asked sharply, descending the stepladder. "I thought you said it was Justine's cottage."

"Justine was the one who called me about it. Zoë's going to live there with her grandmother, who's got some kind of Alzheimer's. You remember Zoë, right? The sweet-faced blonde with the nice set of . . . muffins." Sam grinned as he saw Alex's face. "Help me out. She's one of Lucy's best friends. Do it so I can reap the benefits of Lucy's gratitude."

The ghost stared at Alex with offhand amusement. "Why not?" he asked. "Unless you're scared."

"Why would I be scared?" Alex asked irritably, before he thought better of it.

"Scared of what?" Sam asked, perplexed. "Of Zoë?"

"No," Alex said in exasperation. "Forget it."

"It doesn't have to be complicated," Sam told Alex. "Go fix the house for the nice woman and her grandmother. Maybe you'll get lucky and she'll fix you dinner."

"And if you don't," the ghost added, "we'll know how much of a coward you really are."

"I'll do it," Alex said through gritted teeth. It was clear that the ghost was going to badger him nonstop if he didn't. And he felt the need to prove to the ghost — and maybe to himself — that Zoë Hoffman would pose no problem for him. "Give me her number. I'll find out what she wants and work up a quote. If she doesn't like it, she's welcome to find someone else."

"And you'll give her a good deal, right?"

"I give everyone a good deal," Alex said icily. "I don't rip my customers off, Sam."

"I know that," came Sam's quick response. "Wasn't implying otherwise."

"I'll quote a fair price, I'll do good work, and I'll finish on time. Like I always do. And afterward, if you don't quit bitching about my personal life, I'm going to take this support post and shove it up your —"

"Deal," Sam said promptly.

SEVEN

"Why can't you be the one to meet him at the cottage?" Zoë asked as she and Justine cleared the dining room of the breakfast dishes.

"It's going to be your house," Justine said reasonably, following her into the kitchen. "And you're the one who knows best about what Emma's going to need."

"I still wish you would go with me."

"I can't. I'm meeting the loan officer at the bank. You'll do fine. Just keep the budget in mind."

"It's not the budget I'm worried about," Zoë said, scraping the breakfast plate at the sink with unnecessary vigor. "You know I don't like talking to strangers."

"Alex isn't a stranger. You've met him before."

"For about thirty seconds."

"You just went to Everett and talked with a whole bunch of strangers."

"That's not the same."

"Oh." Justine paused in the middle of loading handfuls of flatware into the dishwasher. "I get it. But I promise he's not going to do anything to make you uncomfortable. He'll be professional."

"Are you sure?"

"Of course I'm sure. He's Sam's brother. He knows Sam would kick his ass if he offended you."

"I suppose."

"You talked to him on the phone to set up the meeting, right? Was he friendly?"

Zoë pondered that. "He wasn't *un*-friendly . . ."

"But he was polite?"

Zoë thought back to the brief conversation they'd had. There had been no pleasantries, not a trace of his brother Sam's easy charm. But yes . . . he had been polite. She nodded in answer to Justine's question.

"The only way to get over your shyness," Justine was saying pragmatically, "is to practice. You know, be friendly, make small talk. Guys aren't all that different from us."

"Yes they are."

"Okay, they are different from us. What I meant was, they're not complicated."

"Yes they are."

"Well, sometimes they can be complicated,

but they are entirely predictable."

Zoë heaved a sigh. She envied Justine's confidence, and she knew that Justine was right: she did need to practice. But the idea of being alone in the lakeside cottage with a man who intimidated her on just about every level was incredibly stressful.

"You know what I do when I'm facing something I dread?" Justine volunteered. "I divide it into steps. So if I were going to meet with Alex at the cottage, I wouldn't let myself think about the whole three-hour ordeal —"

"It's going to take three hours?"

"More like two. So I would start by telling myself, 'Step one. All I'm doing is getting into the car and driving to the cottage.' Don't worry about the rest of it, just do that. And once you're there, say to yourself, 'Step two. All I'm going to do is unlock the door and go inside to wait.' And when Alex shows up: 'Step three. I'll let him in and chitchat for a couple of minutes.' " Justine gave her a self-satisfied smile. "See? None of those things are so terrible by themselves. It's just when you view them all together that you start to feel like you're sprinting away from a rabid tiger."

"Spiders," Zoë said. "I'm not stressed by the idea of a rabid tiger. Spiders are what scare me."

"Fine, but that ruins the metaphor. No one has to sprint away from a spider."

"Wolf spiders chase down their prey. And black widow spiders can move very fast. And there are leaping spiders that —"

"Step one," Justine interrupted firmly. "Find your car keys."

From the moment Alex had pulled up to the lakeside cottage, the ghost had seemed riveted. He'd stopped talking, for once, and stared in open fascination, taking in every detail.

Alex couldn't figure out what he found so interesting. The house was small and rustic, with cedar shake siding, a covered front porch, wide eave overhangs, and a stone chimney. Craftsman details like tapered boxed columns on the porch and a field-stone foundation made it the kind of place that, when properly restored, would have a certain amount of charm. But the cheap carport on the side was a detraction. And it was apparent at first glance that the property management company had done a mediocre job of upkeep. The landscaping was untidy and overgrown, the graveled driveway choked with weeds. If the inside had been as poorly maintained as the outside, there were going to be problems.

Since they were early and Zoë hadn't arrived yet, Alex decided to walk around the exterior to look for mold, damaged siding, or foundation cracks.

"I know this place," the ghost had said in wonder, following Alex from the truck. "I remember being here. I remember —" He broke off abruptly.

Alex glanced at him, sensing the wistfulness in his mood. "You lived here?"

Looking troubled, the ghost said distractedly, "No, I was . . . visiting someone."

"Who?"

"A woman."

"To do what?" Alex persisted.

Although the ghost wasn't capable of blushing, his discomfort was impossible to miss. "None of your business," came the curt reply.

"So you were boning her?"

The ghost glowered at him. "Up yours."

Pleased at having annoyed him, Alex continued to wander around the exterior of the house. The satisfaction faded quickly, though, drowned in the awareness of a yearning so powerful and raw that it almost hurt to be near it. Did the ghost know who or what had inspired the feeling? Alex was tempted to ask him, but somehow that seemed brutish . . . the only way to respect that degree of unexpressed pain was to keep silent.

"She's here," the ghost said, as they heard the crunch of tires on the graveled driveway.

"Great," Alex said dourly. The prospect of talking to Zoë, interacting in even the most mundane way, was enough to make him break into a cold sweat. He reached up to the back of his neck to rub the tense muscles.

The ghost had been right when he'd called Alex a coward. But Alex wasn't worried for his own sake.

The failed marriage with Darcy had confirmed some of the worst things he had ever suspected about himself. It had taught him that intimacy not only gave you the weapons but the will to hurt the people you were closest to. And most of all it had convinced him that he was fated to end up like both his parents. He would inevitably destroy everything and everyone he cared about.

The worst of the damage had become apparent after he and Darcy had separated. They'd continued to have sex on the occasions when she came to the island. "For old time's sake," Darcy had said at one point, but there had been nothing of reminiscence or regret in their savage encounters. Only anger. Retaliation. They'd fucked each other out of mutual resentment, and the worst part was that it had been far better than any experience they'd shared out of affection. He was still haunted by the memories of what they'd done, how they had turned each other into the worst possible versions of themselves.

There was no return to innocence after that.

And there was no place in his life for anyone like Zoë Hoffman. The only act of kindness he could offer was to keep his distance from her.

Before going to the front entrance, Alex said sotto voce, "Stay out of my way and don't distract me while I'm talking to her. People tend not to hire schizophrenic contractors."

"I'll shut up," the ghost promised.

Doubtful. But they both knew that if the ghost pissed Alex off, he would refuse to go through the attic and sift through the heaps of long-forgotten junk that might yield a clue about his former life. And the ghost desperately wanted to find out who he was. Although Alex would never have admitted it, he'd become just as curious. It was impossible not to wonder why the ghost had been condemned to such merciless isolation. Maybe the ghost was paying for his past sins — maybe he'd been some kind of criminal or lowlife. But that didn't explain why Alex had ended up towing him around.

Alex cast a suspicious glance at him, but the ghost didn't appear to notice. He was staring at the house, and Zoë's approaching figure, mesmerized by distant shadows.

To Zoë's consternation, a pickup truck was already parked beneath the carport. Was Alex there already? It was still five minutes before they were supposed to meet.

Her heartbeat quickened to a sharp staccato. She parked beside the truck and consulted the visor mirror, and checked to make certain the buttons of her flower-print shirt were fastened. The top two had been left undone to her collarbone. After a moment's thought, she fastened those as well. Emerging from the VW, she approached the truck and realized it was empty. Had Alex found a way inside the house?

She crossed the gravel in her pink leather flats and went to the front door and found it was still locked. Delving into her bag, she found the keys from the property management company. The first one didn't work. As she extracted the second key and jiggled it into the lock, she became aware of someone approaching from the side. It was Alex, who had been walking around the exterior of the house. He had an athletic, loose-limbed way of moving, his body nearly raw-boned in a black short-sleeved shirt and jeans. He came to stand beside her, a large and brooding presence.

"Hi," she said with forced cheer.

Alex gave her a brief nod, the sunlight sliding across the layers of his dark hair. He was almost inhumanly beautiful, with those angular cheekbones and strongly marked brows, and eyes of frozen fire. Something restless lurked beneath his controlled façade, as if he hadn't had enough food, or enough sleep, or enough *something.* That mysterious and unexpressed need practically glowed through his skin.

No doubt his divorce had taken a physical toll — he could have used a few good meals. Zoë couldn't help thinking of what she would make for him, given the opportunity. Maybe butternut squash soup, graced with hints of tart green apple and smoky bacon, served with yeast rolls brushed with butter and a sprinkle of sea salt.

She turned the key harder in the resisting lock, her mind still occupied with the imaginary dinner. Maybe she would cook something heavier and more filling . . . meat loaf made with pork, veal, and crumbs from rustic French bread. Mashed potatoes swirled with caramelized scallions . . . and a side of green and yellow wax beans sautéed slowly in olive oil and garlic until they were melting-tender —

Zoë's musings were interrupted as the door key snapped in two. To her dismay, she realized that part of the metal had broken off in the lock. "Oh." She flushed and darted a mortified glance at Alex.

His face was inscrutable. "That happens with old keys. They tend to get brittle."

"Maybe we could try to enter through a window."

He glanced at the key ring in her hand. "Is there another house key?"

"I think so. But you'd have to get the broken one out of the lock first . . ."

Without a word, Alex went to his truck, reached inside, and pulled out a vintage red metal toolbox. He brought it to the front porch, and rummaged through a clatter of tools.

Taking care to stay out of the way, Zoë stood beside the door and watched as Alex inserted a metal pick into the jammed lock. In a minute or two, he had jimmied the broken key loose. Deftly he gripped the protruding end with a pair of needle-nosed pliers and pulled out the key.

"You made it look so easy," Zoë exclaimed.

He replaced the tools in the box and stood. She had the impression that it cost him something to meet her gaze. "May I?" he asked, and held out his hand for the key ring.

She gave it to him, taking care to avoid touching his fingers. He sorted through them, tried one, and the door opened with a creak.

The house was dark, musty-smelling, and silent. Alex preceded Zoë into the main room, found a light switch, and flipped it on.

Zoë set her bag by the door and ventured farther into the main living space. Turning a slow circle, she was pleased to discover that the floor plan was simple and open. However, the kitchen was a small galley style, cramped and sadly lacking in cabinet space, floored with ancient linoleum. The only furnishings in sight were an antique chrome kitchen table and three dingy vinyl-upholstered chairs, and a cast-iron woodstove in the corner. Crumpled aluminum blinds covered the windows like a row of skeletons.

Zoë went to unlock a window casing to let in some fresh air, but she couldn't budge it. The window was stuck.

Alex approached, and ran a fingertip along the seam of the window sash and sill. "It's been painted shut." He went to the next window. "This one, too. I'll cut through the paint later."

"Why would someone paint the windows shut?"

"Usually to keep out drafts. Cheaper than weather sealing." His expression conveyed exactly what he thought about the idea. He went to the corner, pulled up a loose section of carpeting, and looked beneath it. "Wood flooring under here."

"Really? Would it be possible to refinish it?"

"Maybe. There's no telling what condition the floor's in until you take out all the carpet. Sometimes they cover it for a reason." Alex went to the kitchen and lowered to his haunches to inspect a section of the wall, where a patch of mold had spread like a bruise. "You've got a leak," he said. "We'll have to take part of the wall out. I saw wood ants on the exterior — they're nesting because of the moisture."

"Oh." Zoë frowned. "I hope it's worth fixing up this place. I hope it's not too far gone."

"It doesn't look that bad. But you'll have to get an inspection."

"How much will that cost?"

"A couple hundred bucks, probably." He set his toolbox on the dingy chrome table. "You'll be living here with your grand-mother?"

Zoë nodded. "She has vascular dementia. It may soon get to the point where she needs a walker or a wheelchair." She went to get her bag, rummaged for a pamphlet, and brought it to him. "These are things that need to be done to make the house safer for her."

After a cursory glance at the pamphlet, Alex gave it back to her.

"Maybe you should keep it," Zoë said.

Alex shook his head. "I know all about ADA codes." With a speculative glance at their surroundings, he continued, "If your grandmother's going to use a walker or wheelchair, you should have laminate floor-ing put in."

Zoë was annoyed by the fact that he had barely looked at the list. His manner was just a hairsbreadth short of patronizing. "I don't like laminates. I prefer real wood."

"Laminate's cheaper and more durable."

"I'll consider it, then. But I would like carpet in the bedrooms."

"As long as it's not too plush. Trying to get a wheelchair across that is like trying to roll through sand." Alex stood at the opening of the kitchen galley and flipped on a light. "I don't think this is a load-bearing wall. I could take it out and turn this area into an island. It would double your cabinets and countertop space."

"Could you? It would be wonderful to have an open kitchen."

Alex took a pad of sticky notes from the toolbox and scrawled a few words on the top one. He reached for a tape measure and went into the kitchen. "Do you know what kind of countertops you want?"

"Oh, yes," Zoë said immediately. "Butcher block." It had always been her dream to have butcher-block countertops, but she'd never had the chance. When she'd started working at Artist's Point, soapstone counters had already been installed.

The measuring tape clicked and rasped a few more times. "If you do a lot of cooking, butcher block is going to show a lot of rough wear. It's expensive. And high maintenance."

"I'm aware of all that," Zoë said. "I've worked in kitchens with butcher-block counters."

"What about engineered stone?"

"I prefer butcher block."

Alex emerged from the kitchen with his lips parted as if he were about to argue. As he saw her defensive expression, however, he closed his mouth and continued to make notes.

Zoë found herself beginning to actively dislike him. His silences were especially unnerving because he didn't reveal a clue about what was behind them. No wonder he was divorced . . . the concept of anyone living comfortably with this man seemed impossible.

Taking care not to look at him, Zoë went to the back of the house, where a pair of French doors opened to a tiny porch with rotted slats. It was a nice little yard, enclosed by a wrought-iron fence, with a wooded copse and Dream Lake just beyond.

"Would it be possible to put in a cat door?" Zoë asked.

"A what?" came his voice from the other side of the room, near the woodstove.

"A cat door. Back here."

"There would be a cat," she heard him mutter.

"What does that mean?" Zoë asked, flushing.

"Nothing."

"Is there something wrong with having a cat?"

Alex pulled out a length of metal tape and began to lay it out along the floor. "I don't care what kind of pet you have. Forget I said anything. And yes, I can install a cat door. Although I can't guarantee that a raccoon or fox won't get in."

"I'll take my chances," Zoë said shortly.

Silence.

While Alex measured the main room and made notes, Zoë went to investigate the narrow kitchen space. As she had expected, there was no microwave, and no dishwasher. She and Justine had previously agreed that part of their budget would include new kitchen appliances, since renovating the kitchen would increase the value of the house. Zoë thought it would be convenient to have a microwave drawer built into the kitchen island. The dishwasher would be next to the sink, naturally, and the refrigerator would have to be in an area where she could open the door without bumping it against a wall.

It might be possible to save money by painting the cabinets and adding new hardware. She opened a cabinet door. The interior was coated with dust. Seeing an object on the middle shelf, Zoë stood on her toes to pull it down. It was an antique eggbeater, rusted metal with a wooden knob. Although it wasn't usable, someone certainly might want it as a decoration. Ruefully Zoë reflected that becoming an eBay seller was practically inevitable, with this and all the other antiques that Emma had saved.

As she set the eggbeater aside, Zoë was startled as a palm-sized object dropped from the edge of the cabinet and landed on the counter.

It was a spider. A *huge* spider.

And it began to hop and bolt toward her with astonishing speed, its articulated legs a blur.

EIGHT

At the sound of Zoë's scream, Alex reacted and reached her in a few seconds. She had bolted from the galley kitchen, her eyes huge in her ashen face. "What is it?" he demanded.

"S-spider," she said hoarsely.

"It's here," the ghost called out from the kitchen. "Damn thing just jumped from one counter to the other."

Dashing into the narrow space, Alex grabbed the antique eggbeater and killed the spider with a few decisive thwacks.

Pausing to look more closely, Alex let out a low whistle. It was a wolf spider, a species that tended to hide during the day and hunt for prey at night. This particular specimen was bigger than anything he'd seen outside of a zoo. A touch of humor quirked one corner of his mouth as he thought of how Sam would have reacted to the situation. Sam would have found a way to capture the spider without harming it and safely transport it outside, all the while lecturing about respect for nature. Alex's view on nature was that any time it ventured inside, it was going to find itself confronting a big can of Raid.

His gaze swept across the kitchen. A loose collection of webbing was anchored at the corner of the ceiling. Spiders spun webs near food sources, which meant there had to be a big supply of insects attracted to the moisture from leaks in the wall.

"Alex," came the ghost's urgent voice from the other room, "something's wrong with Zoë."

Frowning, Alex left the kitchen and found Zoë in the center of the main room, her arms wrapped tightly around her middle. She was breathing in airless pants, as if her lungs had collapsed. He reached her in two strides. "What is it?"

She didn't seem to hear him. Her eyes were wide and unfocused. She was shaking in every limb.

"Did it bite you?" Alex asked, looking over her face, neck, arms, every exposed inch of skin.

Zoë shook her head, wheezing as she tried to talk. Alex found himself reaching out for her and snatching his hands back.

"Panic attack," the ghost said. "Can you calm her down?"

Alex shook his head automatically. He was good at making women angry, but calming them wasn't in his repertoire.

The ghost looked exasperated. "Just talk to her. Pat her back."

Alex gave him an appalled glance. There was no possible way to explain his unwillingness to touch her. The sure knowledge that it would lead to disaster. But Zoë swayed on her feet, looking like she was about to pass out, and there was no choice. He reached for her, his hands closing lightly around her arms. The feel of her skin against his palms, the texture of her flesh, sent a thrill of heat through him, which, in light of the circumstances, was nothing less than depraved.

He had been with women in every imaginable sexual position, but he'd never taken one into his arms with the sole intention of comforting her. "Zoë, look at me," he said quietly.

To his relief, she obeyed. She was panting, gulping painfully as if she couldn't get enough air, when the problem was that she was taking in too much.

"I want you to take a deep breath and let it out slowly," Alex said. "Can you do that?"

Zoë looked at him without seeing him, her eyes desperate and tear-blurred. "My ch-chest —"

He understood immediately. "You're not having a heart attack. You'll be fine. We just need to slow your breathing down." She continued to stare at him, wetness leaking from her eyes, mingling with the pearly mist of sweat on her cheeks. The sight caused something to twist painfully inside his chest. "You're safe," he heard himself saying. "I won't let anything happen to you. Easy . . ." His hand came to the side of her face. Her cheek was cool and plush, like the sepals of a white orchid. Carefully he touched her nose, pressing one nostril shut, holding it like that. "Keep your mouth closed. Breathe through one side of your nose."

With the intake of air restricted, Zoë's breath began to regulate. But it wasn't easy. She gasped and hiccupped, and kept fighting to breathe as if she were trying to insufflate corn syrup through a straw. All Alex could do was hold her patiently, and let her body work it out. "Good girl," he murmured, as he felt her begin to relax. "Just like that." A few more constricted breaths. To his relief, she stopped struggling. He let his hand cradle her face, while his thumb wiped at the stippling of tears on her cheek.

"Take long breaths from deep down."

Looking exhausted, Zoë dropped her head to his shoulder, the pale golden curls tickling his jaw. Alex went very still. "Sorry," he heard her whisper in between broken gasps. "Sorry."

Not as sorry as he was. Because the feel of her had sent a shock of pleasure through him, so pure and searing that it was almost pain. He had known somehow that it would be like this. He found himself gripping her closer, until her body molded to his as if her bones had gone liquid. A few remaining tremors went across her back, and he chased them slowly with his hands. He felt his senses opening to take her in, the incredible lush delicacy of her. She smelled like crushed flowers, a dry and innocent scent, and he wanted to open her shirt and breathe it directly from her skin. He wanted to press his lips against the wild pulse in her throat and stroke it with his tongue.

Heat uncurled and rose through the stillness. The urge to touch her intimately, slide his hands through her hair and inside her clothes, nearly drove him crazy. But it was enough just to stand here with her, disoriented from the desire that flowed all through him.

Through heavy-lidded eyes, he saw a

movement nearby. It was the ghost, only a few yards away, regarding him with lifted brows.

Alex shot him an incinerating glare.

"I think I'll check out the other rooms," the ghost said tactfully, and vanished.

Zoë clung to Alex, who was the one solid thing in the world, the still center of the merry-go-round. Dancing at the edge of her awareness was the mortified knowledge that, after this, she would never be able to face him again. She had made a fool of herself. He would have nothing but contempt for her. Except . . . he was so gentle . . . so concerned. His hand moved over her back in slow circles. It had been a long time since a man had held her — she had forgotten how good it felt. The surprise was that Alex Nolan was capable of such quiet, fluent tenderness. She would have expected anything from him except this.

"Better?" he asked after a while.

She nodded against his shoulder. "I . . . I've always hated spiders. They're like . . . hairy wads of death on eight legs."

"Usually they only bite humans to defend themselves."

"I don't care. I'm still scared of them."

Amusement rustled in his chest. "Most

people are."

Zoë lifted her head to look up at him with wide eyes. "Including you?"

"No." He caressed the edge of her jaw with the backs of his fingers. His face was austere, but his eyes were warm. "In my line of work, you see enough of them that you get used to it."

"I wouldn't," Zoë said vehemently. Remembering the one in the kitchen, she felt her pulse skyrocket. "That one was huge. And the way it dropped out of the cabinet and started hopping toward me —"

"It's dead," Alex interrupted, his hand returning to her back, resuming the calming stroking. "Relax, or you'll start hyperventilating again."

"Was it a black widow?"

"No, just a wolf spider."

She shuddered.

"They're not lethal," he said.

"There must be more. The house is probably full of them."

"I'll take care of it." He sounded so assured and matter-of-fact that she couldn't help but believe him. His face was so close that she could see the shadow of whisker-grain heralding a dark five o'clock shadow. "The only way spiders can get in," Alex continued, "is through cracks and places that aren't sealed. So I'm going to install door sweeps and weather stripping, caulk around all the windows and doors, and put wire mesh over every vent. Trust me, this is going to be the most pestproof house on the island."

"Thank you."

A moment later, it occurred to Zoë that she was still glued to him as tightly as a barnacle on a harbor piling. And her heart was still in overdrive. Standing as close as they were, it was impossible not to notice that he was becoming aroused, the pressure of his body hard and delicious. She couldn't seem to move, only leaned against him in a dry-mouthed paralysis of pleasure.

Alex eased her apart from him, and turned away with a wordless sound.

Zoë still felt the vital imprint of his body everywhere they had touched, a throbbing awareness lingering right beneath her skin.

Desperately trying to think of a way to break the silence, she cast her mind back to what he'd said about pest-proofing. She blurted out, "Will I have to give up the cat door?"

A scratchy sound came from him, as if he were clearing his throat, and she realized he was struggling to hold back a laugh. He threw a quick glance over his shoulder, his eyes bright with amusement. "Yes," he said.

After Zoë stepped out of his arms, Alex became businesslike again. While Zoë cautiously investigated the rest of the small house, he continued to take measurements for a rough floor plan. He tried to focus on anything other than Zoë.

He wanted to take her somewhere, to some dark quiet room, and undress her, and screw her nine ways from Sunday. But she possessed a fragile dignity that, for some reason, he didn't want to undermine. He liked the way she'd stood up to him when they'd argued about the butcher-block countertops. He liked the little smiles that danced out from beneath her shyness. He liked far too many things about her, and God knew no good could come of it. So he was going to do them both a favor and stay away from her.

While Alex peeled off sticky notes and adhered them in a line across the old chrome table, Zoë went to the side door that opened to the carport. "Alex," she said while looking through the dirt-striped window. "Is it difficult to turn a carport into a garage?"

"No. Structurally it's built about the same

as a garage. I'd just have to add sides, insulation, and a door."

"Would you include that in the quote, then?"

"Sure."

Their gazes caught, and an electric awareness crackled between them. With effort, Alex refocused on the pad of sticky notes. "You can go now," he said. "I'm going to be here for a while, getting some measurements and taking pictures. I'll lock up when I leave and have a new key made for you."

"Thanks." She hesitated. "Do you need me to stay and help with anything?"

Alex shook his head. "You'd only get in the way."

The ghost approached the table. "All that charm," he said to Alex in a marveling tone. "Is it natural, or do you have to work on it?"

Zoë approached the table and waited until Alex brought his gaze to meet hers. "I want to . . . well, thank you," she said, her face pink.

"It was nothing," Alex muttered.

"You were very kind," she persisted. "Maybe to return the favor . . . I could make dinner for you sometime."

"Not necessary."

The ghost looked disgusted. "What's

wrong with letting her make you dinner?"

"It would be no trouble," Zoë persisted. "And I'm . . . not a bad cook. You should try me."

"You should try her," the ghost repeated emphatically.

Alex ignored him and looked at Zoë. "My schedule's pretty tight."

The ghost spoke to Zoë as well, even though she couldn't hear him. "He means he'd rather sit somewhere alone and drink like an attention-deficit camel."

Zoë's gaze dropped in response to Alex's refusal.

"In a couple of days," Alex said, "I'll drop by the inn with some drawings. We'll go over them and make changes if necessary. After that, I'll work up a quote."

"Come by any day after breakfast. It ends at ten on the weekdays, eleven-thirty on the weekends. Or . . . come a little earlier and have some breakfast." Zoë touched the surface of the chrome table with a neatly filed fingertip. Her hands were small but capable, the nails clear-varnished. "I like this dining set. I wish there was a way to restore it."

"It can be restored," Alex said. "All it needs is a workover with some steel wool and few coats of spray chrome."

Zoë looked at the table speculatively. "I suppose it's not worth the trouble, with one of the chairs missing."

"The fourth chair is in a corner of the carport," Alex said. "You can't see it because my truck is parked there."

Zoë brightened at the information. "Oh, good. That makes the set worth saving. Otherwise I thought we'd have to sixty-nine it."

Alex looked at her blankly.

She stared back at him with innocent blue eyes.

"You mean eighty-six it," Alex said, his voice carefully monotone.

"Yes, what did I —" Zoë broke off as she realized the slip she'd made. A tide of crimson color washed over her face. "I have to be going," she said in a small voice. She grabbed her bag and scampered from the house.

The door closed with a slam.

The ghost was laughing so hard he was soundless.

Alex braced his hands on the table and lowered his head. He was so turned on he couldn't stand straight. "I can't take this," he managed to say.

"You should ask her out," the ghost eventually said, when he was able.

Alex shook his head.

"Why not?"

"The number of ways I could hurt a woman like that . . ." Alex paused with a faint smile. "Hell. I can't count that high."

After Zoë had told her cousin everything that had happened at the lakeside cottage, Justine wasn't merely amused. She laughed until she nearly toppled off her chair.

"Oh my God," Justine gasped, grabbing a paper towel to blot the tears from her eyes. The sight of Zoë's indignant expression only seemed to make it worse. "I'm sorry, sweetie. I'm laughing with you, not at you."

"If you were laughing with me," Zoë said, "then I would be laughing, too. And I'm not. Because all I can think about is stabbing myself with the first thing I can grab from the nearest utensil drawer."

"Don't even try," Justine said, still snorting. "With the luck you've had today, it would turn out to be a melon baller."

Zoë lowered her forehead to the kitchen table. "He thinks I'm the biggest idiot in the world. And I wanted so badly for him to like me."

"I'm sure he likes you."

"No," Zoë said mournfully, "he doesn't."

"Then there's something wrong with him,

because everyone else in the world does." Justine paused. "Why do you want him to like you?"

Zoë lifted her head and leaned her chin on her hand. "What if I say it's because he's so good-looking?"

"God, that's incredibly shallow. I'm so disappointed in you. Tell me more."

Zoë smiled. "It's not really about his looks. Although he is . . . dazzling."

"Not to mention a carpenter," Justine said. "I mean, all carpenters are sexy, even the ugly ones. But a good-looking carpenter . . . well, that's pretty hard to resist."

"At first I wasn't all that tempted by him, but then he killed the spider. Which was a huge point in his favor."

"Absolutely. I love men who kill bugs."

"And then when I was freaking out and couldn't breathe, he was so . . . gentle." Zoë sighed and colored, remembering. "He was holding me, and talking to me in that voice . . . you know, sort of low and rough around the edges . . ."

"All the Nolans sound like that," Justine said reflectively. "Like they've got a mild case of bronchitis. Totally hot."

A curl dangled in front of Zoë's eyes, and she puffed it away. "When was the last time a man focused on you," she asked reflectively, "as if you were the only thing in the world? Like he was paying attention to your every heartbeat. Like he was trying to absorb the feel of you."

"Never," Justine admitted.

"That was how it felt," Zoë continued. "And I couldn't help thinking about what it would be like, with a man like that. Because whenever men have told me in the past that they wanted me, I always knew that what they really wanted was a notch on the bedpost. And with Chris, even though he was very sweet and considerate, when we were . . . together, in that way . . . it was never . . ."

"Intense?"

Zoë nodded. "But there's something about Alex that makes me think . . ." Her voice faded as she thought better of what she had been about to say.

Justine's velvet-brown eyes darkened with concern. "Zo. You know I'm all for having fun. And I've told you for months that you need to go out with someone. But Alex is not the guy to start with."

"Do we know for certain that his drinking is a problem?"

"If you even have to ask that, it's a problem. And when you get involved with someone like that, you're heading into a love triangle — you, him, and the booze. You don't need his kind of trouble, especially now that you've taken on the responsibility of looking after Emma. I'm not trying to tell you what to do, but . . . never mind, I am. I'm telling you straight up, don't get involved with Alex. There are too many nice, normal guys out there who would all love to be with you."

"Are there?" Zoë asked dryly. "Why haven't I ever met any of them?"

"They're intimidated by you."

"Oh, please. You've seen me on my bad hair days, and when I gained seven pounds over Thanksgiving, and later when I lost them during the most disgusting case of the flu ever . . . there is no reason for any man ever to be intimidated by me."

"Zoë, even on your worst day, you are still the kind of woman that most men fantasize about having wild, crazy monkey sex with."

"I don't want crazy monkey sex," Zoë protested. "I just want . . ." Unable to find the right words, she shook her head ruefully, and swatted back a few dangling curls. "I want solutions," she admitted, "not more problems. And with Alex, there would be nothing but problems."

"Yes. So let me fix you up. I know a ton of guys."

Zoë hated blind dates nearly as much as spiders. She smiled and shook her head, and tried to forget about the feeling of safety she'd found in Alex Nolan's arms. It was a bad habit of hers . . . looking for safety in places where there wasn't any.

NINE

The attic at Rainshadow Road was filled with boxes, a battered wooden trunk, a few pieces of musty broken furniture, and decades' worth of flotsam and jetsam abandoned by previous tenants. Alex reflected that it was a good thing he wasn't afraid of insects or rodents, since there were bound to be a lot of them nesting in so much junk.

"I think you should start over here," the ghost said from the far corner of the room.

"I'm not climbing across that mountain of crap," Alex said, shaking out an industrial garbage bag.

"But the stuff I want to look at is at the back."

"I'll work my way over there eventually."

"But if you —"

"Don't push it," Alex said. "I'm not taking orders from a spook." He plugged his phone into a pair of portable speakers by the door. The app played songs from an

Internet radio service, based on selections previously entered. Because of the ghost's nonstop complaints, Alex had added some big band music to his playlist. And he had secretly found himself starting to like a couple of pieces by Artie Shaw and Glenn Miller, although nothing would have induced him to admit it.

Sheryl Crow's smooth, smoky voice filled the air with a slow rendition of "Begin the Beguine." The ghost wandered over to the speakers. "I know this one," he said in pleasure, and began to hum along.

Alex opened a ragged cardboard box and found it packed with old VHS tapes of B movies. He shoved the box aside and pulled out a faded plaster owl statue. "Where do people get this junk?" he asked aloud. "Or a better question is *why?*"

The ghost was listening intently to the song. "Used to dance to this one," he said distantly. "I remember a woman in my arms. She had blond hair."

"Can you see her face?" Alex asked, intrigued.

The ghost shook his head in frustration. "It's like the memories are hidden behind a curtain. All I can see are shadows."

"Have you ever seen anyone else . . . like you?"

"You mean other spooks? No." The ghost smiled without humor as he saw Alex's expression. "Don't bother asking about the afterlife. I don't know anything about it."

"Would you tell me if you did?"

The ghost met his gaze directly. "Yeah, I'd tell you."

Alex bent back to his work. He unearthed a bag filled with bottles and broken glass. Carefully he placed it inside the box filled with old tapes. The ghost softly sang a few lyrics.

"I wonder what you did, to end up like this," Alex said.

The ghost looked wary. "You think it's a punishment?"

"It sure as hell doesn't look like a reward."

The ghost grinned briefly, then sobered. "Maybe it's something I didn't do," he said after a moment. "Maybe I let someone down, or wasted some chance I should have taken."

"Then why are you stuck here with me? What does that solve?"

"Maybe I'm supposed to keep you from making the same mistake I did." The ghost cocked his head slightly, studying him.

"If I want to waste my life, that's my business. And there ain't crap you can do about it, buddy."

"Be my guest," came the sour reply.

Alex pulled out a box filled with folders.

"What's in there?" the ghost asked.

"Nothing." Alex riffled through the dusty heap of paper. "Looks like notes on college courses from the seventies." He tossed them into the garbage bag.

The ghost went back to the speakers and hummed along to a U2 cover of "Night and Day."

As the hours passed, Alex moved boxes and filled garbage bags, finding nothing of value except a few rolls of wallpaper printed with a wildly mod design of brown stripes and lime green circles, and an antique L. C. Smith and Corona typewriter in a tweed case.

"That could be worth something," the ghost commented, coming to look over Alex's shoulder.

"Maybe fifty bucks," Alex said, annoyed by the ghost's proximity. "Hey . . . personal space here."

The ghost retreated a few inches, but continued to stare at the typewriter. "Look inside the case," he said. "Is there anything in it?"

Alex lifted the typewriter and looked beneath the chassis. "Nope." He flexed his sore shoulders and stood to ease his cramped thighs. "I'm going to call it a day."

"Now?"

"Yes, now. I have to work on the designs for Zoë. And I've got to find a place to live before Darcy has me forcibly ejected from the house."

The ghost stared morosely at the boxes they hadn't touched yet. "But there's so much more to look at."

"We'll come back tomorrow."

The ghost's outrage was nearly palpable, filling the air like a cloud of angry hornets. "A few more minutes," he said stubbornly.

"*No.* I just spent the better part of a day sorting through garbage on your behalf. I have other stuff to do. Paid work. Unlike you, I can't survive on air."

The ghost responded with a baleful glance.

In the silence, Alex organized the clutter, detached his phone from the speakers, picked up the massive plastic bag, and began to lug it out of the attic. Amid the rattling and clanking and rustling of trash, he heard the ghost begin to sing the song he knew Alex hated more than any other.

Down Hawaii way, where I chanced to stray, on an evening I heard a Hula maiden play . . . Yaaka hula hickey dula, Yaaka hula hickey doou . . .

"Quit singing that shit," Alex said. "I mean it." But as he descended to the second floor, the obnoxious tune continued.

. . . Oh, I don't care if you've loved the ladies far and near . . . You'd forget about them all if you could hear . . . Yaaka hula hickey dula, Yaaka hula hickey doo!

TEN

As Zoë put the last of the Friday morning breakfast plates into the dishwasher, she heard a scratch at the back door of the kitchen. She went to open it, and Byron came in with a plaintive meow, his tail held high like a gentleman doffing his hat. He sat and looked at her with expectant green eyes.

Zoë grinned and reached down to smooth his fluffy white fur. "I know what you're after."

She went to the stove, and spooned a few last curds of scrambled eggs from a skillet into Byron's dish. The cat proceeded to eat daintily, his ears and tail twitching with enjoyment.

Justine entered the kitchen. "Someone's here to see you. I wasn't sure what to tell him."

"Is it Alex?" Zoë's nerves jolted pleasantly. "Please send him back here."

"It's not him. It's your ex."

Zoë blinked. She hadn't seen or talked to Chris in more than a year, their contact limited to a couple of impersonal e-mails. As far as Zoë knew, there was no reason for him to come to the island.

"Is he alone or is he with his partner?"

"Solo," Justine said.

"Did he tell you why he's here?" Zoë asked.

Justine shook her head. "Want me to get rid of him?"

Zoë was almost tempted to say yes. It wasn't that she and Chris had parted on bitter terms. In fact, their divorce had been a low-key and bloodless process. As his wife, she had felt betrayed, but as his friend, she couldn't help feeling sympathy for the pain and confusion he'd so obviously been going through. Just after their first anniversary, Chris had come to her with tears in his eyes, and had tried to explain that even though he loved her, would always love her, he had been having an affair with a man who worked at his law firm. Chris had explained that until recently he'd never been able to face his feelings and desires, but he couldn't pretend any longer. Whenever he'd been attracted to men in the past, he had always compartmentalized such feelings, knowing that his conservative family would never approve. However, it had gotten to the point where he could no longer live a lie. And what he regretted most was having caused Zoë disappointment and pain. He had never intended to hurt her.

"Doesn't matter," Justine had said to Zoë, regarding this last point. "He handled it the wrong way. Chris could have come to you and said, 'Zoë, I'm having some complicated feelings,' and then you could have talked about it. Instead, he lied to you repeatedly, until you were blindsided. He cheated on you. And that makes him a jackass, whether he's gay or straight."

Now, contemplating the prospect of seeing Chris, Zoë felt dread settle in her stomach like a lead weight. "I'll talk to him," she said reluctantly. "It wouldn't feel right to turn him away."

"You're such a pushover," Justine grumbled. "Okay, I'll send him back here."

In a couple of minutes, the door opened, and Chris entered cautiously.

He was as handsome as ever, slim and fit, his hair the rich color of wheat. Chris had always been in great shape, and he was scrupulously careful with his diet, rarely eating red meat or drinking a second glass of wine. "No butter, cream, or carbs," he had always told Zoë when she had cooked for him. She had obliged, even though she had found the restrictions more than a little aggravating. The first meal she had made for herself after she had moved out of their apartment had been a huge bowl of spaghetti carbonara, with a sauce of white wine, cream, and three entire eggs, the whole of it covered in a snowy layer of grated Pecorino-Romano and Parmesan cheese and sprinkled with crisp shards of bacon.

Chris smiled when he saw her. "Zoë," he said quietly, and stepped forward.

An awkward moment followed as they moved toward each other in the beginnings of a hug, and ended up clasping hands instead. Zoë was inwardly surprised by how good it was to see him again, and how much she had missed him.

"You look wonderful," he said.

"So do you." But she saw with concern that there was a weathering of sadness around his hazel-green eyes, and lines of tension that had been carved too deep and too fast.

Reaching into the pocket of his impeccably tailored blazer, Chris brought out a small object in a flannel pouch. "I found this behind the dresser the other day," he said, handing it to her. "Remember how hard we looked for it?"

"My goodness," Zoë said as she saw the brooch inside the pouch. It had always been one of the favorites in her collection, a vintage silver and enameled teapot embedded with amethysts. "I thought I'd never see it again."

"I wanted to return it to you in person," Chris said. "I knew how much it meant to you."

"Thank you." She gave him an unguarded smile. "Are you staying on the island for the weekend?"

"Yes."

"Alone?" she brought herself to ask. They were both trying hard to be casual, to mask the awkward edges and corners of a conversation between two people who were trying to reconnect.

Chris nodded. "I needed to get away and do some thinking. I'm renting a waterfront house for a couple of nights. Hoping to see some orcas, maybe do some kayaking." His gaze flicked around the kitchen, taking in the pans that still needed to be cleaned, the remains of breakfast. "I came at a bad time. You're in the middle of stuff —"

"No, it's fine. Do you want to stay for a few minutes and have some coffee?"

"If you'll have some with me."

Zoë motioned for him to sit at the table. She went to brew a fresh pot of coffee. Rather than take a chair, Chris leaned back against the sturdy table and watched her.

"Where is the house you're renting?" Zoë asked, measuring coffee into a filter basket.

"It's at Lonesome Cove." Chris paused before adding, "Apropos name, in my current situation."

"Oh, dear." Zoë went to fill the coffeepot at the sink. "Trouble with . . . your partner?"

"I'll spare you the details. But a lot has been running through my mind. Memories and thoughts . . . and the thing I keep running into, again and again, is that I never really apologized for what I did to you. I handled everything the wrong way. I'm so sorry for that. I'm —" He closed his mouth and set his jaw, but a muscle in his cheek twitched like an overstretched rubber band.

Carefully Zoë brought the pot of water to the coffee machine and poured it in. "But you did," she said. "You apologized more than once. And maybe you could have handled it better, but I can't imagine how difficult it must have been for you. I was so focused on my own hurt feelings that I didn't think about how scary it would be for you to come out. How tough it would be to face everyone's reactions. I forgave you a long time ago, Chris."

"I haven't forgiven myself," Chris said, clearing his throat roughly. "I didn't take responsibility. I told you it wasn't my fault. I didn't want to think about what I was putting you through. For a while I sort of became a teenager again, going through all the phases I missed during adolescence. I'm so sorry, Zoë."

At a loss for words, Zoë started the coffeemaker and turned to face him. Her hands smoothed repeatedly over the bib front of her white chef's apron. "It's okay," she eventually said. "It's *really* okay. I'm fine. But I'm worried about you. Why do you seem so unhappy? Won't you tell me what's wrong?"

"He left me for someone else," Chris said, with a ragged laugh. "Fitting justice, right?"

"I'm sorry," she said gently. "How long ago?"

"A month. I can't eat, can't breathe, can't sleep. I've even lost my sense of smell and taste. I went to a doctor — can you believe there's a level of depression where you can't even smell things?" He let out a shaken sigh. "You were the best friend I ever had. You were always the one I wanted to tell first when anything happened."

"You were my best friend, too."

"I miss that. Do you think . . ." He swallowed audibly. "You think we could ever get back to that? Not like when we were married . . . I mean just the friendship part."

"I can do that part," she said readily. "Have a seat and tell me what happened. And while you do that, I'll make you some breakfast. Just like old times."

"I'm really not hungry."

"You don't have to eat," she said, turning on the stove to preheat a black steel pan. "But I'm going to make something for you."

When they were married, it had been like this nearly every night — Chris would sit and talk to Zoë while she cooked. It felt familiar to slip back into this, even after all the time they'd spent apart. Chris explained the issues he and his partner had faced, the initial exhilaration of their romance fading into the everyday routine of living together. "And then the things that didn't seem to matter before — politics, money, even stupid stuff like whether the toilet paper unwinds from the top or bottom of the roll — all of it became important. We started to argue." He paused as he noticed Zoë breaking eggs into a bowl with one hand. One, two, three. "What are you making?"

"An omelet."

"Remember, no butter."

"I remember." Zoë cast a glance over her shoulder and prompted, "You were telling me about the arguments."

"Yes. He's a different guy when we fight. He's willing to use any weapon, anything you confide in private. Win at all cost —" He paused as Zoë drizzled some clarified butter into a small saucepan. "Hey —"

"It's a French omelet," she said reasonably. "I have to do it this way. Just look the other way and keep talking."

Chris sighed in resignation and resumed. "I wanted his approval too much. Couldn't stand up to him. But he was the first man I ever . . ." He fell silent.

Zoë chopped some fresh herbs — parsley, tarragon, basil — and whisked them into the eggs. She understood the process Chris was going through. She knew how many ways you could find to blame yourself after a breakup, how you recounted a hundred conversations to figure out what you should or shouldn't have said. How you constantly wanted sleep even when you'd already been sleeping too much, and you couldn't eat even though your body was famished.

And how inexplicably foolish you felt when someone else had failed at loving you.

"There's no way of knowing how a relationship will turn out," Zoë said. "You gave it a try."

"Did I ever," Chris said bitterly, still not looking at her. "But I have no more luck being gay than I did being straight."

"Chris . . . hardly anyone ends up with the first person they love."

"Some people don't end up with anyone at all. I don't want to be one of those."

"Justine says if you never find Mr. Right, you should have as much fun as possible with a lot of Mr. Wrongs."

He let out a bleak laugh. "That sounds like Justine."

"And she says you learn something from every relationship."

"What have I learned?" he asked glumly.

Zoë held her hand over the pan, testing the heat as it rose against her palm. When it felt right, she poured the eggs into the pan and began to work them with a fork. "You've learned more about who you are," she said eventually. "And what kind of love you want."

She broke the rich curdles of the egg as they formed, and shook the pan with deft flicks of her wrist, working with the eggs, swirling until the mixture set firmly. Turning the flame on high, she gave the omelet a last caress of high heat, imparting a faint toasted finish to the delicate surface. Tip-ping the pan over a plate, she let the omelet roll out into a pristine sun-colored cylinder.

She garnished the plate with orange slices and fresh lavender petals, and set the plate in front of Chris.

"That looks amazing," Chris said, "but I don't think I can eat anything."

"Try just a bite or two."

Looking resigned, Chris sectioned a bite of the omelet and put it into his mouth. His teeth closed on the combination of textures — tender eggs, the subtle pungency of the herbs, the kiss of sea salt, and a smoky pinch of ground black pepper. Without a word, he took another bite, and another. A slight flush rose in his cheeks as he ate with focused pleasure.

"If I were straight," he said after a moment, "I'd marry you again."

Zoë smiled and poured more coffee into his cup.

While Chris ate, Zoë made apricot lemon teacakes for the afternoon tea that was set out daily for the guests. She mixed the ingredients and poured the batter into a minimuffin pan. As she worked, she told Chris about her grandmother's deteriorating health. He listened with quiet sympathy.

"It's going to be tough on you," he said. "I've known some people who've taken care of relatives with dementia."

"I'll handle it," she said.

"How can you be sure?"

"There's no other choice. My plan is to rise to the occasion, whatever the occasion turns out to be."

"Have you talked to your dad about your decision?"

A wry smile crossed Zoë's lips as she sat at the table. "He and I don't talk. We e-mail. He says he's going to visit us once I get Emma settled at the lakeside cottage."

"Oh, joy." Chris had met Zoë's father, James, on a handful of occasions, and the only thing they'd had in common was that, as males, they both possessed the XY chromosome. After the wedding, Chris had quipped that Zoë's father had walked her down the aisle with all the tenderness of a man mailing a package at the UPS store.

"I don't think Emma will look forward to it any more than I do," Zoë admitted. "They haven't communicated at all since the divorce."

"*Our* divorce?" Chris asked incredulously. "Why?"

"He's against divorce for any reason."

"But he had one."

"He didn't, actually. My mother abandoned us, but there was never a divorce."

Zoë smiled as she added ruefully, "He told me I should have tried to be a better wife, and taken you to counseling, and then you wouldn't have turned gay."

"I didn't turn gay, I *was* gay. Am." Chris shook his head with a perturbed laugh. "Counseling wouldn't have changed that any more than it could have changed the shape of my nose or the color of my eyes. Look, do you want me to talk to him about this? I never dreamed that he would have blamed you for something like —"

"No. That's incredibly sweet of you, but it's not necessary. I don't think my father really blamed me, in his heart. He just takes every chance he gets to be critical. He can't help it. Because blaming other people is easier than thinking about what he might have to blame himself for." She reached over and put her hand on his. "But thank you."

Chris turned his hand palm up and squeezed hers before letting go. "What else is going on in your life?" he asked after a moment. "Is there a Mr. Right in the picture? Or a Mr. Wrong?"

Zoë shook her head. "No time for a love life. My work keeps me busy. And on top of that I'm getting the house ready for my grandmother."

Chris stood to take his plate to the sink.

"You'll let me know if you need help, I hope."

"Yes." Zoë stood as well. She felt relieved, as if their relationship had finally become what it was ultimately supposed to be. Friendship . . . nothing more, nothing less.

"Thank you," Chris said simply. "You're a beautiful woman, Zoë, and I'm not just talking about the outside. I hope to God you find the right guy someday. I'm sorry I got in the way of that." He reached out for her, and she went into his arms and hugged him. "I needed to find out if you still hated me," Chris said above her head. "I'm so glad you don't."

"I could never hate you," she protested.

The kitchen door opened as someone came in. Chris's arms loosened. Zoë glanced at the doorway, expecting to see Justine.

Alex Nolan stood there, hard-faced and unsmiling. In the confines of the kitchen, Alex looked bigger than Zoë had remembered him, and meaner, and she could almost swear that those moments when he'd held her at the lakeside cottage had been nothing but a dream. As his wintry gaze raked over Zoë, an unmistakable tension inhabited his stillness.

"Hi," Zoë said. "This is my ex-husband, Chris Kelly. Chris, this is Alex Nolan. He's going to do the remodeling for the lake house."

"That hasn't been decided yet," Alex said.

Still keeping an arm around Zoë's shoulders, Chris reached out to shake Alex's hand. "Nice to meet you."

Alex returned the handshake in a businesslike manner, his gaze returning to Zoë. "I'll come back another time," he said brusquely.

"No, please stay. Chris was just leaving." Seeing the accordion-pleated folder in his hand, Zoë asked, "Are those the plans? I would love to see them."

Alex returned his attention to Chris. Although his expression betrayed nothing, a sense of hostility seemed to char the air. "You live on the mainland?" he asked.

"Seattle," Chris said equably.

"Got family here?"

"Just Zoë."

The reply was followed by a silence as prickly as a dead juniper bramble.

Removing his arm from Zoë, Chris murmured, "Thanks for breakfast. And . . . for everything else."

"Take care," she said softly.

A metallic jingle cut through the air. Alex was fiddling with his car keys in a show of impatience.

Chris exchanged a private glance with Zoë, his brows drawing together as if to ask silently, *What is his deal?*

Zoë wasn't entirely certain. She gave Chris a bemused little shake of her head.

Her ex-husband left the kitchen, closing the door carefully behind him.

Zoë turned to confront Alex. He was more casually dressed than she had ever seen him, in a gray T-shirt and paint-stained jeans. The worn attire looked good on him, the denim clinging loosely to the hard lines of his body, shirtsleeves taut over sturdy arms.

"Would you like some breakfast?" Zoë asked.

"No, thanks." Alex went to set his wallet and keys on the table. He removed a sheaf of paper from the folder. "This won't take long. I'll point out a couple of things and leave the drawings with you."

"I'm not in a rush," Zoë said.

"I am."

A frown knit between her brows. She came to stand beside him at the table, while he spread out meticulous floor plans, elevations, and interior renderings.

Alex spoke without looking at her. "Later I'll bring some catalogs so you can look at finishes and fixtures. How long have you been divorced?"

Zoë blinked in confusion at the abrupt question. "A couple of years."

He showed no reaction other than a deepening of the brackets on either side of his mouth.

"We'd been best friends since high school," Zoë said. "As it turned out, we should have just stayed friends. I haven't seen Chris for a long time. He just showed up this morning out of the blue."

"What you do with your ex is your own business."

Zoë didn't like the way he'd worded that. "I'm not doing anything with him. We're divorced."

His shoulders hitched in a taut shrug. "A lot of people have sex with their exes."

She blinked in consternation. "What's the point of sleeping with someone after you divorce them?"

"Convenience." At her uncomprehending stare, Alex elaborated, "No dinners, no pretenses, no manners. It's the equivalent of a takeout meal."

"I don't like takeout meals," Zoë said, affronted. "And that's the worst reason I've ever heard to have sex with someone, just because they're convenient. That's . . . that's *swallop*."

He arched a brow, his stony belligerence

seeming to fade. "What's swallop?"

"Something reconstituted. Always terrible. Like dried potatoes, or processed canned meat, or powdered egg product."

One corner of his mouth twitched. "If you're hungry enough, swallop isn't so bad."

"But it's not the real thing."

"Who cares? It's a bodily function."

"Eating?"

"I was referring to sex," he said dryly. "But not every meal — or sex act — has to be a meaningful experience."

"I don't agree. To me, sex is about commitment, trust, honesty, respect —"

"Jesus." He had begun to laugh quietly, not in a nice way. "With standards like that, do you ever get laid?"

Zoë stared at him indignantly.

As Alex looked back at her, his amusement dissolved. He braced his hands on the table on either side of her, their bodies close but not touching. Her breath shortened, and her heart began to beat in a wild staccato.

His face was right above hers, the touch of his breath cool and sweet, like cinnamon gum. "Haven't you ever had sex just for the hell of it?"

Zoë blinked. "I'm not sure what you mean," she managed to say.

"I mean rock-your-world sex with some-

151

one you don't give a damn about. Raw, hard-core, wrong on every level. But you don't care, because it feels too good to stop. You do anything you want because you don't have to talk about it afterward. No rules, no regrets. Just two people in the dark, roughing each other up in all the right ways."

For a split second, Zoë's unruly imagination seized on the idea, and a jolt of heat went to the pit of her stomach. She could feel her pulse beating at the front of her throat. Alex's gaze tracked the visible throb before returning to her dilated eyes. In an abrupt motion, he pushed away from her. "You should try it sometime," he advised coolly. "Looks like your ex is available."

Zoë tucked her hair behind her ears and made a show of retying her apron. "Chris didn't visit me for that," she eventually said. "He just broke up with his partner. He needed to talk it over with someone."

"With you." Alex gave her a sardonic glance.

"Yes," she said warily, sensing the approach of an insult. "Why not with me?"

"A woman who looks like you? If your ex shows up to talk over his problems, cupcake, it's not for your keen psychological insight. It's a booty call."

Before she could reply, the oven timer went off.

Stung, Zoë was tempted to order him out of her kitchen. She picked up a couple of potholders and went to the oven. As soon as she opened the door, the heady fragrance of hot cake poured out in a perfumed steam of apricot and vanilla and heady spices. Taking deep breaths of the opulent sweetness, Zoë reflected that Alex was the most cynical man she'd ever met. How terrible it would be to view the world the way he did.

If he weren't such an arrogant bully, she might have felt sorry for him.

Reaching into the oven with a potholder in each hand, Zoë grasped the heavy-gauge steel pan. As she pulled it out, the burning edge of the pan touched the inside of her arm, and she inhaled sharply. She was so accustomed to minor kitchen mishaps that she didn't say a word, only set the pan calmly on the counter.

Alex was at her side in an instant. "What happened?"

"Nothing."

His gaze shot to the angry red splotch on her arm. Scowling, he pulled her to the kitchen sink and started cold water running from the faucet. "Hold it under there. Do you have a first-aid kit?"

"Yes, but I don't need it."

"Where is it?"

"In the cabinet under the sink." Zoë moved a few inches to the side, so he could open the door and extract the white plastic box. "It's just a little burn," she said, pulling her arm out of the water to look at it. "Not even enough to blister."

Alex took her wrist to reposition her arm under the water. "Keep it there."

"You're overreacting," she told him. "Do you see the marks on my hands and arms? All cooks have scars. This spot on my elbow" — she showed him her free arm — "that was when I tried to rest my arm on the counter after forgetting that I'd just set a hot pan there." She pointed to places on her left hand. "And these marks are from knives . . . this was from trying to pit an avocado that wasn't ripe enough, and this was from deboning fish. Once I stabbed right through my palm while shucking oysters —"

"Why aren't you wearing protective gear?" he demanded.

"I suppose I could wear a chef's jacket," Zoë said, "but on hot days like this, it wouldn't be very comfortable."

"You need Kevlar welding sleeves. I can get you some."

Darting a bemused glance at Alex, Zoë realized he wasn't joking. Some of her irritation faded. "I can't wear welding sleeves in the kitchen," she said.

"You need some kind of protection." Alex took her free hand and examined it with a lingering frown, his fingertips moving from one small white scar to another. "I never thought about cooking being dangerous," he said. "Unless one of my brothers or I were trying to eat something we'd made."

The brush of his fingers caused a ripple of sensation to run up her arm. "None of you can cook?" she asked.

"Sam's not too bad. Our oldest brother, Mark, is limited to making coffee. But it's good coffee."

"And you?"

"I can build a great kitchen. I just can't make anything edible in it."

Zoë made no protest as he adjusted her arm under the water again. He cradled her hand as if it were an injured bird.

"You have scars, too." Zoë dared to put her fingertip against a thin line on the side of his forefinger. "What's that from?"

"Box cutter."

She moved to another healed-over mark, a deep gouge on the pad of his thumb. "And this?"

"Table saw."

Zoë winced.

"Most carpentry accidents come from trying to save time," Alex said. "Like when you need to construct a jig to hold something in place while you're running a router. But instead you wing it, and then you pay for it." He released her hand and opened the first-aid kit, rummaging until he found a small bottle of acetaminophen. "Where do you keep the glasses?"

"The cabinet over the dishwasher."

Alex took a juice glass from the cabinet and filled it with water from the refrigerator dispenser. He gave two tablets to Zoë, and handed her the water.

"Thank you," she said. "I think my arm's okay now."

"Give it a little more time. Burn damage keeps going for a few minutes after it starts."

Resignedly Zoë stared at the water as it streamed over her skin. Alex stayed beside her, making no move to touch her again. Unlike the companionable silences she'd shared with Chris, this silence was tense and voltaic.

"Zoë," he said in a rough-soft murmur. "What I said to you earlier . . . I was out of line."

"Yes, you were."

"I . . . apologize."

Guessing that he was a man who made apologies rarely, and never easily, Zoë relented. "It's okay."

In the charged silence that followed, Zoë became acutely conscious of Alex's solid presence beside her, the steady counterpoint of his breath to her own. He reached out to test the temperature of the water, his forearm heavily muscled and dusted with dark hair.

She glanced discreetly at the hard perfection of his profile, the dark-angel handsomeness of a man who stole his pleasures wherever he could find them. The hints of dissolution — the subtle shadows beneath his eyes, the hollows of his cheeks — only made him seem sexier, elegantly lethal.

An affair with him would cost a woman every ideal she had.

Justine was right — if Zoë wanted to start dating again, Alex was not the one to start with. But Zoë suspected that even though going to bed with him would inevitably turn out to be a mistake, it was almost certainly the kind a woman would enjoy making.

The prolonged exposure to the cold water sent fine tremors through her. The more she tried to steel herself against them, the worse they became.

"Do you have a jacket or a sweater around here?" Alex asked.

She shook her head.

"Should I ask Justine —"

"No," Zoë said immediately. "Justine would call for an ambulance and a team of paramedics. Let's keep her out of this."

Amusement flickered in his eyes. "Okay." He settled a hand on her back, the warmth of his palm sinking through the thin fabric of her T-shirt.

Zoë closed her eyes. After a moment, she felt Alex's arm slide across her shoulders. He was big and warm, his body practically radiating heat. A pleasant sun-bleached, faintly salty smell clung to him.

"I have to tell you something," she managed to say. "About how I know that Chris's visit wasn't a booty call."

Alex's arm loosened. "It's none of my —"

"The reason I'm sure," she said, "is because . . ." She hesitated, the words lodging behind a lump in her throat. Alex might blame her for the failure of the marriage, the way her father and Chris's family had. He might be insulting or even cruel. Or worse, he might not care at all.

There was only one way to find out.

As she forced herself to say it, the lump

broke, and her chest and throat filled with heat. "Chris left me for another man."

ELEVEN

Upon hearing Zoë's words, the ghost, who had been lingering inconspicuously in the background, blurted, "Outta here," and fled.

Stunned, Alex looked down into Zoë's upturned face. Before he could react, she hurried on in a nervous rush. "I didn't know he was gay when we got married," she said. "Chris didn't know, either, or at least he wasn't ready to face it. He genuinely cared about me, and he thought . . . hoped . . . that marrying me would solve all the complications. That I would be enough for him. But I wasn't."

She paused, a deep carnelian flush covering her face. Her free hand dipped under the water, and then she patted her cold wet fingers against her cheeks. The sight of the sparkling droplets sliding down her smooth skin was nearly too much for Alex. Carefully he removed his arm from her back.

Encouraged by his silence, Zoë continued.

" 'A woman who looks like you' . . . I've heard that phrase all my life, and it never means anything good. People who say that always think they know exactly who I am without ever bothering to get to know me. They think I'm dumb, or fake, or conniving. They assume that all I'm interested in is having sex or . . . well, you know what they assume." She slid him a guarded glance, seeming to expect mockery. Finding none, she bent her head and resumed. "I matured a lot earlier than everyone else — by the time I was thirteen, I had to wear a C cup bra. Something about the way I looked caused other girls to not like me, and spread rumors about me in school. Boys shouted things at me when they drove by in cars. In high school, they asked me out only so they could make passes at me and lie to their friends about how far I had let them go. So for a while I stopped going out at all. I didn't trust anyone. But then I became friends with Chris. He was smart and funny and nice, and it didn't matter to him what I looked like. We became a couple — we went everywhere together, helped each other through tough times." A melancholy smile hovered at her lips. "Chris went to law school, and I went to a culinary arts school, but we always stayed close. We talked on the phone all the time, and spent summers and vacations together, and . . . eventually it all just led to marriage."

Alex wasn't quite certain how he'd come to be in this position, standing at a sink with Zoë while she confided in him. He didn't want to hear any of it. He had always hated talking about personal problems — his own, and other people's. But Zoë kept on talking, and he couldn't seem to find a way to shut her down. And then he realized that if he had really wanted to shut her down, he would have by now. He actually wanted to listen, to understand her, and that scared the hell out of him.

He heard himself ask, "Before you got married, did you and he . . ."

"Yes." Zoë's face was partially averted, but he could see the pink curve of her cheek beneath the dark sweep of her lashes. "It was affectionate. It was . . . nice. I wasn't sure if either of us was really into it, but I didn't have enough experience to know how it should be. I thought in time we'd get better at it."

Affectionate. Nice. Alex's brain summoned thoughts of Zoë's luscious naked body, and what he would have done to her, given half a chance. The glinting locks of her hair trailed like curled ribbons, and he couldn't stop himself from touching them, playing with the tousled silk. "When did you find out?"

Zoë took an extra breath as his fingertips reached the curve of her scalp and stroked gently. "He told me he'd been having an affair with another man. A lawyer at the firm. He hadn't meant for it to happen. He didn't want to hurt me. But something was missing in our relationship, and he'd never been able to figure it out."

"Given the fact that he slept with another guy," Alex said, "it's pretty obvious what was missing."

Zoë looked at him quickly, but when she saw the glint of humor in his eyes, she relaxed.

Sliding his hand to the nape of her neck, Alex relished the texture of cool, soft skin, the fine muscles beneath. The kitchen seemed to breathe around them, stirring currents of toasted air that carried the bittersweet zest of lemon rind, the dank sweetness of scrubbed wooden cutting boards, the floating richness of cake, the crisp bite of cinnamon, and the black tang of coffee. All of it whetted a deep thrill of hunger. It seemed as if Zoë were part of the feast all around him, made to be tasted and felt and sensually enjoyed. The only thing that held him back from her was a thread of honor that was stretched nearly to the breaking point. If he let himself do what he wanted, if Zoë didn't stop him, he would end up being the worst thing that ever happened to her. He had to make her understand that.

"In high school," he said, "I was the kind of asshole who would have teased and bullied you."

"I know." After a moment, Zoë said, "You would have called me a dumb blonde."

At the very least. He had been angry at the world. He'd hated all the things he couldn't have. And he would have especially hated someone as gentle and beautiful as Zoë.

She took a deep breath before asking, "Is that how you think of me now?"

Although she'd just handed him the perfect way to put some distance between them, Alex couldn't bring himself to use it. Instead he told her the truth. "No. I think you're smart. I think you're good at what you do."

"Do you think I'm . . . attractive?" she asked hesitantly.

He was nearly drowning in the desire to demonstrate exactly how attractive he found her. "You're sexy as hell. And if I thought you could handle my kind of trouble, we wouldn't be standing here talking. By now I'd have dragged you to the nearest dark corner I could find, and —" He broke off abruptly.

Zoë gave him a look that was difficult to interpret. Eventually she asked, "What makes you sure I couldn't handle you?"

She didn't know what she was asking for, from a man who couldn't remember what it was like to be innocent. Lightly gripping her hair, Alex forced her face close to his. The blond curls danced around his fingers and tickled the backs of his hands. "I'm a bastard in bed, Zoë," he said quietly. "I'm selfish and mean as the devil. I have to have all the control. And I'm . . . not nice."

Her eyes widened. "What do you mean?"

He wasn't about to discuss his sexual preferences with her. "No, we're not going there. All you need to know is that I don't make love to women, I use them. To you, sex is about kindness, honesty, commitment . . . well, I don't bring any of that to bed. If you're as smart as I think you are, you'll believe that."

"I do," Zoë said promptly.

Drawing his head back an inch, Alex stared at her. "Really?"

"Yes." But after a long hesitation, Zoë's

gaze dropped and the corners of her mouth quirked. "No," she admitted, "I really don't."

"Damn it, Zoë —" He broke off in frustration, all the more provoked because she was trying not to smile, as if she thought of him as some big pussycat trying to pose as a tiger. She was playing with fire. She wouldn't begin to understand the depravity that had passed for his love life. He knew who he was, and he knew how to hurt people — God knew he'd done it often enough.

The hint of amusement flitting across her lips drove him crazy. Before he knew what he was doing, he crushed his mouth over hers, holding her head so she couldn't jerk back. He expected resistance. He wanted to scare her off. That was how the lesson would go. But after the first innocent start of surprise, she went soft and easy against him, her fingers lacing into his hair, curving around his skull. Alex was mortified by the force of his own response. He could have no more broken her hold on him than he could have snapped a steel beam in two.

She tasted like lavender sugar. Sweet, dark-flowering kisses, opening in a way that focused all his senses on this one moment, this one blinding perception of pleasure.

Too late, he realized that she wasn't the one playing with fire.

He was.

He reached down to gather her in, all the deep curves and persimmon-smooth skin and silky heat. The feel of her was so lush, so unlike his ex-wife's spareness, that he kept adjusting his hold, trying to fit her more closely against him, and the voluptuous friction aroused him unbearably.

Once, when he was still a teen, he'd been bodysurfing on a trip to Westport with friends, and he'd timed a six-foot wave badly. He'd been tossed and turned like a load of laundry until he'd finally been deposited on the beach, so disoriented that for a few minutes he couldn't remember his own name. He felt like that now, only this time he wanted to dive back in and never come up for air.

His hands went to the inward arc of her waist and moved blindly upward. Reaching the sides of her breasts, he encountered the edges of a bra with sturdy straps designed to support substantial curves. His fingertips followed the straps in restless strokes, up to the tops of her shoulders, back down again.

Her mouth broke from his. Alex stood there panting with fractured breaths. Zoë held his gaze, her eyes pure blue and drowsy and intent. She had no understanding of how close to the edge he was. She reached behind her waist to untie her apron, and then the straps behind her neck. The garment dropped limply to the floor. Rising on her toes, she kissed him again, her fingers touching the sides of his face, stroking tenderly. This moment would haunt him for the rest of his life, the sweet bloom of her mouth, the overpowering heat of his response to her, the way the moments drifted like sparks from a fire and vanished before he could catch them.

He felt her reaching awkwardly for his hands, trying to pull them to her. She wanted him to touch her. God help him, if he started, he wouldn't be able to stop. But his will eroded in the rush of pure feeling, and resisting her was no more possible than stopping his own heart from beating. Zoë took his stiff wrist and shyly urged his hand to the front of her shirt. The backs of his fingers brushed against her breast, the tip jutting distinctly against the elastic webbing of the bra. For a second he couldn't breathe. His hand opened to cup the luxurious weight, his thumb rubbing the peak in savoring circles, until she gasped against his lips.

Alex took his hand from her, having to

secure his balance by gripping the edge of the sink behind her. His equilibrium was gone. It didn't help that Zoë began to nuzzle into his neck with erotic delicacy, nibbling and kissing, the tugs of her lips siphoning up pleasure. His body was nothing but drive and sensation. He reached down to grip her bottom with both hands, pulling her high and tight. Zoë's eyes opened as she felt the searing pressure, blatant even through the layers of their clothing. He urged her closer, letting her feel how much he wanted her, letting the hardest part of him slide with intimate exactness against the softest part of her. She quivered, a vibrant hum in her throat . . . and then she flinched with a cry that had nothing to do with pleasure.

They had both forgotten about the burn on her arm. She had accidently brushed it against his shoulder. It must have hurt like hell. The realization shocked Alex's mind into clarity. He pulled back from her and carefully gripped her arm to look at it. The quarter-sized blotch on her arm was purple, the skin slick and puffy.

Zoë stared up at him, her cheeks fever-colored, her mouth kiss-bruised. Her hand went to the taut plane of his cheek, and he felt the vibration of her palm. She was shaking. Or maybe it was him.

She began to say something, but an unearthly yowl interrupted her.

"What the hell was that?" Alex asked hoarsely, infuriated to be pulled out of the erotic dream, his heart pounding in heavy blows.

They both looked to the source of the noise near their feet. Baleful green eyes stared out from a huge mass of white fur, a thick neck cinched by a glittering band of crystals.

"That's Byron," Zoë said. "My cat."

It was an enormous, weird-looking cat, with a flat face and enough fur to create at least three more of itself.

"What does it want?" Alex asked, revolted.

Zoë bent to pet the cat. "Attention," she said ruefully. "He gets jealous."

Byron began to purr as she stroked him, the sound rivaling a Cessna single-prop engine.

"He can have your attention after I leave." Alex reached over to shut off the water, and picked up the first-aid kit. Grateful for the distraction, he brought the kit to the table and sat down, gesturing to a nearby chair. "Sit there."

Zoë obeyed, giving him a bemused glance.

Alex arranged her arm on the table with the burn facing upward. Finding a tube of antibiotic cream, he applied it in a thick layer, his head bent over the task. His hands weren't steady.

Zoë reached down to pet the massive cat, which was pacing through and around the legs of her chair. "Alex," she asked in a low voice, "are we going to —"

"No."

He knew she wanted to talk about it. But denial was a skill that had been honed over generations of Nolans, and it was going to work just fine in this situation.

In the silence, Alex heard the ghost's sardonic voice. "Is it safe to come back in now?"

Although Alex would have loved to give a scathing reply, he kept silent.

Zoë was befuddled. "You . . . you want to pretend that what just happened didn't happen?"

"It was a mistake." Alex applied a bandage, meticulously sealing the adhesive edges.

"Why?"

Alex didn't bother to soften the impatient edge of his tone. "Look, you and I don't need to know each other any more than we already do. You've got nothing to gain and everything to lose. You need to find some decent guy to go out with — someone who'll take it slow and talk about your feelings and all that sensitive crap. You need a nice guy. And that's not me."

"I'll say," the ghost chimed in.

"So we're going to forget about this," Alex continued. "No discussions, no repeat performances. If you want to find some other contractor for the remodel, I'll totally understand. In fact —"

"No," the ghost protested.

"I want you," Zoë said, and blushed hard. "I mean, you're the right person for the job."

"You haven't even seen the designs yet," Alex said.

The ghost circled them. "You can't quit. I need to spend time at that cottage."

Shove it, Alex thought.

Scowling, the ghost folded his arms and went to lean against the pantry door.

Zoë picked up a few of the pages from the table, studying them.

Alex closed the first-aid kit. "That's how the kitchen will look after the interior wall is taken out and replaced by an island." He had added as much storage as possible, as well as a row of windows that let in abundant natural light.

"I love how open it is," Zoë said. "And the island is perfect. Can people sit on this side?"

"Yes, you can line up about four bar stools." Alex leaned closer to point to the next page. "Here's the configuration on the other side — the microwave drawer, a spice drawer, and a swing-up mixer lift."

"I've always wanted a mixer lift," Zoë said wistfully. "But all of this looks expensive."

"I listed stock cabinets in the specs — they're a lot cheaper than custom. And I've got a supplier who deals in surplus building materials, so we can save on the counter-tops. If the wood flooring is salvageable, that'll cut down on costs, too."

Zoë picked up more pages from the table. "What's this?" She held up a design of the second bedroom. "There's a walk-in closet here, isn't there?"

He nodded. "I included an option for converting that into a full bath."

"A full bathroom in that little space?" Zoë asked.

"Yeah, it's tight." Alex reached over to find the design for the bathroom. He handed it to her. "No room for a cabinet. But I could put a recessed set of shelves in the wall for towels and supplies. I thought . . ." He hesitated. "I thought living so close with your grandmother, you'd probably like to have a little privacy instead of having to share the main bathroom with her."

Zoë continued to look over the rendering. "It's even better than I'd hoped for. How long would it take to get all of this done?"

"Three months, give or take."

A frown puckered her forehead. "My grandmother will leave the nursing facility in a month. I can afford to pay for her to stay an extra couple of weeks, but probably no more than that."

"Could she stay at the inn?"

"It's not set up for her. Too many stairs. And every time we can't rent out a room, it's a loss of income. Especially during the summer."

Alex drummed his fingers lightly on the table, calculating. "I could delay the garage and get some of the subcontractors working simultaneously . . . in six weeks I could make the house livable. But most of the finish work — moldings, casings, paint, would still have to be done. Not to mention replacing the air-conditioning. Your grandmother probably wouldn't take well to all the noise and activity."

"She'll be fine," Zoë said. "As long as the kitchen and main bathroom are done, we'll put up with anything."

Alex gave her a skeptical glance.

"You don't know my grandmother," Zoë said. "She loves noise and activity. She used to be a reporter for the *Bellingham Herald* during the war, before she got married."

"That's cool," Alex said, meaning it. "Back in those days, a woman who wrote for a newspaper was probably a . . ."

"Hot tomato," the ghost said.

". . . hot tomato," Alex repeated, and then snapped his mouth shut, feeling like an idiot. He sent the ghost a discreet glare. Hot tomato — what did that even *mean*?

Zoë smiled quizzically at the old-fashioned phrase. "Yes, I think she was."

The ghost told Alex, "Ask how her grand-mother is."

"I was going to," Alex muttered.

Zoë looked up from the design. "Hmm?"

"I was going to ask," Alex said, "about how your grandmother's doing."

"The therapy is helping. She's tired of staying in the nursing facility, and she's impatient to move out. She loves the island — she hasn't lived here in a very long time."

"She used to live in Friday Harbor?"

"Yes, the cottage is hers — it's been in the family forever. But my grandmother actu-ally grew up at that house on Rainshadow Road. The one you're helping Sam restore." Seeing Alex's interest, she continued, "The Stewarts — that's her family — owned a fish-canning business on the island. But

175

they sold the Rainshadow house a long time before I was born — I'd never set foot in there until I went to visit Lucy."

Hearing an imprecation from the ghost, Alex glanced at him quickly.

The ghost looked stunned and worried and excited. "Alex," he said, "it's all connected. The grandmother, Rainshadow Road, the cottage. I've got to find out how I fit in."

Alex gave him a short nod.

"Don't screw this up," the ghost said.

"Okay," Alex muttered, wanting him to shut up.

Zoë gave him a questioning glance.

"It's okay," Alex revised hastily, "if you want to bring her to Rainshadow Road for a visit. She might get a kick out of seeing it restored."

"Thank you. I think she would. I'm going to visit her this weekend, and I'll let her know. It'll give her something to look forward to."

"Good." Alex watched her as she continued to look over the renderings. It struck him that she was doing something remarkably selfless in sacrificing a year or more of her life to take care of an ailing grandparent. Was she going to have some help? Who was going to watch over Zoë? "Hey," he said softly. "You got someone to give you a hand with this? Taking care of your grandmother, I mean."

"I have Justine. And a lot of friends."

"What about your parents?"

Zoë shrugged in the way people did when they were trying to gloss over something unpleasant. "My father lives in Arizona. He and I aren't close. And I don't even remember my mother. She bailed on us when I was still pretty young. So my dad gave me to my grandmother to raise."

"What's her name?" the ghost asked in wonder.

"What's your grandmother's name?" Alex asked Zoë, feeling like he was playing the old telephone game in which a sentence was repeated until it no longer made sense.

"Emma. Actually, it's Emmaline." Zoë pronounced the last syllable "lin," as if there were no *e* at the end. "She took me in when my dad moved to Arizona. She was a widow at the time. I remember the day Dad dropped me off at her house in Everett — I was crying, and Upsie was so sweet to me —"

"Upsie?"

"When I was little," Zoë explained sheepishly, "she would always say, 'Upsie-daisy,' when she picked me up . . . so I started calling her that. Anyway, when my dad left me with her, she took me into the kitchen and stood me on a chair at the counter, and we made biscuits together. She showed me how to dip the biscuit cutter in flour, so the circles of dough would come out perfectly."

"My mother made biscuits sometimes," Alex said, before he thought better of it. He wasn't in the habit of revealing anything about his past to anyone.

"From scratch or from a mix?"

"From a can. I liked to watch her hit it against the countertop until it split open." Zoë looked so horrified that he was privately amused. "They weren't bad biscuits," he told her.

"I'll make you some buttermilk biscuits right now," she said. "I could whip them up in no time."

He shook his head as he stood from the table.

Standing in the fragrant kitchen with its cherry-print wallpaper, Alex watched as Zoë went to retrieve her apron from where it had landed on the floor earlier. She bent over, her denim capris stretching over a perfect heart-shaped bottom. That was all it took to make him want her again. He had the insane urge to go to her, take her in his arms, and hold her, just hold her and breathe her soft fragrance while the minutes bit through a long quiet hour.

He was tired of denying himself the things he wanted, and of being haunted, and most of all he was tired of picking up the pieces of his life and discovering that most of them were pieces he didn't even want. He'd learned nothing from his failed marriage with Darcy. They had always done what was necessary to satisfy their own selfish needs, taking without giving, knowing it was impossible to hurt each other because the worst hurts had already been inflicted.

"Take a few days to look at this stuff," he told Zoë as she returned to the table. "Talk it over with Justine. You've got my e-mail and phone numbers if you need to ask something. Otherwise I'll be in touch at the beginning of next week." He glanced at the bandage on her arm. "Keep an eye on that. If it starts to look infected —" He stopped abruptly.

Zoë smiled slightly as she looked up at him. "You'll put another Band-Aid on it?"

Alex didn't smile back.

He needed to numb out. He needed to drink until there were a half-dozen layers of smoked glass between him and the rest of the world.

Turning away from her, he picked up his

keys and wallet. "See you," he said curtly, and left without looking back.

TWELVE

"Well, that was fun," the ghost said, as Alex took a right on Spring Street and headed to San Juan Valley Road. "Where are we going now?"

"Sam's place."

"We're going to clear out more of the attic?"

"Among other things."

"What other things?"

Exasperated by the constant necessity of having to explain his every move, Alex said, "I want to catch up with my brother. I haven't talked to him in a while. That okay with you?"

"Are you going to tell him about doing the remodeling for Zoë?"

"Justine may have mentioned it to him already. But if she hasn't, then no, I'm not going to say anything."

"How come? It's not like it's a big secret."

"It's not a done deal," Alex said tersely. "I

may back out."

"You can't."

"Watch me." Alex found perverse satisfaction in riling the ghost.

He expected all kinds of arguments and insults. But the ghost was silent as the truck headed out of the commercial district.

Alex visited Rainshadow Road to help Sam install a pair of carriage lantern sconces on a fireplace wall paved with antique hand-made bricks. As they worked, an English bulldog named Renfield sat on a cushion in the corner and watched them with bulging eyes and an open drooling mouth. Renfield had been a rescue dog, with such abundant health problems that no one had wanted him. Somehow Mark's girlfriend, Maggie, had sweet-talked him into taking in the dog, and although Sam had initially protested, he had eventually caved as well.

It was hardly a surprise that Renfield paid no attention to the presence of a ghost in the room. "I thought dogs were supposed to have a sixth sense about supernatural beings," the ghost had once remarked to Alex.

"On his best day," Alex had replied, "he's only got about three senses working right."

As they worked together on the installation, it was clear that Sam was in the kind of relaxed good mood that could only have come from recently getting laid. As the ghost had predicted, Sam was falling for Lucy Marinn in a major way, although Sam was determined to view it as one of his usual no-commitment deals. "I hit the jackpot with this girl," Sam told Alex. "She is sweet, sexy, smart, and she's fine with having a casual relationship."

It had been a long time since Alex had seen his brother as preoccupied with a woman as he was with Lucy Marinn. Maybe never. Sam always played it cool, never letting his feelings — or anyone else's — get the better of him.

"This casual relationship involves sex?"

"It involves *great* sex. Like, an hour after we're done, my body is still saying 'thank you.' And Lucy doesn't want commitment any more than I do."

"Good luck with that," Alex said. Leveling a light fixture against the wall, he used a chalk pencil to mark the screw hole locations.

Sam's enthusiasm dimmed visibly. "What do you mean?"

"Ninety-nine percent of the women who say they don't want commitment either secretly do want it, or at least they want you to want it."

"Are you saying Lucy's playing me?"

"It could be even worse than that. She could be sincere in thinking she can handle being a jump-off, when in reality she's not equipped for it. In which case —"

"What's a jump-off?"

"A woman you're having a no-strings relationship with. As in, you have sex with her, and then —"

"You jump off." Sam scowled. "Don't call Lucy that. And the next time you ask me how my life is going, remind me not to tell you."

"I didn't ask you how your life was going. I asked you to pass me the half-inch masonry bit."

"Here," Sam said in annoyance, giving him the drill bit.

For the next couple of minutes, Alex drilled pilot holes in the brick and vacuumed the dust out of them. Sam held the light fixture in place as Alex connected the wiring, inserted sleeve anchors into the carriage lantern, and tapped them into the pilot holes. He tightened it with a few deft twists of a wrench.

"Looks good," Sam said. "Let me try the other one."

Alex nodded and picked up the second lantern to hold it against the brick.

"There's something I wanted to mention," Sam said casually. "Mark and Maggie set the wedding date for mid-August. And Mark just asked me to be the best man. Hope that's okay with you."

"Why wouldn't it be?"

"Well, he could only ask one of us. And I guess since I'm the next oldest —"

"You think *I* might have wanted to be the best man?" Alex interrupted with a brief, sardonic laugh. "You and Mark have been raising Holly together. Of course you should be the best man. It'll be a miracle if I show up at all."

"You have to," Sam said in concern. "For Mark's sake."

"I know. But I hate weddings."

"Because of Darcy?"

"Because a wedding is a ceremony where a symbolic virgin surrounded by women in ugly dresses marries a hungover groom accompanied by friends he hasn't seen in years but made them show up anyway. After that, there's a reception where the guests are held hostage for two hours with nothing to eat except lukewarm chicken winglets or those weird coated almonds, and the DJ tries to brainwash everyone into doing the electric slide and the Macarena, which some drunk idiots always go for. The only good part about a wedding is the free booze."

"Can you say that again?" Sam asked. "Because I might want to write it down and use it as part of my speech."

The ghost, who was in the corner of the room, sat with his head resting on his bent knees.

Finishing the wiring for the second sconce, Sam attached it to the brick, tightened the anchor sleeves, and stood back to view his handiwork. "Thanks, Al. You want some lunch? I've got some sandwich stuff in the fridge."

Alex shook his head. "I'm going up to the attic, doing a little more clearing out."

"Oh, that reminds me . . . Holly loves that old typewriter you found. I gave it a couple of shots of WD-40 and reinked the ribbon with a stamp pad. She's been having a blast with it."

"Great," Alex said indifferently.

"Yeah, but here's the interesting thing. Holly noticed the liner of the tweed case was loose, and there was a little corner of something sticking out. So she pulls it out, and it's a weird piece of cloth with a flag and some Chinese characters on it. And there's a letter, too."

The ghost lifted his head.

"Where is it?" Alex asked. "Can I take a look?"

Sam nodded toward the sofa. "It's in the side table drawer."

While Sam put away the tools and vacuumed the remaining dust, Alex went to the table. The ghost was at his side instantly. "Personal space," Alex warned under his breath, but the ghost didn't budge.

A feeling of apprehension crawled down the back of Alex's neck as he opened the drawer and picked up a piece of thin silky fabric, yellowed with age, about eight by ten inches. It was stained in places, the corners dark. A Chinese Nationalist flag dominated the top. Six columns of Chinese characters had been printed under the flag.

"What is it?" Alex wondered aloud, his voice drowned out by the vacuum.

Even so, the ghost heard him, and his reply was soft but audible. "It's a blood chit." The term was unfamiliar to Alex. Before he could ask what it meant, the ghost added quietly, "It's mine."

The ghost was remembering something, emotions emanating like smoke, and Alex couldn't help but catch the edge of them.

The world was smoke and fire and panic. He was falling faster than gravity, ricocheting through blue and cirrus-white, the metal skin of his aircraft twisting like a licorice whip as the forces of heaven and hell wrenched at it. His knees pulled up and his elbows cinched into a fetal position, the last thing every fighter pilot did before dying. It wasn't training, it was the body's primal recognition that it was about to go through more pain and damage than it could endure.

His heart beat out the syllables of a woman's name, over and over.

Alex shook his head to clear it, and looked at the ghost.

"What do you make of it?" he heard Sam ask.

The ghost stared at the silk in Alex's hand. "They gave them to American flyers to carry on missions over China," he said. "In case the plane went down. The writing says, 'This foreigner has come to help in the war effort. Soldiers and civilians should rescue, protect, and provide him with medical care.' We kept them in our jackets — some people sewed 'em in."

In a monotone, Alex heard himself explaining the blood chit to Sam.

"Interesting," Sam said. "I wonder whose it was. I'd like to find out who owned that typewriter, but there's no name in the case."

Alex began to reach for the letter. He hesitated as if he were about to put his hand into an open flame. He didn't want to read what was on that piece of paper. He had a feeling it had never been meant to be seen.

"Do it," the ghost whispered, his face grim.

The paper was stationery-sized and brittle. It wasn't signed. It was addressed to no one.

I hate you for all the years I'll have to live without you. How can a heart hurt this much and still go on beating? How can I feel this bad without dying from it?

I've bruised my knees with praying to have you back. None of my prayers have been answered. I tried to send them up to heaven but they're trapped here on earth, like bobwhites beneath the snow. I try to sleep and it's like I'm suffocating.

Where have you gone?

Once you said that if I wasn't with you, it wouldn't be heaven.

I can't let go of you. Come back and haunt me. Come back.

Alex couldn't bring himself to look at the ghost. It was bad enough to stand at the outer edge of what the ghost felt, trapped in the nimbus of a grief that felt worse than anything he'd ever experienced. It was like being injected with a slow-acting poison.

"I think a woman wrote it," he heard Sam say. "It sounds like a woman, doesn't it?"

"Yeah," Alex replied with difficulty.

"But why was it typed? You'd expect something like that to be handwritten. I wonder how the guy died."

More sadness, coming in aching waves from the ghost. Alex had to clench his fist to keep from striking out at him, even though it would have been like flailing at mist. Anything to make it stop.

"Cut it out," Alex muttered, his throat tight.

"I can't," the ghost said.

"Cut what out?" Sam asked.

"Sorry," Alex said. "I've gotten into a habit of talking to myself. I meant to ask, can I take this with me?"

"Sure, I've got no —" Sam broke off and looked at him closely. "Holy crap. Are you misting up?"

With horror, Alex became aware that his eyes were watering. He was about to start bawling. "Dust," he managed to say. Turning away, he added in a muffled voice, "I'm going upstairs. Work on the attic."

"I'll come up and help you."

"No, I'm on it. You sweep up down here. I

need some private time."

"You get a lot of private time already," Sam said. "Maybe it wouldn't hurt to have some company."

That almost provoked a laugh from Alex. *I haven't been alone for months,"* he wanted to tell his brother. *"I'm being haunted."*

He could feel the weight of Sam's gaze.

"Al . . . you okay?" his brother asked.

"I'm just great," Alex said viciously, heading out of the room.

The ghost's mood hadn't eased by the time they reached the attic. Alex reflected grimly that there was something worse than being followed everywhere by a spook, and that was being followed by a spook who had gone full emo on him.

"It may have escaped your notice," Alex said in a murderous tone, "that I suck at dealing with my own baggage. I'm damned if I can deal with yours."

"At least you know what your baggage is," the ghost said, glaring at him.

"Yeah, which is why I spend half my time drinking to forget it."

"Only half?" came the sarcastic rejoinder.

Alex brandished the handful of printed silk in one hand. "You really think this was yours?"

"Take it easy with that. Yes, it's mine."

Alex held up the letter in his other hand. "And you think this was about you."

The ghost responded with a single nod. His eyes were midnight-dark, his features grim. "I think Emma wrote it."

"Emma." Alex blinked in astonishment, his fury fading. "Zoë's grandmother? You think you and she . . ." Slowly he made his way to the staircase and lowered to the top step. "That's a hell of a leap to take," he said, "with nothing to back it up."

"She was a writer for the *Herald* —"

"I know. And she lived here, and maybe there's some minuscule chance that type-writer might have been hers. But there's no proof of anything."

"I don't need proof. I'm remembering things. I remember *her*. And I know that piece of cloth in your hand was mine."

Alex unfolded the blood chit and looked at it again. "There's no name on this. So you can't be sure it's yours."

"Is there a serial number?"

Alex scrutinized the cloth and nodded. "On the left side."

"Is it W17101?"

As Alex read the serial number . . . *W17101* . . . his eyes widened.

The ghost gave him a superior look.

"You can remember *that* but you can't remember your own name?" Alex asked.

The ghost glanced over the heaps of boxes and objects in the attic, the packed-away memories shrouded by dust and years. "I remember that I was once a man who loved someone." He began to pace, his hands shoved deep in the pockets of his bomber jacket. "I need to find out what happened. If Emma and I got married. If —"

"If you *what?* You died."

"Maybe I didn't. Maybe I came back."

"From a plane crash?" Alex asked sarcastically. "From what I could tell, it was a hell of a lot more than a bumpy landing."

The ghost seemed determined to invent some kind of happy ending for his story. "When you love someone that much, you wouldn't let anything stop you from going back to her. You would survive no matter what."

"Maybe it was all on her side. Maybe to you it was just a fling."

"I still love her," the ghost said with quiet ferocity. "I still feel it. Locked up in here." The ghost put a fist on his own chest. "And it fucking hurts."

Alex believed that. Because it hurt just to be near it.

He watched the ghost resume pacing.

193

If the ghost's image accurately reflected what he had been in life, he'd had the build for a pilot, lean and supple, with enough developed muscle mass to counteract black-outs from the punishing maneuvers of a dogfight. "Kind of tall to be a pilot back in your time," Alex said.

"I could fit in a P-40," the ghost said distantly.

"You flew a warhawk?" Alex asked, fascinated. In his boyhood, he had once built a model of the distinctive shark-toothed World War II plane. "You sure?"

"Pretty sure." The ghost was lost in thought. "I remember being shot at," he eventually said, "and pulling so much g-force that I'd feel the blood leaving my head and everything would get blurry. But I'd hold it until the guy on my tail either gave up or passed out."

Alex fished his phone from his pocket and opened the mobile browser.

"Who are you calling?"

"No one. I'm trying to find out if there's some way to identify a pilot with the serial number on this thing." After a minute or two of searching, Alex found a page of information. He frowned as he read.

"What is it?" the ghost asked.

"Out of luck. No master list. They were

194

issued in bulk from different U.S. and Chinese sources. Some of them were reissued to new pilots after the first ones died. And since the serial numbers were considered classified information, the lists they did have were probably destroyed."

"Look up Emmaline Stewart," the ghost said.

"Not on this phone. The connection's too slow." Alex scowled at the tiny glowing LCD screen. "I need a laptop for this."

"Go to the *Bellingham Herald* site," the ghost insisted. "They'd have to have something about her."

Alex went to the Web site and worked the phone for a minute. "The online archive only goes back to 2000."

"You stink at research. Ask Sam. He could find out everything about Emma in about five minutes."

"People in their eighties," Alex said, "don't usually leave an Internet trail. And there's no way I'm asking Sam — he'd want to know why I'm interested, and I don't want to explain."

"But —"

"You'll see Emma soon enough, when Zoë brings her to the island. And if I were you, I wouldn't get too excited. She's an old lady now."

The ghost snorted. "How old do you think I am, Alex?"

Alex gave him an assessing glance. "Mid to late twenties."

"After what I've been through, age gets pretty damn relative. The body is just a fragile container for a soul."

"I'm not that enlightened," Alex informed him. After attaching his phone to the portable speakers, he went to the box of garbage bags and pulled one out.

"What are you doing?" the ghost asked.

"Going through more of this junk."

"Sam's computer is downstairs," the ghost protested. "You could ask to borrow it."

"Later."

"Why not now?"

Because Alex had to feel like he had some kind of control over his own damn life. The encounter with Zoë that morning, and reading the old typewritten letter, had unsettled him. He needed a break from free-floating emotion and drama and unanswered questions. The only thing he could think of was to do something practical.

The ghost, reading the volatility of his mood, retreated and fell silent.

As a series of Tony Bennett duets played in the background, Alex went through boxes of tax documents, old magazines, broken

196

dishes, moth-eaten clothes, and toys. The floor was littered with dead insects and dirt. Behind one dilapidated box, Alex found an ancient mousetrap with a dried-up rodent carcass. Grimacing, he used a wad of plastic to pick it up and throw it away.

Opening a box, Alex found a stack of leather-bound account books and ledgers. A plume of dust rose as he pulled out the first book, making him sneeze. Kneeling, he sat back against his heels, thighs slightly splayed for balance. He read a few of the brittle age-darkened entries, all of them neatly written in faded black ink.

"What is it?" the ghost asked.

"I think it's an account book from a fish-canning factory." Alex turned a few pages. "Here's an inventory . . . Steam machines, flaying and frying grids, soldering tools, tin plate scissors . . . A whole hell of a lot of olive oil . . ."

The ghost watched as Alex skimmed through the book. "Whoever owned the factory must have had plenty of dough."

"For a while," Alex said. "But this area was overfished until the salmon disappeared for a while. Most of the fisheries and factories went out of business in the sixties." He delved into the box and pulled out more ledgers. Opening another, he found a few handwritten business letters, one concerning a lithographing company that was supplying labels, and another about a state-run committee that was forcing the cannery to lower its prices. He paused to look more closely at one of them. "The factory was owned by Weston Stewart."

The ghost looked at him alertly, recognizing Emma's maiden name.

Alex continued to sift through the ledgers. The entries in the last few books were typed instead of handwritten. A few newspaper clippings and black-and-white photographs had been tucked into the pages.

"What are those pictures?" the ghost asked, approaching.

Alex sensed the ghost's eagerness to hover over him, to get a good view. "Don't crowd me. I'll tell you if there's anything you need to see. These are just exterior shots of buildings." He picked up a newspaper article announcing the closing of the factory. "Place went out of business in August 1960," he said. Sorting through more clippings, he saw one titled "Local Fish Industry on Brink of Collapse" and one describing local complaints about the stench of the waste products coming from the cannery. "Here's an obituary for the factory owner," Alex said. "Weston Stewart. He died less than a year after the cannery closed. Doesn't say what cause. Survived by a widow, Jane, and three daughters: Susannah, Lorraine, and Emmaline."

"Emmaline," the ghost repeated as if the word were a talisman.

A tiny picture of a young woman headed the last newspaper clipping. Her shoulder-length blond hair had been arranged in sculpted waves, her lips rouged with lipstick. She was the kind of woman who was beautiful in spite of technically not being beautiful. Her eyes were clear and curious and melancholy, as if she stared into an unwritten future with nothing to hope for.

"Come take a look at this," Alex said.

The ghost hurried to look over his shoulder. The moment he saw the photo, he made a quiet sound as if he'd been gut-punched.

EMMALINE STEWART, JAMES HOFFMAN TO BE MARRIED SEPTEMBER 7, 1946

After resigning her staff position at the *Bellingham Herald,* Miss Emmaline Stewart has returned home to San Juan Island to prepare for her coming marriage to Lieutenant James Augustus "Gus" Hoffman, who served as a transport pilot in the China-Burma-India theater. During the last two years of the war, Lieutenant Hoffman flew 52 missions across the aerial support route over the Himalayas. Vows will be spoken at 3:30 at an open service at First Presbyterian on Spring Street.

As Alex read the article a second time, he felt emotion closing around him, so heavy and smothering that the more you tried to wade through it, climb out, the deeper and faster you sank.

"Stop," Alex managed to say.

The ghost retreated, his face tearless and drawn. "I'm trying." But he wasn't, and they both knew it. This grief was his way of being close to Emma, the only connection available until he was with her again.

"Just *chill*," Alex said tersely. "I won't be much use to you . . ." — he paused for a deep gasp of air — "if you give me a damned heart attack."

The ghost's gaze followed the faded clipping that had dropped from Alex's fingers. The yellowed paper spun, leaflike, to the floor. "This is what it feels like to love someone you can't have."

Crouched there amid piles of boxed-up memories and dust and shadows, Alex thought that if he were ever capable of feeling that way about anyone — which he doubted — he'd rather take a bullet to the head.

"It'll happen to you," the ghost said, as if he could read Alex's thoughts. "It'll hit you like an ax someday. Some things in life, you can't escape."

"Three things," Alex said unsteadily. "Death, taxes, and Facebook. But falling in love, I can definitely escape."

The ghost let out a huff of amusement. To Alex's relief, the agonizing yearning began to fade.

"What if you could meet your soul mate?" the ghost asked. "You'd want to avoid that?"

"Hell, yes. The idea that there's one soul out there, waiting to merge with mine like some data-sharing program, depresses the hell out of me."

"It's not like that. It's not about losing yourself."

"Then what is it?" Alex was only half listening, still occupied with the viselike tightness of his chest.

"It's like your whole life you've been falling toward the earth, until the moment someone catches you. And you realize that somehow you've caught her at the same time. And together, instead of falling, you might be able to fly." The ghost went to the discarded clipping and stared down at the photo, riveted. "She's a beaut, isn't she?"

"Sure," Alex said automatically, although there was nothing of Zoë's sparkling allure in the photo, only a hint of resemblance.

"Fifty-two missions over the Himalayas," the ghost said, reading the article aloud. He looked at Alex. "They called it the 'Hump.' The transport pilots had to fly fully loaded cargo planes. Bad weather, high altitude, hostile aircraft. Dangerous as hell."

"Were you . . . are you . . ." — Alex reached for the clipping on the floor — "this guy? Gus Hoffman?"

The ghost mused over the possibility. "I flew a P-40. I'm sure of it. Not a cargo plane."

"You were a pilot facing the enemy," Alex said. "What's the difference?"

The ghost looked outraged. "*What's the difference* between a fighter or a transport? You're in a fighter, you're alone. There's no low-and-slow, no coffee and sandwiches, no one else to keep you company. You fly alone, you face the enemy alone, you die alone."

Alex was secretly amused by the pride and arrogance threaded through his tone. "So you were in a P-40. Facts are, you were a pilot, you were in love with Emma, and you remember stuff about the house she grew up in, as well as the cottage at Dream Lake. All this falls in line with you being Gus Hoffman."

"I must have come back to her," the ghost said distractedly. "I must have married her. But that would mean —" He gave Alex a sharp glance. "Zoë could be my grand-daughter."

Alex rubbed his forehead and pinched the corners of his eyes with a thumb and fore-finger. "Oh, great."

"That means hands off from now on."

"You were pushing me to go after her," Alex said in outrage.

"That was before I knew about this. I don't want you becoming part of my family tree."

"Back off, pal. I'm not going near *anyone's* family tree."

"I'm not your pal. I'm . . . Gus."

"Theoretically." Alex glared at him as he stood and whacked the dust from his jeans. He set the article aside and tied the top of the large garbage bag.

"I want to find out what I looked like. And when I died, and how. I want to see Emma. And I —"

"I want some peace and quiet. Not to mention five minutes alone. I wish to hell you could find a way to disappear for a while."

"I could try," the ghost admitted. "But I'm afraid if I do, I might not be able to talk with you again."

Alex gave him a sardonic glance.

"You don't know what it was like," the ghost said, "being alone and invisible to everyone. It was bad enough that even getting to talk to *you* was a relief." He looked contemptuous at Alex's expression. "Hasn't occurred to you to think about that, has it? You ever tried to put yourself in someone else's shoes? Ever taken one minute to wonder about someone else's feelings?"

"No, I'm a sociopath. Just ask my ex-wife."

A reluctant grin spread across the ghost's face. "You're not a sociopath. You're just an asshole."

"Thanks."

"It's good you got divorced," the ghost said. "Darcy wasn't the right woman for you."

"I knew that when I first met her. Which is exactly why I married her."

Pondering that, the ghost shook his head in disgust and looked away. "Never mind. You *are* a sociopath."

THIRTEEN

As soon as the contracts were signed and a schedule of periodic payments had been agreed upon, a large number of decisions had to be made quickly. Zoë had instantly approved of the cream-colored stock cabinetry and the maple for the butcher-block countertops. However, she still had to choose hardware such as knobs, pulls, and plumbing fixtures, as well as tile, carpet, appliances, and lighting.

"This is where it helps to have a limited budget," Alex had told Zoë. "Some of the decisions are going to make themselves when you see the prices." They had agreed to keep to the bungalow style of the house as much as possible, with simple wainscoting, rich wood, and subtle tones with the occasional bright splash of accent color.

Justine had no interest in color palettes or browsing among tile samples, which meant that Zoë would choose the decorating and finishes. "Besides," Justine had said to Zoë, "you're the one who's going to live there, so you decide how it should look."

"What if you end up not liking it?"

"I like everything," Justine said cheerfully. "Go for it."

That was fine with Zoë, who liked going to builders' supply stores and looking through hardware catalogs. And she wanted the opportunity to spend more time with Alex. No matter how much she learned about him, he remained a fascinating stranger. He was not a charmer like his brother Sam, nor did he try to be. There was something unreachable about him, an intransigent remoteness. But somehow that only made him sexier.

Although Zoë had no doubt that Alex drank too much — he certainly hadn't tried to pretend otherwise — so far he had lived up to his reputation for being reliable. Alex arrived early whenever they had agreed to meet. He liked schedules and lists, and he used more sticky notes than anyone Zoë had ever met. She was sure he had to buy them in bulk. He put them on walls and windows, attached them to cables and flooring samples and catalogs, used them as business cards, appointment reminders, and shopping lists. When Zoë didn't know the location of a place he had mentioned, he drew a little map and stuck it on the side of her bag. When they went to an appliance store, he stuck blue squares on all the models of refrigerators, dishwashers, and ovens that were the right dimensions for the kitchen.

"You're wasting trees," Zoë told him at one point. "Have you ever thought of making notes on your phone, or getting a digital tablet?"

"Post-its are faster."

"What about writing a list on one big piece of paper?"

"I do that sometimes," he said. "On jumbo Post-its."

Maybe it was because he was so controlled that the discovery of a quirk was something of a relief to Zoë. She would have liked to learn more about him, to find out his weaknesses. To find out if she could possibly be one of them.

There were, however, no chinks in the armor. Alex had taken to treating her with a calculated politeness that made her wonder if the scene in the kitchen at Artist's Point had been a dream. He asked Zoë plenty of questions about her family and her grandmother. He'd even asked about Grandpa Gus, whom she'd never met and knew next to nothing about, other than he'd been a pilot in the war and afterward had worked as an engineer at Boeing. Eventually he'd died of lung cancer long before Zoë was born.

"So he was a smoker," Alex had said in a faintly censorious tone.

"I think everyone was back then," Zoë replied ruefully. "Upsie told me that my grandfather's doctor said that smoking was probably good for his nervous condition."

Alex had taken particular interest in that. "Nervous condition?"

"PTSD. Back then they called it 'shell shock.' I think Grandpa Gus had it pretty bad. His plane was shot down over the Burmese jungle behind Japanese lines. He had to hide for a couple of days, alone and wounded, before he could be rescued."

After telling Alex about her family's past, Zoë expected him to do the same. But when she tried to find out more about him, asking about his divorce, or his brothers, or even something like why he'd become a contractor, he turned quiet and standoffish. It was maddening. The only way she knew to handle his evasiveness was to be patient and encouraging, and hope that in time he might open up to her.

Zoë had an innate compulsion to take care

of people. It must have been in the Hoffman blood, because Justine had it, too. They both loved to welcome travel-weary or burned-out guests at the inn, most of whom were battling the endless variety of troubles that came along with being human. It was gratifying to be able to offer them a quiet room with a comfortable bed, and a good breakfast in the morning. Although none of that could fix anyone's problems, it was an escape.

"Do you ever get tired of this?" Justine had asked one day, putting away clean dishes while Zoë made cookies. "All this baking and cooking and stuff."

"No." Zoë rolled out cookie dough into a perfectly even sheet. "Why do you ask?"

"No reason. I'm just trying to figure out what you like about it. You know how I feel about cooking. If it wasn't for the microwave, I'd have starved long before you ever started working here."

Zoë had grinned. "I've wondered the same thing about all your jogging and bike-riding. Exercise is the most boring thing in the world to me."

"Being outside in nature is different every day. The weather, the scenery, the seasons . . . it's always changing. Whereas with baking . . . I've seen you make cookies about

209

a hundred times. It's not like you get a lot of excitement."

"I do, too. When I need excitement, I change the shape of the cookies."

Justine had grinned.

Zoë picked out cookie cutters shaped like flowers, ladybugs, and butterflies. "I love doing this. It reminds me of the time early in my life when most of my problems could be solved by a cookie."

"I'm still at that time in my life. I have no problems. No real problems, that is. And that's the key to happiness — knowing how good you've got it while you've still got it."

"I could be happier," Zoë had said reflectively.

"How?"

"I'd like to have someone special. I'd like to know what it's like to really fall in love."

"No you don't. Being single is the best. You're independent. You can go on adventures with no one to hold you back. You can do whatever you want. Enjoy your freedom, Zo — it's a beautiful word."

"I do enjoy it, a lot of the time. But sometimes freedom seems like a word for not having anyone to snuggle with on Friday night."

"You don't have to be in love to snuggle with someone."

"It doesn't feel the same to snuggle with someone you don't love."

Justine grinned. "Are we using 'snuggle' as a metaphor? Because it reminds me of the obituary I read about Ann Landers, where it said one of her most popular columns ever was a poll asking if women would choose cuddling or sex. Something like three quarters of her readers said cuddling." She made a face.

"You would choose sex," Zoë said rather than asked.

"Of course. Cuddling is fine for about thirty seconds, but then it's irritating."

"Physically irritating? Emotionally irritating?"

"Every kind of irritating. And if you cuddle with a guy too often, it encourages him to think you're having a relationship, and it gets all meaningful."

"What's wrong with meaningful?"

"Meaningful is a synonym for serious. And serious is the opposite of fun. And my mother told me that life should always be fun."

Although Zoë hadn't seen Justine's mother, Aunt Marigold, for years, she remembered how beautiful and eccentric she had been. Marigold had raised her only child as a free spirit, just as she had been.

211

Sometimes she had taken Justine to attend festivals with odd names, such as the Beltane Bash or the Old Earth Gather. She had made food Zoë had never heard of before, things like Covenstead Bread with honey and citron, and Groundhog Day cake, and Half Moon cauliflower. After visiting distant relatives, Justine had returned with stories of participating in drumming circles and "drawing down the moon" rituals held in the forest at midnight.

Zoë had often wondered why Marigold never visited the inn, and why she and Justine seemed virtually estranged. When she had tried to ask, Justine had flatly refused to discuss the subject.

"Most parents," Zoë ventured, "tell their children that life *shouldn't* always be fun. Are you sure that wasn't what she said?"

"No, I'm sure it's supposed to be fun. That's why the inn is perfect for me — I like to meet someone new, get to know them superficially, and send them on their way. A continuous supply of short-term friendships."

Unlike Justine, Zoë wanted permanence in her life. She had liked the stability of marriage, and the companionship, and she hoped to marry again someday. However, the next time she would have to choose very carefully. Even though the divorce with Chris had been cordial, she never wanted to go through something like that again.

As for Alex Nolan, he wasn't the kind of man who would fit in with her plans. Zoë decided that she would focus on cultivating a friendship with him, nothing more. She knew herself well enough to be certain that she was not a short-term-affair kind of person. And she would have to take Alex at his word, when he claimed that she wouldn't be able to handle him as a lover. *"I have to have all the control,"* he'd told her in that raw-velvet voice, and, *"I'm not nice."* Which had been intended to warn her away, but at the same time had aroused a wild curiosity about what he'd meant.

Alex was relieved to begin the physical work of the remodel, starting with the teardown of the kitchen wall. He and two guys from his crew, Gavin and Isaac, prepared the area with plastic and removed fixtures and outlets. Gavin, a trade-level carpenter, and Isaac, who was in the process of getting LEED certified for green construction jobs, were both serious about their work. Alex could trust them to show up on time and get the job done as safely and efficiently as possible. Wearing goggles and dust masks, the three of them took the wall down to the studs with pry bars. They tore out chunks of plaster, occasionally reaching for a reciprocal saw to cut through stubborn nails.

The hard physical work felt good to Alex, helping him expend some of the pent-up frustration that had accumulated during the past few days with Zoë. She had qualities that annoyed the hell out of him. She was unreasonably perky early in the morning, and she always seemed to want to feed him. She read cookbooks as if they were novels, and she recounted restaurant menus in astonishing detail, seeming to expect he would find the subject as fascinating as she did. Alex had never been fond of people who looked on the bright side of life, and Zoë had made it into an art form. She neglected to lock doors. She trusted salespeople. She started a conversation with the appliance dealer by telling him exactly how much she had to spend.

Everywhere Alex went with Zoë, whether it was the hardware store or the flooring company or a sandwich shop to get a couple of cold drinks, men checked her out. Some of them tried to be discreet, but some made no attempt to hide their fascination with her jaw-dropping beauty and her grade-A rack. The fact was, Zoë was eye candy, and short of disfiguring herself there was nothing she could do about it. At the sandwich shop, a pack of four or five guys leered until Alex had moved in front of Zoë and sent them a look of imminent death. They had all backed off. He'd done the same thing at other times, in other places, silently warning them away even though he had no right. She didn't belong to him. But he kept watch over her anyway.

It would be a full-time job to fend off the poachers. Until he'd met Zoë, Alex would have scoffed at the idea that beauty could be a problem for someone. But it would be difficult for any woman to be subjected to that kind of relentless attention. It explained the reason for Zoë's innate shyness — the wonder was that she ever dared to go out at all.

Now that the work on the Dream Lake cottage had started, Alex wouldn't have to see Zoë for at least a month, except in passing. It would be a relief, he thought. He would get his head clear.

The first payment was due tomorrow. Justine had offered to drop it in the mail, but Alex had asked to pick it up at the inn in the morning. He needed to take it directly to the bank. He'd laid out his own money for the initial supplies and expenses, and since the divorce there wasn't a hell of a lot of surplus cash in the coffers.

After working late on the cottage with Gavin and Isaac, Alex went home. He was so tired from the day's exertions that he didn't bother scrounging for dinner. He didn't even reach for the bottle of booze, only took a shower and went to bed.

When the alarm went off at six-thirty, Alex felt like hell. Maybe he was coming down with something. His mouth was parched, and his head ached ferociously, and the effort to lift a toothbrush felt like bench-pressing a kettlebell. After a long shower, he dressed in jeans and a tee with a flannel shirt over it, but he was still cold and shaking. Filling a plastic cup with water from the sink, he drank until a wave of nausea forced him to stop.

Sitting on the edge of the tub, he struggled to keep the water down, and wondered wretchedly what was wrong with him. Gradually he became aware of the ghost standing at the bathroom doorway.

"Personal space," Alex reminded him. "Get out."

The ghost didn't move. "You didn't have anything to drink last night."

"So?"

"So you're in withdrawal."

Alex looked at him dumbly.

"Hands aren't steady, right?" the ghost continued. "Those are the DTs."

"I'll be fine after I have some coffee."

"You should probably have a shot of booze. Guy who drinks as much as you, it's better to wean off slowly rather than go cold turkey."

Alex was swamped with incredulous outrage. The ghost was wildly overstating the case. He drank a lot, but he knew what he could tolerate. Only drunks got the DTs, like the homeless guys in alleys or the barflies who drank the nights away. Or his father, who'd died of a heart attack while recreational diving at a tourist resort in Mexico. After a lifetime of alcohol abuse, Alan Nolan's coronary arteries had been so blocked that, according to the doctors, he would have needed a quintuple bypass surgery had he lived.

"I don't need to wean off anything," Alex said.

It would have been easier to take if the ghost had been mocking or superior, or even apologetic. But the way he looked at Alex, with a sort of gravity touched with pity, was too offensive to bear.

"You might want to take the day off and rest," the ghost said. "Because you're not going to get much work done."

Glaring at him, Alex lurched to his feet. Unfortunately the motion was too much for his outraged digestive system, and he was forced to lean over the toilet, retching.

After a long time he made it to his feet again, rinsed his mouth and splashed his face with cold water. Looking into the mirror, he saw a pale, haggard complexion and puffy eyes. He recoiled in horror, having seen his father in this shape about a thousand times while growing up.

Gripping the sides of the sink, he forced himself to raise his head and stare in the mirror again.

This wasn't who he wanted to be. But it was what he'd become, what he'd made of himself.

Had there been any tears in him, he would have wept.

"Alex," came the quiet voice from the doorway. "You're not afraid of work. You're used to tearing things down. Rebuilding."

Even as sick as Alex was, the metaphor didn't escape him. "Houses aren't people."

"Everyone's got something that needs fixing." The ghost paused. "In your case, it happens to be your liver."

Alex struggled to strip off his shirts, having sweated through both of them. "Please," he managed to say. "If there is any mercy in you . . . don't talk."

The ghost obliged, retreating.

By the time Alex had gotten dressed again, the shaking had subsided, but the clammy hot-and-cold feeling kept crawling over him. His nerves were strung tight. The difficulty in finding the work boots he wanted, the same ones he'd worn the previous day, sent him into a full-blown fury. As soon as he laid his hands on the boots, he threw one of them at the wall so hard that it ruined the paint and left a dent in the Sheetrock.

"Alex." The ghost reappeared. "You're acting crazy."

He hurled the other boot, which shot through the ghost's midsection and left another dent in the wall.

"Feel better now?" the ghost asked.

Ignoring him, Alex retrieved the boots and jammed them on. He tried to think above the violent pounding of his head. He had to get the check from Justine and take it to the bank.

"Don't go to Artist's Point," he heard the ghost say urgently. "Please. You're in no shape. You don't want anyone to see you like this."

"By 'anyone' you mean Zoë," Alex said.

"Yes. You'll upset her."

Alex gritted his teeth. "I don't give a damn." Grabbing his car keys, wallet, and heavy black sunglasses, he went to his truck and pulled it out of the garage. As soon as he drove onto the main road, the sunlight seemed to split his skull open with the precision of surgical instruments. He groaned and swerved, looking for a place to pull over in case he needed to puke.

"You're driving like you're in a video game," the ghost said.

"What do you care?" Alex snapped.

"I care because I don't want you to kill anyone. Including yourself."

By the time they had arrived at Artist's Point, Alex had sweated through another T-shirt, and he was trembling with what felt like fever chills.

"For pity's sake," the ghost said, "don't go through the front entrance. You'll scare the guests."

Much as Alex would have loved to defy him, the ghost had a point. Surly and exhausted from the effort of driving, he pulled around to the back of the inn and parked near the kitchen entrance. The smell of food drifted outside, causing the hot sting of nausea in his throat. As his sunglasses slipped down his nose on a fresh bloom of sweat, Alex ripped them off and flung them across the gravel with a curse.

"Get control of yourself," he heard the ghost say tersely.

"Fuck off."

A retractable screen door covered the kitchen's back entrance. Through the fine solar mesh, Alex saw that Zoë was alone in the kitchen, making breakfast. Pots simmered on the stove, and something was baking in the oven. The smell of browning butter and cheese nearly made Alex recoil.

He tapped on the doorjamb, and Zoë looked up from a cutting board piled high with hulled strawberries. She was dressed in a short pink skirt and flat sandals, and a white ruffly top, and an apron tied at the waist. Her legs were toned and gleaming, calf muscles neatly rounded. The blond curls had been drawn up to the top of her head, a few escaping to dangle against her cheeks and neck.

"Good morning," she said with a smile. "Come in. How are you?"

Alex avoided her gaze as he entered the kitchen. "I've been better."

"Would you like some —"

"I'm here for the check," he said curtly.

"Okay." Although this was certainly not the first time he'd ever been brusque with her, Zoë gave him a questioning glance.

"The first payment's due," Alex said.

"Yes, I remember. Justine handles the office work, so she'll write the check for you. I'm not sure which account to write it from."

"Fine. Where is she?"

"She just went out for an errand. She'll be back in five or ten minutes. The big coffee machine is broken, so she's picking up some carafes of breakfast blend from a local place." A timer went off, and Zoë went to take a dish out of the oven. "If you want to wait for her," she said over her shoulder, "I'll pour some coffee and you can —"

"I don't want to wait." He needed the check. He needed to leave. The heat and light of the kitchen were killing him, and yet he had to clench his teeth to keep them from chattering like one of those plastic windup skulls from a joke shop. "She knew the check was due today. I texted her."

Zoë set the casserole dish on a pair of trivets. Her smile had vanished, and her voice was even softer than usual as she replied. "I don't think she knew you would be here this early."

"When the hell else would I come? I'm going to be working on the cottage all day." The anger rushed through him in stronger and stronger waves, and he was helpless to do anything about it.

"What if I run it out to you after breakfast? I'll drive out to the cottage, and —"

"I don't want to be interrupted at work."

"Justine will be here soon." Zoë went to pour some coffee into a white porcelain cup. "You . . . don't seem well."

"Bad sleep." Alex went to the counter and tugged at the roll of paper towels. The roll spun out. He let out a few foul curses as a stream of paper toweling shot from the dispenser.

"It's all right." Zoë came to him instantly. "I'll fix it. Go sit down."

"I don't want to sit down." He took a paper towel and blotted his sweating face, while Zoë deftly rerolled the long white cylinder. Although he tried to keep his mouth shut, words tumbled out, the syllables shredded like they'd been pulled across razor blades. He was jittery and furious, wanting to throw something, kick something. "Is this how you two run a business? Agree to something, and then no follow-through? We're going to rewrite the payment schedule. My time may not be important to you, but I have to count on things being done when they're supposed to be done. I've got to get to work. My guys are probably already there."

"I'm sorry." Zoë set a cup of coffee on the counter beside him. "Your time is important to me. Next time I'll make certain the check is waiting for you first thing in the morning."

Alex hated the way she talked to him, as if she were humoring a lunatic or soothing a barking dog. But it worked anyway. He felt the anger drain so abruptly that he was dizzy. And he was so tired that he could barely stay on his feet. Jesus. There was something really wrong with him.

"I'll come back tomorrow," he managed to say.

"Have this first." Zoë nudged the cup toward him.

Alex looked down at the coffee. She had put cream in it. He always drank his coffee black. But he found himself reaching for the cup, taking it with both hands. To his stunned mortification, the cup shook violently, liquid sloshing over the edge.

Zoë was staring at him. He wanted to swear at her, turn away, but her gaze held his and wouldn't let go. Those round blue eyes saw too much, things he had spent a lifetime concealing. She couldn't help but see how close he was to crumbling. But there was no judgment in her expression. Only kindness. Compassion.

He had a sudden urge to drop to his knees and rest his head against her in exhausted supplication. Somehow he kept standing, swaying on stiff legs.

Carefully Zoë laid her hands over his, so they were both holding the cup. Even though her hands were half the size of his, her grip was surprisingly firm, subduing the shaking. "Here," she whispered.

The cup lifted to his mouth. Her hands kept his steady. He took a swallow. The liquid was hot and smooth, soothing his sandpaper throat, melting through the chill of his insides. It was slightly sweet, and the touch of cream had softened the bitterness, and it was so unexpectedly good that he found himself desperately gulping the rest. His veins hummed with a gratitude that bordered on worship.

Zoë's hands eased from his. "More?"

He nodded with a hoarse, wordless murmur.

She made another cup, stirring cream and sugar into it, while sunlight broke through the shuttered window and embossed her hair with bright ribbons. It occurred to him that she was making breakfast for a crowd of paying guests. There were still things cooking on the stove, in the oven. And not only had he interrupted her work, he had stood there and ranted about his own schedule like it was so much more important than hers.

"You're busy," he muttered in the prelude to an apology. "I shouldn't have —"

"Everything's fine." Her voice was gentle. She set the cup of coffee at the table, and pulled a chair back. Clearly she intended for him to sit for this one.

He cast a wary glance around the kitchen, wondering what the ghost would make of this, but thankfully he was nowhere to be seen. Alex went to the table and sat. He drank the coffee slowly, able to do it on his own as long as he was careful.

Zoë worked at the counter. The clink of utensils, the sounds of pots and plates being deftly wielded, was oddly relaxing. He could sit here and no one was going to bother him. Closing his eyes, he let himself sink into the feeling of temporary peace. Of sanctuary.

"Another?" he heard her ask.

He nodded.

"First try some of this." She set a plate of food in front of him. As she leaned closer, he could smell her skin, fresh and sweet, like she had been steeped in sugared tea.

"I don't think I can —"

"Just try." She put flatware on the table

and went back to the stove.

The fork was as heavy as a lead mallet. Alex looked at the plate. It contained a neat portion of something with layers of bread, the top lightly puffy and golden-brown. "What is it?"

"A breakfast strata."

As Alex took a cautious bite, he discovered that the whole of it was infused with a mild custardy lightness. It was like a quiche but infinitely more delicate, the texture perfect for delivering the ripe hint of tomato and mild cheese. The flavor of basil came through last, hitting his tongue with a clean, pungent note.

"Do you like it?" he heard Zoë ask. He couldn't even reply. Hunger had come raging, and he had given over entirely to the single-minded act of eating.

Zoë brought a glass of cold water. When the plate was empty, Alex set down his fork, and drank the water, and silently evaluated his physical condition. The change was nothing short of miraculous. His headache was fading, and the tremors were gone. He was sated with taste and warmth . . . it was like being drunk on food.

"What was in that?" he asked, his voice distant as if he were speaking from a dream.

Zoë had replenished his coffee cup. She

leaned her hip against the table as she faced him. Her cheeks were satiny from the heat of the stove. "French bread I made myself. Heirloom tomatoes I bought at the farmer's market. The cheese was made on Lopez Island, and the eggs were laid this morning from wyandotte hens. The basil was grown in the herb garden out back. Would you like another helping?"

Alex could have eaten an entire pan of it. But he shook his head, deciding it was better not to push his luck. "I should leave some for your guests."

"There's more than enough."

"I'm fine." After taking a swallow of coffee, he looked intently at her. "I wouldn't have thought —" He broke off, not able to describe what had just happened to him.

Zoë seemed to understand. A faint smile played at the corners of her mouth. "Sometimes," she said, "my cooking has a kind of . . . effect . . . on people."

The back of his neck prickled, not unpleasantly. "What kind of effect?"

"I don't let myself think about it too much. I don't want to ruin it. But sometimes it seems to make people feel better in a sort of . . . magical way." Her smile turned rueful at the edges. "I'm sure you don't believe in things like that."

"I'm surprisingly open-minded," Alex said, conscious of the ghost wandering back into the kitchen.

"Well, look at you." The ghost sounded relieved. "You're not going to keel over and die."

Zoë's attention was diverted as her cat meowed at the back door, its furry bulk visible through the screen. As soon as she let Byron inside, he sat and looked at her, flicking his tail impatiently.

"Poor little fluff-monster," Zoë cooed, putting a spoonful of something in a dish, setting it on the floor.

The cat gobbled up the treat ferociously, looking like the kind of pet that would eat its owner.

"Isn't it against the health code to let him in here?" Alex asked.

"Byron's not allowed near the dining or food-prep areas. And he only visits the kitchen for a few minutes a day. Most of the time he sleeps on the porch or in the back cottage." She came to collect Alex's plate. The front of the apron gaped to reveal just enough lush cleavage to make him lightheaded. He dragged his gaze up to Zoë's face.

"You get grumpy," she said gently, "after you've had too much to drink."

"No," Alex said, "I get grumpy when I've stopped."

She looked at him closely. "You mean for good?"

Alex gave her an abbreviated nod. There were countless reasons for him to quit, but the one that mattered most was that he didn't want to need anything that much. He'd been caught off guard by the realization of how dependent he'd become on booze. It had been easy to delude himself into thinking it wasn't a problem because he wasn't disheveled and homeless, had never been arrested. He was still functional. But after what had happened that morning, he couldn't deny that he had a problem.

It was one thing to be a heavy drinker. It was another to become a full-blown alcoholic.

Zoë went to take his dishes to the sink. "From what I've heard," she said over her shoulder, "it's not an easy habit to break."

"I'm about to find out." Alex stood from the table. "I'll be back tomorrow morning for the check."

"Come early," Zoë said without hesitation. "I'm making oatmeal."

Their gazes met across the room.

"I don't like oatmeal," Alex said.

"You'll like mine."

Alex couldn't seem to tear his gaze away. She was so soft-looking, so radiant, and he let himself think, just for a moment, about the way she would feel under him. The magnitude of his attraction to her was nearly overwhelming. He wanted things from her that he'd never wanted from anyone, things beyond sex, and none of it was possible. It was like standing at the edge of a cliff, fighting not to fall while the wind pushed at his back.

As Zoë returned his stare, rampant color washed over her face, contrasting with the brilliant pale gold of her hair. "What is your favorite food?" she asked, as if the question were profoundly intimate.

"I don't have a favorite food."

"Everyone has a favorite."

"I don't."

"There must be some —" A timer interrupted her. "Seven-thirty," she said. "I have to pour coffee for the first guests. Don't go, I'll be right back."

When Zoë returned, however, Alex was gone. A sticky note had been applied to the backsplash above the sink, with a word written in black ink:

THANKS

Zoë took the note in her hand, drawing her thumb over the surface. A sweet, terrible ache filled her chest.

Sometimes, she thought, you could rescue a person from trouble. But some kinds of trouble, a person had to rescue himself from.

All she could do for Alex was hope.

FOURTEEN

Alex was tormented by nightmares from midnight to dawn, his body jerking as if he'd been hit with an electric current. He dreamed of demons sitting at the foot of his bed, waiting to tear at him with long sharp claws, or of the ground opening beneath him and letting him fall into endless darkness. In one dream he was hit by a car on a dark road, the impact knocking him backward onto hard midnight asphalt. He stood over the unconscious body on the road, looking down at his own face. He was dead.

Startled awake, Alex sat up in bed. He was soaked in sweat, the sheets sticking to him in a clammy film. A bleary glance at the clock revealed that it was two in the morning.

"Son of a bitch," he muttered.

The ghost was nearby. "Go get some water," he said. "You're dehydrated."

Alex lurched from the bed and went into

the bathroom. He drank some water, turned on the shower, and stood there for a long time with the hot spray pounding on the back of his neck. He wanted a drink. It would make him feel better. It would take away the dreams, the god-awful sweating. He wanted the taste of alcohol, the sweet burn of it in his mouth. But the fact that he wanted it so badly was enough to steel him against it.

After finishing the shower, Alex dragged on some pajama pants and pulled a blanket from the bed. Too exhausted to change the sheets, he went to the living room. Breathing heavily with effort, he collapsed onto the couch.

"Maybe you should go to a doctor," the ghost commented from the corner. "There must be something they could give you to make this easier."

Alex rolled his head slowly against the arm of the couch. "Don't want it to be easier." His tongue felt too big for his mouth. "I want to remember exactly what this is like."

"You're taking a risk, trying to do this on your own. You might fail."

"I won't."

"How can you be sure?"

"Because if I do," Alex said, "I'm going to end it."

The ghost gave him a sharp look. "End your life?"

"Yeah."

The ghost was silent, but the air seethed with worry and anger.

As Alex's breathing slowed, memories slid around the headache. "By the time my brothers and sister left home," he said after a while, his eyes closed, "both my parents were drinking nonstop. And when you live with a drunk, the sum total of your childhood is about thirty minutes. The good days were when they forgot I was there. But when either of them remembered they still had a kid in the house, that was when it sucked. It was a minefield, living with them. You never knew when you'd set your foot wrong. Sometimes asking my mom for food or trying to get her to sign a school permission slip would make her explode. One time I changed the TV channel when my dad was sleeping in the recliner, and he woke up just long enough to backhand me. I learned never to ask for anything. Never need anything."

It was the most that Alex had ever told anyone about the way he'd grown up. He'd never explained that much even to Darcy. He wasn't sure why he'd wanted the ghost to understand.

There was no sound or movement, but Alex had the impression of the ghost settling for the night, occupying a shadow in the corner. "What about your brothers or your sister? Did any of them try to help?"

"They had their own problems. There's no such thing as a healthy, normal family surrounding a drunk. The trouble belongs to everyone."

"Either of your parents ever take a shot at this?"

"You mean quit drinking?" Alex let out a quiet breath of amusement. "No, they both rode that train off the tracks."

"While you were still on board."

Alex changed position on the sofa, but it didn't help the feeling of being uncomfortable in his own skin. His nerves were raw, his senses smarting. The nightmares were ready to come creeping back as soon as he tried to sleep. He could feel them waiting nearby like a pack of wolves.

"I dreamed I died," he said abruptly.

"Earlier tonight?"

"Yeah. I was standing over my own body."

"Part of you is dying," the ghost said pragmatically. At Alex's shocked silence, the ghost added, "The part of you that drinks to avoid pain. But avoiding pain only makes it worse."

"Then what the hell am I supposed to do?" Alex asked in weary hostility.

"At some point," the ghost replied after a while, "you may have to stop running and let it catch up to you."

After a few hours of broken sleep on a couch that resembled a torture rack, Alex showered, dressed, and made his way to Artist's Point like one of the walking dead. He hoped to hell that he wouldn't have to see Justine — he wasn't going to be able to tolerate her today.

To his relief, Zoë was alone. She welcomed him into the kitchen, urging him to sit at the table immediately. "How are you this morning?"

He gave her a sullen glance. "If you measure headaches using the Fujita scale, I just reached F-5."

"I'll get you some coffee."

The vicious throb at the front of his skull made him want to gouge his eyes out. Carefully he lowered his forehead to his arms and tried to think past the jitters. "Why don't you bring me a six-pack of Old Milwaukee tall boys to go with it," he said in a muffled voice.

Zoë set a cup on the table. "Try this first."

Alex fumbled for the coffee.

237

"Let me —" Zoë began, reaching out to steady his hands.

"I don't need help," he growled.

"Okay," she said calmly, backing off.

Her patience annoyed him. The cherry-printed wallpaper hurt his eyes. His head was pounding like a thrash band concert.

Once he got the cup to his mouth, he drank as if his life depended on it. He asked for another.

"Have some of this first," she said, placing a shallow bowl in front of him.

The bowl contained a golden cakelike square spangled with candied fruit cut into strips no thicker than a cat's whisker. Cinnamon-scented steam rose to his nostrils. Zoë poured a splash of whole milk into the bowl and gave Alex a spoon.

The baked oatmeal was chewy and tender, crisp at the edges, the crumbly sweetness infused with a sunny citrus tang. As the milk soaked into the oatmeal, the texture loosened and each spoonful became more moist and delicious than the last. It was the farthest thing possible from the gray-slurry oatmeal of his youth.

As he ate, the toxic feeling left him, and he relaxed and began to breathe deeply. Something like euphoria settled over him, a mellow warmth. Zoë moved around the kitchen, stirring contents of pots, pouring milk into pitchers, and chatting lightly without requiring a response. He had no idea what she was talking about — something that had to do with the difference between a cobbler and a brown Betty, none of which made any sense to him. But he wanted to wrap the sound of her voice around him like a clean cotton blanket.

His days fell into a pattern: every morning before work he went to the kitchen at Artist's Point and ate whatever Zoë put in front of him. The half hour he spent with her was the time around which everything else was structured. After he left, the sense of well-being faded hour by hour until he reached the raw and ragged evenings.

His sleep was riddled with nightmares. Often he dreamed he was drinking again, and he awoke smothered in shame. Even the knowledge that it had only been a dream, that he hadn't fallen off the wagon, failed to ease the panic. What got him through the nights was knowing that he would see Zoë soon.

She always said "good morning" as if it actually were one. She set plates of beautiful food in front of him, every bite blooming with color and fragrance, flavors nudg-

239

ing each other forward in clever ways. Soufflés so light they seemed to have been inflated by a wish, eggs Benedict blanketed with hollandaise the color of sunflowers. She created symphonies of eggs and meat, poems of bread, melodies of fruit.

The kitchen was more personal to Zoë than her bedroom. It was her artistic space, arranged exactly as she wanted it. The open pantry, lined floor to ceiling with shelving, held rows of deeply colored spices in glass cylinders, and huge old-fashioned penny candy jars filled with flour, sugar, oats, vivid yellow cornmeal, plump beige pecan halves. There were bottles of pale green olive oil from Spain, inky balsamic vinegar, Vermont maple syrup, wildflower honey, jars of homemade jam and preserves, bright as jewels. Zoë was as particular about the quality of her ingredients as Alex was about making angles plumb and square while framing a house, or using the right carpentry nail for a given task.

Alex loved to watch Zoë work. She moved around the kitchen with a kind of clunky-ballerina quality, graceful movements often coming to the abrupt finish of a heavy pot being lifted with both hands, or an oven door closing decisively. She wielded a sauté pan as if it were a musical instrument, gripping the handle and jerking it back with a sharp elbow motion so that the contents appeared to jump and toss themselves.

On the seventh morning that Alex ate breakfast at the inn, Zoë served him a plate of buttermilk grits sprinkled with cheese and spicy red crumbs of fried chorizo sausage. She had stirred some of the sausage renderings into the grits, charging them with salty, earthy richness.

As he ate, Zoë came to the table and sat beside him, sipping her own coffee. Her nearness made him slightly uneasy. She usually worked while he had breakfast. He stole a glance at the finespun skin of her inner arm, noticing the healed-over burn mark. He wanted to press his lips to it.

"The cabinets have come in," he told her. "We'll start installing them later this week, and I'll build the kitchen island."

"Build it? I assumed you would order a premade one."

"No, it'll be a little cheaper — and look more custom — if we make one by trimming down some stock cabinets, finish the outside with beadboard, and add the countertop." He smiled as he saw her expression. "It'll look great. I promise."

"I wasn't doubting you at all," she said. "I'm just impressed."

Alex drowned his smile in the cup of coffee. "I'm not doing anything special," he said. "Just basic carpentry."

"It's special when it's my house."

"In another week, I'll need to know what paint colors you want."

"I've almost got them all picked out," she said. "Soft white for the beadboard and trim, and butter yellow for the walls, and pink for the bathrooms."

Alex gave her a skeptical glance.

"It's a nice pink," she said, laughing. "A blush tone. Lucy helped me pick it out. She says pink is a great color for bathrooms because the reflected glow is flattering."

The image jumped into his mind before he could stop it . . . Zoë, stepping out of the bath, surrounded by pink walls, tender wet curves gleaming in steam-misted mirrors.

Rising to her feet, Zoë went to check on something in the oven. "Would you like some water?"

He was hot from head to toe. "Yes, thanks." Picking up his cell phone, he glued his gaze to it, reminding himself desperately to keep his distance from Zoë.

She stopped beside him and set a glass of ice water by his plate. She was close enough that he could breathe in her fragrance, cottony and flowery, with hints of smoke from the chorizo, and all he could think of was how much he wanted to turn and press his face against her, and lock his arms around her hips. He stared at his phone, scrolling blindly through text messages he had already read.

Zoë lingered beside him. "You need a haircut," she murmured, a smile in her voice. He felt a light touch on the back of his neck . . . her fingers . . . sliding softly through the hair at his nape. His hand clamped on the phone until the casing threatened to crack.

He managed a quick, irritable shrug that caused Zoë's hand to fall away. She went back to the stove, and he heard the sound of something being whisked in a pot. She was speaking casually about her plans to go to the floating fish market attached to the main dock in Friday Harbor, they had just brought in a fresh catch of halibut. Struggling to clear away the haze of lust, Alex did math problems in his head. When that didn't work, he resorted to gripping his fork so that the tines dug sharply into the heel of his hand. That settled his rampaging desire just enough that he could walk. He pushed back from the table and stood, muttering something about going to work.

"Tomorrow, then," Zoë said too brightly. "Pumpkin ginger pancakes."

"I can't make it tomorrow." Realizing how brusque he'd sounded, Alex added, "I've got to get to work earlier, now that we're putting up Sheetrock."

"I'll make you something to go," Zoë said. "Stop by, and I'll hand it through the doorway. You won't even have to come in."

"No." Exasperated, he couldn't think of any way to soften the refusal.

The ghost entered the kitchen. "Are we leaving?"

"Yes," Alex said reflexively.

"So you will come by?" Zoë asked in confusion.

"No," he snapped.

Zoë followed him to the back door, looking tense and miserable. "I'm sorry. I didn't mean to offend you."

The ghost looked perplexed and indignant. "What does she mean? What happened? I told you before —"

"Don't start," Alex warned him wrathfully. Glancing down at Zoë's worried face, he amended, "Don't start jumping to conclusions. There's nothing to be sorry for."

"There's *something* to be sorry for," the ghost insisted. "Because from what I can tell, hormones are flying through the air like a biblical plague."

Zoë stared up at Alex as if she were trying to read his thoughts. "Then why did you react like that when I touched you?"

Alex shook his head in baffled annoyance.

"Obviously you didn't like it," Zoë said, flushing deeply.

"*Damn* it, Zoë." The only way he could stop himself from grabbing her was to slam his hands on the counter, on either side of her. She jumped a little, her eyes turning round. "I liked it," Alex told her gruffly. "If I liked it any more, I'd have you bent over the counter right now, and it wouldn't be to help you roll out biscuit dough."

The ghost groaned. "Spare me," he said, and made a fast exit.

Zoë colored at his deliberate crudity. "Then why —" she began.

"Don't give me that," Alex said testily. "You know why. I'm a drinker in the process of drying out. I've just been divorced, and I'm a paycheck away from being broke. I don't know of any more damning combination of qualities a man could have. Except maybe being impotent on top of it."

"You're not impotent," she protested. After a brief hesitation, she asked, "Are you?"

Alex covered his eyes with one hand and

began to laugh. "Sweet Jesus," he said feelingly, "I wish I were." After a moment, seeing the hurt confusion on her face, he sobered and let out a sigh. "Zoë. I don't do friendship with women. And the only other possibility is sex, which is not going to happen." Alex paused, seeing a snowy dusting of flour on the crest of her cheek. Unable to resist, he reached out and brushed it off gently with his thumb. "Thank you for getting me through this past week. I owe you for that. So the best thing I can do for you in return is stay away long enough for you and me to get some distance from this."

Zoë was quiet, staring at him, weighing his words. An oven timer went off, and a hint of rueful amusement hitched the corners of her mouth into apostrophes. "Every moment of my life is measured by oven timers," she said. "Please don't go yet."

He stayed, watching as she went to pull a pan of biscuits from the oven. The smell of hot bread flooded the kitchen.

Returning, Zoë stood very close to Alex. "I know you're right," she said. "And I know what I've got ahead of me. Probably more than I can handle. My grandmother will be here in a month, and after that . . ." She gave a helpless little shrug. "So I know my limits, and I think I know yours. But the

246

problem is —" A nervous breath of laughter. "Sometimes you meet a really nice guy, but no matter how you try, you can't seem to make yourself want him. But that's not nearly as bad as when you meet the wrong guy, and you can't make yourself *not* want him. You feel hollow inside, just waiting and wishing and dreaming. You feel like every moment is leading to something so amazing that there's no name for it, and if you could just get there with him, it would be such a . . . relief. It would be all you'd ever need." She let out a trembling sigh. "I don't want distance from you. Maybe I shouldn't have said that, but I have to let you know how I —"

"I already know," he said coldly, dying inside. "Give it a rest, Zoë. I've got to go."

Zoë nodded. She didn't even look offended. Somehow she knew that it was the only way he could leave her, that some things couldn't be seasoned to make them go down easier.

Alex reached for the door handle, but she stopped him with a touch on his wrist.

"Wait," she said. "One more thing."

Even though she was no longer touching him, the skin of his wrist had come alive with craving. It was getting worse, he thought with something like despair, this need that threatened to turn him inside out.

"From now on I'll never mention anything about this again," Zoë said, "or tell you about my feelings, or even try to be friends with you. But in return, I want one favor."

"The cat door," Alex said in resignation.

She shook her head. "I want you to kiss me. One time."

"What? No." He was aghast. *"No."*

"You owe me a favor."

"Why the hell do you want that?"

Zoë looked stubborn. "I just want to know what it feels like."

"I kissed you once before. Right here."

"That doesn't count. You were holding back."

"You want me to hold back," he assured her grimly.

"No I don't."

"Zoë, damn it, this is not going to change anything."

"I know that. I don't expect anything to change." She was practically vibrating with nerves. "I just want it as a sort of . . . amuse-bouche."

"What's an amuse-bouche?" he managed to ask, afraid of the answer.

"It's a French term for a tidbit the waiter brings from the chef at the beginning of a meal. Nothing you order or pay for, it's just . . . given." At his stunned silence, she added helpfully, "The literal translation is 'to please the mouth.' "

Alex gave her a dark glance. "You want a favor from me, it's going to involve crown molding or adding extra can lights. I draw the line at amusing your bouche."

"*One kiss* is impossible? Twenty seconds of putting your lips against mine scares you that much?"

"Now you're going to time it," he said sardonically.

"I'm not going to time it," she protested. "That was just a suggestion."

"Well, you can forget it."

She looked offended. "I don't understand why you're angry."

"Like hell. We both know you're trying to prove a point."

"What point is that?"

"You want to make sure I know what I'm giving up. You want me to be sorry about not going after you."

She opened her mouth to deny it. But she hesitated.

"If I did kiss you," Alex said, "the only reason I'd do it would be to make you sorry as hell that you asked for it." He gave her a hard look, willing her to back down. "Still want it?"

"Yes," Zoë said promptly, and closed her eyes and lifted her face.

Alex was right, of course. Any kind of relationship between them was a bad idea, for many reasons. But she still wanted him to kiss her.

She stood with eyes closed, braced for whatever he would do. An electric quietness surrounded them. She felt him move nearer, and his arms went around her so slowly that a shiver crossed over her like rough light. There was the curious sensation she remembered from before, of being absorbed, drawn in, as if he were feeling her with all his senses, drinking in every breath and blush and heartbeat.

One of his hands came up to her face, angling her jaw upward, his fingers shaping over the fragile bones. A soft brush against her mouth, and another, ephemeral kisses that made her lips feel swollen. Her balance faltered, but he gripped her against the support of his body and held her steady. Bending his head lower, he dragged his mouth along the thin, blood-heated skin of her throat. She felt the tip of his tongue rest against a pulse point, and she went weak, her hands clutching at his shoulders. Slowly he kissed his way up to her jaw, while one of his hands cupped the back of her head to lift it, and finally she felt the full, hard pressure of his mouth on hers, making her dizzy with wholesale relief.

Soft plangent sounds rose in her throat. She reached up to grip his head with her hands, anything to keep his mouth on hers. But the kiss dissolved with a muffled laugh, and he looked down into her dazed face with a tender, mocking amusement she had never seen from him before.

She struggled to speak between ragged breaths. "Alex . . . please . . ."

"Shhh." His lashes half lowered over eyes that were startlingly bright in the heightened color of his face. His gently restless hands moved over her hair, her body, her back.

"I want . . ." she tried to say, but the dazzle of heat made it impossible to think. She tried again. "I want . . ."

"I know what you want." The hint of a smile burned out, and his head bent again.

He opened her mouth with his, sent his tongue deep. The kiss turned rougher, wetter, acquiring a subtle erotic rhythm. To her mortification, her hips began to roll forward, seeking the hard pressure of him. She couldn't stop herself. If only she could be somewhere else with him, some quiet and shadowy place where nothing would bother them. Just the two of them away from the rest of the world. The pleasure thickened, her thoughts dissolving. Sensations blended into a sweet ache that seemed to come from outside and inside at the same time. She arched feverishly, trying to bring herself closer against him.

Alex pulled his mouth from hers, and crushed her against his chest. "No more," he said, sounding shaken. "Zoë . . . no . . . be still . . ."

She shuddered as he held her, his breath rushing in hot bursts against her hair. Linking her arms around his lean waist, she let her fingertips make a timid foray into the top edges of his back pockets, while his heartbeat pressed against hers. It felt as if she might fall to pieces without his hard grip holding her together.

"We're even now," she heard him whisper.

She managed a nod, her face hidden.

"I didn't mean to do it that way." Alex nipped softly at the outer curve of her ear. "I was going to make it hurt, just a little."

"Why didn't you?"

A long, wondering hesitation. "I just couldn't."

He eased her away. Zoë forced herself to look into his eyes, and saw that the same force of will that had impelled him to stop drinking was now being repurposed.

This wouldn't happen again. He wouldn't allow it.

An oven timer went off again, and she jumped at the piercing sound.

Alex smiled slightly, breaking their shared gaze, and turned away.

Zoë went to the oven without looking back. She heard the back door open and close.

Neither of them had said anything.

Sometimes silence was easiest, when the only word left was good-bye.

FIFTEEN

A month passed, and somehow the new direction of Alex's life held. The ghost had not expected to learn anything from Alex during their enforced association, but as it turned out, he did. Alex had to wrestle his addiction hour by hour, sometimes even minute by minute, but he was about as stubborn as it was possible for a man to be. To the ghost, quitting drinking looked a lot like jumping into the water and hoping that somehow you'd figure out how to swim before you went under.

Alex distracted himself with work, and plenty of it. He did such meticulous handwork on the Dream Lake cottage that any master craftsman would have been proud to claim it. Alex worked long into the nights, sanding, buffing, staining, painting, and in the process he consumed enough candy bars to send a normal person into diabetic shock. Thanks to the ghost's nagging, Alex also ate regular meals throughout the day, although he would have to eat a lot more to make up for the deficit of calories he'd been used to consuming in the form of alcohol.

Alex saw Zoë on two occasions, once to collect paint swatches. That had lasted about a minute and a half, and then he was gone. The second time, Zoë had come to the cottage for Alex to show her the progress on the remodel. He had been businesslike. Zoë had been restrained. Gavin and Isaac, for their parts, had been so mesmerized by Zoë that neither of them had so much as hammered a nail while she was there.

From all appearances, Zoë's visit had barely affected Alex. He knew how to build a wall, how to fortify it until nothing could break through. There was no way for Zoë to reach Alex now, and that was probably for the best. Still, the ghost couldn't stop feeling regretful about it. And Alex refused to discuss exactly what, if anything, he still felt for Zoë. The subject was off-limits.

The ghost understood.

A woman could do that to you — reach that place in your soul where the best and worst of you was kept. And once she was there, she owned that place and never left.

That was why he hadn't told Alex about his newfound memories of Emmaline Stewart, the scenes unrolling in front of him like a moving-picture show.

Emma had been the youngest and liveliest of Weston Stewart's three daughters. She was bookish, and funny, and just farsighted enough that she'd occasionally needed reading glasses. Wonderful cat-eye glasses with thick black frames, which she loved to wear to goad her mother, Jane. Emma would never catch a man, wearing those glasses, her mother had said. And Emma had claimed that she would catch the right man by wearing those glasses.

The ghost remembered being alone in the cottage with her, after sharing a picnic beside Dream Lake. She had read to him, a piece she had written about local high schools that had forbidden female students to "paint" their faces, meaning to use lipstick, cheek rouge, or powder. High school girls across Whatcom County had objected to the regulation, and Emma had interviewed principals of three different schools about the controversy.

"The wearing of lipstick leads to the ruin of the first barrier of a girl's nature," Emma had quoted one of the principals, her eyes bright with amusement behind the glasses. *"Next come cigarettes, then liquor, and after that, unmentionable acts will occur."*

"What unmentionable acts?" he had asked her, kissing her cheek, her neck, the soft little space behind her ear.

"You know."

"I do not. Describe one for me."

Emma had laughed deep in her throat. "No."

But he had persisted, kissing and teasing, trying to pull her hands to his body. She had giggled and feigned reluctance, knowing how to provoke his desire.

"Just tell me which body parts are involved," he'd said, and when she'd still refused, he'd made suggestions about just what might constitute an unmentionable act.

"Dirty language isn't going to get you anywhere," she'd told him primly.

He had grinned. "It's already gotten me past the first four buttons of your blouse."

And she'd flushed and gone still as he murmured softly to her, pulling all the little buttons free of their moorings . . .

The remembered physical intimacy with Emma was intoxicating. And yet the desire and pleasure that a soul could experience was far deeper and more profound than any mere physical sensation.

The day that he would see her again was approaching. But the fierce anticipation was tempered by the feeling that something was wrong, that there was something he needed to know, to set right. He was grateful for the time Alex spent at the cottage; it had given him enough gossamer filaments to be woven into a memory or two. But that wasn't enough. He needed to go back to Rainshadow Road . . . something had happened there that he needed to remember.

After going through the storage space where she and Justine kept odd pieces of furniture and framed pictures and other items they had never found use for, Zoë had gathered an assortment of objects for the Dream Lake cottage. Among them were a set of vintage metal bowling alley lockers, each square little door painted a different color . . . a retro wall clock shaped like a coffee cup . . . a teal blue Victorian cast-iron bed frame. She had also tagged some pieces of furniture from Emma's former apartment that had been sent to Friday Harbor, things like a set of leather club chairs, a wicker trunk table, a collection of teapots that would be displayed on a set of built-in bookshelves. The quirky mixture would fit well into the new clean lines of the remodeled house, and Zoë knew that her grandmother had always enjoyed touches of whimsy in her surroundings.

It had been six weeks since Alex had

started remodeling the cottage. True to his word, the kitchen had been completed, and so had the main bedroom and bathroom. Since the original wood flooring had turned out to be unusable, Zoë had agreed to let Alex install laminate flooring in a honey maple shade, and she had to admit that it looked beautiful and surprisingly natural. The second bedroom and pocket bathroom still had to be completed, and the garage hadn't been built yet, which meant that Alex would be spending time at the cottage after Zoë and Emma had moved in. Zoë wasn't certain how she felt about that. On the recent occasions when she'd seen him, the strain of mutual discomfort had made them both awkward.

Alex looked healthier, more well-rested, the shadows gone from beneath his eyes. But his rare smiles were as thin as a knife blade, his mouth was hard with the bitterness of a man who knew he would never have what he truly wanted. His remoteness wouldn't have bothered Zoë nearly so much if she hadn't seen the other side of him.

With Justine's help, Zoë would spend a couple of days getting the cottage ready with dishes, bed linens, pictures, and other things to make it cozy and welcoming. Then she would go to Everett and bring her grandmother back to the island.

Emma's nurses had provided frequent updates about her physical therapy and the course of medications they had put her on. They had also warned her that Emma had already started to show signs of "sundowning," which meant that late in the day or in the evening, she might become agitated, and ask repetitive questions more frequently than usual.

Over the course of several conversations, Colette Lin, the elder-care consultant, had also helped Zoë to understand what to expect in the future. That whenever some of Emma's abilities were lost, they were not likely to come back. That she would have sequencing problems, doing things in the wrong order, until something as simple as making a pot of coffee or doing laundry would be impossible. Eventually she would deteriorate to a point when she would start to wander and get lost, and then she would have to be taken to a secure locked facility for her own safety.

It was difficult to read Emma's moods, especially over the phone, but she seemed to be facing her illness with the same mixture of pragmatism and humor she'd shown all her life. "Tell everyone my dementia is early-onset," she'd told Zoë with a mischievous chuckle. "That way they'll think I'm younger." And another time, "Every night, no matter what you make us for dinner, tell me it's my favorite meal. I won't remember if it is or not." When Zoë had told Emma that she'd found a home-care nurse to stay at the cottage in the mornings while she worked, Emma's only question was, "Does she do manicures?"

"I know that inside she has to be scared," Zoë told Justine, the night before they started to move things into the cottage. "It's like little pieces of her are being chipped away, and there's nothing anyone can do to stop it."

"But she knows she'll be safe. She knows you'll be there."

"She knows that right now." Zoë began to pet Byron, who had just crawled onto her lap. "But she may not always know it."

After handing a glass of wine to Zoë, Justine poured another and sat on the other side of the sofa. "It's weird, when you think of it," she said. "About what you are, when you take away the memories and desires."

"You're nothing," Zoë suggested morosely.

"No, you're a soul. A soul on a journey . . . and life on earth is just part of that journey."

"What do you think happens after we die?"

"According to my family — at least, on my mother's side — some souls are lucky enough to go up to the ultimate life force. Heaven. Whatever you want to call it." Justine crossed her legs and settled more comfortably into the corner of the sofa. "But other souls, who've made mistakes during their lives on earth, have to go to a sort of waiting place."

"What kind of waiting place?"

"I'm not exactly sure. But it's their chance to understand what they did wrong and learn from it. The coven calls it 'Summerland.' "

Byron curled himself into a doughnut shape on Zoë's lap and began to purr. Zoë sipped her wine and studied her cousin with a perplexed smile. "Did you just say 'coven'? As in witchcraft?"

"Oh, it's just a joke my mother and her friends have," Justine said with a dismissive little wave of her hand. "They've called their group a coven forever. They even named it. The Circle of Crystal Cove."

"Are you part of it?"

Justine made a scoffing sound. "Do you ever see me with a broomstick?"

"I don't even see you vacuum." Zoë

smiled down into her wineglass, but looked up as a thought occurred to her. "What about that old besom broom in your closet?"

"My mother gave it to me as a rustic decoration. I like to keep it near my clothes because it smells like cinnamon." She made a comical face as she saw Zoë's expression. "What?"

"What's the word for when people go astray from their religion?"

"Lapsed."

"I think you might be a lapsed witch."

Although Zoë said the words lightly, Justine gave her a strangely intent glance before asking with a grin, "Would it make any difference to you if I was?"

"Yes. I'd want you to cast a spell to make my grandmother better."

Her cousin's expression softened. "I'm afraid spells can't take her off the path she's on. If I tried, things would only get worse." She stretched out a long leg and rubbed Byron's furry bulk with her foot. "All I can do is be a friend to you both," she said. "For whatever that's worth."

"It's worth a lot."

The next morning, after making breakfast at the inn, Zoë called Emma. "Guess what I'm doing today?" she asked brightly.

"You're coming to visit me," her grandmother guessed.

"Close. Today and tomorrow I'll be busy getting the cottage ready, and the next day, you and I are moving in together. Just like old times."

"Come get me now, and I'll help."

Zoë smiled, knowing that even though the offer was sincere, Emma wouldn't be of any practical use. "I can't change the schedule," she said. "Justine and I have everything worked out. Her boyfriend Duane is going to help us, and —"

"The man from the motorcycle gang?"

"Well, it's not really a gang, it's a biker church."

"Motorcycles are noisy and dangerous. I don't like men who ride them."

"We like the ones who have big muscles to help us move furniture."

"Is Duane the only one helping you? Those club chairs are very heavy."

"No, Alex will be there."

"Who is he?"

"The contractor. He has a pickup with a trailer hitch."

Mischief edged her grandmother's tone. "Does he have big muscles, too?"

"Upsie," Zoë chided, and felt her color rise as she remembered the hard strength of Alex's body pressed to hers. "Yes, as a matter of fact he does."

"Is he attractive?"

"Very."

"Married?"

"Divorced."

"Why did he —"

"Don't get any ideas," Zoë said, laughing. "I'm not interested in a love life right now. I want to focus on taking care of you."

"I'd like to see you find a good man before I'm gone," Emma said wistfully.

"You'd better hang around then, because at this rate it's going to take me a while." Hearing the back door of the kitchen open, Zoë turned to see Alex walking in. She smiled at him, her heart beginning to beat faster.

"When are you coming to get me?" Emma asked.

"The day after tomorrow."

Her grandmother sounded perturbed. "Did I already ask that?"

"Yes," Zoë said gently. "It's fine." At the periphery of her vision, she saw Alex looking at a pan of muffins on the counter, and she gestured for him to take one. He complied without hesitation. Zoë went to pour him some coffee, while she said on the phone, "I'd better get busy now."

But the minor mistake had made Emma

anxious. "Someday I'll look at you," she said, "and I'll think 'that's the nice girl who makes me dinner' and I won't know you're my granddaughter."

The words caused a painful tug in Zoë's chest. She swallowed hard and poured some cream into Alex's coffee. "I'll still know who you are," she said. "I'll still love you."

"That's awfully one-sided. What good is a grandmother who doesn't remember anything?"

"You're more to me than what you remember." Zoë slid an apologetic glance to Alex, knowing that he disliked to be kept waiting. But he seemed relaxed and patient, his gaze averted as he ate the muffin.

"I won't be myself," Emma said.

"You'll still be you. You'll just need a little more help. I'll be there to remind you of things." At her grandmother's silence, Zoë said softly, "I've got to go, Upsie. I'll call you later today. In the meantime, you'd better start packing. I'm coming to get you the day after tomorrow."

"The day after tomorrow," her grandmother repeated. "Bye, Zoë."

"Bye. Love you."

Ending the conversation, Zoë slid the phone into her back pocket and stirred some sugar into Alex's coffee. She handed it to him.

"Thanks." His face was unreadable as he looked down at her.

Zoë's throat was so tight that she wasn't sure she could talk.

Seeming to understand, Alex filled the silence by saying easily, "I've already loaded the boxes into the pickup. I'll take you and Justine to the cottage, and you can start putting away the dishes and books and that stuff. When Duane gets there, we'll hitch up the trailer and move the furniture from storage." He paused to take a swallow of coffee, his gaze sweeping briefly over her.

Zoë had dressed in a pair of jeans, a shapeless T-shirt, and a pair of old sneakers. And unlike Justine, who was slender and long-stemmed no matter what she wore, Zoë didn't have the figure for baggy clothes. On a woman with her breasts and hips, anything that didn't fit well was unflattering.

"This outfit makes me look dumpy," Zoë said, and was instantly annoyed with herself. "Forget I just said that," she told him before he could reply. "I'm not fishing for compliments, I'm just feeling insecure. About everything."

"It's normal to feel that way," Alex said, "when you're facing a lot of challenges. But 'dumpy' is never a word that could apply to you." He drained the coffee cup and set it down. "And if you need a compliment . . . you're a great cook."

"Can you tell me one that's not about my cooking?" she asked wistfully.

That almost made him smile — she could see the subtle deepening at the corners of his mouth. "You," he said after a moment, "are the kindest person I've ever known."

Before Zoë could recover from that, he started for the door. "Get your bag," he said in an offhand tone. "I'll take you to Dream Lake."

The cottage on Dream Lake Road was spotless and light-filled and beautiful, the rows of new casement windows glittering in the sunshine. It smelled agreeably of fresh paint and scrubbed wood. They carried boxes inside, Alex taking two heavy crates of dishes to the new kitchen island. Following him, Zoë was surprised to see the retro dining set, finished with a gleaming coat of new silver chrome, the chairs reupholstered with liqht aqua vinyl that approximated the original hue. She set down the box she was carrying and stared at the dining set in amazement. "You restored it," she said, running her fingers over the shiny white table-top.

Alex shrugged. "Just gave it a few shots of chrome spray."

She wasn't fooled by his nonchalance. "You did a lot more than that."

"I worked on it now and then when I needed distraction. You don't have to use it, by the way. You can sell it and use the money for another dining set."

"No, I love this. It's perfect."

"It goes with your bowling lockers," he agreed.

Zoë grinned. "Are you making fun of my decorating style?"

"No, I like it." Seeing her dubious expression, he added, "Really. It's cute."

Her smile lingered. "I suppose your decorating style is very tasteful."

"It's impersonal," he said. "Darcy always said that no one would ever be able to tell a thing about either of us by looking at our house. I kind of liked it that way."

Noticing a couple of objects in the center of the table, Zoë picked one up. It was a little plastic strap with a buckle, and something that looked like a miniature transmitter. "What is this?"

"It's for the cat." He retrieved the other object on the table, a tiny remote control of some kind, and showed it to her. "This goes with it."

She shook her head, mystified. "Thank you, but . . . Byron doesn't need a shock collar."

That drew a brief grin from him. "It's not a shock collar." Taking her by the shoulders, he steered her to the door that led to the back patio. "It's for that."

A small Plexiglas square in a frame had been set into the wall beside the main door. Alex pressed a button on the remote control, and the clear pane slid upward with a quiet whoosh.

Her mouth fell open. "You . . . you put in a cat door?"

"The collar will activate it automatically, but only when Byron approaches directly. So nothing else will get in, including spiders." At Zoë's silence, he added, "It's a gift. I figured you'd be busy enough with your grandmother, you didn't need to be opening the door a dozen times a day for a cat." Alex pointed to a sticky note on a nearby cabinet. "Those are directions for how to use it. The instruction manual is in the —" He broke off as Zoë reached for him. Reflexively he snatched her wrists in his hands before she could put them around his neck. The remote control clattered to the floor.

"I was just going to hug you," Zoë said on a breath of laughter. No gift had ever pleased her as much. She was too filled with delight to be cautious.

His grip on her wrists was gentle but inexorable. His face had gone taut, grim, as if he'd just found himself in mortal danger.

"One hug," she whispered, smiling.

Alex shook his head slightly.

Zoë watched, fascinated, as a band of color crossed the crests of his cheeks and the bridge of his nose. The front of his throat rippled with a swallow. How remarkable his eyes were, striations running through the light blue-green irises like spokes of starlight. He looked at her as if he wanted to eat her alive. And instead of being nervous, she was filled with giddy excitement.

Since he was still holding her arms, she lifted on her toes and leaned close, until her lips caught gently at his. She kept her wrists yielding in his grip, understanding that he was fighting some inner battle. She sensed the moment that he lost. Slowly he brought her hands behind her back, pressing them toward the base of her spine until her breasts were arched upward. His mouth came to hers. He held her in a way that made movement impossible — she could only answer him with her mouth, her lips clinging desperately.

Still kissing her, he let go of her wrists and lifted his hands to her face, cradling her cheeks. He seemed determined to pull in every sensation and make it last forever. Neither of them was rational, there was no room left for thought. Only for feeling. Only for wanting. Zoë reached under his T-shirt until the skin of his back was against her palms. She drew them slowly along the muscles on either side of his spine. He reacted with a quiet grunt and pushed her back against the edge of the wooden countertop, and tugged the front of her shirt upward. His breath was rough, but his hands were gentle on her breasts, squeezing and stroking as he kissed her. He licked inside her mouth, hot and deep. His fingers slipped beneath the top edge of her bra until his knuckles brushed a sensitive peak. The tender flesh went tight, and she felt the sweet ache of his touch all through her. He caught the tip and tugged, gently harrowing until the pleasure made her writhe. She struggled to get closer to him, rising on her toes, while he kissed her as if he were feeding on her, openmouthed and wet and slow —

Someone opened the front door.

Too startled to react, Zoë felt Alex yank her shirt back down. He grabbed a box from the island and carried it to the counter area near the sink.

"We're here," Justine announced, shouldering her way inside the cottage with a box in her arms. "Duane's right behind me. Wow. Would you look at this place. Fantastic!"

It was difficult to think past the cloud of dream-colored heat that surrounded her. "Isn't it beautiful?" Zoë asked, feeling swoony and unsteady as she retrieved the tiny remote control from the floor.

"It's beautiful *and* a great investment," Justine replied. "I'll have no trouble renting this place out someday. Nice work, Alex."

"Thanks," he muttered, using a jackknife to open the box.

"Out of breath already, old man?" Justine asked with a grin. "It's a good thing Duane's here to help with the heavy lifting."

"Look at this, Justine," Zoë said hastily, before Alex could say a word. "Alex installed a special door for Byron."

The electronic pet door was duly admired, while Duane entered the cottage with another couple of boxes.

Duane was a good-hearted man who attended his biker church regularly. He tended to be rowdy and impulsive, but he was loyal to his friends and always ready to help someone in need. His appearance was so intimidating — muscle-bulked arms protruding from leather vests, both arms sleeved with tattoos from wrist to shoulder, his face half obscured with boot-shaped sideburns — that it had taken Zoë a while to feel comfortable around him. But he seemed devoted to Justine, with whom he'd been going out for almost a year.

"I'm not the falling-in-love type," Justine had once told her breezily, when Zoë had asked if the relationship with Duane might deepen into something permanent.

"You mean you're leery of falling in love, or is there something about Duane —"

"Oh, I'm not leery of it. And Duane is great. It's just that I can't love anyone."

"You're a very loving person," Zoë had protested.

"To friends and family, yes. But I can't love someone in the romantic way you're talking about."

"But you have sex," Zoë had said, bemused.

"Well, sure. People can have sex without love, you know."

"Someday," Zoë had said wistfully, "it

would be nice to try both at the same time."

More labeled boxes were brought in, including those containing Emma's belongings. After Alex and Duane had left to get the furniture out of storage, Justine and Zoë unpacked shoes and handbags. They put them away on the shoe racks and shelves in the closet of the main bedroom. "I don't remember all these built-ins being listed on the invoice," Justine said. "It looks like Alex has been doing some extra work around here. Have you paid him on the side?"

"No, he did it without even asking," Zoë said. "He really wants to make the house comfortable for Emma."

Justine's mouth twisted with wry amusement. "I don't think Emma was the one he did it for. Is there something going on between you and the human iceberg?"

"No, nothing at all," Zoë said emphatically.

Justine's brows lifted. "I would have believed you if you said 'a little flirtation here and there,' or 'we've gotten to be friends.' But 'nothing at all' . . . nope, I'm not buying it. I've seen the way he looks at you when he thinks no one is noticing."

"What way?"

"Like he's a starving climber who's just been rescued after three days with no supplies, and you're a Cinnabon."

"I don't want to talk about it," Zoë said.

"Okay." Justine continued lining up shoes.

After a moment, Zoë burst out, "It's not going to go beyond kissing. He's made that clear."

"I'm glad to hear that, because you already know my opinion." Justine began to open another box.

"He's a better man than you think he is," Zoë couldn't resist saying. "He's a better man than *he* thinks he is."

"Don't do it, Zoë."

"Don't do what?"

"You know what I'm talking about. You're thinking about doing it, and you're trying to find all kinds of ways to justify it because of your attraction to emotionally unavailable men."

"The other day," Zoë retorted, "you told me that you were emotionally unavailable to men. Does that mean no one should have sex with you?"

"No, it means only a certain kind of man should have sex with me, or he's going to get burned. And if he does, it's his own fault."

"Fine. If I get burned as a result of becoming involved with Alex, or anyone, I won't ask for your sympathy." Zoë's irritable tone caused Justine to glance at her in surprise.

"Hey, I'm on your side."

"I know that. And I'm even pretty sure you're right. But it still feels like I'm being bossed around."

Justine pulled shoes out of the box. "Doesn't matter anyway," she said after a moment. "You're going to be so busy with Emma, you won't have the time to fool around with Alex."

Later Duane and Alex carried furniture and mattresses into the house and set various pieces where Zoë indicated. The afternoon sun was ripening by the time the heavy work had been completed. Now it was just a matter of putting an array of smaller items in their places, which Zoë would finish tomorrow.

Alex carried Zoë's old dressmaker's mannequin into the smaller bedroom, which hadn't yet been painted. He unwrapped the mover's blanket from around the mannequin. It was richly covered in a treasure garden of brooches made with crystals, gemstones, enamel, or painted lacquer. "Where do you want this?" he asked Zoë.

"That corner is fine." Zoë had left most of her brooch collection pinned to the mannequin, having only removed about a half

277

dozen of the more valuable ones. Taking them out of her bag, she went to pin them back onto the mannequin.

"I'm sorry this room isn't finished yet." He frowned as he glanced around the small space. The carpeting was new, but the room still had to be repainted and the old light fixtures replaced. Although a new wall-to-wall closet had been framed, it hadn't been drywalled or fitted with doors.

"You've done an amazing amount of work," Zoë replied. "And the most important things were the kitchen and my grandmother's room, which are beautiful." Scrutinizing the mannequin, Zoë pinned a brooch on an empty space. "I'm either going to have to stop collecting," she said, "or get another mannequin."

Alex stood next to her, looking over the array of jewelry. "When did you start the collection?"

"When I was sixteen. My grandmother gave this to me for my birthday." She showed him a flower covered with crystals. "And I bought this to celebrate graduating from culinary school." She held up a red enameled lobster with gold antennae before fastening it to the mannequin's chest.

"What about that one?" Alex asked, looking at an antique gold-framed ivory cameo.

"A wedding present from Chris." She smiled. "He told me if you own a cameo for seven years, it becomes a lucky charm."

"You're due for some luck," he said.

"I think people don't always know when lucky things are happening to them. Or they only realize it later. Like the divorce from Chris. It turned out to be the best thing for both of us."

"That wasn't luck. That was bailing out after a mistake."

She made a little face at him. "I try not to think of the marriage as a mistake, but more like something fate put in my path. To help me learn, and grow."

"What did you learn?" he asked with a mocking gleam in his eyes.

"How to be better at forgiving. How to be more independent."

"Don't you think you could have learned that stuff without some higher power putting you through a divorce?"

"You probably don't even believe in a higher power."

He shrugged. "Existentialism has always made a lot more sense to me than fate, God, or chance."

"I've never been sure exactly what existentialism is," Zoë confessed.

"It's knowing the world is crazy and

meaningless, so you have to find your own truth. Your own meaning. Because nothing else makes sense. No higher power, just human beings stumbling through life."

"But . . . does having no faith make you happier?" she asked doubtfully.

"To existentialists, you can only be happy if you can manage to live in a state of denial about the absurdity of human existence. So . . . happiness is out."

"That's horrible," Zoë said, laughing. "And way too deep for me. I like things I can be sure of. Like recipes. I know that the right amount of baking powder makes a cake rise. And eggs bind the other ingredients together. And life is basically good, and so are most people, and chocolate is proof that God wants us to be happy. See? My mind works on the most superficial level possible."

"I like how your mind works." As he held her gaze, there was a brief, hot flicker in his eyes. "Call if you have any problems," he said. "Otherwise I won't see you for a couple of days."

"I wouldn't dream of bothering you during your time off. You've worked practically nonstop since the project started."

"It's no hardship to work," he said, "when I'm being paid well."

"I appreciate it anyway."

"I'll come to the cottage on Monday. From now on I won't start until about ten, so your grandmother will have time to get up and have breakfast before all the noise starts."

"Will Gavin and Isaac come with you?"

"No. Just me, that first week. I don't want to overwhelm Emma with too many new faces all at once."

Zoë was touched and a little surprised by the realization that Alex had considered her grandmother's feelings so carefully. "What are you going to do this weekend?" she asked, obliging Alex to stop at the doorway.

He gave her an opaque glance. "Darcy's visiting. She wants to stage the house to sell faster."

"I thought you said it was already impersonal. Isn't that the point of staging?"

"Apparently not always. Darcy's bringing an expert in target staging. The theory is that you're supposed to fill the house with colors and objects that make potential buyers connect emotionally with the place."

"Do you think that will work?"

He shrugged. "Regardless of what I think, it's Darcy's house."

So Alex would be spending at least part of the weekend, if not all of it, in the company of his ex-wife. Zoë remembered what he'd once told her, that he and Darcy had slept together after the divorce out of sheer convenience. It would probably happen again, she thought, while depression settled over on her. There was no reason for Alex to turn down an offer of sex if Darcy was willing.

Maybe it wasn't depression. It felt worse than that. It felt as if she'd made a pie with poisoned fruit and eaten all of it.

No, definitely not depression. It was jealousy.

Zoë tried to smile through the feeling as if she didn't care. The effort made her mouth hurt. "Have a good weekend," she managed to say.

"You, too." And he left.

He always left without looking back, Zoë thought, and jabbed another brooch into the glittering mannequin.

"What was all that crap about?" the ghost asked in a surly tone, walking beside Alex. "Existentialism . . . life is meaningless . . . you can't really believe that."

"I do believe it. And stop eavesdropping on me."

"I wouldn't have to if there was anything else to do." The ghost scowled at him.

"Look at yourself. You're being haunted by a spirit. That's about as unexistential as you can get. The fact that I'm with you means it doesn't all end with death. And it also means that someone or something put me in your life for a reason."

"Maybe you're not a spirit," Alex muttered. "You could be a figment of my imagination."

"You have no imagination."

"Maybe you're a symptom of depression."

"Then why don't you take some Prozac, and see if I disappear?"

Alex paused at the door of his truck and regarded the ghost with a contemplative scowl. "Because you wouldn't," he finally said. "I'm stuck with you."

"So you're not an existentialist," the ghost said smugly. "You're still just an asshole."

SIXTEEN

"You look good," were the first words Darcy uttered when Alex opened the front door. Her tone was inflected with mild surprise, as if she'd expected to find him sprawled in a pile of empty cough syrup bottles and drug paraphernalia.

"So do you," Alex said.

Darcy lived and dressed as if she were the subject of a fashion magazine layout, ready for photographs to be taken at random angles. Her exterior was a hard, brilliant gloss of perfect makeup and retail chic. Her blouse was unfastened one more button than necessary, her hair flat-ironed and expertly highlighted. If she had any deeper goals than acquiring money by any and all means available, she had never expressed them. Alex didn't blame her for that. He knew without a doubt that she would marry again soon, to some wealthy and well-connected man from whom she would eventually garner an immense divorce settlement. Alex didn't blame her for that, either. She had never pretended to be anything other than what she was.

Pleasantries were exchanged as Darcy introduced the stager, an artfully made-up woman of indeterminate age, with layered hair that had been sprayed until it didn't move. Her name was Amanda. Darcy and the stager wandered through the sparely furnished house, occasionally asking questions that obliged Alex to follow in their wake. The place was scrupulously clean, every wall freshened with touch-up paint, the lighting and plumbing in perfect working order, the landscaping tidy with beds of new mulch.

Darcy had set a Vuitton overnight bag inside the front entranceway. Alex glanced at it with a frown, having hoped that Darcy wouldn't stay after the stager had left. The prospect of making conversation with his ex-wife was depressing. They had run out of things to say to each other even before the divorce.

The prospect of having sex with his ex-wife was even more depressing. No matter if his body was clamoring to fire one off, no matter if Darcy was hot and willing . . . it wasn't going to happen. Because the problem with having tried something new and amazing was that you could never go back and take the same pleasure in the thing you used to enjoy. You could never erase the awareness that somewhere out there was a better experience you weren't having. You knew you were eating a canned biscuit after you'd tried a fluffy, tender homemade one with a crisp buttered top, the whole of it split open and doused with honey.

"You should tell Darcy before she decides to stay," the ghost said, lounging nearby.

"Tell her what?"

"That you're not going to sleep with her."

"What makes you think I'm not?"

The ghost had the effrontery to grin. "Because you're looking at that bag like it's full of live cobras." The smile changed, gentling at the edges. "And Darcy doesn't fit with your new direction."

The ghost had been in a strange mood the past few days, impatient, eager, worried, and most of all filled with a burning quick-silver joy at the knowledge that he would see Emma soon. It rattled Alex to be in the vortices of such intense moods — he was having enough trouble keeping his own emotions in check. Probably the thing he missed most about drinking was how it had kept him anesthetized from that kind of turmoil.

What Alex did appreciate was that the ghost had been making an effort to give him as much space as possible, trying not to interfere. The remark he'd just made about Darcy was the only vaguely manipulative thing he'd said in days. He hadn't uttered a word about the way Alex had kissed Zoë at the cottage. In fact, he'd actually pretended not to notice. For his part, Alex had tried like hell to forget it.

Except that part of his brain had locked around it, viselike, and wouldn't let go. Zoë's sparkling blue eyes looking up into his, the provocative way she had lifted on her toes and molded herself against him. He had never been so overwhelmed by anyone, by the idea that he might actually have made a woman happy for a moment. And she had moved with him so easily, letting him do whatever he wanted. She would be like that in bed, open to anything. Trusting him.

Christ.

If that happened, before long he would have turned her into someone else entirely, someone cynical, angry, guarded. Like Darcy. That was what happened to women who got mixed up with him.

After a couple of hours of discussing ideas

and looking at photos and designs on an electronic tablet, Amanda said it was time to leave. She didn't want to miss the late afternoon ferry.

"I'll take Amanda to Friday Harbor and pick up something for dinner," Darcy told Alex. "How does Italian sound?"

"You're staying overnight?" Alex asked reluctantly.

Darcy looked sardonic. "You saw my bag." A quick blink of annoyance as she saw his face. "You don't have a problem with that, I hope. Considering the fact that it's my house."

"I'm maintaining it and paying the bills until it sells," he said. "Not a bad deal for you."

"True." She smiled, her gaze provocative. "Maybe I'll give you a bonus later."

"Not necessary."

A little over an hour later, Darcy returned with takeout boxes of pasta marinara and salads. They plated the food and sat at the kitchen table, just as they had done while they were married. Since neither of them cooked, they had lived on takeout and frozen dinners, or had eaten at restaurants.

"I got a bottle of Chianti," Darcy said, rummaging in the drawer for a bottle opener.

"None for me, thanks."

She cast a surprised glance over her shoulder. "You're joking, right?"

The ghost, who was sitting on one of the counters with his long legs dangling, asked rhetorically, "Since when does he joke about anything?"

"I just don't feel like it tonight," Alex said to Darcy, and sent the ghost a hard glance.

"Okay," the ghost said, easing off the counter, sauntering away. "I'll leave you two lovebirds alone."

Darcy took two wineglasses from the cabinet, filled them both, and brought them to the table. "Amanda says we need to make the house look warmer. It's going to be easy, since the house is already uncluttered and everything is in neutrals. She's going to bring colorful pillows for the sofa, some silk trees, centerpieces for the tables, things like that."

Alex looked at the glass of Chianti, the liquid glowing pomegranate red. He remembered the taste of it, dry and violety. It had been weeks since he'd had a drink. One glass of wine wouldn't hurt. People drank wine with dinner all the time.

He reached for the glass but didn't pick it up, only ran his fingertips along the smooth circular base of the stem. He pushed it away an inch.

Dragging his gaze to Darcy's face, he focused on what she was saying. She was talking about her latest promotion — she was a marketing communications manager for a massive software company, and she had just been put in charge of the internal business group newsletter, which would go out to thousands of people.

"Good for you," Alex said. "I think you'll be great at it."

She grinned at him. "You almost sound like you mean it."

"I do. I've always wanted you to be successful."

"That's news to me." She drank deeply of her wine. Extending a long leg, she rested her foot on his thigh. Delicately her toes began to burrow into his lap. "Have you been with anyone?" she asked. "Since our last time?"

He shook his head and caught her wiggling foot, keeping it still.

"You need to let off steam," Darcy said.

"No, I'm fine."

A disbelieving smile touched her lips. "You're not trying to turn me down, are you?"

Alex found himself reaching for his wineglass, his fingers closing lightly around the gleaming bowl. He cast a wary glance around the kitchen, but the ghost was nowhere to be seen. Lifting the glass, he took a sip, and the flavor of wine filled his mouth. He closed his eyes briefly. It was a relief. It promised that he would feel better soon. He wanted more. He wanted to guzzle it without pausing for breath.

"I've met a woman," he said.

Darcy's eyes narrowed. "You're interested in her?"

"Yes." It was the truth, not to mention the biggest understatement of his life. But of course he had no intention of doing anything about it.

"She doesn't have to know," Darcy said.

"I would know."

Darcy's voice was coolly mocking. "You want to be faithful to a woman you haven't even had sex with yet?"

Alex carefully pushed her foot from his lap. He looked at her, really looked at her for the first time in a while, noticing a flicker of something . . . unhappiness, loneliness. It reminded him of the reluctant compassion he'd felt when Zoë had told him what it had been like to be let down by her husband.

Darcy had been let down by a husband, too. By him.

Alex wondered how it could have been so

easy to make vows he had never intended to keep. Neither of them had, but it hadn't seemed to matter to Darcy any more than it had to him. *It should have mattered,* he thought.

With an effort, he poured the wine into the sink and set the glass aside. The fragrance spilled into the air, fruit and tannin and oblivion.

"Why did you do that?" he heard Darcy ask.

"I've stopped drinking."

She looked incredulous. Her brows lowered. "For God's sake, one glass of wine won't hurt."

"I don't like who I am when I'm drinking."

"I don't like who you are when you're not drinking."

He smiled without amusement.

"What's going on?" Darcy demanded. "Why are you pretending to be someone you're not? I know you better than anyone. I've lived with you. Who is this woman you're seeing? Is she a Mormon or Quaker or something?"

"It doesn't matter."

"This is bullshit," Darcy said, but somewhere in the snapping tension of her voice, he heard a bewildered note. He felt more compassion for her in that moment than he had in the sum total of their marriage. Once he'd read or heard something to the effect that it was never too late to save a relationship. But that wasn't true. Sometimes too much damage had been done. There was an invisible line of "too late" in a marriage, and after it had been crossed, the relationship would never thrive.

"I'm sorry," he said, watching her drain a glass of wine the way he'd wanted to a few moments earlier. "You got a raw deal, marrying me."

"I got the house," she reminded him smartly.

"I'm not talking about the divorce. I'm talking about the marriage." Part of him warned against lowering his guard. But Darcy deserved the truth. "I should have been a better husband to you. I should have asked how your day was, and paid attention to the answers. I should have gotten us a damn dog, and made this place seem like a home instead of a corporate suite at the Westin. I'm sorry I was a waste of your time. You deserved a lot more than you got."

Darcy stood and approached him. Her face had turned red, and to his astonishment he saw the glitter of tears in her eyes. Her jaw was trembling. As she drew closer, he had the wildly uncomfortable thought that she might try to embrace him, which was not at all what he wanted. But her hand shot out, and the sound of a slap rang through the kitchen. The side of his face went numb, then turned to fire. "You're not sorry," Darcy said. "You're not capable of it."

Before he could say anything, Darcy continued with low-voiced vehemence. "Don't you dare make me out to be the poor little mistreated wife, pining for love. You think I ever expected love from you? I wasn't stupid. I married you because you could make money, and you were good in bed. And now you can't do either of those things. What's the problem, you can't get it up now? Don't look at me like I'm a bitch. If I am, it's because of you. Any woman would be, after being married to you." She snatched up the wine bottle and her glass, and stormed off to the guest bedroom. It seemed the entire house vibrated from the slam of the door.

Slowly massaging his jaw, Alex went to lean against the counter, pondering Darcy's behavior. He had expected just about any other reaction than the one he'd gotten.

The ghost came to stand beside him, a glint of friendly sympathy in his dark eyes.

Alex took a deep breath and let it out slowly. "Why didn't you say something?"

"When you started to drink the wine? I'm not your conscience. It's your battle. I'm not going to be hanging around with you forever, you know."

"God, I hope you're right."

The ghost smiled. "You did the right thing, telling her that stuff."

"You think it might have helped her?" Alex asked dubiously.

"No," the ghost said. "But I think it helped you."

Darcy left without a word the next morning. Alex spent most of the weekend working on the house at Rainshadow Road, clearing out the rest of the attic and insulating a knee wall. On Sunday evening he texted Zoë to ask if Emma was at the cottage and if everything had gone well.

"Got here just fine," Zoë texted immediately. *"She loves the cottage."*

"Need anything?" he couldn't resist texting back.

"Yes. Making apple pie. Need help with it tomorrow AM."

"Pie for breakfast?"

"Why not?"

"ok," he texted.

"gn"

"gn"

Although *gn* was standard text shorthand for "goodnight," it could, in certain contexts, be interpreted as "get naked." Alex's mind summoned images of Zoë's clothes dropping to the floor, and it set off a deep pang of lust.

The feeling was quickly supplanted by a nervous thrill emanating from the ghost.

"Chill," Alex said curtly. "Listen, when we go there tomorrow, if you're emoting all over the place, I'm hauling ass out of there. I can't work like this."

"Sure." But it was clear the ghost wasn't even listening.

"This is what it feels like to love someone . . ." the ghost had once told him. Alex didn't want to know how it felt, even secondhand.

"She's still sleeping," Zoë said softly, opening the front door of the cottage to let Alex in. "I thought I should let her rest as long as possible."

Alex stopped at the threshold, looking down at her. There were smudges of exhaustion beneath her eyes, and her hair was unwashed, and she was dressed in khaki shorts and a modest tank top. She was

296

weary and luminous, her face innocently clean of makeup. He wanted nothing more than to hold and comfort her.

Instead he said, "I'll come back later."

The ghost, who was behind him, said shortly, "We're staying."

"Have breakfast with me," Zoë said, catching at Alex's hand, pulling him inside.

The air smelled like butter and sugar and warm apples. Alex's mouth watered.

"Instead of pie," Zoë said, "I made apple crisp in a skillet. Sit at the island, and I'll get some for us."

He began to follow her into the kitchen, pausing as he saw that the ghost had stopped in front of a bookshelf in the living room. Although he couldn't see the ghost's face, something about his utter stillness alerted Alex. Casually he wandered to the bookshelf to see what had caught the ghost's attention.

One shelf contained a row of framed pictures, some of them sepia-toned and faded with age. Alex smiled slightly as he saw a snapshot of Emma holding a cherubic blond toddler who could only have been Zoë. Beside it was an old black-and-white photo of three girls standing in front of a 1930s sedan. Emma and her two sisters.

His gaze moved to a photo of a man with

a seventies haircut and sideburns, and a broad, lantern-jawed face. He was the kind of man who wore his dignity like a three-piece suit.

"Who's this?" Alex asked, picking up the framed picture.

Zoë looked over from the kitchen. "That's my dad. James Hoffman Jr. I've asked for a more recent photo, but he never remembers to send one."

"Any pictures of your mom?"

"No. My dad got rid of them all after she left us." At Alex's intent glance, Zoë forced a quick smile. "No need for pictures — apparently I look just like her." The brittle smile didn't fully conceal the pain of having been abandoned.

"Did you ever find out why she left?" Alex asked gently.

"Not really. My dad would never talk about it. But Upsie said she thought my mother got married too young and couldn't handle the responsibility of having a child." She let out a little breath of amusement. "When I was little, I thought she must have left because I cried too much. So for most of my childhood, I tried to act happy all the time, even when I didn't feel like it."

You still do, Alex thought. He wanted to go to her, put his arms around her, tell her that with him she never had to pretend something she didn't feel. It took the force of his entire will to stay where he was.

The ghost spoke gruffly. "Ask her about this."

The last picture on the shelf was a wedding portrait. Emma, young and attractive and unsmiling. And the groom, James Augustus Hoffman Sr. . . . stalwart and heavy-jawed. His resemblance to his son was unmistakable.

"This was your grandpa Gus?" Alex asked.

"Yes. He wore glasses later on. They made him look just like Clark Kent."

"Is that me?" the ghost asked in a hushed tone, staring at the photo.

Alex shook his head. The ghost, with his lean face and dark-eyed handsomeness, wasn't at all similar to Gus Hoffman.

The ghost looked torn between relief and frustration. "Then who the hell am I?"

Alex straightened the pictures on the shelf with care. When he looked up from the task, the ghost had gone to Emma's room.

Feeling uneasy, Alex went to the kitchen island and sat on a bar stool. He hoped to hell the ghost wasn't going to scare Emma into a damned heart attack. "Who made breakfast at the inn this morning?" he asked Zoë.

"Justine and I have a couple of friends who like to help out and make a little extra money now and then . . . so I put some breakfast casseroles in the freezer and left instructions for heating everything."

"You're going to wear yourself out," Alex said, watching her spoon the apple crisp, with its crumbly browned topping, into two bowls. "You need to rest."

She smiled at him. "Look who's talking."

"How much sleep have you been getting?"

"Probably more than you," she said.

In a couple of minutes they were sitting side by side at the island, and Zoë was telling him about bringing her grandmother over on the ferry, and how much she had liked the cottage, and about the variety of medications she was taking. And while she talked, Alex ate. The oatmeal topping crumbled between his teeth with a crunch that quickly turned into something marvelously chewy and melting, a tart ambrosia of apples inflected with cinnamon and a zing of orange.

"I would ask for this on death row," Alex told her, and although he hadn't meant it to be funny, she laughed.

The sound of the pet door heralded Byron's entrance from outside, the massive cat sauntering into the kitchen as if he owned the place.

"The cat door is working perfectly, as you can see," Zoë said. "I didn't even have to train Byron — he knew exactly what to do." She sent a fond look to the Persian, who wandered into the living room and jumped onto the sofa. "If only the collar wasn't so ugly. Would it cause any technical problems if I decorate it?"

"No. But don't decorate it. Leave him some dignity."

"Just a few sequins."

"It's a cat, Zoë. Not a showgirl."

"Byron likes being decorated."

Alex gave her an apprehensive glance. "You don't ever dress him up in little outfits. You're not one of those people."

"No," she said instantly.

"Good."

"Maybe just one little Santa's helper outfit around Christmas." She paused. "And last Halloween I dressed him in a —"

"Don't tell me any more," Alex said, trying not to laugh. "Please."

"You're smiling."

"I'm gritting my teeth," he said.

"It's a smile," Zoë insisted cheerfully.

It wasn't until midway through another serving that Alex wondered about the ghost and Emma. The door of the main bedroom was closed, no sound or movement of any kind. But Alex became aware of a free-floating sweetness filling the air, an elation that surrounded them until he couldn't avoid breathing it in, absorbing it in his pores. The feeling was made even more potent by its complexity, just as a pinch of salt enhanced the flavors of a cake. The swirling, dizzying joy made his chest uncomfortably tight, as if it were being pried open. He looked down, fiercely concentrating on the wood grain of the butcher-block countertop.

Don't, he thought, without even knowing whom he was saying it to.

Emma.

The ghost approached the sleeping figure on the bed, the delicacy of her skin illuminated by a spill of morning light from the half-shuttered windows. She was still beautiful . . . it was there in the structure of her bones, the skin embossed with thousands of joys and sorrows that he hadn't been there to share. Had he been able to share a life with her, his face would have been sketched with the same stories, the same inscriptions of time. To wear your life on your face . . . what an amazing gift.

"Hiya," he whispered, looking down at her.

Her lashes flickered. She rubbed her eyes and sat up, and for a moment he thought she might be able to see him. Anxious joy awakened.

"Emma?" he said quietly.

She got out of bed, her body slim and fragile in a set of lace-trimmed pajamas. Going to the window, she stared outside at the view. Her hands fluttered and went to her eyes, and a sob escaped through her fingers. The sound would have broken his heart, if he'd had one. As it was, the sight of the tears shining in the light nearly shattered the soul that he was.

"Don't cry," he said urgently, even though she couldn't hear him. "Don't be upset. My God, I love you. I've always —"

Her breathing took on the velocity of panic. She limped to the door, crying harder with each step.

"Emma. Be careful, don't fall —" Flooded with grief and worry, the ghost followed her into the main room.

Alex and Zoë were sitting at the island. Their heads lifted at the same time as Emma staggered forward.

Zoë's face went white with alarm. She jumped from the bar stool and rushed to

303

her grandmother. "Upsie, what happened? Did you have a bad dream?"

"Why are we here?" Emma sobbed, trembling. "How did I get here?"

"You came with me yesterday. We're going to live here together. We talked about it, Upsie —"

"I can't. Take me home. I want to go h-home." Emma could barely speak through the sobs.

"This is home," Zoë said softly. "All your things are here. Let me show you —"

"Don't touch me!" Emma retreated to the corner, growing more distraught with every passing moment.

Alex gave the ghost a hard look. "What did you do to her?"

Although the muttered words had been intended for the ghost, Zoë replied. "She hasn't had her medicine this morning. Maybe I shouldn't have waited —"

"No, not you," Alex said impatiently, and Zoë blinked in confusion.

"She can't see or hear me," the ghost said. "I don't know what started this. Help her. *Do something.*"

"Upsie, please come sit down," Zoë begged, reaching for her, but Emma swatted at her hands and shook her head wildly.

Alex moved forward, approaching Emma.

"Be careful," the ghost snapped. "She doesn't know you."

Alex ignored him. The contrast between them — Alex, so physically powerful, Emma, frail and shivering — alarmed the ghost. For a moment he thought Alex might physically restrain Emma or do something to scare her. Perhaps Zoë thought the same thing, because she put a hand on his arm and began to say something.

But Alex was entirely focused on the older woman. "Mrs. Hoffman. I'm Alex. I've been waiting to meet you."

The unfamiliar voice drew Emma's attention. She looked at him with startled wet eyes, her chest heaving with a few hiccupping sobs.

"I've been working on this place to get it ready for you," Alex continued. "I'm the woodwork guy. And I've been helping my brother restore the old Victorian at Rainshadow Road. You used to live there, right?" He paused, a smile lurking in the corners of his mouth. "I usually play music while I'm working. Want to hear one of my favorites?"

To the ghost's astonishment, and Zoë's, Emma nodded and wiped her eyes.

Alex drew the phone from his pocket, fiddled with it for a few seconds, and turned up the micro speaker volume. Johnny Cash's baritone seeped through the air in a raggedy, melancholy version of "We'll Meet Again."

Emma stared at Alex in wonder. Her tears stopped, and the sobs eased into unsteady sighs. Alex held her gaze as they listened to the first few bars of the song. And then, incredibly, he sang a bar or two, his voice soft but true.

Zoë shook her head, watching as if hypnotized.

Alex smiled and extended a hand to Emma. She took it as if she'd just walked into a dream. He drew her closer, and put his arm around her. The music hung in the air like floating ribbons as the pair moved in a shuffling foxtrot, with Alex being mindful of Emma's weaker left leg.

A young man trying to forget his past . . . an old woman trying desperately to remember hers . . . but somehow they had found a connection in this liminal moment.

The ghost was spellbound. Disbelieving. He'd gotten to know Alex so thoroughly that he would have sworn nothing could surprise him. But he had never expected this.

Alex, lowering his cheek to Emma's hair. Holding her with a tenderness he must have carried in some secret cache in his heart.

306

Emma leaned into the vibration of his low crooning.

The ghost remembered dancing with Emma at a nighttime party held outdoors. The dance area had been lit with strings of little painted metal lanterns.

"I don't really like this song," Emma had said.

"You told me it was your favorite."

"It's beautiful. But it always makes me sad."

"Why, love?" he'd asked gently. "It's about finding each other again. About someone coming home."

Emma had lifted her head from his shoulder and looked at him earnestly. "It's about losing someone, and having to wait until you're together in heaven."

"There's nothing in the lyrics about heaven," he'd said.

"But that's what it means. I can't bear the idea of being separated from you, for a lifetime or a year or even a day. So you mustn't go to heaven without me."

"Of course not," he had whispered. "It wouldn't be heaven without you."

What had happened to them? Why hadn't they married? He couldn't fathom that he would have left to fight in the war without first having made Emma his wife. He must have proposed to her . . . in fact, he felt sure that he had. Maybe she had refused him. Maybe her family had stood in the way. But he and Emma had loved each other so much, it seemed impossible that any force on earth could have kept them apart. Something had gone unspeakably wrong, and he had to figure out what it was.

The song finished with a near spectral chorus of voices. Slowly Alex lifted his head and looked down at Emma.

"He used to sing that to me," she told him.

"I know," Alex whispered.

She squeezed his fingers until the veins showed on the back of her hand like delicate blue lace.

Zoë came forward to slip an arm around her grandmother's shoulders, pausing only to tell Alex in a distracted tone, "Thank you."

"No problem."

As Zoë guided her to a chair at the dining table, Emma said, "You were right, Zoë. He does have big muscles."

Zoë darted a mortified glance at Alex. "I didn't say that," she protested. "I mean, I did, but —"

His brows lifted into mocking arcs.

"What I mean is," Zoë said awkwardly, "I don't sit around discussing the size of your —" She broke off and went crimson.

Alex averted his face to hide a grin. "I'll

get my tools from the truck," he said.

The ghost followed him outside.

"Thanks," the ghost said, as Alex hefted a couple of tool buckets from the back of the truck. "For taking care of Emma."

Alex set the buckets on the ground and faced him. "What happened?"

"She woke up distraught. I don't know why."

"You sure she can't see or hear you?"

"I'm sure. Why did you play that song for her?"

"Because it's your favorite."

"How did you know that?"

Alex looked sardonic. "You sing it all the time. Why do you look so pissed off?"

After a long moment, the ghost said morosely, "You got to hold her."

"Oh." Alex's face changed. He gave the ghost a sympathetic glance, as if he understood the torture it was to be so close to the person you loved beyond anything, and yet not be able to touch her. To comprehend that you were only a shadow, an outline, of the physical being you once had been.

In the yearning silence, Alex said, "She smells like rose perfume and hairspray and the air just after it rains."

The ghost drew closer, hanging on to every word.

"She has the softest hands of anyone I've ever met," Alex said. "They're a little cool, the way some women's are. And her bones are as light as a bird's. I could tell she used to be a good dancer — if it wasn't for her weak leg, she'd still be able to move well." He paused. "She has a great smile. Her eyes light up. I'll bet she was as fun as hell when you knew her."

The ghost nodded, comforted.

Zoë served breakfast to her grandmother and went to the bathroom for her medication. She saw her reflection in the mirror, cheeks too red, eyes too bright. She felt as if she had to relearn how to breathe.

Thirty-two bars of music. The length of an average song. That was all the time it had taken for the earth to spin off its axis and go tumbling into a net of stars.

She loved Alex Nolan.

She loved him for every reason and no reason.

"You are everything that's ever been my favorite thing," she wanted to tell him. *"You are my love song, my birthday cake, the sound of ocean waves and French words and a baby's laugh. You're a snow angel, crème brulée, a kaleidoscope filled with glitter. I love you and you'll never catch up, because I've*

gotten a head start and my heart is racing at light speed."

Someday she would tell him how she felt about him, and he would leave her. He would break her heart the way people did when their own hearts had been broken long ago. But that didn't change anything. Love would have its way.

Squaring her shoulders, Zoë brought the medicine to Emma, who was already midway through the bowl of apple crisp. "Here are your pills, Upsie."

"He has the hands of a carpenter," Emma said. "Strong. All those calluses. I used to be sweet on a man with hands like that."

"Did you? What was his name?"

"I don't remember."

Zoë smiled. "I think you do."

Alex came into the house, carrying tool buckets to the threshold of Zoë's bedroom. "All right if I go in?" he asked. "I want to work on the closet."

Zoë had trouble returning his gaze, her face blazing with renewed color. "Yes, it's fine."

His attention turned to Emma. "I have to put up some Sheetrock, Mrs. Hoffman. Think you can handle some hammering for a little while?"

"You must call me Emma. Once a man

has seen me in my pajamas, it's too late for formality."

"Emma," he repeated, with a swift grin that left Zoë light-headed.

"Oh, my," Emma murmured, after Alex had gone into the bedroom and closed the door. "What a divine-looking man. Although he could do with some fattening up."

"I'm trying," Zoë said.

"If I were your age, I would already have lost my head over him."

"I stand to lose a lot more than my head, Upsie."

"Don't worry," Emma said. "There are worse things than having your heart broken."

"Like what?" Zoë asked skeptically.

"Never having it broken. Never giving in to love."

Zoë considered that. "So what do you think I should do?"

"I think you should cook dinner for him one night, and tell him that you're dessert."

Zoë couldn't help laughing. "You are trying to get me into trouble."

"You're already in trouble," her grandmother said. "Now go ahead and enjoy it."

SEVENTEEN

"Use your left hand," Zoë instructed patiently, standing with Emma at the laundry closet next to the kitchen pantry. She was reading from a booklet provided by Emma's physical therapist, describing ordinary household tasks that would strengthen muscles weakened by a minor stroke.

Emma opened the door of the washer with her left hand and looked at Zoë.

"Now reach in and grasp a piece of clothing, and drop it into the dryer. Here, hold my hand for balance —"

"I'll hold on to the edge of the machine," Emma said testily.

Alex paused at the doorway of Zoë's bedroom, where he had been installing a pocket bathroom in the small space that had originally been a closet. He watched the pair of them with silent amusement, while the ghost sat atop the washing machine with his legs dangling.

"Don't grab two things at once," Zoë cautioned, as her grandmother dropped a couple of shirts into the dryer.

"It'll get done faster," Emma protested.

"The point isn't to be efficient. The point is to make your fingers open and close as many times as possible."

"What am I supposed to do after this?"

"Transfer the dry clothes to the laundry basket one at a time. And then we'll do some dusting to give your wrist a workout."

"Now I see why you wanted me to live with you," Emma said.

"Why?" Zoë asked.

"Free maid service."

Alex snickered.

Noticing the sound, Zoë gave him a mock frown. "Don't encourage her. You two have spent too much time around each other — I can't tell who's a worse influence on who."

" 'Whom,' " Emma said, delving into the washer for more clothes. " 'Who' is used when it's the subject of a verb, 'whom' when it's the object."

Zoë grinned fondly at the top of her head. "Thank you, grammar police."

Emma's voice resonated in the dryer. "I don't know why I can remember that but not the name of the paper I wrote for."

"The *Bellingham Herald.*" Zoë exchanged

a glance with Alex as he crossed the room and went to the kitchen sink for a glass of water. He'd become used to those looks by now, the worry she couldn't quite conceal, the need for reassurance that no one was able to provide.

During the two weeks since Emma had come to live on Dream Lake Road, she had experienced moments of forgetfulness, confusion, agitation. Some days she was alert and competent, some days she was in a fog. There was never any predicting how she would feel or what she would remember from one day to the next.

"Don't hover, Zoë," Emma said irritably one afternoon. "Let me watch a TV program in peace." Apologizing, Zoë went to the kitchen, where she kept stealing concerned glances at Emma.

"You're still hovering," Emma said.

"How can I be hovering when I'm twenty feet away?" Zoë protested.

"Alex," Emma asked, "would you take my granddaughter for a walk?"

"I can't leave you alone," Zoë said. "Jeannie isn't here."

Jeannie, a part-time home-care nurse, came early every morning to take care of Emma, and usually left around lunchtime. Her unflappable poise made it comfortable for Emma to accept her help with private matters like dressing, bathing, and physical therapy.

"Just for fifteen minutes," Emma persisted. "Go outside and get some fresh air with Alex. Or go by yourself, if he won't keep you company."

Alex picked up Emma's cell phone from the kitchen island and entered his number on it. "I'll walk with Zoë, Emma, as long as you promise not to move while we're gone." He went to hand the phone to her. "Any problems, you call me. Got it?"

"Got it," Emma said with satisfaction.

Observing all this, the ghost frowned. "I don't like this idea."

"She'll be fine," Alex said, and swerved his gaze to Zoë. He made his voice gentle. "Come with me. Nothing's going to happen to Emma."

She was still reluctant. "You're in the middle of your work day."

"I can take a break." Extending his hand, Alex gave her an expectant look.

Slowly Zoë reached out and put her hand in his.

Something as casual as the feel of her fingers in his made him hot and ravenous. He savored every small, accidental contact between them, the brush of her arm, the silky tickle of her hair against his ear as she leaned to set a plate in front of him. He noticed every detail about her, the bruise on her shin where she had bumped it against something, the flowery scent of the new soap she'd bought at the farmer's market.

There was no word for this kind of relationship, for the way she made him feel. The clasp of their hands contained something more than shared warmth, more than skin pressed to skin . . . it felt as if they were holding something together, keeping it safe.

Even when he made himself let go, he could still feel the clasp of their hands and the invisible imprint of that mysterious secret something between them.

Emma settled back into the sofa to watch TV, looking more than a little satisfied. Byron hopped up and crept into her lap.

The ghost stood over Emma. "You little schemer," he said in soft amusement. "You want them to be together. You have rotten taste in men, you know that?"

Although he wanted badly to stay with her, he eventually felt the inevitable traction of his connection with Alex, and he was forced to go outside.

■ ■ ■ ■

"I can't help it," Zoë said, as she and Alex walked on the side of the road beneath a canopy of big leaf maples and Pacific madrones, the forest ground padded with licorice fern and sword fern, and blackberry bramble in the places where enough sun had penetrated. "I know I'm worrying too much, and micromanaging. But I don't want her to get hurt. I don't want her to need something she's not getting."

"What she needs — what you both need — is an occasional break from each other. You should go out at least one night a week."

"Do you want to go to a movie with me?" Zoë dared to ask. "Maybe this weekend?"

Alex shook his head. "My brother Mark's getting married in Seattle."

"Oh, that's right. I'd forgotten. Lucy's going with Sam. Are you taking anyone?"

"No." Alex was already regretting the impulse to take a walk with Zoë. Being alone with her was the surest way to give him that giddy, intoxicating feeling he dreaded, the hundred-proof shot of exhilaration that threatened to crack his chest open.

"Lucy and Sam seem happy together,"

Zoë said. "Do you think it might turn into something serious?"

"As in marriage?" Alex shook his head. "There's no reason for them to do that."

"There's a great reason."

"Joint filing on their tax return?"

"No," Zoë said with an exasperated laugh. "*Love.* People should marry because they love each other."

"People who want to stay in love should do their best to avoid marriage." As he saw her smile fade, Alex felt ashamed and vile. "Sorry," he said. "I hate weddings. And this is the first one where I won't be able to —" He scowled and shoved his hands in his pockets as they walked.

Zoë understood instantly. "There'll be an open bar at the reception?"

He gave a single nod.

Another gentle question. "You haven't told anyone in your family that you've stopped drinking?"

"No."

"Maybe you should let them help you. Give you moral support. If they knew —"

"I don't want support. I don't want anyone watching and waiting for me to fail."

He felt Zoë's arm slip through his, her fingers curving around his forearm.

"You won't fail," she said.

The day of Mark and Maggie's wedding, held on a retired ferry on Seattle's Lake Union, was sunny and clear. But even if it had rained, the bride and groom would have been too much in love to notice. After champagne was served and Sam made a toast, the guests filled their plates at the elaborate buffet. Alex retreated to the stern of the ferry and occupied one of the chairs by the railing. He'd never liked to make small talk, and he especially didn't want to keep company with people who were holding champagne or cocktails. It was strange to face this situation without having alcohol as a crutch. It felt almost as if he were trying to impersonate himself. He would have to get used to it.

He noticed Sam dancing with Lucy Marinn, who still wore a leg brace from her biking injury. They swayed together, flirting and kissing. Sam looked at Lucy in a way he'd never looked at anyone before, evincing the invisible alchemy that sometimes happened to people who were busy making other plans. They had become a couple. Alex was fairly certain that Sam wasn't even aware that it had happened. The dumbass still thought he was a single guy having a carefree relationship.

Alex lurked in the corner, drinking iced Cokes in highball glasses. The ghost lounged beside him, silent and brooding.

"What are you thinking about?" Alex eventually asked beneath his breath.

"I keep wondering if Emma loved her husband," the ghost said.

"Do you want her to have loved him?"

The ghost struggled to answer. "Yes," he eventually said. "But I want her to have loved me more."

Alex smiled, swirling the ice in his drink.

The ghost stared pensively at the sun-struck water. "I did something wrong," he said. "I hurt Emma. I'm sure of it."

"You mean before you died?"

The ghost nodded.

"You probably pissed her off by enlisting," Alex said.

"I think it was worse than that. I need to remember before something happens."

Alex gave him a skeptical glance. "What do you think's going to happen?"

"I don't know. I have to spend as much time as possible with Emma. I remember more when I'm with her. The other day —" The ghost stopped. "Time to shut up. Maggie's coming this way."

Mark's red-haired wife — now Alex's sister-in-law — approached him. She was holding a white porcelain coffee cup. "Hi, Alex." She was radiant with happiness, her brown eyes glowing. "Are you having a good time?"

"Yeah. Nice wedding." He began to stand up from his chair.

"Don't get up," Maggie urged, motioning for him to remain in the chair. "I just wanted to check on you. There are a few women who are dying to meet you, by the way. Including one of my sisters. If I bring her over, would you —"

"No," he said quickly. "Thanks, Maggie, but I'm not in the mood for small talk."

"Can I get you something?"

He shook his head. "Go dance with your husband."

"Husband. I like the sound of that word." Maggie smiled and gave him the cup she was holding. It was filled with steaming black coffee. "Here. I thought you might like this."

"Thanks, but I'm —" Alex broke off as he saw her discreetly retrieve his half-finished glass of Coke and ice from the little table next to his chair.

"She thinks you're plastered," the ghost said helpfully. "You've had about four drinks and now you're sitting here in the corner talking to yourself."

"They were nonalcoholic drinks," Alex said.

"Oh, of course," Maggie said brightly.

The ghost snorted. "She's not buying it."

With a self-mocking smile, Alex took a sip of bitter black coffee. Given his past, it was entirely reasonable to think that he might get drunk on such an occasion. And Maggie, being a sweetheart, was trying to handle it in a way that would spare his pride. "I'm not talking to myself, by the way," he said. "There's an invisible guy sitting right beside me."

Maggie laughed. "I'm glad you told me. Otherwise I might have accidentally sat on his lap."

"Feel free," the ghost said without hesitation.

"He wouldn't mind," Alex told Maggie. "Have a seat."

"Thank you, but I'll leave you and your friend to your conversation." She bent to kiss his cheek. "Drink the whole cup of coffee, okay?" And she left, taking his half-finished Coke with her.

EIGHTEEN

When Alex went to the Dream Lake cottage on Monday morning, the home-care nurse, Jeannie, met him at the door with an expression that instantly warned something was wrong.

"How's it going?" Alex asked.

"It was a tough weekend," she said quietly. "Emma had a downturn."

"What does that mean?"

"The term for it is TIA. Transient ischemic attacks. Tiny blockages that stop the blood flow to the brain. They're so minor that you may not notice any stroke symptoms, but the damage adds up. With the kind of mixed dementia that Emma has, there'll be a steady decline with these occasional downward steps."

"Does she need to see a doctor?"

Jeannie shook her head. "Her blood pressure is fine, and she's not having any physical discomfort. Many times after a step-down, a patient will show signs of temporary improvement. Today, Emma's doing well. But as time goes on, the moments of confusion and frustration will last longer and happen more often. And the memories will keep disappearing."

"So what exactly happened? How can you tell that a TIA occurred?"

"According to Zoë, Emma woke up on Saturday with a slight headache and some confusion. By the time I got there, Emma was determined to make herself breakfast — she insisted on frying an egg at the stove. It didn't go well. Zoë kept trying to help her — put a pat of butter in the pan first, turn the heat lower — but Emma was having a tough time trying to do something she'd always done, and that made her frightened and angry."

"She took it out on Zoë?" Alex asked in concern.

Jeannie nodded. "Zoë is the most convenient person for her to vent her frustration on. And even though Zoë understands, it's still stressful." Jeannie paused. "Yesterday Emma repeatedly asked for the car keys, messed up Zoë's computer when she tried to get on the Internet, and kept arguing with me to get her some cigarettes."

"Does she smoke?"

"Not for forty years, according to Zoë. And cigarettes are the worst possible thing for someone in Emma's condition."

The ghost, who stood just behind Alex, muttered, "Hell, let her have them."

The nurse wore a resigned expression. Alex couldn't help wondering how many times she had accompanied patients along this path, watching their inevitable deterioration, steering families through the pain and confusion of losing someone day by day. "Does it ever get easier?" he asked.

"For the patient or —"

"For you."

The nurse smiled. "You're very kind to ask. I've been through this with many patients, and even knowing what to expect . . . no, it doesn't get easier."

"How long does she have?"

"Even the most experienced doctors can't predict —"

"In your personal opinion. You've been in the trenches, you probably have some idea. What's your take on how it's going to progress?"

"A matter of months. I think she's headed for a major stroke or an aneurysm. And maybe that's for the best — I've seen it when it's a long and drawn-out process. You wouldn't want that for Emma, or Zoë."

"Where is Zoë?"

"She went to the inn as usual, and then to buy groceries." Jeannie stepped back to let him into the house. "Emma is awake and dressed, but I think she would do better without a lot of noise today."

"I'll stick to caulking and painting."

The nurse seemed relieved. "Thank you."

Entering the main room, Alex saw that Emma was watching television with a throw blanket over her lap, in spite of the warmth of the day. The ghost was already at her side.

Even if Jeannie hadn't told Alex what had transpired over the weekend, he would have known that something had changed. There was a new delicacy about Emma, a touch of radiance at her outline, as if her soul were no longer fully contained in her skin.

"Hi, Emma," Alex said, approaching her. "How are you feeling?"

She gestured for him to have a seat. Taking the ottoman near the sofa, Alex sat and faced her, leaning forward until his forearms were braced on his knees. Emma looked fine to him, her gaze clear and direct, her expression calm.

"I'm going to do some straightening up," Jeannie said as she headed to the bedroom. "Do you need anything, Emma?"

"No, thank you." The older woman waited

until the nurse was out of earshot. Her gaze returned to Alex. "He's here, isn't he?"

Startled, Alex kept his face expressionless. She could sense the ghost? But what had made her assume that Alex had a connection to him? His thoughts moved at a rapid pace. Emma was in a vulnerable condition. He had to be careful. But he wasn't going to lie to her.

So Alex settled for giving Emma a blank look and saying, "Who?"

"Damn it, Alex," the ghost exploded, "now's not the time to play dumb. Tell her I'm here, I'm with her right now, and I love her, and —"

Alex sent him a quick scowl, silencing him.

Emma's gaze was steady. "The way I used to feel whenever he was near . . . I knew that if I ever felt that again, it was because he'd found a way to come back. But it only seems to happen when you're near. He's with you."

"Emma," Alex said gently, "as much as I want to talk to you about this, I don't want to stress you out."

A little smile stretched the dry, feathery contours of her lips. "You're afraid to give me a stroke? I have them all the time. Believe me, no one will notice any extra thrombosis. Especially me."

"It's your call."

"I've never talked about him to anyone," Emma said. "But I'm forgetting things every day. Soon I won't even remember his name."

"Then tell me."

Emma lifted her fingers to her lips as if to pat a tremulous smile into place. "His name was Tom Findlay."

The ghost stared at her, riveted.

"I haven't said his name in so long." A glow came to Emma's cheeks, like light shining through pink glass. "Tom was the kind of boy that all the mothers warned their daughters about."

"Including yours?" Alex asked.

"Oh, yes, but I didn't listen."

He smiled. "I'm not surprised."

"He worked at my father's factory on the weekends, cutting tin plate and soldering cans. After he graduated high school, he became a carpenter — he taught himself out of books. He was smart, and he had the hands for it. Like you. Everyone knew when he built something, it was done right."

"What kind of family did Tom come from?" Alex asked.

"There was no father. His mother had already had Tom by the time she came to live on the island, and there were rumors that . . . well, not nice rumors. She was very beautiful. My mother told me she was a kept woman. There were relationships with prominent men in town. I think that for a while my father was one of them." She sighed. "Poor Tom was always getting into fights. Especially when other boys would say something about his mother. The girls had eyes for him — he was so handsome — but no one dared to go out with him openly. And he was never invited to the nice parties or picnics. Too much of a hell-raiser."

"How did you meet him?"

"My father hired him to install a stained-glass window that had been shipped from Portland. My mother objected and wanted to pay someone else to do it. But my father said that for all Tom's wild ways, he was the best carpenter on the island, and the window was too valuable to take chances with."

"What did the window look like?"

Emma hesitated so long before answering that he thought she might have forgotten. "A tree," she finally said.

"What kind of tree?"

She shook her head, looking evasive. She didn't want to discuss it. "After Tom installed the window, my father had him do other things around the house. He built a set of shelves, and did some cabinetry work, and made a beautiful mantel for the parlor fireplace. Since I was hardly immune to the charms of a handsome young man with a wicked reputation, I talked to him while he worked."

"You flirted with me," the ghost said.

"But I wouldn't go out with him," Emma told Alex, "because I knew my mother would never approve. One night I saw him at a dance in town. He came up to me and asked if I was too much of a scaredy-cat to dance with him. Of course I had to take the dare."

"You wouldn't have danced with me otherwise," the ghost said.

"I told him the next time he'd have to ask like a gentleman," Emma told Alex.

"Did he?" Alex asked.

She nodded. "He was so bashful about it — stammering and blushing — that I fell in love with him right then."

"I didn't stammer," the ghost protested.

"We kept our relationship secret," Emma said. "We saw each other all through the summer. This cottage was our favorite meeting place."

"I proposed to you here," the ghost said, remembering.

"Did you ever talk about getting married?" Alex asked Emma.

A shadow crossed her face. "No."

"We did," the ghost insisted. "She's forgotten, but I did propose to her."

Wondering at the contradictions, Alex asked gently, "Are you sure, Emma?"

She looked directly at him. "I'm sure I don't want to talk about it."

"Why not?" the ghost implored. "What happened?"

Alex wasn't about to push Emma for answers she didn't want to give. "Can you tell me what happened to Tom?"

"He died in the war. His plane crashed in China. His squadron had been assigned to protect cargo lifters flying the Hump, and they came under attack." Her shoulders slumped, and she looked tired. "Afterward, I received a letter from a stranger. A Hump pilot. He flew one of those big clumsy planes carrying troops and supplies . . ."

"A C-46," the ghost murmured.

"And he wrote to tell me that Tom had died a hero, that he had shot down two of the enemy in the air, and helped to save the lives of all thirty-five men on the cargo plane. But his Warhawk was outmaneuvered. The Japanese fighters were so much lighter and more agile than our P-40s . . ." She looked distressed and shaky, her fingers plucking fitfully at the throw blanket.

Alex reached out to engulf her hands in a warm grip. "Who wrote the letter to you?" he asked, although he thought he might know the answer.

"Gus Hoffman. He sent me the piece of cloth that had been sewn into Tom's jacket."

"A blood chit?"

"Yes. I wrote back to thank him. We corresponded for two years. Only as friends. But Gus wrote that if he made it back home, he wanted to marry me."

"I'll bet he did," the ghost said grimly. The air seethed with jealousy.

"And you said yes?" Alex asked Emma.

She nodded. "I suppose I thought if I could never have Tom, it didn't matter whom I married. And Gus wrote lovely letters. But then his plane was shot down. It reminded me so much of losing Tom. When I found out that Gus had survived, I was very relieved. He had a head wound . . . they operated to remove shrapnel . . . and he was sent back to the States on medical discharge. After he left the hospital, I married him. But there were problems."

"What kind of problems?"

"It had to do with the head wound. It changed his personality . . . flattened it, somehow. He was still intelligent, but his emotions were gone. He was indifferent to

333

everything. Like a robot. His family said he wasn't the same man."

"I've heard of that happening with some brain injuries," Alex said.

"He never got better. He never really cared about anything. Even our son." Blinking like an exhausted child, Emma pulled her hands from Alex's and settled back against the sofa. "It was a mistake. Poor Gus. I need to rest now."

"May I help you to your room?" Alex asked.

She shook her head. "I like it here."

He stood and reached down to lift her feet to the ottoman.

"Alex," Emma said as he rearranged the throw blanket and drew it up to her shoulders.

"Yes?"

"Let him help you," she whispered, closing her eyes. "For his sake."

Alex shook his head, slightly mystified.

The ghost looked shaken. "My God, Emma."

Hearing the sound of a car pulling into the carport, Alex went outside. It was Zoë, back from the grocery store. She hopped out of the car and opened the back, reaching for a pair of canvas bags filled with groceries.

"I'll get those," Alex said, walking toward her.

Zoë started at the sound of his voice and looked at him in surprise. "Hi," she exclaimed brightly. She looked stressed as hell, her face pale, her eyes tired. "How was the wedding?"

"It was fine." He took the bags from her. "How are you?"

"Great," she said, too quickly.

Alex set the bags down and turned Zoë to face him. She was standing a step above him, all fast-breathing tension and locked muscles. "I heard that Emma was a handful this weekend," he said bluntly.

Zoë avoided his gaze. "Oh, we had a rough patch. But it's fine now."

Alex discovered that he couldn't stand it when she put up a front for him. He settled his hands at her hips. "Talk to me."

Zoë stared at him, looking flustered. In the silence, he brought her against him slowly. She took an anxious breath, her composure unraveling. Wrapping his arms around her, he surrounded her with all his warmth and strength. She fit against him perfectly, her head tucked into the crook of his neck and shoulder.

He slid his hand into her hair and sifted lightly through the blond curls. "What did

Emma do to your computer?"

Zoë's voice was compressed against his shoulder. "She zoomed the screen out so far that the icons are ginormous and I can't close the magnifier. And somehow she made copies of the task bar so there are at least eight of them, and I can't make them go away. And to top it all off, she somehow managed to turn the entire screen upside down."

"I can fix that stuff," he said.

"I thought Sam was the computer genius."

"Trust me on this: don't ever let Sam near your computer. By the time he leaves, he's changed all your passwords, illegally hooked you up to the Department of Defense grid, and Bluetooth-enabled everything in your house until you can't use your toaster because it's not discoverable." He felt the shape of Zoë's smile against his neck. Smoothing her hair back, he murmured near her ear, "You don't need a genius. You just need a guy who can do some troubleshooting."

"You're hired," she said, her face still hidden.

He pressed his lips to her hair. "What else can I do?"

"Nothing." But her arms had crept tentatively around him.

"Think of something," he coaxed.

"Well . . ." Her voice turned watery. "I called my father this morning. To tell him that if he's going to visit, he'd better do it soon. Or Emma isn't going to remember him by the time he gets around to it."

"What did he say?" Feeling that she had tensed again, Alex began to rub her back.

"He's coming this weekend, with his girlfriend, Phyllis. They're going to stay at the inn. He's not especially happy about it, but he's doing it. I'm going to make a special dinner for them and Upsie and Justine, and . . ." Her voice faded as his hand slid lower on her spine, massaging in small circles.

"You want me to be there?" he prompted gently.

"Yes."

"Okay."

"Really?"

"I'd love to."

"I'm so glad you —" She stopped and gripped handfuls of his shirt.

His hand stilled instantly. "Did I hurt you?"

Zoë looked up at him with dilated eyes, her cheeks flushed. Slowly she shook her head, looking as if she'd been hypnotized.

Desire shot through him as he realized

she was aroused by the way he'd been touching her. For few white-hot seconds, all he could think about was her naked body caught under his like a flower pressed between the pages of a book.

"There's one more thing I need from you," she said. The sound of her voice could have been classified as a legal sexual stimulant.

Alex couldn't seem to make his arms let go. He had to pry his hands from her one finger at a time. "Let's talk about that later," he said gruffly, and steered her into the house.

NINETEEN

Although Emma stabilized during the next few days, Zoë noticed that she was more forgetful and distracted. Emma needed frequent reminders to get through her morning routine — she might forget to have breakfast or to take a shower. Or when she was in the shower, she might miss a step such as using shampoo or conditioner.

Near the end of the week, Justine spent the afternoon with Emma, taking her to the salon to have her hair done. Afterward, they had lunch down by the docks. Zoë was grateful to have the break, and Emma had been in a great mood when Justine dropped her off.

"She lectured me for at least an hour about what kind of guys I should go out with," Justine told Zoë the next morning, as Zoë washed dishes at the inn.

"No bikers," Zoë guessed.

"Exactly. And then she forgot that she'd

just lectured me, and told me the whole thing again."

"I'm sorry."

"No, it was fine. But jeez, that kind of repetition would drive me crazy if I had to live with her."

"It's not that bad. Some days are worse than others. For some reason she's better when Alex is around."

"Really? Why is that?"

"She likes him. She really tries to focus when he's there. He's been doing tile work in the little bathroom he built where the old closet used to be. So the other day I found her sitting on the bed, chatting up a storm while he was gluing tile and grouting."

"So even grandmothers think carpenters are hot."

Zoë laughed. "I guess so. And Alex is very patient with her. Very sweet."

"Ha. That's the first time I've ever heard someone call Alex Nolan sweet."

"He is," Zoë said. "You can't imagine what a difference he's made to Emma."

"And to you?" Justine prompted, looking at her closely.

"Yes. He's going to be here for dinner on Saturday night. I asked him for moral support, since my dad's going to be there."

"You've got me for moral support."

Zoë started to scrub a baking pan in the sink. "I need all the support I can get from as many people as possible. You know how my dad is."

Justine sighed. "If it makes Saturday night easier for you, Alex Nolan is welcome. I'll even be nice to him. What are you going to make, by the way?"

"Something special."

Justine had bounced on her heels in anticipation. "Your dad does not deserve the dinner you're making for him. But I'm glad I get to reap the benefits."

Zoë refrained from telling her cousin that she wasn't really cooking for her father's benefit, or even for Emma's. It was for Alex. She was going to speak to him in a language of fragrance, color, texture, taste . . . she was going to use all her skill and instinct to create a meal he would never forget.

Justine met Alex at the front door of the inn and welcomed him inside. Her hair was a loose curtain of dark silk, as opposed to the usual ponytail. She was strikingly attractive in slim cigarette pants and flats, and an emerald top with a deeply scooped neckline. But there was something subdued about her this evening, her usual vibrancy diminished.

"Hi, Alex." Her gaze went to the glass jars

in his hands, filled with lavender bath salts and tied with filmy purple bows. "What are those?"

"Hostess gifts." He handed them to her. "For you and Zoë."

"Thanks," she said, looking surprised. "That's nice. And lavender is Zoë's favorite smell."

"I know."

Justine studied him intently. "You two have been getting close lately, huh?"

He was instantly wary. "I wouldn't say that."

"You don't have to. The fact that you're here for this dinner makes it pretty clear. Zoë's relationship with her dad is an emotional minefield. He's never given a damn about her. I think he's the reason she's always been attracted to men who are guaranteed to let her down."

"Are you leading to a point?"

"Yes. If you hurt Zoë in any way, I'll put a curse on you."

Justine looked so sincere that Alex couldn't help asking, "What kind of curse?"

"Something lifelong and incapacitating."

Although Alex was tempted to tell Justine to mind her own business, part of him was touched by her fierce concern for her cousin. "Understood," he said.

Seeming satisfied, Justine led him toward the inn's private library.

"Is Duane here tonight?" Alex asked.

"We broke up," Justine muttered.

"Can I ask why?"

"I scared him."

"How could you . . . never mind, let's change the subject. When did Zoë's dad get here?"

"Late last night," she said. "He and his girlfriend, Phyllis, spent most of the day with Emma."

"How is she doing?"

"She's having a pretty good day — every now and then she got a little mixed up and kept asking who Phyllis was. But Phyllis has been really nice. I think you'll like her."

"What about James?"

Justine gave a snort. "No one likes James."

They entered the library, where a long mahogany table had been set with crystal and white linen, and decorated with a row of green hydrangea blossoms floating in glass bowls. Emma stood with her son and his girlfriend near the fireplace, which was filled with lit candles set in assorted mercury glass candlesticks.

Emma beamed as she saw him. She was wearing a plum silk dress, her light blond hair shining in the candle glow. "There you

343

are," she exclaimed.

Alex went to her and bent to kiss her cheek. "You look beautiful, Emma."

"Thank you." She turned to the brunette by her side. "Phyllis, this handsome devil is Alex Nolan. He's the one who's remodeling the cottage."

The woman was tall and large-boned, her hair cut in an efficient bob. "Nice to meet you," she said, giving Alex a firm handshake and a friendly smile.

"And this," Emma continued, gesturing to a squarely built man of medium height, "is my son, James."

Alex shook his hand.

Zoë's father greeted him with all the pleasure of a substitute teacher who had just been assigned to a misbehaving classroom. He had the kind of face that appeared boyish and aged at the same time, his eyes flat as pennies behind heavy-rimmed glasses.

"We visited the cottage today," James told him. "You seem to have done a competent job."

"That's James's version of a compliment," Phyllis interceded quickly. She smiled at Alex. "It's a terrific lake house. According to Justine and Zoë, you've transformed the place."

"There's still more left to do," Alex said.

"We're starting on the garage this week."

As the conversation continued, James divulged that he was the manager of an electronics store in Arizona, and Phyllis was a veterinarian who'd been certified as an equine specialist. They were considering the idea of buying a five-acre horse farm. "It's on the edge of a ghost town," Phyllis said. "At one point the town had the richest silver mine in the world, but after all of it was extracted, the town dried up."

"Is it haunted?" Emma asked.

"Some people claim there's a ghost in the old saloon," Phyllis told her.

"Isn't it odd," James asked dryly, "that you never hear of ghosts haunting a nice place? They always pick some broken-down house or a dusty old abandoned building."

The ghost, who had been wandering beside the bookshelves and perusing the titles, said sarcastically, "It's not like I got a choice between an attic or the Ritz."

Emma responded with a serious expression. "Ghosts usually haunt the places where their suffering was greatest."

James laughed. "Mother, you don't believe in ghosts, do you?"

"Why shouldn't I?"

"No one has ever managed to prove that they exist."

"No one's proved that they don't exist, either," Emma pointed out.

"If you believe in ghosts, you might as well believe in leprechauns and Santa Claus."

Zoë's laughing voice came from the doorway as she brought in a pitcher of water. "Dad always told me Santa Claus wasn't real," she said to the room in general. "But I wanted to believe in him. So I asked a higher authority."

"God?" Justine asked.

"No, I asked Upsie. And she said I could believe in whatever I wanted."

"So much for my mother's firm grasp on reality," James said acidly.

"I grasp reality," Emma said with dignity. "But sometimes I like to choke it into submission."

The ghost regarded her with an approving grin. "What a woman."

Zoë laughed and glanced at Alex. "Hi," she said softly.

Alex had temporarily lost the power of speech. Zoë was impossibly beautiful in a sleeveless black dress with straps and a twist front, the stretchy fabric clinging lightly to spectacular curves. Her only accessory was a brooch pinned at the lowest point of the vee neckline, an Art Deco half-circle encrusted with white and green rhinestones.

"I forgot about music," Zoë told him. "Do you have a playlist on your phone? Maybe some of those old tunes that Upsie likes? There's a dock with speakers on that bookshelf."

When Alex was slow to respond, the ghost said impatiently, "The jazz list. Put on some music."

Alex shook his head to clear it, and went to set his phone into the dock. In a minute, the sultry strains of Duke Ellington's "Prelude to a Kiss" floated into the air.

Sitting beside Emma at the table, Alex watched as Zoë brought in a tray of white porcelain spoons. She set one in front of him. It contained a small, perfectly seared scallop nestled into a little dab of something green.

"It's a scallop and fried pancetta on artichoke puree," Zoë said, smiling down at him. "Eat it all in one bite."

Alex took it into his mouth. The salty pancetta crackled against the sweet scallop, the smoky bite of black pepper warming the smooth artichoke. He heard a few hums of delight around the table.

Zoë lingered beside Alex, her lashes lowering as she watched his reaction. "Do you like it?" she asked.

It was the best thing he had ever tasted.

"Are there more? Because I could skip the rest of dinner and just have these."

Zoë shook her head with a grin, reaching to collect the empty spoon. "Amuse-bouche," she told him, and went to the kitchen to bring out the next course.

"This is so much fun," Phyllis exclaimed, swaying a little in her seat as Benny Goodman's "Sing Sing Sing" began. She held up the wine bottle invitingly. "Alex, would you like some?"

"No, thanks," Alex said.

"Abstinence makes the heart grow fonder," Emma murmured, and patted his shoulder.

Somehow James had heard from across the table. "Mother, you've got the saying wrong."

"Actually," Alex said, smiling down at Emma, "she got it exactly right."

The next course was a small plate of fiddleheads, tightly coiled fronds of young ferns. After being blanched in hot water until they had turned a brilliant green, the fiddleheads had been tossed in a warm vinaigrette of browned butter, fresh lemon, and sea salt. Toasted walnuts were sprinkled on top, along with snowy flakes of fresh Parmesan cheese. The guests exclaimed over the salad, tongues rolling the flavors inside

348

their cheeks. Phyllis and Justine giggled together at their own efforts to scrape every last drop from the salad plates. Zoë's gaze often touched on Alex, as if she savored his obvious pleasure in the food.

Only James seemed unaffected. Midway through the dish, he set down his fork, looking disgruntled. He lifted a glass of red wine to his mouth and drank a deep swallow.

"You're not going to finish your salad?" Phyllis asked incredulously.

"I don't care for it," he said.

"I'll help you, then." Phyllis reached over and began to spear his remaining fiddleheads enthusiastically.

Zoë, who had just begun on her own salad, looked at her father with concern. "Can I get you something else, Dad? A dish of field greens?"

He shook his head, looking like an airport traveler waiting for his boarding pass number to be called.

Billie Holiday's ebullient rendition of "I'm Gonna Lock My Heart" danced across the dining table. Soon Justine and Zoë brought out individual bowls of mussels, their abundant steam perfumed with white wine, saffron, butter, parsley. The guests picked up the dark, gleaming shells with their fingers, and used tiny forks to spear the

349

sweet tidbits inside. Empty bowls were set on the table for the discarded shells.

"My God, Zoë," Justine exclaimed after her first taste of the mussels. "This *sauce*. I could just drink it."

A relaxed and jovial mood spread through the room, accompanied by the busy clacking of shells. It was a dish that required activity, involvement, conversation. The broth was indecently good, a savory elixir that washed exquisite, truffly sensation through his mouth. Alex was about to ask for a spoon, having decided there was no way in hell he was giving back his bowl until he'd consumed every drop. But homemade French rolls were being passed around, crisp on the outside, fine textured and chewy on the inside. The diners tore the bread with their fingers and used the pieces to sop up the rich liquid.

The discussion turned to the half-day whale-watching trip that Phyllis and James had arranged to take the next morning, and an alpaca farm that Phyllis wanted to visit.

"Have you ever treated an alpaca?" Zoë asked Phyllis.

"No, most of my patients are dogs, cats, and horses." Phyllis smiled reminiscently as she added, "Once I diagnosed a guinea pig with a sinus infection."

"What's your weirdest case ever?" Justine asked.

Phyllis grinned. "That's a tough one. I've seen a lot of weirdness. But not long ago a man and a woman brought in their dog, who'd been having stomach problems. The X-rays showed a mysterious obstruction, which I removed with an endoscopic camera. It turned out to be a pair of red lace panties, which I put in a plastic bag and gave to the woman."

"How embarrassing," Emma exclaimed.

"It gets worse," Phyllis said. "The woman took one look at the panties, clocked the man with her purse, and left the office in a fury. Because the underwear didn't belong to her. And the man was left to pay the bill for a dog who had just outed him as a cheater."

The story was greeted with raucous laughter.

Glasses were refilled and little fingerbowls filled with water and rose petals were brought out. They rinsed their fingers and dried them on fresh napkins. A palate-cleansing sorbet was served in frosty lemons that had been hollowed into small cups, the iced puree flecked with lemon zest and mint.

When Zoë and Justine went to the kitchen for the next course, Phyllis exclaimed, "I've never had food like this in my life. It's an *experience.*"

James frowned. Inexplicably, he had become more dour and subdued with every passing minute. "Don't be dramatic."

"For goodness' sake, James," Emma said. "She's right. It is an experience."

He grumbled beneath his breath and poured more wine into his glass.

Zoë and Justine returned with plates of crisp-skinned quail, brined with salt and honey before it had been roasted in the oven. The quail was accompanied by quenelles, or small delicate dumplings, made with minced chanterelle mushrooms and a sweet, nutlike kiss of hyacinth.

Alex had eaten quail before, but not like this, enlaced with a pungent, toasted, deeply rich flavor. Conversation turned languid, faces flushed, eyes blinked slowly as repletion settled over the room. Coffee and handmade chocolate truffles were served, followed by pots-de-crème, vanilla and egg creams and honey baked in a water bath. The luscious emulsion dissolved in the mouth and slid gently down the throat, coating the taste buds in rapture.

James Hoffman alone had been silent amid the exclamations of the group. Alex couldn't fathom what was wrong with the man. He had to be ill, there was no other possible reason why he had eaten so little.

Apparently reaching the same conclusion, Phyllis asked James in concern, "Are you okay? You hardly touched your food all through dinner."

He looked away from her, focusing his gaze on the pot-de-crème in front of him, blotchy color appearing on his cheeks. "My dinner was inedible. It was bitter. All of it." He stood and tossed his napkin to the table, and cast a furious, resentful glance at the stunned faces around him. His gaze settled on Zoë's blank face. "Maybe you did something to my food," he said. "If so, your point was made."

"James," Phyllis protested, blanching. "I ate from your plate, and your food was exactly like mine. Your taste buds must be off tonight."

He shook his head and strode from the room. Phyllis hurried after him, pausing to turn back at the doorway and say sincerely to Zoë, "It was magnificent. The best meal of my life."

Zoë managed a smile. "Thank you."

Justine shook her head after Phyllis had gone. "Zoë, your dad is crazy. This dinner was amazing."

"She knows it was," Emma said, gazing at Zoë.

Zoë looked back at her with resignation. "It was the best I could do," she said simply. "But that's never been enough for him." She stood from the table and gestured for them to stay in their chairs. "I'll be right back. I'm going to put on another pot of coffee." She left the library.

Seeing Justine begin to stand, Alex said quietly, "Let me."

She frowned but remained seated as he headed after Zoë.

Alex wasn't entirely certain what he would say to Zoë once he reached her. For the past two hours, he had watched her set plate after plate of magnificent food in front of a father who would never appreciate such offerings. He understood the situation all too well. From his own experiences, Alex knew that parental love was an ideal, not a guarantee. Some parents had nothing to give their children. And some, like James Hoffman, blamed and punished their children for things they'd had nothing to do with.

Zoë was occupied with measuring grounds into the basket of the small coffeemaker. Hearing his footsteps, she turned to face him. She looked expectant, oddly intent, as if she wanted something from him. "I wasn't surprised," she said. "I knew what to expect from my father."

"Then why did you make this dinner for him?"

"It wasn't for him."

His eyes widened.

"If you hadn't agreed to come here tonight," Zoë continued, "we would have gone to a restaurant. I wanted to cook for you. I planned every course trying to think of what you would enjoy."

Frustration and bewilderment tangled inside him. He had the sense of being manipulated in the softest possible way, like silken nets being drawn around him. A woman didn't do these things purely for the sake of kindness or generosity. There had to be something behind it, a motive he would only discover when it was too late.

"Why would you do that for me?" he asked roughly.

"If I were an opera singer, I would have sung you an aria. If I were an artist, I would have painted your portrait. But cooking is what I'm best at."

He could still taste the flavor of the pot-de-crème, clover and wildflowers and deep amber nectar. The taste bloomed on his tongue and tightened his throat with sweetness, and flowed through him until he could have sworn the honey scent was even rising from his pores. Without meaning to, he reached Zoë in two strides and took her by the arms. The feel of her, voluptuous and silky, sent his blood racing. Emotion and sensation swirled together in a volatile mixture, and all it would take was a single spark to obliterate him. He was so hard, so hungry for her. So tired of trying to keep apart from her.

"Zoë," he said, "this has to stop. I don't want you to do things for me. I don't want you to think about ways to please me. You've already ruined me. For the rest of my life, I'll never be able to look at another woman without wanting her to be you. You're woven all through me. I can't even dream without you being there in my head. But I can't be with you. I hurt people. It's what *I'm* best at."

Her face changed, her mouth rounding in an O of tender dismay. "Alex, no."

"I'll hurt you," he said ruthlessly. "I'll turn you into someone we both would hate." The truth came from the deepest part of his soul. *You're nothing. You deserve nothing. You have nothing to give anyone except pain.* Knowing that, believing it, was the only way the world made sense.

As Zoë held his gaze, he saw anger gathering on her face. The sight relieved him. It meant she would strike him, reject him. It meant she would be safe.

Her hand came to his cheek. But softly.

Her fingers were gentle against his jaw, her thumb brushing his lower lip as if to erase the razor-edged words. It threw him into hot confusion to realize that her anger wasn't directed at him. "No," she murmured, "you've twisted it all around. You're the one who's been hurt. You're not trying to protect me. You're trying to protect yourself."

He shoved her hand away from him. "It doesn't matter who the hell I'm trying to protect. The point is, some things are broken too bad to be fixed."

"Not people."

"Especially people."

Seconds passed, sawing deep through the silence.

"If either of us gets hurt," Zoë said carefully, "it's still better than never taking a chance."

"You want to take a chance on something hopeless," he said in a scornful tone.

She shook her head. "Something hopeful."

In that moment Alex hated her for what

she was trying to do, for making him want to believe her. "Don't be stupid. Don't you get what having a relationship with me would do to you?"

"We're already having the relationship," she said in exasperation. "We have been for a while."

Alex seized her, wanting to shake some sense into her. But instead he was gripping her close against his hammering heart, forcing her to stand on her toes. He didn't kiss her, only held her with his head bent so that he could feel her breath on his face.

"I want you," she whispered. "And you want me. So take me home and do something about it. Tonight."

The sound of the kitchen door made him flinch, but he still couldn't let go of Zoë.

"Oops," he heard Justine mutter. "Sorry."

Zoë turned her face toward her cousin. "Justine," she said, sounding remarkably calm, "you don't have to drive Emma and me back to the cottage. Alex is going to do it."

"He is?" Justine asked warily.

Zoë's warm blue eyes stared up into his. Daring him. Entreating.

All right, then. He had finally reached the point where he didn't care. He was sick of struggling and needing, and never having.

He didn't give a damn about anything except getting what he wanted.

Alex gave her a single nod.

Against every instinct he possessed.

TWENTY

Emma was sleepy and contented on the drive back to Dream Lake, not to mention relieved that Zoë hadn't been upset by her father's behavior.

"Of course I wasn't," Zoë said with a light laugh. "I know how he is. I'm glad he brought Phyllis, though. I like her."

"I do, too," Emma said. A reflective pause. "It must say something good about James, that he can attract a woman like her."

"Maybe he's different when he's away from us," Zoë said. "Maybe when he's in Arizona, he's more positive."

"I hope so," Emma said doubtfully.

Alex was quiet, occupied with a fierce inner battle. He knew that he should drop Zoë and Emma off at the cottage and leave at once. He even thought there was a chance he could do that. The odds were seventy–thirty in favor of leaving.

Maybe sixty–forty.

Alex wanted Zoë so badly there was no room left for anything else. He was molten inside, but in the past few minutes his heart had shut down and turned glacier-cold. The difference in temperature, the tension between fire and ice, threatened to crack his chest in a thermal downshock.

The ghost, occupying the backseat next to Emma, was silent. There was no doubt that he'd sensed Alex's turmoil. He understood something was wrong.

"Alex is coming in for a drink," Zoë told Emma as they got out of the car.

"Oh, how nice." Emma linked arms with her granddaughter as they headed to the front door.

"Would you like something, too, Upsie?"

"At this hour? No, no, I've had a lovely day, but I'm tired now." She glanced over her shoulder. "Thank you for driving us, Alex."

"No problem."

They went into the house, and Zoë murmured to Alex, "I'll just be a few minutes. There's lavender lemonade in the fridge."

She went into Emma's room and closed the door.

Lavender lemonade. Alex suspected it would taste like leftover water from a flower vase. But heat was thrumming in his body, turning his skin dry and parching his mouth. He went to the refrigerator, found the pitcher of lemonade, and poured a glass.

It was tart and light, wonderfully cool. He drank deeply, sitting on one of the bar stools at the kitchen island. The ghost was nowhere in sight.

A heavy mass of emotion had gathered inside, and he struggled to separate it into identifiable parts. Lust, first and foremost. Anger. Maybe a trace of fear, but it was so mixed up with the anger that he couldn't be sure. And worse than anything was a terrible knifing tenderness he'd never felt for anyone in his life.

The women he'd been with in the past, including Darcy, had all been experienced, confident, seasoned. With Zoë it would be different. The familiar terms for sex . . . nailing, boning, banging . . . did not apply. She would expect him to be gentle . . . gentlemanly . . . God help him, he'd have to figure out how to fake that.

The bedroom door opened and closed quietly. Zoë had slipped off her high heels. She walked toward him in that damned black dress, the gathered fabric hugging every luxurious curve. Alex didn't move from the bar stool. A tightening feeling spread over him, the lust threatening to annihilate him, and her along with him.

"She's asleep now," Zoë whispered, coming to stand in front of him. Her smile was tremulous. He reached out and touched the pure line of her throat, pale as moonglow. His fingertips trailed softly downward to her collarbone. The light touch drew a shiver from deep within her.

He pulled her closer between his spread thighs and gripped one strap of her dress, dragging it down a few inches. Pressing his mouth to the side of her neck, he kissed the smooth skin, working his way down. Gently he bit the fine, firm muscle at the top of her shoulder. A gasp escaped her. He could feel a blush in her, burning its way to the surface. For a moment it was enough just to hold her like this, to savor the female form caught between his thighs, the veil of her hair sliding against his face and neck.

"You know this is a mistake," he said gruffly, lifting his head.

"I don't care."

He sank his hand into her hair and kissed her, opening her mouth with his, searching aggressively with his tongue, then caressing in softer, deeper strokes. She tensed against him, a sound caught in her throat, her hands groping around his shoulders.

He had never known such intense need,

more than could be satisfied in ten lifetimes. He wanted to spread her out like a feast, kiss and taste every part of her. Reaching behind her, he found the hidden zipper of the dress, and it gave way with a metallic hiss. His hand slipped inside the shadowed opening, fingers spreading across the satiny warmth of her back. The pleasure of touching her shot through him. His mouth traveled over her throat, and he breathed her name, rubbing the syllables into her skin with his lips and tongue —

A harsh caterwaul came from behind him. Startled, he nearly jumped out of his shoes. He turned to see the big, baleful cat glaring at him.

Zoë pulled away from Alex, her eyes wide. Seeing the cat, she laughed breathlessly. "I'm sorry. Poor Byron." She bent to pet the Persian.

"Poor *Byron?*" Alex asked incredulously.

"He's insecure," she explained. "I think he needs reassurance."

Alex gave the cat a narrow-eyed glance. "I think he needs to be drop-kicked from the front doorstep." His attention was diverted as Zoë held up the gaping front of her dress with one hand.

"Let's go into the bedroom," she said. "He'll settle down in a few minutes."

Following Zoë, Alex turned and closed the door in the cat's face. After a moment of silence, they heard a drawn-out yowl, accompanied by scratching.

Zoë gave Alex an apologetic glance. "He'll be quiet if we leave the door open."

There was no way he was letting a cat watch while he had sex. "Zoë, do you know what the word 'cockblocked' means?"

"No."

"It's what your cat is trying to do to me."

"I'll give him some catnip," Zoë said in a moment of inspiration. Opening the door, she paused at the threshold and told him, "Don't change your mind while I'm gone."

"I can't change my mind," he said darkly. "I've already lost it."

Zoë put a spoonful of dried catnip into a brown paper grocery bag, and set it sideways on the kitchen floor. Byron purred and arched against her hand, pleased to have her attention focused on him. "Be a good boy and stay in here, okay?" Zoë whispered.

The cat sniffed at the grocery bag and crept in. The paper crackled and sagged as Byron executed a slow roll inside.

Returning to the bedroom, Zoë closed the door.

Alex had taken off his shoes and was sitting on the edge of the bed, which was covered with a flowered duvet. He looked big and vaguely dangerous in the confines of her bedroom. The glow from the lamp played over the hard perfection of his features, the gleaming black layers of his hair.

"We may have to get creative," he said. "Not being forewarned, I don't have any kind of protection for you."

"I bought some just in case," she admitted.

One of his brows arched. "You were pretty sure I'd end up at your place."

"Not sure," she said. "Just optimistic."

"Bring them to me." The raw velvet of his voice caused the back of her neck to prickle in excitement.

Zoë went to the tiny bathroom and closed the door. After undressing and slipping into a soft pink robe, she found the box of condoms, and returned to the bed.

Alex's gaze traveled slowly over the robe, down to her exposed ankles and bare feet, and back to her flushed face. Taking the box from her, he opened it, took out a packet, and set it on the night table. To her surprise, Alex took out another packet and set it beside the first. She blinked and felt her face turn hot. Sending her a pointed glance, Alex put a third packet on the nightstand.

Zoë couldn't hold back an airless giggle. "Now *you're* being optimistic," she said.

"No," came his measured reply, "I'm sure."

She thought with private amusement that there were situations in which a touch of male arrogance was not necessarily a bad thing.

Alex set aside the box and stood. He unbuttoned his charcoal gray shirt and let it drop to the floor. His vee-neck undershirt was crisp white against tanned skin. Tentatively Zoë reached for the hem of the tee, the bleached cotton holding the warmth and salty-clean scent of his body. She pulled it upward, and he moved to help her. As the undershirt was stripped away, his body was revealed, elegant in its spare, hard strength. For a split second, she wondered if he would be gentle enough, careful enough. It had been so long since she'd been intimate with anyone.

He focused on her, taking in her dazed expression. "Worried?" he asked quietly, his hands coming to her arms, caressing over the robe.

"No, I . . ." She gave him an unsteady smile. "I just want to remind you that I'm not very skilled."

"I got it covered," he said. Pulling her closer, he nuzzled against her hair, the heat of his breath sinking to her scalp.

Yes. That much she knew. The awareness of his experience sent a nervous flutter through her stomach.

Alex drew her to the bed and lay beside her. His callused hand came to the side of her face, warmth and roughness cradling her cheek. He kissed her, slow and insatiable, the taste of him sweet and edged with lemonade tartness. She opened eagerly to the flavor and rolled to press closer to him, trembling in excitement at the feel of the hard masculine form all along hers. Her hands wandered over the arousing textures of him, the silky-coarse hair on his chest, the sleek hardness of his shoulders, the shaven bristle of his jaw.

He nuzzled beneath her jaw and worked his way to the hollow behind her ear, and touched his tongue to her earlobe. Shivering, she turned to find his lips with hers. More of those dizzying wholemouthed kisses, a little deeper, rougher.

Heat had accumulated beneath the pink robe. She wriggled to be free of the confining fabric, she was smoldering, suffocating. Clumsy with desire, she fumbled at the fabric belt. The knot defied her efforts, tightening adamantly until she began to wrench at it in frustration.

Lifting his head, Alex saw what she wanted. "I'll do it," he said, reaching for the belt. "Lie still."

Zoë rolled to her back, gasping. Heat had gathered in her mouth and at the roots of her hair, and between all her fingers and toes. Everywhere. She clenched her thighs against a simmer of wetness. She had never wanted anything as much as she wanted him inside her . . . she was anxious and aroused, lost in the middle of a dream that might end too soon.

"Alex," she said desperately, "you don't have to bother with doing a lot of extra stuff."

"What stuff?" he asked, busy with the belt of her robe.

She couldn't prevent a moan of relief as the garment loosened. "Foreplay. I don't need any right now. Because I'm ready."

His hands stilled. He looked down at her flushed face, a glint of amusement in his eyes. "Zoë. Do I ever go into the kitchen and tell you how to make a soufflé?"

"No."

"That's right. Because that's your area of expertise. And this is mine."

"If I were a soufflé," she said, struggling

369

to pull her arms from the robe, "I would be overdone by now."

"Trust me, you're not — oh, *God.*" The sides of the robe had fallen apart, revealing the abundant pink and white curves of her body. Looking down at her, Alex shook his head slowly. "This is dangerous. This is how people die."

With a shy grin, Zoë pulled her arms free of the robe, her breasts bouncing with the movement.

Alex said something incomprehensible, his color rising.

"Take me now," she urged, sliding her arms around his neck. "I don't want to wait."

"Zoë . . ." He wasn't breathing well. "With a body like yours, skipping foreplay is not an option. In fact . . . any time you spend out of bed is wasted."

"Are you saying I'm only good for sex?"

"No, you're good for a lot of other things," he said, his gaze locked on her breasts. "I just can't think of any of them right now."

Her laugh was muffled as he kissed her. He slid lower, dragging his mouth along her throat, his breath hot against her skin. His hand cupped beneath her breast, lifting it as he took the straining tip into his mouth, his tongue tracing liquid circles. She closed her eyes against the soft balm of lamplight, her senses humming with pleasure as he tugged gently, repeatedly.

There was no world outside this bed, nothing but the two of them. He touched between her thighs where she was wet and sensitive, and her hips rode upward reflexively. His thumb separated the seam of vulnerable flesh, rubbing lightly, the grooved scar sliding deliciously through the wetness. She was so close, so desperate for the climax that hovered just out of reach, that her eyes stung with frustrated tears.

Inside the blur of light and shadow, he was whispering for her to trust him, let him take care of her. His hand cupped her, one of his fingers entering the softness. Reaching deep inside, he traced a subtle pattern, his knuckles wriggling gently.

Her trembling hand slid down to his wrist, where she could feel the intricate movements of bone and tendon. The bedroom was silent as they both concentrated on the secret movements within her. A new tension began at the quick of her body and spread in supple pulses. His face was dark and intent above her hers, his fingers slow and clever.

"What are you doing?" she asked through dry lips.

His lashes lowered over a flick of blue fire, and he bent to murmur near her ear. "Writing my name."

"What?" she asked, disoriented.

"My name," he whispered. "Inside you."

The maddening stroking of fingertip and knuckles never stopped. Sensation gathered and began to roll forward as the heel of his hand pressed her rhythmically. Her head fell back against his supportive arm, and she felt his mouth caress her throat.

"That's . . . more than four letters," she managed to say weakly.

"Alexander," he explained. "And this . . ." A low, erotic tickle. "This is my middle name."

"Wh-what is it?"

She felt him smile against her skin.

"Guess," he murmured.

"I can't. Oh, please —"

"I'll tell you," he murmured, "as long as you don't come before I finish."

Impossible to lock the pleasure out. Impossible to ignore the sensations rushing so hard and fast. She strained and stiffened, gripping his shoulders. The shudders began, pleasure spilling in waves, each crest rolling higher until she thought she might pass out. He gathered her against him, took her sobs into his mouth, brought her through the feeling and spun it out even longer.

The release was so absolute that Zoë couldn't move for minutes afterward, her limbs twitching as if with an electric current. Alex began a leisurely project of kissing her from head to toe. On the way back up, he parted her legs with deliberate caresses, his mouth skimming up the tender inside of her thigh until she jolted.

"You don't need to do that," she said, twisting. "I've already . . . no, really. Alex —"

He looked up at her across the rapid rise and fall of her stomach. "Area of expertise," he reminded her.

"Yes, but . . ." She stuttered as he gripped her legs behind the knees, pushing them up and apart. "You can ruin a soufflé by overworking the batter."

His quiet laugh vibrated against the most sensitive part of her, causing her legs to quiver. "You haven't been overworked," he murmured. "Yet." He nuzzled against her, his shaven cheek gently rasping the delicate skin. She struggled to breathe, her heart pounding in a violent rhythm.

"Turn off the light?" she pleaded, a fierce blush racing over every inch of her.

A slow shake of his head, his mouth nudging deeper. She fell back with a little yelp, startled by the slippery-hot stroke of his tongue.

"Shhh," he whispered, right against her, and the rush of his breath inflamed her even more. Another stroke . . . a teasing flutter . . . a swirling taste inside. She gripped handfuls of the flowered duvet, her thoughts dissolving in the burning physical awareness of what he was doing to her. He played with her deliberately, paying attention to every moan and twitch and squirm.

Eventually he lifted his head and whispered, "More." But the word was tipped upward in a question, and he waited for her reply.

"Yes." Anything he wanted. Anything at all.

Alex left the bed, and she heard the sounds of his jeans dropping to the floor, and the efficient rip of one of the foil packets on the nightstand. He returned to her, lowering his body over hers, the hair on his chest teasing her breasts. Her breath hastened as she felt the intimate pressure of him.

He settled deeper, every movement careful and easy. She moaned as she felt her body yielding to the steady pressure.

"Am I hurting you?" she heard him whisper.

She shook her head blindly. The sensation was overpowering, but he was so gentle, filling her slowly, letting her take him by degrees. And all the while he brushed kisses against her mouth and throat, whispering that she was sweet, soft, beautiful, that nothing had ever felt this good, nothing ever would again.

It was like a dream, this slow, inexorable possession, both of them intent on coaxing her body to take as much of him as she could. And then he was sealed against her, and her back was flat against the bed, her body weighted and impaled. She turned her face into the brutal swell of his bicep, his skin salt-flavored and delicious against her parted lips. He began to rock against her, a lascivious friction that prodded and rubbed and caressed. The pleasure was shattering. She stiffened, her legs spreading as she was thrown into a blinding climax. His thrusts lengthened, centering straight and deep, and then Alex shuddered, and held her as if the world were about to end.

"Tell me," she said a long time later, in the dark. Her voice was lower than usual, liquid, as if it had been heated to a melting point.

Alex's hand wandered idly over her sated body. "Tell you what?"

"Your middle name."

He shook his head.

She tugged gently at his chest hair. "Give me a hint."

He took her hand and brought it to his mouth, kissing her fingers. "It's a U.S. president."

She traced the fine, firm edge of his upper lip. "Past or present?"

"Past."

"Lincoln." As he shook his head, she continued to guess. "Jefferson. Washington. Oh, give me another hint."

His mouth curved against her palm. "Born in Ohio."

"Millard Fillmore."

That drew a low laugh from him. "Millard Fillmore wasn't born in Ohio."

"Another hint."

"A Civil War general."

"Ulysses S. Grant? Your middle name is Ulysses?" She snuggled next to him, smiling against his shoulder. "I like that."

"I don't. A thousand playground fights started with someone calling me by my middle name."

"Why did your parents name you that?"

"My mother was originally from Point Pleasant, Ohio, where he was born. She claimed we were distant relatives. Since

Grant was a notorious alcoholic, I could almost believe it."

Zoë kissed his shoulder.

"What's your middle name?" Alex asked.

"I don't have one. And I always wanted one — I didn't like having only two initials for a monogram. When I married Chris, I finally got three. But I went back to being Zoë Hoffman after the divorce."

"You could have kept your married name."

"Yes, but it never seemed to fit me." She smiled and yawned. "I think deep down, you always know."

"Always know what?"

Her eyes closed, an overwhelming weariness settling over her. "Who you are," she said drowsily. "Who you're supposed to become."

The ghost lay beside Emma's sleeping form, her hair and face silver-limned as a stray moonbeam slipped through the partially shuttered window. He listened to the soft flow of her breathing, the occasional disruptions as she drifted through dreams. Lying beside her, so close that they would have touched if he'd had a physical form, he could remember the feeling of being young with her, the thrill of being alive and in love, the promise that everything was still before them. With no idea of the evanescence of life.

A memory came to him, of Emma fragile and distraught, her eyes swollen from crying.

"Are you sure?" he asked, the words coming with difficulty.

"I went to the doctor." Her hand pressed against her stomach, not in the protective way of an expectant mother, but clenched in a fist.

He felt ill, furious, blank. Scared out of his mind. "What do you want?" he asked. "What should I do?"

"Nothing. I don't know." Emma began to cry, with the rusted aching sounds of someone who had already been crying a long time. "I don't know," she repeated hopelessly.

He put his arms around her, and held her firmly, and kissed her burning wet cheeks. "I'll do the right thing. We'll get married."

"No, you'll hate me."

"Never. It's not your fault."

Silence.

"I want to marry you," he said.

"You're lying," she choked, but her sobs quieted.

Yes, he was lying. The idea of marriage, a baby, made him die inside. Marriage would be a prison. But he loved Emma too much to hurt her with the truth. And he'd known the risks of having an affair with her. A nice girl, from a fine family, facing ruin because she loved him. If it killed him, he wouldn't let her down. "I want to," he repeated.

"I — I'll talk to my parents."

"No, I'll talk to them. I'll take care of everything. You just calm down. It's not good for you to get upset."

But Emma was shaking with relief, holding him tightly, struggling to get even closer. "Tom. I love you. I'll be a good wife. You won't be sorry, I swear it."

The memory faded, and the ghost was left with feelings of shame and dread. For God's sake, what had been wrong with him? Why had he been so afraid of the thing he had wanted most? He'd been an idiot. If only he'd had it to do over again, everything would be different. What had happened to the baby? And why had Emma lied when she'd told Alex that she and Tom had never talked about getting married? Why hadn't the wedding ceremony taken place?

He looked at Emma's still face. "I'm so sorry," he whispered. "I never meant to hurt you. You're all I ever wanted. All I ever loved. Help me find a way back to you."

TWENTY-ONE

Since a relationship with a Nolan had a limited shelf life, Alex was not surprised when Sam and Lucy broke up in mid-August. He was sympathetic, however. For the past couple of months, Sam had been happier than Alex had ever seen him. Clearly Lucy had meant a lot to him. But Lucy had been offered some kind of art grant that would require her to move to New York for a year. She was going to take it. And Sam, being Sam, wasn't about to interfere with that or ask her to stay for the sake of a relationship that was headed nowhere.

Since Alex had been doing some work on an upstairs staircase at Rainshadow Road, he happened to be there on the day that Lucy came to break up with Sam. While Alex pounded shims into the treads and risers of the stairs, the ghost went to check out what was happening.

"Lucy just broke up with Sam," the ghost reported about ten minutes later.

Alex paused in his hammering. "Just now?"

"Yeah. Clean and simple. She told him she had to move to New York, and he didn't try and stop her. I think it's hit him hard. Why don't you go downstairs and talk to him?"

Alex gave a snort. "About what?"

"Ask him if he's okay. Tell him there are other fish in the sea."

"He doesn't need me to tell him that."

"He's your brother. Show a little concern, why don't you? And while you're at it, you might want to mention that you have to move in with him."

Alex scowled. Darcy had recently e-mailed him that she was filing for a temporary order from family court to kick him out of their house. Her house.

Moving in with Sam would be cheaper than renting an apartment, and in lieu of paying rent, Alex could continue the restoration work at Rainshadow Road. God knew why Alex felt so compelled to work on the place. It wasn't even his. But he couldn't deny his attachment to it.

It had been three weeks since he had started having sex with Zoë — the best three

381

weeks of his life, and also the worst. He rationed out his time with her, when he wanted to see her every minute of the day. He invented excuses to call her, just to listen to her talk about a new recipe or explain the differences between Tahitian, Mexican, or Madagascar vanilla. He found himself smiling at odd times during the day, thinking of something she had said or done, and that was so unlike him that he knew he was in serious trouble.

He wished he could blame Zoë for being demanding, but she knew when to push and when to back off. She managed Alex more adeptly than anyone else ever had, and even though he knew he was being managed, he couldn't bring himself to object. Like the night he'd told her he couldn't stay, she'd made a pot roast that had filled the entire cottage with a dark succulent fragrance, and so of course he had relented long enough to have dinner, and after that he'd found himself in bed with her. Because pot roast, as she must have known, was an aphrodisiac to any man from the Pacific Northwest.

He tried to limit the number of nights he spent with her, but it wasn't easy. He wanted her all the time, in every way. The sex was amazing, but even more astonishing was how much he wanted Zoë for other reasons. The things that had once annoyed him — the perkiness, the stubborn optimism — had somehow become his favorite things about her. She constantly sent out cheerful thoughts like party balloons that he couldn't bring himself to pop.

The one thing Zoë couldn't delude herself about was Emma's condition, which was going downhill. Recently the home-care nurse, Jeannie, had given her some cognitive tests: word repetition, and drawing clock faces on pieces of paper, and simple coin-counting games. Emma scored significantly lower on the same tests she had taken a month earlier. More distressing was that Emma had lost the awareness of hunger, as well as what constituted a balanced meal. Had Jeannie and Zoë not been there to remind her, she might have gone days without eating, or gotten herself something like corn chips and yellow mustard for breakfast.

It worried Zoë to realize that her grandmother, always so impeccably groomed, no longer seemed to notice or care if her hair had been brushed or her nails had been filed. Justine came at least twice a week to take Emma to the salon or to the movie theater. Alex sometimes kept Emma occupied after dinner while Zoë cleaned the kitchen or took a bath. He played cards with Emma, grinning at her flagrant cheating, and he had even put on music and danced with her while she criticized his foxtrot technique.

"Your foot-turn is too late," Emma complained. "You're going to trip me. Where did you learn to dance?"

"I took lessons at a place in Seattle," Alex said as they crossed the room to the melody of "As Time Goes By."

"You should get your money back."

"They worked miracles," he told her. "Before the lessons, the way I danced looked like a pantomime of washing my car."

"How long did you go?" Emma asked dubiously.

"It was an emergency weekend crash course. My fiancée wanted me to be able to dance at our wedding."

"When did you get married?" Emma demanded testily. "No one told me about that."

Although he'd talked to her about his marriage to Darcy, Alex realized she had forgotten. He said in a matter-of-fact tone, "It's over now. We're divorced."

"Well, that was fast."

"Not fast enough," he said ruefully.

"You should marry my Zoë. She can cook."

"I'm not marrying again," he said. "I was terrible at it."

"Practice makes perfect," she told him.

That night, as Alex stayed at the cottage and held Zoë while she slept, he finally figured out what the sweetly painful chest-clutching sensation was, the one that had plagued him since he'd first met her. It was happiness. And it made him exquisitely uncomfortable. He'd heard about certain addictive substances that if you did it once, you'd already done it more than once. That was the nature of his attraction to Zoë — instant, full-blown, no hope of recovery.

Three days after Sam and Lucy's breakup, Alex stopped by Rainshadow Road to pick up some tools he'd left there. A delivery truck followed him along the drive, and parked in front. Two guys proceeded to unload a huge flat crate. "Someone's gotta sign for this," one of them told Alex as they carried the crate up the front steps. "It's insured up the ass."

"What is it?"

"Stained-glass window."

From Lucy, Alex surmised. Sam had told him that Lucy had been making a window for the front of the house. The one that Tom Findlay had installed so long ago had been broken and removed, and replaced with a single pane. Sam had said something about Lucy coming up with the design during her stay at Rainshadow Road, some image she'd seen in a dream.

"I'll sign for it," Alex said. "My brother's out in the vineyard."

The delivery guys laid the massive window on the floor and partially uncrated it to make certain no damage had occurred in transit. "Looks okay," one of them said. "But you find anything after we're gone, hairline cracks or somethin', call the number on the bottom of the receipt."

"Thanks."

"Good luck," the guy said affably. "Gonna be a bitch to install."

"Looks like it," Alex replied with a rueful smile, signing for the package.

The ghost stood beside the window and stared down at it, transfixed. "Alex," he said in a peculiar voice. "Take a look."

After the delivery guys left, Alex went to glance at the window, which featured a winter tree with bare branches, a gray and lavender sky, and a white moon. The colors were subtle, the glass layered and fused to give it an incandescent 3D effect. Alex didn't know much about art, but the skill that had gone into this window was obvious. It was masterful.

His attention returned to the ghost, who was utterly still and silent. The entrance hall had turned chilly in spite of the summer heat. It was sorrow, so raw that Alex felt his throat and eyes sting. "Do you remember this?" he asked the ghost. "Is it like the one you put in for Emma's father?"

The ghost was too upset to speak. He responded with a single nod. More sorrow, filling the air until every breath was an icy scourge. He was remembering something, and it wasn't good.

Alex took a step back, but there was nowhere to go. "Cut it out," he said gruffly.

The ghost pointed to the second floor, and gave Alex a beseeching stare.

Alex understood instantly. "All right. I'll install it today. Just . . . no drama."

Sam came into the house. To Alex's disgust, his lovelorn brother wasn't nearly as interested in the window as he was in the question of whether Lucy had included a note with it. Which she hadn't.

Taking out his phone, Alex began to dial Gavin and Isaac. He would pull them off work on Zoë's garage just for the afternoon, and have them come over here. "I'm going to call some of my guys to help me put the window in," he said. "Today, if possible."

"I don't know," Sam said glumly.

"About what?"

"I don't know if I want to install it."

Feeling a new wave of despair coming from the ghost, Alex said in exasperation, "Don't give me that crap. This window *has* to go into this house. The place needs it. There was one just like it a long time ago."

Sam looked puzzled. "How do you know that?"

"I just meant that it seems right for the place." Alex walked away, dialing his phone. "I'll take care of it."

Right after lunch, Gavin and Isaac met Alex at the vineyard house, and they installed the stained-glass window. The project went fast, owing to the precision of Lucy's measurements. She had constructed the window so that it fit perfectly into the existing framework. They sealed the edges with clear silicone caulk, and taped it into place, using cardboard spacers folded into accordion shapes to protect the glass from the tape. After a twenty-four-hour drying period, they would add wood trim around the edges.

The ghost watched them intently. There were no wisecracks, questions, or comments, only silent, sullen gloom. He refused to explain anything about the window or the memories it had jarred loose.

"Don't you think I'm entitled to some answers?" Alex demanded later that evening. "You could at least give me a clue about what's going on with that damn window. Why did you want me to install it? What's put you in such a foul mood?"

"I'm not ready to talk about it," came the infuriating reply.

The next morning Alex stopped by Rainshadow Road to check on the silicone caulking before he headed to Zoë's cottage. He took his BMW, figuring he might as well enjoy it another couple of days before he sold it back to the dealership. Back when he'd bought the sedan, he and Darcy had wanted a high-end vehicle to take on their weekend trips to Seattle. It had suited their lifestyle, or at least the lifestyle they'd aspired to. Now he couldn't figure out why it had seemed so important.

Along the drive he passed Sam, who had been out walking in the vineyard. Slowing the car, Alex rolled down the window and asked, "Want a lift?"

Sam shook his head and motioned him to go on. His expression was dazed and distracted, as if he were listening to music no one else could hear. Except there were no headphones in sight.

"He looks weird," Alex said to the ghost, continuing to drive to the house.

"Everything looks weird," the ghost replied, staring out the window.

He was right. A strange radiance had permeated the scene. All the colors of the vineyard and garden were softer, more vivid, every blossom and leaf feeding brightness into the air. Even the sky was different, silver where it touched the water of False Bay, gradually deepening to a blue that almost hurt his eyes.

Getting out of the car, Alex took a deep breath of the floral earthy freshness that laced the breeze. The ghost was staring at the second-floor window. It didn't look the same. The color of the glass had changed — but that had to be a trick of the light, or the angle they were viewing it from.

Alex bounded into the house and up the stairs to the landing. Something had definitely happened to the window — the winter tree was now covered with luxuriant greenery, leaves made of glass gems crossing the window in sparkling profusion. The moon was gone, and the glass sky was flushed with pink, orange, lavender, all blending into daylight blue.

"The window's been replaced," Alex said in bewilderment. "What happened to the other one?"

"It's the same window," came the ghost's reply.

"It can't be. All the colors are different. The moon is gone. There are leaves on the branches."

"This is how it looked when I installed it all those years ago. Down to the last detail. But one day —" The ghost broke off as they heard Sam entering the house.

Climbing the stairs, Sam came to stand beside Alex. He stared at the window, rapt and preoccupied.

"What did you do to it?" Alex asked his brother.

"Nothing."

"How did —"

"I don't know."

Flummoxed, Alex looked from Sam to the ghost, who were both occupied with their own thoughts. They seemed to have a better idea of what was going on than he did. "What does it mean?" he asked.

Without a word Sam left, taking the stairs two at a time, heading out to his truck with long ground-eating strides. The truck engine roared as the vehicle sped along the drive.

Annoyance edged Alex's confusion. "Why

is he hauling ass like that?"

"He's going after Lucy," the ghost said with calm certainty.

"To find out what happened to the window?"

The ghost gave him a sardonic glance and began to pace around the landing. "Sam doesn't care about what happened to the window, the important thing is *why* it happened." At Alex's uncomprehending silence, he said, "The window changed because of Sam and Lucy. Because of how they feel about each other."

That made no sense. "You're saying this is some kind of magic mood window?" Alex asked with a snort of disbelief.

"Of course not," the ghost said acidly. "How could that be possible if it doesn't fit in with your existential beliefs? It's probably another psychotic delusion. Except that Sam seems to be in on this one." He went to the wall and lowered himself to the floor, one arm curled loosely around a bent knee. He looked weary and ashen. But he couldn't be tired — he was a spirit, beyond the thrall of physical weakness. "As soon as I saw the window in the crate yesterday," the ghost said, "I remembered what happened to me and Emma. What I did."

Alex braced his arms on the balcony railing and stared at the window. The jeweled green leaves sparkled in a way that gave the illusion of movement, a soft breeze blowing through the tree limbs.

"I was a couple of years older than Emma," the ghost said, emotions rising through the air like incense. "I avoided her whenever possible. She was off-limits. Growing up on the island, you knew which people you could be friendly with, which girls you could spark and which ones you couldn't."

"Spark?"

The ghost smiled slightly. "That's the word they used for kissing."

Alex sort of liked that. Sparks . . . kisses . . . creating fire.

"Emma was out of my league," the ghost continued. "Smart, classy, rich family. She could be headstrong at times — but she had the same sense of kindness as Zoë. She would never hurt anyone if she could help it. When Mr. Stewart hired me to install the stained-glass window, his wife told all three daughters to keep out of my way. Don't socialize with the handyman. Emma ignored her, of course. She sat and watched me work, asking questions. She was interested in everything. I fell for her so hard, so fast . . . It was like I'd loved her before I'd even met her.

"We met in secret all through the summer and part of autumn — we spent most of our time at Dream Lake. Sometimes we'd take a boat out to one of the outer islands and spend the day. We didn't talk much about the future. The war was going on in Europe but everyone knew it was just a matter of time until we got into it. And Emma knew I was planning to enlist. After basic training, the Army Air Corps could turn a civilian with no flight experience into a qualified pilot in a couple of months." He paused. "Early November in '41 — this was before Pearl Harbor — Emma told me she was pregnant. The news hit me like an anvil, but I told her we'd get married. I talked to her father and asked for his consent. Although he wasn't exactly thrilled about the situation, he wanted the wedding to happen as soon as possible, to avoid scandal. He was pretty decent about it. It was the mother who I thought might kill me. She believed Emma was lowering herself by marrying me, and she was right. But there was a baby on the way, so no one had a choice. We set the wedding date for Christmas Eve."

"You weren't happy about it," Alex said.

"Hell, no, I was terrified. A wife, a

baby . . . none of that had any connection to who I was. But I knew what it was like to grow up without a father. There was no way I'd let that happen to the baby.

"After Pearl Harbor, every guy I knew headed to the local recruiting office to sign up. Emma and I agreed that I'd hold off enlisting until after the wedding. A few days before Christmas, Emma's mother called and told me to come to the house. Something had happened. I knew it was bad from the sound of her voice. I got there just as the doctor was leaving. He and I talked on the front porch for a few minutes, and then I went upstairs to Emma, who was in bed."

"She'd lost the baby," Alex said quietly.

The ghost nodded. "She started bleeding in the morning. Just a little at first, but it got worse hour by hour, until she had a miscarriage. She looked so small in that bed. She started crying when she saw me. I held her for a long time. When she quieted down, she took off the engagement ring and gave it to me. She said she knew I hadn't wanted to marry her, and now that the baby was gone, there was no reason. And I told her she didn't have to make any decisions right then. But for a split second I was relieved, and she saw that. So she asked me if I thought I would be ready for marriage someday. If she should wait for me. I told her no, don't wait. I said even if I made it through the war and came back, she would never be able to count on me. I told her love didn't last — she'd feel the same way about some other guy, someday. I even believed it. She didn't argue with me. I knew I was hurting her, but I thought it would spare her a lot more pain in the future. I told myself it was for her own good."

"Cruel to be kind," Alex said in agreement.

The ghost barely seemed to have heard him. After a contemplative silence, he said, "That was the last time I ever saw her. When I walked out of that bedroom and headed to the stairs, I passed by this window. The glass had changed. The leaves had disappeared, and the sky had darkened, and a winter moon had appeared. An honest-to-God miracle. But I couldn't let myself think about what it meant."

Alex couldn't understand what the ghost thought was so appalling and shameful in such a confession. He'd acted honorably in offering to marry Emma when circumstances had merited. There had been nothing wrong about breaking off the engagement after the miscarriage — Emma had hardly been left alone and destitute. And Tom was going to enlist anyway.

"You did the right thing," Alex volunteered. "You were honest with her."

The ghost looked at him with a flare of incredulous anger. "That wasn't honesty. It was cowardice. I should have married her. I should have made sure that no matter what happened, she would have always known that she meant more to me than anything else in the world."

"Not to be insensitive" — Alex began, and scowled at the ghost's humorless laugh — "but you probably would have died in the war anyway. So it's not like you would have gotten any more time together."

"You don't get it, do you?" the ghost asked in disbelief. "*I loved her.* And I failed her. I failed both of us. I was too much of a coward to take a chance. Some men go their whole lives dreaming of being loved like that, and I threw it away. And all my chances to make it right went smashing down to the ground along with me and that airplane."

"Maybe you were lucky. Have you thought of that? If you'd lived through the war and made it back to Emma, you might have ended up with a lousy marriage. The two of you might have ended up hating each other. Maybe you were better off the way things turned out."

"Lucky?" The ghost looked at him with horror, fury, disgust. He stood and wandered aimlessly around the landing. A couple of times he paused to glance at Alex as if at some mildly repellent curiosity. Eventually he stopped in front of the window and said in a hostile tone, "I guess you're right. It's better to die young, and avoid all the miserable, messy business of loving other people. Life is pointless. Might as well get it over with."

"Exactly," Alex said, resenting the moralizing. After all, he was willing to make his choices and pay for them, just as the ghost had. It was his right.

Staring at the window, with all its flourishing colors, the ghost said with quiet malevolence, "Maybe you'll be lucky like I was."

TWENTY-TWO

"Maybe you'll be lucky like I was."

Although Alex hadn't wanted to admit it, the words had bothered him more than the ghost would have suspected. He knew he'd been a jerk, telling the ghost that he might have been better off dying young. It was all kinds of wrong to say something like that, even if it was what you believed.

The thing was, Alex wasn't entirely sure what he believed anymore.

Introspection had never been his strong suit. He'd grown up thinking that if you expected nothing and then got nothing, you wouldn't be disappointed. If you didn't let someone love you, you'd never have your heart broken. And if you looked for the worst in people, you'd always find it. Those beliefs had kept him safe.

But he couldn't help remembering a line in that grief-stricken letter Emma had typed so long ago . . . something about her prayers being trapped like bobwhites beneath the snow. The ground-roosting birds, sleeping in a tight circle in winter, welcomed the falling snow that covered them with a layer of insulation. But sometimes the snow iced over, trapping them in a hard shell that they couldn't escape from. And they starved and suffocated and froze to death. Unseen, unheard.

There were times he had felt like Zoë was breaking through the layers of protection. She had given him some of the few moments of happiness he'd ever known in his life. But he would never be able to inhabit the feeling fully because of the unshakable conviction that it wouldn't last. And that meant Zoë was a danger to him. She was a weakness he couldn't afford.

He was different from his brothers, who were both more easygoing, more comfortable with giving and receiving affection. From what he remembered of their sister Vickie, she had been like that, too. But none of them had still been living at home when their parents had sunk to the worst of their alcoholism. None of them had been neglected for days or weeks at a time in a silent house. None of them had been given cups of booze to keep them quiet on weekends.

Despite his own issues, Alex couldn't find

it in himself to begrudge Sam's newfound happiness. Sam had gotten back together with Lucy. He had told Alex that the relationship was serious, and he was going to marry Lucy someday. Their plan was that Lucy would accept the year-long art grant in New York, and she and Sam would maintain a long-distance relationship until she came back to Friday Harbor.

"So it'll be convenient to have you move in at Rainshadow Road," Sam told Alex. "I'm going to go to New York at least once a month to visit Lucy, while you keep an eye on things for me."

"Anything to get rid of you," Alex said, unable to hold back a smile as Sam gave him a jubilant high five. "Jeez. A little too happy. Can you bring it down a notch? Just so I can stand being in the same room with you?"

"I'll try." Sam poured some wine for himself and looked askance at Alex. "Want a glass?"

Alex shook his head. "I'm not drinking anymore."

Sam gave him a brief, arrested glance. "That's good." He began to set aside his wine, but Alex gestured for him to keep it.

"Go ahead, I'm fine."

Sam took a sip of wine. "What made you

decide to stop?"

"I was getting too near the invisible line."

Sam seemed to understand what he meant. "I'm glad," he said sincerely. "You look better. Healthier." A deliberate pause. "Looks like going out with Zoë Hoffman has its benefits."

Alex frowned. "Who told you that?"

Sam grinned. "This is Friday Harbor, Alex. A supportive close-knit community where we all live to know the sordid personal details of each other's lives. It would be easier to list who *hasn't* told me. You've been seen out with Zoë about a hundred times, you've been remodeling her cottage, your truck has been parked in her driveway overnight . . . I hope you didn't think any of this was a secret."

"No, but I didn't figure on everyone being so damn interested in my private life."

"Of course they are. It's no fun to gossip about something that's not private. So about you and Zoë —"

"I'm not talking about it," Alex informed him. "Don't ask me how the relationship is going, or where it's headed."

"I don't care about that stuff. All I want to know is how hot the sex is."

"Mind-blowing," Alex said. "Orgasms on a cellular level."

"Damn," Sam said, looking impressed.

"All the more amazing in light of the fact that there's usually an old lady in the house, and a cat howling outside the door."

Sam laughed quietly. "Well, you'll have a chance at some time alone with Zoë next week. I'm going to New York for a few days to help Lucy settle into her new apartment. So if you've moved your stuff here by then . . ."

"It'll take me half a day at most," Alex said. Hearing a text message alert from his phone, he pulled it from his back pocket. It was from his real estate broker, who had recently been approached with a potential offer for Alex's Dream Lake parcel. Although Alex had said he wasn't interested in selling — he wanted to develop the land himself — the Realtor had insisted that this offer was worth considering. The buyer, Jason Black, was a video game designer for Inari Enterprises. He was looking for a place to build some kind of a learning community retreat. The project would be huge, with several buildings and facilities. Whoever built it would make good money. "And here's the interesting part," the Realtor had told Alex. "Black wants it all built LEED certified, with all the latest environmental and energy-saving requirements. And when

I told his broker that you were accredited and you'd had experience building green-certified homes . . . well, now they're interested in talking to you. There's a chance you could sell the property with the stipulation that you'd be hired as the builder."

"I like working on my own," Alex had said. "I don't want to sell. And the idea of having to answer to a video game geek — how do I know he's not a flake?"

"Just meet with him," the Realtor had pleaded. "We're not just talking good money, Alex. We're talking *sick* money."

Glancing at his brother, it occurred to Alex that Sam might be familiar with the game company. "Hey, do you know anything about Inari Enterprises?"

"Inari? They just came out with Skyrebels."

"What's that?"

"What rock have you been living under? Skyrebels is the fourth installment in the Dragon Spell Chronicles."

"How could I have missed that?" Alex wondered aloud.

Sam continued with enthusiasm. "Skyrebels is the most played game out there. They sold over five million in the first *week* of release. It's a role-playing open

world format that features nonlinear emer-
gent play, and it's got this incredible graphic
fidelity with self-shadowing and motion blur
—"

"In English, Sam."

"Let's just say it's the biggest, best, coolest
time waster of a game ever known to man,
and the only reason I don't play it twenty-
four hours a day is because I occasionally
need to take a break for food or sex."

"So have you heard of Jason Black?"

"One of the top game creators of all time.
Kind of mysterious. Usually a guy in his
position speaks at a lot of gaming industry
events and award shows, but he keeps a low
profile. He has a couple of front men to do
appearances and speeches for him. Why are
you asking?"

Alex shrugged and said vaguely, "Heard
he might want to buy property on the island."

"Jason Black could afford to buy the entire
island," Sam assured him. "If you have a
chance to do anything associated with him
or Inari, take it and run."

"Is it a game like Angry Birds?" Zoë asked
a few days later, when Alex told her about
Skyrebels.

"No, this is an entire world, like a movie,

where you can explore different cities, fight battles, hunt for dragons. There's a potentially unlimited number of scenarios. Apparently you can take time out from the main quest to read books from a virtual bookshelf or cook virtual meals."

"What is the main quest?"

"Damned if I know."

Zoë smiled as she scraped cooled melted white chocolate from a small saucepan into a bowl. She and Alex were alone at the house on Rainshadow Road. Sam had gone to visit Lucy in New York, while Justine had volunteered to stay with Emma at the Dream Lake cottage. "I'm not doing it for Alex, I'm doing it for you," she had told Zoë. "You should have an occasional night when you don't have to worry about Emma."

Setting aside the empty saucepan, Zoë said, "Why would anyone want to spend that much time in a virtual world instead of the real one? You could go to all the trouble of making a virtual meal, but you still wouldn't have a real dinner to eat."

"Gamers don't want a real dinner," Alex said. "They like things you can eat with one hand. Potato chips. Pop-Tarts." He laughed at her expression, and watched, intrigued, as Zoë used a spatula to mix the white

406

chocolate into a bowl of whipped cream. "Why are you stirring it like that?"

"I'm folding it. If you stir it the regular way, it won't be fluffy." She cut the rubber spatula vertically through the bowl of whipped cream and liquid white chocolate, swept it across the bottom of the bowl and up the side, and over the top of the mixture. Each time she finished the movement, she rotated the bowl a quarter turn. "See? This way it keeps the mixture light. Here, try it."

"I don't want to ruin it," Alex protested as she gave him the spatula.

"You won't." She put her hand over his, and showed him the motion. He stood behind her, his arms around her, while she guided his hand deftly. "Down, across, up, over. Down, across, up, over . . . yes, that's the technique."

"I'm starting to get excited," he said, and she laughed.

"It doesn't take much for you."

He gave the spatula back to her, and nuzzled into her curls as she finished folding the batter. "What are we making this stuff for?"

"White chocolate strawberry shortcake." She dipped a fingertip into the rich whipped cream and turned in his arms. "Taste."

He tasted the cream from her finger. "My

God. That's good. Give me another."

"No more after this," Zoë said sternly, dipping her finger once more into the bowl. "We need the rest for the shortcake."

Her finger was drawn into the warm suction of his mouth. "Mmmn." Bending his head, he shared the taste with her, his tongue sweet like white chocolate. Zoë relaxed against him, her lips parting. The kiss lengthened, turning lazy and deep, while his hands slid over her arms and shoulders. Grasping the hem of her T-shirt, he began to pull it upward, and she stopped him with a little squeak of protest.

"Alex, no. We're in the kitchen."

His lips dragged gently to her neck. "No one's here."

"The windows . . ."

"There's no one for miles around." He stripped the shirt away from her. His mouth caught hers with a sensual greed that made the down on her neck and arms rise. When she felt him pulling down her bra straps, she tensed uneasily but let him do it. His fingers, so clever and sure, went to the back of her bra and unfastened the tiny hooks. One . . . two . . . three. The straps and elastic webbing fell away.

His hand covered her breasts with warm, stimulating pressure, his palms rubbing softly, and then his thumbs flicked until the tips were rosy and hard. She leaned back against the hard edge of the counter, forcing words between shallow gasps. "Please . . . upstairs . . ." She wanted the dark enveloping privacy of a bedroom, the softness of a bed.

"Here," Alex insisted softly. He took off his own shirt and dropped it to the floor, all toughness and masculine brawn, his body rampantly aroused. His eyes were light and devil blue as he reached into the bowl of frothy cream and scooped some with two fingers. She blinked as she realized what he intended.

"Don't even think it," she wheezed, giggling, trying to slide away. "There's something wrong with you." But his free hand gripped the front edge of her shorts, anchoring her in place, and he dabbed the chilled white chocolate mixture over the tips of her breasts. She closed her eyes, trembling as he bent to lick and suck the sweetness from her. He stood and kissed her again, his mouth delicious and hungering. His hands were in her shorts, his palms hot against her skin. She couldn't think, could hardly breathe. *Just let him,* her body urged, the pleasure unfolding in wanton blooms. Let him ease her shorts and panties off, let him kiss the vulnerable curve of her stomach and grip her bottom with his hands. Let him kneel in front of her, his mouth following the taste of her excitement.

Her legs shook, and she leaned back against the cold granite counter for support. Gooseflesh covered her skin everywhere. He reached for the bowl of cream. A dab of cool sweetness between her thighs. He opened her with his mouth, his tongue flickering. Down, across, up, over. The rhythm was persistent, merciless, allowing her no time to think, lavishing her with a feeling so intense that it shortened the spaces between her heartbeats. She heard herself making sounds like a distraught dreamer, her hips moving in tight circles against his mouth. Her flesh swelled, and he licked deeper, rougher, faster, sending her into a commotion. She cried out, their surroundings shimmering in a brilliant blur. He stayed with her, stroking while the release melted through her, until she was moaning and spent.

Rising to his feet, Alex tugged at the zipper of his jeans. His arms went around her, pulling her upward against the stiff shape of his erection. She wrapped her arms around his neck, her head falling to his shoulder. There was no need for condoms, she had started taking the pill. Reaching down, he angled her hips and positioned himself, and she gasped as a heavy upward thrust nearly lifted her toes from the floor. Her body closed around him, working at the hard invasion until he groaned and thrust again. She was weightless, anchored only by the force of him inside her, shudders of pleasure rebounding from her flesh to his and back again. The breath hissed between his teeth as he came in rough pulses, his arms curling tightly around her. They stood locked and shivering, exchanging soft, sated kisses that soon turned greedy . . . the kind of kisses you shared with someone you might not have for always, but you could have for right now.

They went upstairs to Alex's bed, with its cool white sheets and the screened windows open to the salty breeze from False Bay. As Alex kissed and caressed her, the September moon shed cold lavender light into the room. She felt the pull of it, the moon tide of emotion and energy rising as Alex made love to her as if he owned her. As if he wanted the feel of him to sink deep in her nerve memory and never be erased.

He was so strong over her, so deliberate, filling her with heavy lunges while the moonlight wrapped around them. His hand went beneath her bottom, lifting her into his movements. The lust gathered to an agonizing pitch, and she groaned the moment before it uncoiled, but he backed off, slowing, not letting her come. He circled his hips, teasing until she writhed. She gasped out a few pleading words, telling him she wanted him, needed him, she would do anything for him. It wasn't enough. He brought her to the edge and retreated until they were both sweating and shaking with desire, and he breathed her name with each thrust as he drove her at a slow, merciless pace. She felt hot pleasure-tears leak from her eyes, and he kissed them, pressing wordless gasps against her cheek.

And then she understood what Alex wanted, what he was trying to force from her even though he wasn't aware of it. The moment she gave it to him, she would lose him. But she had known from the beginning that this was where they'd been heading. Withholding the truth wouldn't change what was real, what was inevitable.

Turning her face, she spoke close to his ear. "I love you."

She felt the jolt that went through him, as if she'd just hurt him. But he began to thrust harder, losing control. "I love you," she said again, and he crushed his mouth over hers, his hips pumping roughly. She felt herself splintering, rapture spilling and spreading. Tearing her mouth free, she repeated the words as if they were an incantation, a charm to break a spell, and he buried his face against her neck and found his own shattering release.

TWENTY-THREE

In the morning they treated each other with the forced casualness of two people desperately trying to pretend nothing had changed, when everything had. Zoë found it unbearable, trying to pretend to be light and cheerful when she could see the way Alex was pulling back from her. They talked impersonally while he drove her to the cottage. It was positively gruesome, Zoë thought privately, feeling miserable and defiant. She knew with every fiber of her being that Alex loved her but would never admit it, that he wanted her to love him but would never allow it.

The home-care nurse's car was in the driveway. Justine had already returned to the inn.

Pausing at the front door, Zoë turned to face Alex. "Last night was fun," she said brightly. "Thanks."

He leaned forward and brushed a light,

dry kiss against her lips. His gaze didn't quite meet hers. "It was fun," he agreed.

"Will I see you later?" Zoë asked. "Maybe tonight?"

Alex shook his head. "I'm going to be busy the next couple of days with this Inari stuff. But I'll call you."

"No . . . don't," she heard herself say.

Alex looked at her then, his eyes questioning.

Zoë didn't want to keep up pretenses. The idea of waiting and wondering while their relationship drained like sand in an hourglass was too depressing. She had to be honest with him. "What I said last night . . . I'm sorry it freaked you out. But I can't take it back. And I don't want to."

"I don't —"

"Please let me finish," she said with a wavering smile. "If this is the point where you feel like breaking it off, that's okay." She reached up to touch his taut cheek. "The only thing is . . . if you want this to go on, we can't pretend last night didn't happen. You have to be okay with me loving you . . . or else we shouldn't see each other anymore."

He was silent for a long moment, his face expressionless. "Maybe we should take a break."

"Okay," she whispered, her heart plummeting.

It was over. He was right there with her, but the distance between them might as well have been infinity.

"Just for a few days," he said.

"Absolutely." She wanted to plead with him. *"Don't leave me. Let me love you. I need you."* Somehow she managed to lock the words away before they could escape.

"But if you need anything," Alex said, "call me."

Never. She wouldn't do that to him, or herself.

"Yes." Zoë turned and fumbled in her bag for her key, and somehow managed to unlock the front door. "Bye," she said without turning back, her eyes burning. And she went inside and closed the door.

The ghost didn't say anything until they had returned to Rainshadow Road. Alex felt sick and exhausted. He hadn't slept all night, he'd just watched Zoë while she had pretended to sleep. He longed to jump into the truck and go back to her, but at the same time he couldn't handle it if she said those three words again. That had been the deal breaker. He knew he was screwed up — hell, he'd never doubted it — but this wasn't something he could joke about or sneer at or ignore. This was painful.

He went to the kitchen and saw the place at the counter where Zoë had leaned while he'd undressed her. He remembered the intense pleasure of the previous night, the earth-shattering joy and tenderness of a physical act that could only be described as making love. He'd never known anything like it before . . . he hoped he never would again.

His gaze touched on a bottle of half-finished wine, a cork wedged in the top. Sam's wine. Despite the early hour, Alex wanted a drink more than he ever had in his life. Whenever something went wrong, something in his gut clamored for booze. He wondered if that would ever change. Swallowing an excess of saliva, he went to the sink and splashed cold water on his face.

The ghost spoke behind him. "So this is it, I guess."

"I'm not listening," Alex said hoarsely, but the ghost was undeterred.

"Zoë committed the unforgivable crime of saying she loves you — for what reasons I can't begin to imagine — and now you're bailing on her. You know what's funny? I heard Darcy tell you dozens of times how much she hated you, and you couldn't seem to get enough of that. Why is it easier to tolerate a woman who hates you than one who loves you?"

Alex turned, swiping at the excess water on his face, pushing back wet locks of hair. "It won't last."

"That's what I used to think," the ghost said. At Alex's stony silence, the ghost looked grim and defeated. "I've never understood why I've been shackled to you. I probably never will. There's no point in any of this. I should be with Emma, not you. What's going to happen to her when she passes on and I'm not there?"

"Nothing will happen. She's going to die whether you're there or not. She'll end up where she's supposed to be, and you'll end up where you're supposed to be, and God willing, I'll be left alone."

"You don't believe in God. You don't believe in anything. You asked if I could find a way to disappear, and I told you I was afraid that if I tried, I wouldn't be able to talk to you anymore. Now I don't care. Might as well be invisible." He saw Alex's gaze alighting on the wine bottle once more. His mouth twisted with scorn. "Go ahead and have a drink. What does it matter? I'd pour one for you if I could."

In the blink of an eye, he was gone.

The kitchen was quiet.

"Tom?" Alex asked, almost stunned by the complete absence of movement or sound.

No reply.

"Good riddance," Alex said aloud. He went to the wine bottle, his hand closing around it. The weight of the liquid inside, the inky slosh of it against the glass, wrenched him with sudden craving. He pulled the cork from it with his teeth and began to take a swig. Out of the corner of his eye, however, he saw a shadow slide across the floor.

In an explosive movement, Alex hurled the bottle at the dark shape, and the glass shattered everywhere. Wine hit the cabinet in splatters. The rich smell of cabernet flooded the room. Alex sat and leaned back against a cabinet, gripping his head in his hands, while red liquid pooled on the floor and spread outward.

"What kind of curse?" Justine asked, flipping busily through a tattered old book in the kitchen while Zoë made breakfast. "Let's see. Impotence? Warts, boils? Digestive upset, halitosis, hair loss . . . I think we'll let him keep his sex drive, but we'll make him so hideous no one will want him."

Zoë shook her head in bemusement, using an ice cream scoop to fill muffin pans with batter. That morning she had admitted to Justine that she and Alex had broken up a few days earlier, and Justine had practically gone on a rampage. She seemed convinced that she could exact some kind of supernatural revenge on Zoë's behalf.

"Justine," she asked mildly, "what are you looking at?"

"A book my mother gave me. Lots of good ideas in here. Hmm, maybe a plague of some kind . . . frogs or something . . ."

"Justine," Zoë said, "I don't want to curse anyone."

"Of course you don't, you're much too nice. But I don't have that problem."

Setting aside the scoop, Zoë went to the table where Justine was sitting. She glanced at the grimy, ancient-looking book, which was filled with bizarre symbols and mildly alarming illustrations. A touch of something weirdly gelatinous dripped down the side. "Good Lord. Justine, make sure to wash your hands after handling that disgusting thing . . . there's goo over all the pages."

"No, not all the pages, it's just chapter three. It always oozes a little."

Grimacing, Zoë brought some Windex and paper towels to the table. "Cover it back up," she commanded, gesturing to the piece of cloth the book had been wrapped in.

"Wait, let me just find a quick little spell —"

"Now," Zoë said inexorably.

Scowling, Justine wrapped the book in the cloth and held it in her lap, while Zoë cleaned the table.

"I don't know if you're being serious or just having fun," Zoë said, "but there is no need for spells or curses. If a man doesn't want to be with me, he's allowed to make that decision."

"I agree," Justine said. "He's allowed to make that decision. And I'm allowed to make him suffer for it."

"Do not put a spell on Alex. You didn't put one on Duane, did you?"

"If you ever see him without his sideburns, you'll know why."

"Well, I want you to leave Alex alone."

Justine's shoulders slumped. "Zoë, you're the only real family I've ever had. My dad's gone, and my mom is one of those women who should never have had a child. But somehow I got lucky enough to have you in my life. You're the only really good person I've ever known. You know enough about me to hurt me worse than anyone else ever could, but you would never do that. No sister could love you as much as I do."

"I love you, too," Zoë said, sitting next to her, smiling through a sheen of tears.

"I wish there were a spell to find a man who would treat you the way you deserve. But spells don't work that way. I knew right away that Alex was dangerous for you, and the worst thing in the world is to see someone you care about headed toward danger and not be able to stop them. So I don't think a curse — a small one — is entirely unwarranted."

Zoë leaned against her, and they sat together silently.

Eventually Zoë said, "Alex is cursed enough, Justine. You couldn't do anything to him that would be worse than what he's already been through." Standing, she went back to the counter to finish filling the muffin pan. "Do you want a plastic bag to keep that revolting book in?"

Justine held the book defensively. "No, it needs to breathe."

As Zoë put the muffin pan into the oven, her cell phone went off. Her heart skipped a beat, as it had for the past few days every time someone called. She knew it wasn't Alex, but she couldn't help wanting it to be him. "Would you get that for me?" she asked. "It's in my bag on the back of the chair."

"Sure."

"Wipe your hands first," Zoë said hastily.

Making a face at her, Justine sprayed Windex on her hands and scrubbed them with a paper towel. She reached into Zoë's bag for the phone. "It's your home number," she said, lifting it to her ear. "Hi, this is Justine, Zoë's in the middle of something. Can I take a message?"

A moment of silence. "She'll be there soon." Another pause. "I know, but she'll want to come. Okay, Jeannie."

"What is it?" Zoë asked, sliding another muffin pan into the oven.

"Nothing serious. Jeannie says Emma's blood pressure is slightly elevated, and she seems confused. Mixing up her words a little more than usual. Jeannie's giving her medicine and says there's no need for you to go over there, but you heard what I said."

"Thanks, Justine." Zoë's frown deepened. Removing her apron, she tossed it to the counter. "Take those muffins out in exactly fifteen minutes, okay?"

"Yes. Call me when you can. Let me know if you end up having to take her to the ER."

Zoë reached the cottage in fifteen minutes flat. She hadn't seen Emma that morning — when Jeannie had arrived, Emma had still been sleeping. It had been the latest in a string of rough nights. Emma's sundowning was getting worse, with confusion and irritability in the evenings. She wasn't sleeping well. Jeannie had made several helpful suggestions, such as encouraging Emma to take naps during the day, and listening to soothing music just before bedtime. "Dementia patients tend to get overwhelmed near the end of the day," Jeannie had explained. "Even the simple things are a lot for them to handle."

Although Zoë had been warned what to expect, it was stressful to see her grandmother behaving in ways that weren't at all like her. When Emma couldn't find a pair of embroidered slippers, she had mortified Zoë by accusing Jeannie of stealing them. Fortunately Jeannie had been kind and calm, and not at all offended. "She'll do and say many things she doesn't mean," she had said. "It's part of the disease."

Entering the cottage, Zoë saw her grandmother sitting on the couch, her face lined and tired. Jeannie was sitting beside her, trying to brush her tangled hair, but Emma pushed her hand away irritably.

"Upsie," Zoë said with a smile, approaching her. "How are you feeling?"

"You're late," Emma said. "I didn't like my lunch. Jeannie made me a hamburger, and it was too raw inside because I wouldn't eat it if I didn't. Because I didn't like my lunch and you make lunch when it's not raw but I won't eat."

Zoë struggled to maintain her calm expression, while panic surged inside. Even for Emma, this "word salad" was unusual.

Jeannie stood and brought the hairbrush to Zoë, murmuring, "Stress. She'll get better once the blood pressure medication takes effect."

"I didn't like my lunch," Emma insisted.

"It's not lunchtime yet," Zoë said, sitting beside her, "but when it is, I'll make you whatever you want. Let me brush your hair, Upsie."

"I want Tom," Emma said gravely. "Tell Alex to bring him."

"Okay." Although Zoë wanted to ask who Tom was, she thought that it was better just to agree, until Emma's blood pressure lowered. Gently Zoë drew the brush over her hair, pausing to pull apart a tangle. Emma fell silent for a while, seeming to enjoy the feeling of Zoë's hands in her hair. The simple task helped them both to relax.

How many countless times Emma had done the same thing for Zoë, when she was a little girl. Emma had always finished by telling her that she was beautiful, inside and out, and those words had taken root inside her. Everyone should have someone who loved them unconditionally . . . and for Zoë, it had always been Emma.

When Zoë was done, she set aside the brush and smiled into her grandmother's face. "Beautiful," she said, "inside and out."

Emma's arms went around her. They hugged each other in a moment of pure quiet joy, with no thought of the past or future. They focused on what they had right now, together.

Emma rested for most of the afternoon, while Jeannie kept an eye on her blood pressure. Finally satisfied that the hypertension had subsided, Jeannie left for the day. "Try to get her to sip some water at every opportunity," she told Zoë. "She keeps forgetting to drink, and we don't want her to become dehydrated."

Zoë nodded. "Thank you, Jeannie — I can't tell you how much I appreciate everything you do for Emma. And for me. We couldn't do without you."

The nurse smiled at her. "I'm glad to help. By the way, you may want to give Emma one of the prescription sedatives after dinner, to get a head start on the sundowning. She had a lot of rest today, and even though she needed it, sleeping tonight may be a dicey proposition without a little help."

"Got it. Thanks."

Having discovered that Emma stayed calmer when the television was off during the evening, Zoë played some quiet music instead. The strains of "We'll Meet Again" floated softly through the air. Emma listened as if mesmerized.

"When is Alex coming?" she asked.

The question made Zoë's heart ache. She missed Alex the most in the evenings, the relaxed conversation while he helped put away the dishes, the way he would hold her and rub her back. One night he had discovered that his laser measure, with its red dot of light dancing across the floor, would drive Byron wild. Alex had sent the cat in circles across the room, chasing after the dot, and then he would switch it off so that Byron thought it was trapped beneath his paw. Watching their antics, Emma had laughed so hard she'd nearly fallen off the couch. On another evening, having learned that Emma was having trouble remembering where things were kept in the kitchen cabinets, Alex had labeled each door with a sticky note, one for plates, another for glasses, another for flatware, and so forth. The sticky notes were still there, making

Zoë's heart twinge every time she saw them.

"I don't know when Alex will be here," she told Emma. *Or if he'll ever come back.*

"Tom is with him. I want Tom. Can you call Alex?"

"Who is Tom?"

"A rascal." Emma smiled slightly. "A heartbreaker."

An old boyfriend. Zoë smiled back at her. "Were you in love with him?" she asked softly.

"Yes. Yes. Call Alex and ask him to bring Tom."

"A little later, after my bath," Zoë said, hoping Emma would forget about it as the sedative kicked in. She gave her grandmother a quizzical smile, wondering what connection she had made between her old boyfriend and Alex. "Does Alex remind you of Tom?"

"Oh, yes. Both tall and dark-haired. And Tom was a carpenter. He made such beautiful things."

There was no telling whether Tom had been real, Zoë thought, or was perhaps a figment of Emma's imagination.

"I'm tired," Emma murmured, twisting one of the buttons along the front of her flower-printed pajamas. "I want to see him, Lorraine. I've waited for so long."

Lorraine had been one of Emma's sisters. Swallowing hard, Zoë leaned over and kissed her. "I'm going to take my bath," she whispered. "Rest here and listen to the music."

Emma nodded, staring at the windows, the sky darkening to twilight.

Zoë drew a bath and sank into the hot water with a sigh. She would have liked to soak for a while, but allowed herself only about ten minutes, reluctant to leave Emma unsupervised for any longer than that. Letting the water out of the tub, she dried herself and dressed in a nightgown and a robe.

"Much better," she said with a smile, walking into the main room.

There was no reply. The couch was empty.

"Upsie?" Zoë glanced around the silent kitchen, and strode into her bedroom. No sign of Emma anywhere.

Zoë's pulse began to race. So far Emma hadn't yet started to wander, which was usually a feature of a more advanced stage of dementia. But there had been a definite downturn today. And she had been so insistent on seeing this mysterious Tom, and having Alex bring him . . . Rushing to the front door, Zoë saw that it was unlocked. She darted outside, her breath

429

coming in frantic bursts. "Upsie, where are you?"

Alex had just concluded a walk to the periphery of his Dream Lake parcel with a Realtor and a lawyer, both of whom worked for Inari Enterprises. They had met for dinner in town, and afterward had gone to the property. They had strolled along a bull-dozed trail to the lakefront, ostensibly to get a feel for the land, but mainly to get a bead on what kind of guy Alex was. The meeting had gone well as far as Alex could tell.

Night was falling by the time he got into his truck. As he turned the key in the ignition, his phone vibrated, and he glanced at the small screen. The sight of Zoë's number caused a tumult of eagerness. He was starved for the sound of her voice. Without even thinking, he answered.

"Hi," he said. "I've been —"

"Alex." Zoë sounded desperate, shaky. "I'm sorry, I — please help me. I need help."

"What is it?" he asked instantly.

"Emma's missing. I just took a bath, and . . . she's only been gone for fifteen minutes, but she wandered off and I've been calling for her." Zoë was sobbing and talking at the same time. "I'm outside right now. I've gone all around the outside of the

430

house and she won't answer, and it's dark
—"

"Zoë. I'm close by. I'll be right there." All
he could hear was the broken sound of her
crying. He was fiercely glad that she had
turned to him for help. "Sweetheart. Did
you hear me?"

"Y-yes."

"Don't be scared. We'll find her."

"I don't want to call the police. I think
she would try to hide from them." More
crying. "She's had part of a sedative. And
tonight she kept talking about you, and
s-some guy named Tom, and she wanted
me to ask you to bring him. I think she went
out looking for you."

"Okay. I'm less than a minute away from
the cottage."

"I'm sorry," Zoë choked. "Sorry to bother
you, but —"

"I told you to call if you needed something. I meant it."

He'd meant it even more than he'd realized. Even in these circumstances, talking
with Zoë was a relief beyond measure. It
was like being able to breathe again. He realized he wasn't going to be able to walk
away from Zoë this time. Something had
changed in him, or . . . no, something had
not changed. That was the point. His feel-

ings for Zoë hadn't changed and never would. She was a part of him. The revelation astonished him, but there was no time to think about it now.

As he drove, he scanned the heavily forested road for any sign of Emma. She couldn't have gotten far in such a short amount of time, especially not while sedated. The only thing he worried about was the lake being in such proximity. "Zoë," he said, "have you gone to the waterfront yet?"

"I'm headed there right now." She sounded calmer now, although she was still sniffling.

"Good. I'm pulling into the driveway. I'm going to check out the woods on the other side of the road and work back to the house. What is she wearing?"

"Light-colored pajamas."

"We'll find her soon, sweetheart. I promise."

"Thank you." He heard the sound of her unsteady sigh. "You never called me that before."

She ended the connection before he could answer.

Alex jumped out of the truck and nearly yelped as he came face-to-face with the ghost. "Jesus!"

Tom gave him a sardonic glance. "No, it's

just me."

"It's about time you showed up."

"This has nothing to do with you," Tom informed him. "I just want to help find Emma. Start calling for her."

"Emma," Alex shouted. "Emma, are you out here?" He stopped as he heard the sound of a distant female voice, but he recognized it immediately as Zoë's. Continuing to search, he went into the woods, periodically calling Emma's name.

Tom strayed from Alex as far as he could, wandering among the trees. "She wouldn't have gone any farther than this," he said. "I don't think she crossed the road — let's head back toward the house."

Night was lowering fast, opaque and plum-colored where it draped over the lake.

"Emma," Alex called out. "It's Alex. I'm here with Tom. Come out so I can see you."

The twin high beams of a car slanted outward from a deep curve in the road. It was coming fast, too fast for such a narrow lane, so Alex retreated to the side, waiting for it to pass.

"Alex," came Tom's voice, harsh with fear.

At the same moment, Alex saw Emma's slight form wavering unsteadily toward the center of the road. She looked uncertain, wide-eyed, her skin brilliant in the stark glare of headlights. The car was coming around the curve. By the time the driver saw her, it would be too late.

Zoë, who had just returned from the lake, approached the opposite side of the road from Alex. Her face contorted with horror as she saw Emma standing in the path of the oncoming vehicle.

Alex sprinted toward Emma, a rush of adrenaline making him lightning-fast. He reached her, shoved hard, and felt a massive impact that knocked him to the ground. Everything spun, the world turning too fast, his flesh translating to fire. But the scalding premonition of pain vanished instantly. He wasn't hurt. He'd just had the wind knocked out of him.

It took him a few seconds to recover himself. Dazedly he sat up, looked around, and saw with relief that he'd succeeded in pushing Emma out of the way. She had stumbled against Zoë, who had caught her. They'd fallen to the ground, but Zoë was already helping Emma up.

Everything was all right. Everyone was fine.

That was a close one, he was about to say, when Zoë looked at him and gave an anguished scream. She began to sob, *Alex, no, no . . .* running toward him, tears streaming down her face.

"It's okay," Alex said, amazed that she would be so concerned for him. A rush of overwhelming tenderness swept over him. He stood and began to walk toward her. "The car just bumped me. I've got a couple of bruises, nothing more. I'm fine. I love you." He couldn't believe he'd just said it, for the first time in his life. And it was so damned easy. "I love you."

"Alex," she choked. "Oh, God, please, *no . . .*"

And she rushed right past him.

No, not past. *Through* him.

Startled, he turned to see Zoë dropping to the ground, huddling over a crumpled shape on the road. Her shoulders shook violently, and she crooned a few broken words.

"That's . . . me?" Alex asked in bewilderment, backing away. He looked down at his arms and legs. They weren't there. *Nothing* was there. He was invisible. His gaze returned to the two figures on the road . . . the body Zoë was crouching over. "That's me," he said, his emotions racing across the spectrum from joy to despair.

He wanted to cry, he could feel the agony of sorrow, but his eyes remained dry.

"You never get used to grief without tears," came a quiet voice beside him.

"Who'd have thought one of the things you miss the most is crying?"

"Tom." Alex turned and seized his forearms desperately. He was shocked to be able to feel the texture and strength of a human form. "What do I do now?" he asked.

"Nothing." Tom stared at him with grim compassion. "All you can do now is watch."

Alex's gaze returned compulsively to Zoë. "I love her. I have to be with her."

"You can't."

"Goddamn it, I didn't get to say good-bye to her!"

"Easy with the language," Tom said. "You're not one for hedging your bets, are you?"

"There are things she needs to know. My life can't be over yet. I didn't have enough time with her."

Tom looked exasperated. "What do you think I've been trying to tell you, you lunkhead?"

"If there is a God, I'd like to tell Him to —"

"Shut up." The ghost shook free of him impatiently. "I just heard something."

All Alex could hear was Zoë's broken crooning.

Tom stared distractedly up at the sky, wandering away a couple of steps.

"What are you doing?" Alex demanded.

"Someone's trying to tell me something. I hear a voice. A couple of voices."

"What are they saying?"

"If you would just shut your piehole long enough for me to hear them, I'll —" His attention returned to the sky. "Okay, I get it. Yes. Uh-huh. Right." After a moment, he looked at Alex. "They're letting me help you."

"Who's they?"

"Not sure. But they said we only have about fifteen seconds left before it's too late."

"Too late for what?"

"*Quiet.* They just told me how to fix this, and I'm trying to remember everything."

"Fix what? Fix me?"

"Don't distract me. Shut up and go stand next to the body."

The body. *His* body. Alex wanted so damn badly to be alive, to inhabit that broken carbon shell even for a few moments. Just long enough to tell her what she meant to him. Standing over the prone form, he saw his own still face. Zoë's hand caressed his motionless jaw, her fingers trembling against his parted lips. The sounds she made were like the fabric of a soul being torn apart. He would never have dreamed anyone could feel such grief for him.

Precious seconds were ticking away.

"Tom," he said desperately, his gaze locked on Zoë. "Nothing's happening."

"I'll take care of my part of this." The ghost was at his side. "You do your part."

"Which is?"

"Focus on Zoë. Tell her what you'd say if you had a couple of extra minutes with her. Pretend she can hear you."

Alex knelt over her, longing to stroke her hair and dry her tears. But he couldn't hold her. He couldn't feel or smell or kiss her. All he could do was love her. "I'm so sorry," he said urgently. "I don't want to leave you. I love you, Zoë. You were the one miracle I believed in. You made up for all the rest of it. I wish you could hear me. I wish you could know that." He felt dizzy, felt himself fragmenting, the bonds of spiritual matter dissolving. The remnants of consciousness slipped between the blurred margins of life and afterlife. His last few seconds were slipping away. Words were no longer possible. Only thoughts were left, moving outward like a row of toppling dominoes. *No matter what I become . . . I will love you. No force of heaven or hell could stop me, and damn anyone who tries. I will love you forever.*

Everything went dark, the stars extinguished as the sky collapsed and the world folded in on itself.

"Blaspheming to the end," Alex heard someone say dryly. "Can't say I was surprised."

Alex recognized Tom's voice. He felt like he'd been encased in lead, his limbs too heavy to move. And then it hit him: he was in a body. He had a physical form.

"Wasn't easy to get you in there," Tom informed him. "Like trying to put toothpaste back in the tube."

Gathering sensations in a frantic rush, Alex perceived that he was lying on asphalt, his neck angled uncomfortably because of the way Zoë was clutching his head against her chest. His lungs felt like they were about to burst.

"Try breathing," Tom suggested.

Alex pulled in a rush of cool, blessed air, blinked his eyes open, and began to move.

Zoë let out a startled cry. "Alex!" Her shaking hands moved over him. "But . . . you were . . . your chest was all . . . there was no way you could have . . ." Overcome, she covered her mouth with one hand, staring at him in terrified wonder.

With effort, Alex levered himself to a sitting position. He grasped Zoë's wrist and pulled it away, and crushed a hard kiss against her lips. He tasted the salt of her tears. "I love you," he said hoarsely.

Breathing in sobs, Zoë stared at him with streaming eyes.

Tom spoke to him urgently. "Help Emma. She needs to go inside the house."

Emma was kneeling nearby, watching them blearily, the breeze blowing locks of silvery hair across her face.

Alex struggled to his feet and pulled Zoë up with him.

"Maybe you shouldn't try to walk," Zoë protested.

"I'm fine."

"Alex, you were *hurt.* I saw it."

"I know what it must have looked like," Alex said gently. "But everything's okay. I promise."

The driver of the car, a distraught middle-aged woman, was babbling about insurance and phone numbers and calling paramedics. Alex said to Zoë, "If you could take care of her, I'm going to bring Emma inside." Without waiting for a reply, he bent to scoop Emma into his arms. He carried her to the cottage. She was astonishingly light in his arms.

"Thank you for saving me," Emma said.

"No problem."

"I saw the car hit you."

"Just a little bump."

"The front grille was caved in and the headlight was smashed," she told him.

"They don't make cars the way they used to."

She gave a raspy little chuckle.

Alex carried her into the house and directly to the bedroom. After setting her on the bed, he removed her slippers and pulled the covers up to her chest.

"I was looking for Tom," Emma said, reaching up to pat his cheek.

Alex bent to kiss her forehead. "He's here," he murmured.

"I know."

Zoë entered the room and fussed over her grandmother, asking worried questions, coaxing her to take a sip of water. As Alex left the room, he heard Emma say a bit testily, "Let me sleep, Zoë. I love you, too. Let me rest."

When Zoë finally turned out the lights and left the bedroom, Tom went to lie quietly beside Emma.

"I wanted you," she whispered after a moment. "I couldn't find you."

"I'll never leave you again," Tom told her. He didn't know if she could hear him, but he sensed that she was relaxing, settling into sleep.

A plaintive murmur. "I don't remember anything."

"You don't have to," Tom replied, smiling at her in the darkness. "I found all your memories tonight. I'm keeping them safe for you . . . they're waiting inside me like a heartbeat. And I'll give them to you when the time is right."

"Soon," she whispered, turning toward him with a sigh of relief.

"Yes, love . . . very soon."

Zoë gestured for Alex to follow her. She led him to her room, her throat tight, her eyes flooding with fresh tears.

He looked down at her with infinite concern. "What's the matter?"

"I was so scared," she said in a watery voice, blotting her sore eyes with the sleeve of her robe.

"I know. I'm sorry I pushed Emma like that. But she seems okay now —"

"I meant *you*." She went to the tiny bathroom, found a tissue, and blew her nose vehemently. Her jaw quivered as she continued. "I saw you get hit by that car —"

"Bumped."

"Hit," she said, letting out a coughing sob,

442

"and you were all s-smashed up on the ground, and I th-thought you were —" Breaking off, she swallowed painfully against another burst of crying. She would never recover from the sight of him unconscious on the road. The fear still hadn't left her. Her shaking hand touched his shoulder, just to make certain he really was there, that he was alive.

He took both her hands and brought them to his chest, where she could feel the strong, steady thump of his heart. "Zoë. I have so much to say to you, it could take all night. A year. No, a lifetime."

"Take as long as you want," she said with a sniffle. "I'm not going anywhere."

Alex put his arms around her, gathering her into a deep, secure embrace. So strong. So vital. He was silent for a long time, understanding somehow that she needed the feel of him. She laid her head against his chest, breathing in the scents of dirt and tar and night air.

Pushing aside her hair, Alex pressed a few light, hot kisses against the side of her face. "When you told me you loved me," he said quietly, "I got scared. Because I knew when a woman like you says that, it means . . . everything. Marriage. A house with a porch swing. Children."

"Yes."

He sank his hand into her hair and tilted her head back. He looked into her eyes with a sober intensity that she couldn't doubt. "I want those things, too."

She had been shaking with nerves and fear before, but she felt shaky in a new way now, because she understood that he meant it.

His mouth caressed hers, a searing pressure that lingered until her knees went weak. "We'll take it at your pace," he said. "As fast or slow as you want."

"I don't want to wait," she told him, her hands creeping up his warm, hard back. "I don't want to spend a night without you ever again. I want to move in together right away, and get engaged, and set a wedding date, and . . ." She stopped and gave him a sheepish glance. "Is that too fast?"

Alex laughed quietly. "I can keep up," he assured her, and took her to bed.

Alex awakened in a wash of morning light. He lay still, relishing the feeling of waking up in Zoë's bed, his head half buried in lavender-scented pillows. His arm swept across the white sheets, reaching for her, but all his hand encountered was empty space.

"Zoë's in the kitchen," he heard Tom say.

Opening his eyes, Alex did a double take as he saw that Tom wasn't alone. A slender young woman stood beside him, their hands clasped. Her blond hair was arranged in smooth curls and parted on the side. She had a lovely, slightly angular face, her eyes bright with intelligence.

Alex sat up slowly, keeping the sheet pulled up to his waist. "Good morning," he said, dazed.

She gave him a familiar smile of mischief. It was more than a little disconcerting to see Emma's smile in this drastically younger version of herself. "Good morning, Alex."

His wondering gaze slid over the two of them. The air was luminous with happiness, emotion translated to light. Tom had lost the ever-present shadow of loneliness, his dark eyes snapping with joyful vitality.

"Everything's okay, then," Alex said, giving them both a questioning glance.

"Glorious," Emma said. "Everything is the way it should be."

Tom's gaze lingered on Emma before returning to Alex. "We came to say good-bye," he said. "We've got places to go."

"Do you?" It hit Alex that the ghost was finally leaving him. They were both free. What Alex had never expected was that he would feel so forlorn at the prospect. "I've never been so damn glad to get rid of anyone," he managed to say.

Tom grinned. "I'll miss you, too."

There were things Alex needed to say . . . *I will never forget you and your obnoxious singing and smartass comments, and the way you saved my life. You became the friend I didn't even know I needed. And you made me realize that the worst thing isn't dying, but dying without ever having loved someone.* However, it didn't seem that they would have the time or opportunity to talk. And he saw from Tom's gaze that he understood all of that, and more.

"Will I see you again?" Alex asked simply.

"Yeah," Tom said, "but not for a while. You and Zoë have a long life ahead of you. And a big family to start on — two boys and a girl. And one of them is going to grow up to be —"

Emma interrupted hastily. "Alex, pretend you didn't hear any of that." Turning to Tom, she clicked her tongue reprovingly. "Still a troublemaker. You know you weren't supposed to tell him anything."

"It's your job to keep me in line," Tom told her.

"I'm not sure anyone could manage that," she retorted. "You're a tough case."

Tom lowered his head to hers until their

foreheads touched. "Not for you," he murmured.

They were silent for a moment, their pleasure in each other's company almost palpable.

"Let's get going," Tom murmured. "We've got some lost time to make up for."

"About sixty-seven years," she told him.

He smiled into her eyes. "We'd better get started, then." Sliding an arm around Emma's shoulders, he guided her to the doorway. Stopping at the threshold, they turned to look back at Alex.

He saw them through a sudden blur. He had to clear his throat roughly before he could speak. "Thanks. For everything."

The other man smiled in understanding. "You and I both got it wrong, Alex: love does last. In fact . . . it's the only thing that does."

"Take care of Zoë," Emma told him gently.

"I'll make her happy," Alex said in a gravelly voice. "I swear it."

"I know you will." She held his gaze for a long, affectionate moment. "Work on that foxtrot," she eventually said, and gave him a wink.

The next moment, they were gone.

Putting on his jeans, Alex went barefoot to the kitchen, where a pot of coffee was brewing. But Zoë wasn't there.

Seeing that the door to Emma's room was ajar, he realized she had gone to check on her grandmother. He found Zoë sitting on the edge of the bed with her head bent. Although he couldn't see her face, he could hardly miss the glitter of tears falling into her lap.

"Alex —" she said in a suffocated voice. "My grandmother —"

"I know, sweetheart." He held out his arms, and she went to him at once. He wrapped her in his arms and murmured against her hair, telling her that he loved her, he would always be there for her. She buried her face against him and breathed in shuddering sighs, until her tears finally slowed.

After a while, Alex eased Zoë from the bedroom and closed the door. "She's happy now," he said, keeping an arm around her. "She wanted me to tell you that."

"Are you sure?" she asked, looking bewildered.

"Very sure," he replied firmly. "She's with Tom."

Zoë pondered that for a moment. "I don't know anything about Tom." She wiped a last smudge of moisture from her cheek. "I don't know if I like the idea of her going off with a man I don't know."

Alex smiled down at her. "I can tell you a few things about him . . ."

EPILOGUE

A week after Emma's funeral, Zoë went back to work at the inn. It was a beautiful September morning, sunny and clear. The farmers' markets had begun to feature dazzling varieties of apples, along with squash, eggplant, carrots, and fennel. The orca pods had begun to travel farther away from the island as the salmon had finished their runs and reached the mainland spawning rivers. Wintering loons and ducks had begun island-hopping to feast on marine life, and bald eagles busied themselves with adding sticks to their massive nests.

As Zoë made breakfast, she wondered why it was so quiet at the inn. Justine had dashed in and out of the kitchen with barely a word to her. And although Alex had promised to stop by for breakfast after running a couple of errands, he still hadn't shown up. The guests, for that matter, were oddly silent, with none of the usual conversation and clinking of coffee cups.

Before Zoë could venture out of the kitchen to find out what was going on, Justine appeared.

"Is breakfast ready?" Justine asked without preamble.

"It will be in about fifteen minutes." Zoë gave her a quizzical smile. "What's happening? Why is everyone so quiet?"

"Never mind that. Someone's at the front door, asking for you."

"Who is it?"

"Can't tell you. Take off your apron and come with me."

"Couldn't you just send them back here?"

Justine shook her head and tugged Zoë along with her. They went through the hallways and into the empty dining room.

"Where are all the guests?" Zoë asked, mystified. "What did you do with them?"

Her question was answered by the sight of a crowd in the entrance hall. And they were all grinning at her. Zoë flushed as she realized they had gathered as a part of some surprise intended for her. "It's not my birthday," she protested. Laughter rippled through the group. They parted, and the front door opened. Cautiously Zoë went out to the front porch.

Her eyes widened as a five-piece swing

band began to play.

Alex emerged, handing her a small bouquet. He smiled down at her. "I arranged for us to have a dance."

"I can see that." Zoë took the bouquet, inhaled the fragrance of fresh flowers, and looked up at him with shining eyes. "Any particular reason?"

"Just wanted to practice my foxtrot."

"All right." Laughing, Zoë set the bouquet on a porch rail and went into his arms, letting him draw her into a smooth, easy dance. Other couples joined in, young and old, and passersby stopped to listen. A few children began to hop and swirl in time to the ebullient music. "Why this particular morning?" Zoë asked Alex. "And why on the front porch of the inn?"

"I'm in the mood to make a public declaration."

"Oh, no."

"Oh, yes." Leaning closer, Alex murmured in a confidential tone, "I have a present for you."

"Where is it?"

"My back pocket."

Her brows lifted. "I hope it's not a brooch. You could hurt yourself."

Alex grinned. "It's not a brooch. But before I give it to you, I need to know something. If I got down on one knee in front of all these people and asked you a yes-or-no question . . . what would you say?"

Zoë looked up into his warm blue eyes. They were eyes a woman could gaze into for a lifetime. She stopped dancing and stood on her toes to kiss him. "Try it and find out," she whispered against his mouth.

And he did.

A READING GROUP GUIDE

1. Do you believe in ghosts? If so, why? If not, why not? Have you had any experience with supernatural events in your life?

2. What factors do you think have brought Alex Nolan to the bad state he is in when the novel opens? And in what ways do you see Alex's story mirrored in the ghost's?

3. Zoë and Alex are opposites in every way. Do you believe this made their attraction more compelling?

4. Of the three Nolan brothers, why do you think Alex is the most damaged, even though they all come from the same family background?

5. What was the turning point for you in Alex and Zoë's relationship? When did you truly believe that these two belonged

together? Was there any moment in the book when you felt that they should not be together?

6. How realistically do you think the author handled Alzheimer's disease in this novel?

7. In the context of the novel, do you believe that the childlike aspects of Alzheimer's make one more open to the possibilities of the supernatural?

8. What elements of Friday Harbor itself make it come alive to you? Is Friday Harbor a place you'd like to visit? To live? Why or why not?

9. Why do you think the ghost could not cross over and what do you believe occurred to make it possible?

10. What is the author trying to say about true love and the power of love?

For more reading group suggestions, visit www.readinggroupgold.com.

ABOUT THE AUTHOR

Lisa Kleypas is the award-winning author of over thirty novels. Her books are published in fourteen languages and are bestsellers all over the world. She lives in Washington State with her husband and two children.

The employees of Thorndike Press hope you have enjoyed this Large Print book. All our Thorndike, Wheeler, and Kennebec Large Print titles are designed for easy reading, and all our books are made to last. Other Thorndike Press Large Print books are available at your library, through selected bookstores, or directly from us.

For information about titles, please call:
　(800) 223-1244

or visit our Web site at:
　http://gale.cengage.com/thorndike

To share your comments, please write:
　Publisher
　Thorndike Press
　10 Water St., Suite 310
　Waterville, ME 04901

MRcS

SCHOLASTIC GUIDES

HOW TO WRITE
POETRY

SCHOLASTIC GUIDES

HOW TO WRITE
POETRY

PAUL B. JANECZKO

SCHOLASTIC
REFERENCE

Sincere thanks to Sarah Sabasteanski,
my "research assistant" and e-mail buddy,
for answering all my questions.

Library of Congress Cataloging-in-Publication Data
Janeczko, Paul B. • How to write poetry / Paul B. Janeczko • p. cm.
—(Scholastic guides) • Includes bibliographical references and index.
Summary: Provides practical advice with checklists on the art of writing poetry.
1. Poetry—Authorship—Juvenile literature. [1. Poetry—Authorship.] I. Title.
II. Series. PN1059.A9J36 1999 808.1–dc21 98-26866 CIP AC
ISBN 0-590-10077-7
10 9 8 7 6 5 4 3 2 1   99 00 01 02 03 04

Printed in U.S.A. 23
First Printing, April 1999

Book design by Nancy Sabato
Composition by Brad Walrod

With affection and admiration,
this book is for
Susan Bean, Connie Burns, and Karen Guter,
who love kids and love words.

P.B.J.

CONTENTS

INTRODUCTION

ONE OF THE QUESTIONS THAT COMES UP ALL THE TIME when I talk to young writers is, "Why did you start writing poetry?" It's a good question and one that I've thought about quite a bit. I started writing poetry when I realized that some of the things I wanted to say could best be said in poetry. Poetry is special. Like a lot of writing I do, writing poetry is fun. Don't get me wrong. Writing anything well takes hard work, but there is still the element of enjoyment running through it like silver through the side of a mountain. But the kick I get from writing a good poem is different.

The first poems I recall writing were haiku that I wrote in college. In graduate school I wrote more poems in different forms. I fell in love and wrote about how *wonderful* the girl was and how *wonderful* I felt when I was with her. I fell out of love and wrote poems about how unfair life was, how miserable I felt. Now, when I look back at those poems, I can see ways that I could make some of them better. (Most are beyond help!) Even though the poems may not have been very good, they gave me the chance to explore my feelings in concrete and vivid language. That is part of the power of poetry. Writing poetry gives you the chance to fall in love with language again and again.

CHAPTER ONE
GETTING READY

"WHERE DO YOU GET YOUR IDEAS?" I'VE HEARD THAT question from students and adults more times than I can count. I'm afraid that many people feel that writers have some special access to ideas that other people don't have. Like some 800-number that supplies ideas if you have your credit card handy! But that's simply not true.

FINDING IDEAS AND SAVING THEM

Most writers will tell you the same thing about ideas: They are all around you. However, if you want to write, you need to look and listen carefully. You also need to save your ideas. If you don't, there is a good chance that they will slip away from you like quarters at an arcade. Good ideas do not, of course, guarantee good writing. That takes hard work, imagination, and a willingness to take chances.

There are lots of ways to save your ideas. An obvious place is in a pocket notebook. (Don't leave home without it!) It should be small enough to fit into your pocket or backpack but thick enough to give you plenty of wide-open spaces to write down your observations and thoughts. When I drive in my car, even on short trips around town, I always carry a microcassette tape recorder with me. It didn't take me long to realize that to drive and write notes at the same time is dumb. So, if I get an idea while I'm in my car, I can easily push the record button and save my ideas on a tape and play it back whenever I have time.

I am guilty of saving ideas in odd places—old napkins, backs of envelopes, on the palm of my hand—but, like most writers, I've come to realize that it is best to keep my ideas in a book. That's why my journal is invaluable. I recommend that if you are serious about writing, you give some thought to keeping a journal or a writer's notebook. Although a journal is a great place to jot down brilliant ideas, it can be much more than that.

WRITING TIP FROM A POET

My journal is the heart of my writing. There I record dreams, memories, funny happenings and wild ideas. Free to play, I write in different directions and colors; I draw; I tape in leaves, notes from kids, boarding passes. From such compost, poems, stories and even novels grow.

George Ella Lyon

What *is* a journal? Good question. Some people think it's a book in which you write things that happened to you each day. But if that's a journal, what's a diary? Another good question. So maybe before you can decide if you want to keep a journal, you need to know the difference between a diary and a journal.

For starters, both are, of course, books that you write in. But since a diary usually has a space for each day of the year, it comes with the expectation that you will write something each day and that your writing will be limited to the space provided for that day.

A journal is different. With a journal there are no expectations to write something every day. Nor is there any space limitation. You can write as often as you like in a journal. You can write a few sentences or many pages. And a journal can hold more than just writing. You might think of it as a gigantic shoe box that can hold all sorts of treasures and memories. It can be a best friend. It can be a mirror to help you see yourself. It can be a mailbox where you store letters. It can be a sketchbook and a photo album. A journal can be a combination of all these things.

Remember that your journal is *your* book, so it should reflect you and your personality. It is a place to express yourself. If you like to paint, you might think of it as a blank canvas. If you like to write, you might think of it as . . . well, as a lot of blank pages. A journal can be different things for you.

- It can be a place for you to experiment with words, lines, colors, and shapes.
- It can be a place where you write things that you can't (or don't want to) write for a class assignment.
- It can record the story of your life or the history of your family and friends.
- It can be a place to collect quotations that are funny or inspirational; quotations from novels, poems, comedians,

and friends that show the power of our magnificent language.

- It can be a place where you save your deepest confessions. Likewise, it can be a place for you to figure out a problem.
- It can be a place to write letters to mail as well as letters that will remain in your journal. Letters to yourself, to people you will never see again, to people you love, to people with whom you are in heated disagreement.
- It can be an album of photos of family, friends, places you've enjoyed, people you admire, and people you'd like to meet.
- It can be a sketchbook for your drawings, paintings, and doodles.

But no matter what you put in your journal, it should be a place where you can freely explore your creativity. A place where you can comfortably take a close look at your personality, hopes, and fears. A place where you can be *you*.

WRITING TIP FROM A POET

I often get my ideas from juxtapositions of unusual things—something clicks inside my head, and I take note. It's like the exercise where you're supposed to pick out the one thing in a list that doesn't belong—I pick it out, then write about how it got there.

Jim Daniels

A Word About Privacy

Although you can let anyone look at your journal, most people want to keep their journals private. But there are few things more tempting than a journal left unattended. The best way to keep your journal private is to be sure it's not a temptation for someone else. In other words, hide it. That doesn't mean you have to pry up a floorboard and stash it underfoot. But it might mean keeping it out of sight in a closet, in your backpack, or at the bottom of one of your drawers. Some people write a brief message at the beginning of the journal to those who might find the book, accidentally or not. Something like: *You have picked up my personal journal. Please respect my privacy and return the journal to me without reading it. Thank you.* While this sort of message will work with honorable people, others may simply ignore it. So, the best advice is to keep your journal out of sight of anyone who might be tempted to read it.

The Right Tools

Any good craftsperson will tell you that to do a job right you need the right tools. The same is true for your journal. Since you are hoping that your journal will be your longtime companion, you want to make sure that you get the tools with which you will feel comfortable.

✦ A Book   You have many different possibilities when you are looking for the book to use as a journal. Walk into any good stationery store or discount store and you will find many books to choose from. Which is the right one? That's easy: the one that feels most comfortable for you. Some people like a large sketch-book with big, snow-white pages. Other journal writers (like me) have got to have lines on their pages. You might prefer a basic spiral notebook. Some writers I know use a three-ring binder because they feel it gives them greater flexibility to move the pages around. And you can take a stack of composition paper with you and leave the binder at home. You might like a stenography pad. I like to use those composition books with the black-and-white marbleized covers. The point is simple: Choose a book that *feels* right for you.

✦ PENS AND MARKERS   I am a pen freak. I love the feel of a good pen, usually a fountain pen. I love the way the ink flows so smoothly from a quality fountain pen. Many of my friends think I am crazy to care so much about a pen. They are happy to settle for a simple ballpoint pen with a gnawed end. I say they don't know what they're missing. As with the notebook, you must pick a pen that feels good to you. It might be a fountain pen or a felt-tip marker that writes blue or a ballpoint pen that writes green or even a pencil. It's strictly your choice.

In addition to a pen, you might want some colored pencils and markers to jazz up your writing. Maybe some highlighters to emphasize some words, phrases, or ideas in your writing. You might also use highlighters to draw a connection between ideas. For example, when you reread your journal, you might notice that your boyfriend or parents are mentioned a lot. One way to keep track of such a subject is to highlight it with a yellow marker. Or, you might highlight in pink every time you have an idea or see an image that might be the start of a poem.

The Right Time and Place

One of the wonderful things about a journal is you can write in it whenever you like. And wherever you like. Having said that, however, it is a good idea to think about setting aside a special time and place to write in your journal. Again, what works for you is best. Because I usually wake up before my wife and daughter, I sometimes take advantage of that quiet morning time to write in my journal. On other days, I write in my journal when I am finished working for the day. What's a good time for you to write in your journal? At the end of school? Before dinner? Before you turn off the light at night?

As far as a place is concerned, I prefer to write at a desk or at a table. Other people feel just as comfortable writing propped up in bed or sprawled on the sofa. Do you have "your place" where you feel most comfortable? It might be a place where you go when you want to shut out the world. Your room? The tree house you used to play in? A quiet corner of the library? You can write in your journal anyplace, but finding "your place" helps make the whole process special.

A Checklist of Pitfalls

To help you get the most out of your journal and maintain a sense of enjoyment when you write, let me offer some suggestions. It will be helpful if you remind yourself of these things from time to time, particularly when you find yourself dreading your journal as if it were some big, hairy dog with bad breath coming to slobber in your face.

✓ *It's okay if you don't write in your journal every day.* Or, even every other day, for that matter. The journal is there to serve you, not to be your master. When you feel guilty because you haven't written in your journal for a few days, it is time to repeat this suggestion to yourself over and over until you believe it. Write in your journal when you have something to say or something to add to the book.

✓ *Never criticize what you write.* One of the biggest obstacles for writers who want to experiment with their language is that nasty voice most of us have that tells us that what we are doing is stupid, not very good, or a flat-out waste of time. You know the voice. Yours might whisper to you. Mine is shrill, like a rusty nail being yanked out of a plank. Don't listen to that voice. Your journal is yours. What you write or draw won't be perfect. But it doesn't have to be. It just has to be honest.

✓ *Neatness doesn't count.* It's okay if you make mistakes in your journal. When you do, don't be afraid to cross them out. Draw arrows if you find a section that belongs somewhere else. If you drop a blob of catsup on a page, wipe it up and write around the pink stain. If you are too worried about keeping a "perfect" journal, you may be too afraid to take a chance. And it's only when you take a chance with your writing that you will learn what you can do.

✓ *Spelling doesn't count.* If your journal becomes the kind of book it can be, there will be times when you will be writing so fast that you won't want to stop to consider spelling rules. Fine. If spelling mistakes in your journal bother you that much, go back and correct them later. But don't dampen a burst of enthusiasm to grab a dictionary.

✓ *Don't throw out anything.* Keep everything that you write in your journal. You never know what will come of it. I can't tell you how many times early in my career I nearly tossed out a pile of notes because I thought they were worthless, only to later realize that in all that junk there were a couple of ideas worth hanging on to.

✓ *Date every entry.* Since one of the reasons to keep a journal is to record your life, it's helpful to know, for example, when you thought about the value of friendship or when you were feeling elated or left out. If you look back over your journal, dated entries may help you see a pattern or notice recurring themes in your life.

✓ *Your journal is for you.* You are certainly free to share your journal entries with whomever you choose. Your girlfriend, for example. However, be careful that you do not wind up writing things for someone else. When you know that someone else is going to read your journal, you may not be as honest as you would be if the book was for your eyes only. Always remember that your journal is just that: *your* journal.

READING

While you are capturing your thoughts and experiences in your journal, don't forget that you cannot be a good writer — poet or prose writer — if you are not a reader. So, make that one of the things you do whenever you have a few spare minutes: Read some poems. All kinds of poems. Rhyming and non-rhyming poems. Short poems. Long poems. Only by reading what other poets have written will you be able to get some sense of what your poems can be like. At first, you will copy the poets you admire. That's fine. Everybody does it when they're beginning. But as you write more poems, you will gain more confidence in your own talent and ability, and you will rely less on imitating the work of other poets. Even when you are on your own as a poet, it will be important for you to keep reading poetry.

If you're not sure where to find books of good poems, you're in luck. Throughout this guide I've scattered the titles of some poetry books that I think you will enjoy. Beyond that, I've included a longer list of poetry books at the end of the guide.

Don't limit yourself to the books on that list. Go to the library and cruise the poetry section. You may be surprised by what you discover. I can't count the times I've browsed the stacks and discovered some wonderful poets, who were, at the time, unknown to me.

When you take a book of poems and start reading, don't feel that you have to like or understand every poem you read. That's not going to happen. And it's okay if you don't like a lot of what you read. Just ask yourself why you don't like a poem. What did the poet do or not do that put you off? Was it the subject? Was it the language? Didn't you like the fact that the poem rhymed? Or didn't rhyme? By answering these kinds of questions, you will begin to develop your own sense of what makes a good poem. And, as you write, you will try to make sure that your poem reflects what you have learned from other poets.

This book will not, of course, teach you everything you need to know about writing poetry. That's not its purpose. Rather, as the title suggests, these pages will serve as a guide for you, i.e., something that points you in the right direction and helps you avoid some of the pitfalls of writing. Like any other art, poetry writing takes practice. The more you practice and think about what you are writing, the more you read poems and books about writing poetry, the better your poems will become.

Notice that I said this book is meant to be a guide for writing poems, not a blueprint. There are no rigid blueprints for writing good poems. No follow-these-steps-and-you-get-a-good-poem, although some rhyming poems follow a specific form. Good writing of any kind takes trial and error. In some ways it's like taking a trip. You know where you want to go, and you think you know the route you will take. But once you get on the road, you may run into detours, dead ends, side trips, and pit stops for rest. Eventually, you will arrive at your destination, but you will have had a more adventurous time of it.

Sometimes when you write a poem, you may think you know what the poem is going to be. But as you write and tinker your way through several drafts, you find that the poem wants to be something else. Maybe you thought you wanted to write a poem about a party, but the poem wound up being about friendship. As a writer, you must learn to trust your intuition. When a poem wants to go its own way, let it. See where it takes you. You may be pleasantly surprised.

So, if you're ready to write some poems, sharpen your pencil, grab your journal, and let your imagination loose!

WRITING TIP FROM A POET

Poetry is a secret kingdom. If you engage all your senses—seeing, touching, listening, smelling, and tasting—the gates open. Seemingly unimportant things begin to speak: salmon-colored geraniums, a smooth beach stone, your mother's voice when she calls your name, the diesel smell of the school bus, and that first bite of a Snickers bar. Details are the beginnings of poetry and the doors to your kingdom.

Christine Hemp

SOMETHING TO READ

If you want more sound advice about writing poetry, check out these books:

- *Gonna Bake Me a Rainbow Poem*, Peter Sears, Scholastic, 1990.
- *Knock at a Star: a Child's Introduction to Poetry*, X.J. Kennedy and Dorothy M. Kennedy, Little, Brown, 1985.
- *The Place My Words Are Looking For*, edited by Paul B. Janeczko, Bradbury Press, 1990.
- *Poem-Making: Ways to Begin Writing Poetry*, Myra C. Livingston, HarperCollins, 1991.

CHAPTER TWO
STARTING TO WRITE

A S YOU FILL YOUR JOURNAL WITH LOTS OF GOOD stuff—things that are important or fascinating to you— you're that much closer to writing some poems. The things and feelings you can write poems about are all around you and inside you. A poet is, in some ways, like a scientist. They both observe and report. True, the form of their reports will be dif- ferent—a poet writes a poem and a scientist writes a prose report—but the process they go through is frequently the same.

THE WRITING PROCESS

Although it varies from writer to writer and even from one piece of writing to the next, the writing process usually involves the same steps:

- Brainstorming, when you doodle and jot down ideas, thoughts, feelings, and images;
- Drafting, when you take your first crack at the poem;
- Editing, when you go over your poem and look and listen for ways to make it better;
- Revising, when you make improvements in your poem;

❀ Publishing, when your poem is complete and you decide it's time to share it with someone.

The process is never exactly the same. And there is no set time for the process to play itself out. On occasion, you have probably written a poem in a short time, with only a little editing and revising. Other poems may have taken you much longer to write. If you're lucky, you have a trusted reader who can help the process by listening to a new poem and offering some comments and suggestions.

Let me share one example of how the writing process worked for me. I wasn't thinking about writing a poem. I was simply driving on a country road past a farmhouse and saw a man and a dog walking across a pasture. I thought I spotted some sort of flower on the front porch. The skies had darkened and I could almost feel the approaching storm. I was struck enough by the scene that I pulled onto the shoulder of the road and whipped out my pen and small notebook. I quickly jotted down some notes, enough to save the scene.

When I got home, I took my jottings and used them to recreate the scene in my mind. Then I brainstormed a list of details:

- man and dog walking through pasture
- white farmhouse in distance
- black or brown dog barking
- dark thunderclouds
- lightning flashing
- rain pouring down

- wash on the line, flapping
- grayish sky
- like the ocean
- bright flower in window (like a lighthouse?)

As I looked over the list, I tried again to visualize the scene. Then I grabbed a pen and a pad of paper and began doing what poets do all the time: looking for the best way to create a vivid image that would bring the scene to life for a reader. Over time I created what I considered to be a good poem. At that point I put the poem away in a folder, where it rested out of sight for a few weeks. When I looked at the poem again, I saw problems that I had not seen in the rush of enthusiasm that often goes with a first draft. So, I took some more time to edit, revise, and tinker with my poem before I wound up with a version that satisfied me:

LIGHTNING RIDES
Lightning rides
the sea slate sky,
dog follows master
over crests of pasture.
In a window
of the white farmhouse,
a beacon:
a single geranium.

What I wanted to do in the poem was create an image of the scene I had seen that afternoon. To make sure the image was clear, I had to make sure I used vivid words. So, for instance, I wrote *sea slate sky* instead of settling for simply comparing the color to the ocean. Quite by accident, I saw that I could use terms usually associated with the ocean to stitch the poem together: *sea slate sky, over crests of pasture, a beacon.*

It's important to remind you that I did not set out to write a poem that would describe a farmhouse setting in terms of the ocean. I merely wanted to vividly describe the scene I had seen. It was through the process of writing that I discovered the magic of this poem.

ACROSTIC POEMS

For your first poem, try writing an acrostic about a subject that you know very well: yourself. If you've done a lot of writing in your journal, you probably have learned quite a bit about yourself. This poem will give you a chance to use some of that information. Here are some acrostic poems that students of mine wrote to introduce themselves to me:

JOSH
Jokes
Oranges
Spaghetti
Holy cow!

LAUREN

Loves her mom
Also likes to cook
Unlikes to clean her room
Ruins some things
Eats a lot
Nonlikes spaghetti

KURT

Kind most of the time.
Usually
Rely on my shooting video games
To take out my anger

You noticed that the subject of each poem is a person, the poet. That subject is the title of each poem. But also note how each letter of the title is the first letter of each line of the poem. You can write an acrostic poem with a single word in each line, or you can have longer lines. It all depends on what you have to say.

Begin your draft by writing your name at the top of a page in your journal. Make a list of some important things about yourself. Think of some of the things you would tell someone who was interested in getting to know you better. You might want to include your likes and dislikes. Some of your personality traits. Interesting comments about yourself. Be honest. Remember that you don't need to show this poem to anyone.

A pitfall to avoid is staring at the letters of your name and wondering what in the world you can possibly say about yourself that would begin with that letter. If you try to write your poem that way, you will, most likely, wind up doing more sitting and staring than writing. Rather, think of what you want to say about yourself. Look at the list of things about yourself that you brainstormed. Look for ways you can work those ideas into the letters of your name.

As you work on your acrostic poem, you might want to keep this checklist in mind:

✓ You can write your acrostic poem as a list, with a different item on each line.

✓ Or, you can write your poem as a sentence or two that continue through the poem, like "Kurt."

✓ Your poem can also be a combination of these two possibilities.

✓ Make sure you have selected items that capture the essence of your subject.

✓ The first letter of each line must come from the title or subject of your poem.

Remember that you can, of course, write an acrostic poem about any subject. All you need to do is substitute the subject for your name and write the poem as you did the one about yourself. It can be about someone or something concrete and real—friend, father, soccer, Mozart—or it can be about something abstract, like love, loneliness, or friendship. If you write about something abstract like love, make sure your poem *shows* love with specific examples.

Try This . . . When you have had time to tinker with your draft and think you have a good poem, try writing another, perhaps with a different slant or emphasis. Your first acrostic poem might be about your total personality. Try writing one that emphasizes your likes. Perhaps, for example, you might write one that reflects your love of sports or reading. You might write an acrostic poem about your role in the family. If you are an only child or the oldest child, how can you write a poem about that role? Or, think about how you would change your name if you could, then write an acrostic about that name.

❖ ❖ ❖

SOMETHING TO READ

✦ *Autumn: An Alphabet Acrostic* (Clarion Books, 1997) by Steven Schnur is a collection of well-crafted acrostic poems that captures the sights and sounds of the season.

Poetry is sound. It's a lot of other things, too, of course, like structure and meaning and rhythm, but sound cannot be ignored when you are writing a poem. Not only the sound of individual words, but the sounds the words make when they are together on the page. You are trying to create a music with the words in your poem. It might be sweet music or it might be harsh music, but you must have your ears open when you write (and read) poetry.

If you've never really given much thought to the sound of words, I suggest you start collecting words. Save a few pages of your journal for your word collection. You'll be making what I call a Poet's Wordbank. What words should you collect? That's up to you, but I suggest you start with your favorite words. My list of favorite words is long, but here are a few at the top of that list: *ointment, hawkweed, contraption, billow,* and *siesta.* What are your favorite words? Words you like the sound of. Words that give you an image. Write your list in your journal.

You can makes columns of words in your journal. You can find interesting words in newspapers and magazines and paste them in your journal. Look in atlases, nature books, computer books, seed catalogs, prayer books, and art books. Make all sorts of wild combinations: *Picasso's hard drive, pink river, yawning mushrooms.* Read the words aloud. Listen to the sounds. You can make a collage or a mobile with the cut-out words. Or, write them on file cards, which will allow you to share and swap them with friends. Listen to the sounds. You can use some of the words in your Poet's Wordbank.

Will collecting words make you a better poet? Not necessarily. But it could very well make you more attentive to the sounds of words, and you cannot be a good poet without that. So, start collecting. There's no rush or deadline. Just keep your eyes and ears open and keep some space free in your journal for the words you collect.

Try This . . . Before you read another word, open your journal to a fresh page and write down some of your favorite words. Don't stop to think or analyze your choices. Just write.

◆　◆　◆

Sound Effects

As you listen closely to words—those you say and those you write—you'll hear how words sometimes follow patterns to create sounds. Although there is a long list of terms related to sound in poetry, you should be aware of three basic terms:

▧ Alliteration is the repetition of the initial consonants of words. If you have ever tried to get through a tongue twister, you've used alliteration. For example, *Peter Piper picked a peck of pickled peppers* is an example of alliteration.

Other examples are such phrases as *setting sun, totally terrible territory, nasty nonsense,* and *far-flung favorite.* Examples of alliteration abound in poetry. See how Samuel Taylor Coleridge used alliteration when he wrote, "So fierce a foe to frenzy." One of my favorite couplets, written by British poet Alexander Pope, happens to be full of alliteration:

> The bookful blockhead, ignorantly read,
> With loads of learned lumber in his head.

- Assonance is the repetition of the vowel sounds in words. For example, note the *oo* sound in *zoom, loon,* and *ruin* or the *ee* sound in *heat, three,* and *meet.* Notice how John Masefield used assonance in this line: "Slow the low gradual moan came in the snowing." Can you hear the *o* sound in four words? Assonance occurs frequently in the work of a master poet such as William Shakespeare, so it is easy to find many examples. Here's one: "Shall ever medicine thee to that sweet sleep."
- Onomatopoeia is a word that makes the sound of the action it describes. For example, *thump, bang, honk, moo, ring,* and *hiss.* In a sense, these words make their own sound effects. Robert Burns wrote how "The birds sit chittering in the thorn." Describing branches covered with ice, Robert Frost wrote that "they click upon themselves."

Try This . . . Read some poetry out loud. Pick some new poems as well as your old favorites. Be on the lookout for examples of alliteration, assonance, and onomatopoeia. When you find examples, see if you can hear what they add to the poem. Jot down good examples in your journal.

◆ ◆ ◆

REPETITION

The sound devices described above can help hold a poem together and create music. Repetition can serve the same purpose. You have noticed how this is particularly true of many of the songs you hear on the radio, many of which have words and lines repeated. This is nothing new. Early ballads used repetition effectively, especially refrain, the exact repetition of words or phrases. Edgar Allan Poe's famous poem about the death of his young wife begins with this stanza, or group of lines:

> It was many and many a year ago,
>   In a kingdom by the sea,
> That a maiden there lived whom you may know
>   By the name of ANNABEL LEE;
> And this maiden she lived with no other thought
>   Than to love and be loved by me.

In each of the six stanzas of the poem, Poe repeats his dead wife's name at least once (in capital letters, no less) to emphasize how deep his love was and how great his loss. Notice how the repetition at the end of the fifth and into the final stanza adds to the power of the poem:

And neither the angels in heaven above,
    Nor the demons down under the sea,
Can ever dissever my soul from the soul
    Of the beautiful ANNABEL LEE:

For the moon never beams, without bringing me dreams
    Of the beautiful ANNABEL LEE:
And the stars never rise, but I feel the bright eyes
    Of the beautiful ANNABEL LEE:
And so, all the night-tide, I lie down by the side
Of my darling — my darling — my life and my bride,
    In the sepulchre there by the sea —
    In her tomb by the sounding sea.

EDGAR ALLAN POE

Warning: There is a danger in overusing any of the sound techniques, of using them simply to show off. So, when you use alliteration, for example, make sure that you have a good reason for doing so. And if you use a refrain, make sure you are repeating something that is important to your poem. Otherwise, you run the risk of boring your reader to the point where she will not finish reading your poem.

SOMETHING TO LISTEN TO

Your school or public library may have recordings of poets reading their work. Check some out and give a listen to the magic of the words. Here are a few suggestions to get you started:

✤ *How to Eat a Poem*, Eve Merriam, Harper Audio, 1990.

✤ *The Butterfly Jar*, Jeff Moss, Bantam Audio, 1992.

✤ *The Dragons Are Singing Tonight*, Jack Prelutsky, who even sings his poems, Listening Library, 1994.

✤ *The Best of Michael Rosen*, by the hilarious British poet, Wetlands Press, 1995.

CHAPTER THREE
WRITING POEMS THAT RHYME

N OW THAT YOU'VE HAD A CHANCE TO WARM UP A BIT BY writing some acrostic poems, you might want to try writing some poems that rhyme. The three short poems that follow—synonym poem, opposite, and clerihew—will let you work with rhythm and rhyme as you compose some humorous short poems.

SYNONYM POEMS

A synonym poem is as short as a rhyming poem can be: two lines. (You do know what a synonym is, right? Just in case you don't know, a synonym is a word that means the same thing or almost the same thing as another word.) When you have two lines of poetry that rhyme, it's called a couplet, so each synonym poem is made up of one couplet. Read these synonym poems and see if you can tell how these poems are written:

> SCHOOL LUNCH
> Burgers, prunes, and warm spaghetti
> To eat this stuff I'm not ready

THIN
Scrawny, slender, skinny, slight
Your plump friends tell you you're too light

WEIRD
Bizarre, strange, and spooky things
Books and stories by Stephen King

OUTLAW
Pirate, bandit, thief, or crook
At them the judge should throw the book

Look over this checklist of things to keep in mind when you write your synonym poem:

✓ Each poem is made up of two lines of poetry that rhyme.

✓ The title is the subject of the poem.

✓ The first line contains three or four synonyms for the subject.

✓ The second line of each poem can do one of two things: it can describe the subject a little more, as in "Weird," or it can tell how the poet feels about the subject, as in "School Lunch."

✓ Each line generally has seven or eight syllables arranged in a way that gives the poem its rhythm. If you're not sure what the rhythm of these poems is, read the examples out loud without the titles. You will hear the rhythm.

✓ A synonym poem can be funny.

Before you start drafting your synonym poem, do some brainstorming on paper. When you know what you want to write about, put that word at the top of a journal page. Since a synonym poem is essentially a descriptive poem, a good subject will be something that you can describe. Maybe a person, place, or thing. But it could also be an emotion — anger, joy, or sadness, for example — or an adjective — such as tall, heavy, or round.

Once you have a good subject, make a list of words that are synonyms for that word. Feel free to use a thesaurus from the library or one that is part of a word processing program for your computer. A thesaurus, a book that lists and may define synonyms and antonyms for other words, is a wonderful storehouse of great words that we often know but might not be able to think of when we need them. (And isn't "thesaurus" an interesting word? I picture some sort of vegetarian dinosaur.)

When your list has a dozen or so words, look for the ones that will make up your first line of poetry. Write them out. How do they sound together? Do they work with each other to make a suitable rhythm? Or, do they quarrel with one another and sound as if they don't quite belong in the same line? If that's the case, you might simply need to move a couple of words around within the line. Sometimes that helps the rhythm. If moving some words doesn't help, go back to your list to find substitutes.

When you have a first line that sings a slick song for you, look for a good second line that will complete your poem. Remember that your second line will describe the subject a little more or tell how you feel about it. And, don't forget the rhythm of the poem. If you're not sure how your poem sounds, read it out loud. You will hear things when you read something aloud that you may very well miss when you read it silently. Even if you know your poem sounds good, read it out loud for the sheer joy of hearing the words work together so smoothly.

📖 Try This . . . Once you've written a couple of good synonym poems, you might want to write a cycle of poems, three or four poems that are somehow related. For example, you could write a cycle of synonym poems about sports, the seasons, members of your family, or your friends. Because these poems are so short, they are perfect to put on a card, maybe with a drawing, and send to someone. You could send your best friend a synonym poem for her birthday. Or, wouldn't your parents be surprised if you wrote a poem about them and gave it to them on their anniversary!

◆　◆　◆

WRITING TIP FROM A POET

Some teachers think kids never should rhyme, because rhymes can sound too forced: "My reindeer/drinks brain beer," or something. Yet, I've seen kids' poems containing wonderful rhymes: wish/squish, pewter/computer. Like learning to play the piano, rhyming takes practice. But if you want to, why shouldn't you start?

X.J. Kennedy

OPPOSITES

An opposite is another descriptive poem that is, well, the opposite of a synonym poem. You might even call it an antonym poem. (An antonym is a word that means the opposite of another word. Some obvious antonyms are *good/evil* and *high/low*.) One difference between a synonym poem and an opposite is that in an opposite you describe something by what it's not. Confused? Maybe some examples will help you. As you read these poems, see if you can tell what makes a good opposite:

What is the opposite of kind?
A goat that butts you from behind.

The opposite of chair
Is sitting down with nothing there.

What is the opposite of new?
It might be stale gum that's hard to chew,
A hotdog roll as hard as a rock,
Or a soiled and smelly forgotten sock.

You can probably see right away that opposites are more challenging than synonym poems. But, as the challenge increases, so does the potential for more enjoyment when you write a good poem. Here is a checklist of the ingredients of a good opposite:

✓ It is, obviously, about opposites.

✓ It is written in couplets. But, where the synonym poem can only be one couplet—two rhymed lines—the opposite can be two, four, six, eight, ten lines, or more, as long as you write it in couplets.

✓ An opposite will frequently, though not always, begin with the question: *What is the opposite of* _____? If you decide to start your poem with a question, the rest of the poem will answer that question. However, as the examples show, you could also begin your poem with something like: *The opposite of* _____ *is* _____.

✓ Like any well-crafted piece of writing, a good opposite will contain specific details, not simply generalities.

✓ Although the rhythm of an opposite is not as predictable as the rhythm of a synonym poem, you must make sure that your poem does have its own music.

You can begin an opposite the same way you started to write your synonym poem, although you may find that you spend more time trying to find a good subject because not everything has an opposite. For example, encyclopedia. In addition to being a tough word to rhyme with, finding its opposite will be tough. So, take some time to brainstorm some things, persons, and feelings that truly do have opposites. For example, school, your sister, or anger might be a good subject for you. Sometimes it helps to use an adjective as a subject. Words such as *happy, dreary, short,* and *cozy* are begging to be used in an opposite. Write good subjects for opposites in your journal. A good idea is like a good friend. You never can have enough.

When you find a good subject for an opposite, write it at the top of a fresh page of your journal. Then start writing down ideas that are the opposite of your subject. *Do not* (I repeat: *do not*) look for words that will rhyme with your subject. If you do, you will worry too much about rhyme instead of about what your poem says. Trust me: Once you have a list of good opposite words, you'll find the rhyme you need.

When you start the draft of your first opposite, I suggest that you make it easy on yourself and begin with the question, *What is the opposite of* _____? After all, that could be half of your poem! However, after you have written a rhyming second line, you need to ask yourself if the poem is complete. Some two-line opposites are simply not finished. For example:

> What is the opposite of school?
> It would be something very cool.

What is the opposite of tall?
I'd say it's something small.

Can you hear how these poems need another couple of lines to finish the job? They are good starts, but they are lacking the specific details that a good poem will always have. (In your journal, you might want to write additional couplets that would complete these too-short opposites.)

Try This . . . Don't be satisfied writing all two-line opposites. While they certainly are fun to write, push yourself to look for more specifics that are the opposite of your subject. Challenge yourself to write a four-line opposite and even a six- or eight-line opposite. It'll take patience and work, but you will have every reason to be proud of yourself when you write a clever opposite of six or eight lines.

◆　◆　◆

SOMETHING TO READ

If you want to read some wonderful opposites, go to your library and look for:

✦ *Opposites* and *More Opposites* by Richard Wilbur, Harcourt Brace, 1973 and 1991.

POETCRAFT: CREATING IMAGES

When you write a poem you are trying to create an image (or a series of images) that will help the reader to experience what you experienced. You may want to put the reader in a scene, real or imaginary. You might want the person to feel an emotion the way you felt it. You are going for the total effect of your words.

One way to help the reader connect with your poem is to include details that appeal to the senses: sight, sound, smell, taste, and touch. That's not to say that you are going to include all the senses in every poem you write. But it does mean that you need to be aware of which senses you need to explore to make your poem a vivid reading experience. Since we live in a visual culture—we watch TV and movies, read books and magazines—we tend to think of an image as visual, while ignoring the other senses. There are a number of ways to create strong images, but they all ask that you use vivid, specific language.

You can create clear images by using strong verbs. If I said to you, "My friend went down the street," I would be guilty of using a weak verb: *went*. Can you think of other verbs that more accurately show how my friend "went" down the street? How about these possibilities:

My friend *ran* down the street.

My friend *wobbled* down the street.

My friend *hopped* down the street.

My friend *danced* down the street.

My friend *sprinted* down the street.

Each of these verbs gives a different picture of how my friend "went" down the street, doesn't it? Can you think of other strong verbs you can use instead of "went"?

Try This . . . On a page of your journal, write down some vivid verbs that you could use in place of the weak verbs listed below. Pick verbs that create an image.

said

looked

moved

gave

hit

When you have given your list some thought, look up these verbs in the thesaurus and see what other strong verbs you can find. Add them all to your Poet's Wordbank.

◆　◆　◆

What about your adjectives? Can you find a more precise way to say, "The car was *blue*"? You could make a comparison and say, "The car was *as blue as a robin's egg*." Or, you could check a thesaurus to find that some other words for blue are: *azure, sapphire, aquamarine, turquoise, navy, lapis lazuli,* and *indigo.* These words are not interchangeable, of course, but that is the point. Each of them describes a more specific variation of blue.

Try This . . . Check a thesaurus and find synonyms for these words:

mad

silly

glowing

rapid

pleasant

If you're not sure of the exact meaning of some of the synonyms, look them up in a good dictionary. Add the best words to your Poet's Wordbank.

◆　　◆　　◆

WRITING TIP FROM A POET

When you write a poem, you are like a magician conjuring up mental pictures in the mind of your reader. So choose your words carefully. The word *daisy* will evoke a sharper image than the word *flower*. The word *birch* will bring to mind a different picture than the word *tree*. *Seagull* or *eagle* will conjure up mental scenes that are totally different from those brought on by the word *bird*. When I hear the word *cardinal* I think of the bright red ones that come to my feeder in the winter.

WHAT'S IN A WORD?
Say "bird,"
and a sparrow appears

inside you and ruffles
its feathers.

Say "cardinal,"
and the bird turns red.
Suddenly it is winter.
With a lot of snow. And look!
There are sunflower seeds
in the feeder.

Siv Cedering

CLERIHEWS

During World War II, a man by the name of E. C. Bentley
wrote a regular column for a London newspaper. In that column he included short rhyming poems about historical and literary figures, written in a form that he had invented when he
was a student. And, since his middle name was Clerihew, that's
what he called this new type of poem. Here's one that he wrote:

Edgar Allan Poe
Was passionately fond of roe.   [fish eggs]
He always liked to chew some
When writing anything gruesome.

E. C. BENTLEY

And here are a couple that were written by student writers:

That famous lady, Mona Lisa
Whose smile has been a real teasa
Will never tell this world we're in
What's behind her fabled grin.

Basketball ace, Dr. J
Is seven feet tall so they say.
His only hang up is buying shoes.
But that's why they invented canoes.

When you begin to draft your first clerihew, keep the items on this checklist in mind:

✓ A clerihew is about a celebrity.

✓ It pokes gentle fun at that person, so it tends to be humorous. (Please do not write mean-spirited clerihew. That's not what these poems are about.)

✓ It is always made up of two couplets.

✓ The first line ends with a person's name, so you must rhyme with that name. (The first line of Bentley's clerihew contains only the name of the subject. But, if you'd like, you can begin your first line with a couple of words that identify the subject. In other words, your first line should not be something like, *There once was the Mona Lisa.*)

As usual, before you start writing, brainstorm some good subjects for your poems. You can start by listing some categories of celebrities. For example, movie stars, athletes, characters in books, and rock musicians. Next, write down the names of specific people in those categories, trying to include people who have some quality or characteristic you can poke fun at. It might be a basketball player's shaved head or a movie starlet's behavior in public. Jot down some things you think you'd like to say about your subject.

Once you have zeroed in on a good subject, start drafting your poem. The first line is the easy one because you know it must end with the celebrity's name. The other lines will be more challenging, but also more fun to write. Remember to have fun with your clerihew. Because you must rhyme with a person's name, this is a good time to try out some outrageous rhymes.

When you've completed your draft, read your clerihew out loud. How does it sound? Is it smooth and graceful? If it's not, take a careful look at the poem and see what you can do to improve the rhythm. Can you make it smoother by changing a word or two? (Check your thesaurus.) Or, perhaps major surgery is needed. Don't worry about it. That's what rewriting is all about: finding a way to make your writing better.

Try This . . . If you've written about a contemporary person, why not put your poem on a poster with a magazine picture of your subject? Or, you can draw a caricature of the celebrity. You could even do a series of poem posters about people in the same field, say, NBA superstars or rap singers.

◆　◆　◆

Something to Read

Although many of Bentley's clerihews are dated and very British, you can find all of them in *The Complete Clerihews of E. Clerihew Bentley,* Oxford University Press, 1982.

CHAPTER FOUR
WRITING FREE VERSE POEMS

AS I MENTIONED EARLIER, THERE ARE NO STEP-BY-STEP directions for writing a good poem. There are certain things that happen in a good poem, of course, but they may fall into place at different times during the writing process. What you want to say and how you want to say it may come easily in one poem, but your next poem may be more difficult to complete. You may decide that an image you thought was clear is really muddled. Or, after you've written a number of drafts and tinkered with the poem for a while, new words may come to mind.

A good poem is original. It uses clear language to say something in a compelling way. The American poet Robert Francis said that a poem is like an arrow; it should wound the reader. He meant that a good poem should touch the reader (as well as the writer). That can happen in a number of ways. A poem might scare or anger him. Or, a poem might get a snicker or a belly laugh. A poem can touch like a hand on her shoulder in troubled times. Maybe it will bring a tear to her eye. Perhaps the poem will surprise the reader with a good ending.

But at the heart of every good poem, every poem that touches a reader, is the language. And don't worry if you think you can't be a poet because you don't have a good vocabulary. More often than not, the language of a poem is simple, ordinary language that the poet uses in inventive ways. When the right words combine, they frequently make meanings beyond the words themselves.

And it's all done with words. No high-tech special effects. No computer-enhanced remastered sound. No trick photography. Words. Those things we've used since we were babies. And when you sit down to write a poem, you have the power of the words at your fingertips. If you work at a poem, you can share your feelings with your readers. You can share how you see the world. And, if you write well, your readers will be touched by your gift.

In this section of the guide you will learn some of the basics of writing free verse poems. A free verse poem is a poem that is free of a set rhythm and rhyme. Among other things, I will talk about imagery, figurative language, rhythm, line breaks, and word choice. You will have a chance to write four types of poems: a list poem, a poem of address, a persona poem, and a narrative poem. Learning these types of poems will give you the tools to write about many of the topics and situations that interest you.

This seems like a good time to say something about the model poems I've included. Remember that the poems I've used as examples are like this book. They are meant to be guides, not blueprints. If your poem doesn't "fit" the model, that's fine.

Write *your* poem and don't worry about how close it is to the poem you are using as your model. I encourage you to experiment. Use what works for you and ignore what doesn't seem right for you. The more poems you write, the more confident you will be about taking chances. And when you do that, you will surprise yourself with the energetic and original poems you will write.

LIST POEMS

The list poem is a great place to start when you want to write free verse poems. Although it looks easy to write, writing a truly good list poem takes more effort than simply jotting down a list. When we hear the word *list* we probably think of a column of words on a sheet of paper, like a shopping list or a list of your favorite movies or foods. Well, some list poems are like that. Here's one by Anne Waldman:

THINGS THAT GO AWAY
& COME BACK AGAIN

Thoughts
Airplanes
Boats
Trains
People
Dreams
Animals
Songs
Husbands
Boomerangs
Lightning
The sun, the moon, the stars
Bad weather
The seasons
Soldiers
Good luck
Health
Depression
Joy
Laundry

ANNE WALDMAN

But not all list poems have (mostly) one-word lines like Waldman's poem. Walt Whitman broke many of the rules of established poetry late in the nineteenth century when he wrote sprawling free verse poems in his magnificent book, *Leaves of*

Grass. Read aloud these opening lines from "I Hear America Singing," and you will hear the poem's music:

I hear America singing, the varied carols I hear,
Those of mechanics, each one singing his as it should
    be blithe and strong,
The carpenter singing his as he measures his plank or
    beam,
The mason singing his as he makes ready for work, or
    leaves off work,
The boatman singing what belongs to him in his boat,
    the deckhand singing on the steamboat deck,
The shoemaker singing as he sits on his bench, the
    hatter singing as he stands,
The wood-cutter's song, the ploughboy's on his way in
    the morning, or at noon intermission or at sundown,
The delicious singing of the mother, or of the young
    wife at work, or of the girl sewing or washing,
Each singing what belongs to him or her and to none
    else,
The day what belongs to the day—at night the party of
    young fellows, robust, friendly,
Singing with open mouths their strong melodious songs.

WALT WHITMAN

Your list poems will very likely fall in between these ex-
tremes, perhaps like this poem:

A History of Pets

Butch, black cocker spaniel, collected
stinks, dirt, and open wounds into which our
father poured gentian violet. Did not
come back one morning. A brown and white mutt
—I don't recall its name—was shot by our
mother, beheaded, and pronounced rabid
by health folks who provided all five of us
with fourteen Friday nights of shots. There was
Hooker, half-Persian cat who'd claw your back-
side through the open backed kitchen chairs and swing
by his hooks till you pulled him loose. Short-Circuit,
affectionate cat that walked crooked, that'd been
BB-shot in the head. Goat. Skunk. Some snakes.

DAVID HUDDLE

You may have noticed one thing these list poems have in common. They all describe or name things. Waldman names things and feelings. Whitman describes the "songs" of Americans. Huddle describes pets. (You might also notice that by naming and describing the pets he grew up with, Huddle gives us a good idea of how chaotic it must have been living in his home!)

I hope you see how these poets, particularly Whitman and Huddle, included specific details in their poems. Whitman writes about the carpenter "singing as he measures his plank or beam" and about the shoemaker "singing as he sits on his bench." And Hooker, one of Huddle's pets, was a "half-Persian cat who'd claw your back-/side through the open backed kitchen chairs and swing/by his hooks till you pulled him loose." It is rich details like these that make a poem, list poem or otherwise, come alive.

📖 Try This . . . One type of list poem is a history poem, which details a part of the writer's life. If you've moved a lot, you might consider writing a history of the houses you've lived in or the schools you've attended. If you've been to summer camp, you could list some of the new things you tried. When you come up with some ideas, make sure you write them down in your journal before you forget them. Then, using Huddle's poem as a model, try your own history poem.

◆　◆　◆

Here's a poem written by a student as a variation on Huddle's poem:

A HISTORY OF THE FAULTY SHOES
Tiny white lacy slippers
    that I kicked off when I was a baby
Sweet little pink jellies
    that I wore on the swing set and broke the strap
Soft leather moccasins
    that had beads that fell off

Bright pink sneakers
   that were hard to lace up
Little purple velcro tennis shoes
   that had a hole in the heel
Shiny black party shoes
   that got scratched on the sidewalk
White leather sandals
   that got wet in the sprinkler and shrank
Green All-Stars
   that rubbed at the toe
Black Mary-Janes
   that I still wear today
But who knows?

AMANDA GRANUM

Another type of list poem you can write is the "how-to" poem. The boy who wrote the next list poem built it on things he says to get out of doing his homework:

HOW TO GET OUT OF HOMEWORK
I'm feeling sick
Look at what the dog's doing
Five more minutes
That's a beautiful necklace
Oh, just a little longer
But, I just reached dark castle and I can't stop now
There's a bomb in my bedroom

There's a killer outside
The baby's sick
But this book is stretching my mind in ways
    homework can't
I'm feeling sleepy
I might wake the baby
I just heard a gunshot
Was that the phone?
After dinner?
The cat's outside
So is the dog
I'm hungry
I don't feel like it.

JARED CONRAD-BRADSHAW

While this poet used excuses to build his poem, you can also write a poem that is a set of directions, and you know how important clear directions are when you are trying something new.

Try This . . . In your journal make a list of subjects that might make an interesting how-to poem. Include things that are fairly simple. "How to Build a Car" would be too complicated. Something like "How to Make the Perfect Pizza" or "How to Be a Best Friend" might be more suitable. But you can also write zany how-to poems. For example, "How to Be a

Gerbil" or "How to Make a Rainbow" might make interesting poems.

Once you've made a list, pick the subject that interests you the most and begin drafting your how-to poem. Remember to include the words that will best help readers follow your directions.

❖　❖　❖

The history poem and the how-to poem are only two types of list poems. To get an idea of other kinds of list poems, take a look at this list of list poem subjects that was generated by a class of young writers I worked with:

Things that never die	Things that come in handy
Things that annoy me	Things that are quiet
Achievements	Things I like about my friends
Things that stink	Memories I'd forgotten
Things that are gross	Make-believe places
Siblings	The perfect friend
My grandmother's house	What to do in study hall
Bad cooks	Nighttime
Irritating sounds	Lies I've told
What money can do	Embarrassing moments
Things I can't do & why	My mistakes
What cats do	What my teachers do at home
Lucky things	Attic
What to do if . . .	When I'm alone I . . .

📖 Try This . . . Pick a topic from this list and begin drafting your list poem. Remember that these topics are suggestions, so feel free to change them to work for you.

◆   ◆   ◆

Here's a list poem by a young poet who uses one of the topics as a title and starting line:

"WHEN I'M ALONE I . . ."
think about my life
it's gone up in smoke
cry
listen to my cat
hear music play
hold my breath
scream
sleep
never dream
sing along
clean
sneak a puff
hold my breath
watch the news
have some coffee
fix a meal
do the dishes

sweep the floor
strum my guitar
mess up and start again

OLLIE DODGE

I said earlier that writing a good list poem was more difficult than merely writing a list. But that is how you start, by writing a list of anything you can think of that's related to your subject. For example, suppose you want to write a poem called "Things That Drive Me Crazy." The first step is simple: Brainstorm a list of things that drive you crazy. Don't censor yourself. Don't listen to the voice that might be telling you, "This poem will never work," or "What a lame idea that is!" Write down whatever comes to mind. Take your time with your list. You might think you are finished, but if you let the list rest for a few days, you will more than likely come up with other items to add to it.

When you have a good, long list, read it over carefully. Can you see some things on the list that are related to other things? You might realize, for example, that half of the items on your list of things that drive you crazy are about your younger brother. Great! That should tell you that your poem wants to be "Things About My Brother That Drive Me Crazy." Copy those things on a new page of your journal and let them be the basis for your poem.

As you look at your list for your new poem, you may think of other things to add. Maybe you repeat some things that can be crossed out of your draft. Be careful to include in your poem only those things that give the reader a clear picture of how your brother annoys you.

When you think you have all the things that you want to include in your poem, examine the order in which they appear. Do you have a reason for putting things where you do? You should. You might want to start off your poem with little annoying things and work your way up to the more important ways in which your brother bugs you. Or, you might want to list the aggravating things he does in a "typical" day, starting with things he does or says in the morning and ending with what he does or says in the evening.

As you work on the draft of your list poem, read it out loud. How does it sound? Have you placed words together that start with the same consonant? Perhaps some words have the same vowel sounds. (You can read more about the sounds of words in POETCRAFT: SOUND on page 21.) What sort of rhythm does your poem have? Short lines will give it a more hurried feel than long lines. Does the rhythm fit with the subject of the poem? If you are writing about the joys of running on the cross-country track team, you might want to create a smooth rhythm to match the rhythm of distance running.

WRITING TIP FROM A POET

One way to deal with writer's block is to write free, to daydream in writing. When you write quickly, recklessly, there's often something uncovered you previously didn't know about. Another way is by reading. What others have written well can also open us up in unexpected ways.

Mark Vinz

Something to Read

In *Near the Window Tree* (Harper & Row, 1975), Karla Kuskin offers a generous selection of poems (and illustrations) as well as some prose anecdotes and suggestions for writers.

POETCRAFT: WORD CHOICE

A basic skill that good poets must master is word choice. The poet's job is to find the best words for each line of the poem that she is working on. Rarely will a poet settle for the first words that hit the page. Sometimes finding the right word might involve using the thesaurus. It might mean trying different words and listening to how they affect the poem. Or, it might mean just letting the right word come to you while the poem sits in your drawer. As Mark Twain said, the difference between the right word and the almost right word is like the difference between lightning and a lightning bug. So, don't settle for a good word when a little work and thought will give you the right word.

With my first draft of "Bingo," I was interested in getting my ideas down on the paper. Who would be in the poem? What would they do? What story did I want the poem to tell? At this brainstorming part of the writing process, I wasn't overly concerned with word choice. I knew that I could find the right words as the poem worked its way through many drafts. I focused on finding vivid and expressive words, sometimes even surprising words.

BINGO
Saturday night
Dad washed, I dried
the supper dishes
while Mom armed herself
for Early Bird bingo at seven
in the church basement:
her lucky piece
(a smooth quarter she'd won the first time out),
seat cushion,
and a White Owls box of pink plastic markers.

Dad read the paper
watched TV with me
until Mom returned,
announcing her triumph with a door slam
and a shout
"I was hot!"

Flinging her hat,
twirling out of her jacket,
she pulled dollar bills
from her pockets
before setting them free
to flutter like fat spring snow.

"Ninety-two dollars!" she squealed
as Dad hugged her off the floor.
"Ninety-two dollars!"

In bed I listened to
mumbled voices
planning to spend the money —
on groceries
school clothes
a leaky radiator —
and wished she'd buy
a shiny red dress
long white gloves
and clickety-click high heels.

Notice in the opening stanza that I used *armed* instead of
prepared, because I wanted to suggest in a single word how
seriously the mother takes her bingo. She gathers things as
though readying herself for battle. Also, I was very specific
about what she took with her.

In the third stanza, I changed *dropping* to *flinging* because I think it shows her exuberant attitude, and I added *twirling* to heighten that feeling. And when I wrote "setting them free/ to flutter like fat spring snow" (notice the repetition of the *f* sound), I wanted the reader to see the bills falling in slow motion.

I ended the poem with specific items that I hoped would emphasize the contrast between how the parents planned to spend the winnings — "on groceries/school clothes/a leaky radiator" — and what the young narrator wished his mother would buy with the money: "a shiny red dress/long white gloves/clickety-click high heels."

Even though most of the details in this poem are made up, I hoped that choosing the right words would make the scene come alive. Choosing the right words for your poem takes time and work, but it lets you speak from your heart about your subject.

Try This . . . Choose a draft of a poem that you haven't looked at for a while. Read through the poem, looking for words that do not quite create the image you were trying for. Look in the thesaurus for words that would work better. After you substitute strong, vivid words for weak, vague words rewrite the poem and read it to a friend to get his reaction to the changes you've made. Are you more satisfied with the new version? Can you see other changes that would improve the poem?

◆　◆　◆

POEMS OF ADDRESS

A poem of address is a poem that is written *to* somebody or *to* something. Although the reader will learn about the object or person that is the subject of the poem, a poem of address is not *about* that person or thing. That's an important point to keep in mind as you work on this poem. If you don't stay focused on writing a poem of address, it could easily turn into simply another poem about the subject.

When you start thinking of a subject, you might want to consider writing a poem to a person with whom you have some unfinished business. Perhaps your best friend has moved away or a treasured relative has died, and you never had a chance to tell her how much she meant to you. Or, perhaps you admire your father or one of your teachers. A poem of address is a good way to express those feelings.

A poem of address that deals with such unfinished business is:

GRANDMOTHER

O Yaya, I miss you.
I know I never enjoyed
our Sunday lunches with you
inside the dining room
not out in the sun.
You were old
I was young.
I never talked to you
unless I was forced
but I didn't know
how much I loved you.
Now you are gone
I miss our lunches,
the dining room is empty,
the chairs pushed in tight.
And the maid has left.
So have you
and I wish you'd come back
because I miss you.

KATE MANTHOS

Of course, there are lots of other reasons for writing a poem of address. Perhaps you're angry at the neighbor's dog who always starts barking on a Saturday morning when you have a chance to sleep in. You could also write to a friend who let you down or to people who pollute our rivers and air. You could also write a poem of address out of thanks. Maybe your big sister gives you a ride to the mall every now and then. Maybe your mother tries to understand without prying when something is bothering you. Or, you might address your poem to the assistant principal who believes your excuses for being late to school ... most of the time.

One of the neat things about a poem of address is that you can write one to have fun. You can write one to your favorite character in a book, TV show, or computer game. You can write one to the person who invented your favorite food (like chocolate, pizza, or frozen waffles). Maybe you want to write a poem to the snow that caused school to be called off the Friday your not-quite-finished research project was due.

Try This . . . You can also write a poem of address to an object. Such as to your armpits because they always seem to sweat at the wrong times. You could write a poem to one of our modern conveniences like the microwave oven, the computer, the VCR, or the compact disc player. Look around. There are lots of objects that you could write a poem to.

❖ ❖ ❖

SOMETHING TO READ

In *Neighborhood Odes* (Scholastic, 1994) Gary Soto writes odes (poems of celebration and admiration) about a sprinkler, fireworks, weight lifting, family photographs, and *la tortilla*.

Another book of celebratory poems by Soto is *Canto Familiar* (Harcourt Brace, 1995).

When you think you have a suitable topic, quickly jot down the reasons why you want to write a poem to this person or thing. Be specific. That list will likely wind up being the backbone of your poem. If you're angry, try to list the reasons why. If you're writing out of admiration, try to capture your feelings about your subject. Why do you admire it? If you are writing a poem on a fun subject, don't forget to be playful. You still need to be specific, but in a playful poem there is room for exaggeration, overstatement, and downright goofiness, as in this poem:

HICCUPS
Dear Hiccups,
You're the enemy of my mouth and throat.
You're the worst thing that could ever—hic—happen!
If you ever should disturb me again,
I shall toss you out of my vocal chords.
You're like hail on an angry alligator.
So, catch my drift, dear hiccups—hic—
and get far, far away.
Get out—hic—DEAR, AWFUL HICCUPS!
—hic—

                                    JENNIFER NUSSINOW

POETCRAFT: FIGURATIVE LANGUAGE

A good way to describe something—such as a person, a place, or a feeling—is to compare it to something else. We do this all the time in our conversation when we say things like, "She's as light as a feather" or "My brother is a pig." Although these comparisons are not very original, notice that they compare things that are dissimilar—a girl and a feather, a boy and a pig—and both create images that appeal to the senses. A feather is something we can see and feel, while we can see, hear, touch, and smell a pig.

You can make your writing come alive by using vivid, original comparisons. When you compare something to something else, you are using a metaphor. When you make a comparison that uses "like" or "as," that is a simile. Usually, a metaphor will be more of an attention grabber than a simile in your poem. A simile is more mild mannered. For example, notice the way I used metaphors in this poem:

REVEREND MONA
When the elders said she was too old,
Reverend Mona
surrendered her tabernacle
next to Fast Frankie's Pawn Shop
and dropped out of sight

long enough for people to wonder.
She returned,
a shaggy boat
leading a wake of dogs—
shepherd,
Husky,
mutts—
to preach on a bench
near a crescent of marigolds,
while her hounds sat,
a congregation in restless prayer.

I walked away
before our eyes could meet.

You can see how I compare Reverend Mona to a boat "leading a wake of dogs" and call her dogs "a congregation in restless prayer." Both metaphors help give the reader a sharp picture of this woman and her pack of dogs. Both comparisons would have been weaker, I think, if I had put in a "like" or an "as" and written them as similes.

Here is a checklist of a few questions to answer as you try to come up with fresh metaphors:

✓ How would you describe that object or place?

✓ How does it make you feel?

✓ What does it remind you of?

✓ What object, emotion, or experience could you compare it to?

Try This . . . In your journal, write metaphors for these things:
    a swiftly flowing river
    a calm, blue lake
    a snake coiled on a rock
    a long, dark hallway
    a partially torn basketball net

◆   ◆   ◆

Although metaphors may sound stronger than similes, similes are still a wonderful way to create vivid images in your poems. Here are a few of the similes I've used:

- eyes as dark as a night river
- with cuffs stiff
  as the ace of spades
- hands as tough and smooth
  as the underside of a tortoise
- as graceful as a coatrack
- perched on counter stools
  like gulls on a pier

As you work on your metaphors and similes, you will learn

how to skillfully make them a part of your poems. One thing to keep in mind when you make a comparison is to be certain that your reader will understand the things you are comparing. If I tell you that my new jacket is "as brown as a Siberian mud snake," that wouldn't help you visualize the color of my jacket because you have never seen a Siberian mud snake. (I know because I just made it up!) However, if I tell you that my jacket is as brown as a new football, then you get a good idea of the color.

Good similes make your poems come alive because they link two things that aren't ordinarily thought of as being similar. This is what good writing is all about: letting the readers see things in new ways.

Try This . . . In your journal, write fresh comparisons for the following:

His eyes are like _____.

Her snowball throwing is like _____.

The trees are as tall as _____.

The sun was as hot as _____.

The (cold/hot) water felt like _____.

◆ ◆ ◆

Another type of figurative language is personification, which is when you give human qualities to inanimate objects. For example, we might say, "The wind howled through the night," or "The old house groaned in the fierce hurricane."

Notice how Elinor Wylie gives the sea murderous human qualities in her poem:

SEA LULLABY

The old moon is tarnished
With smoke of the flood,
The dead leaves are varnished
With colour like blood,

A treacherous smiler
With teeth white as milk,
A savage beguiler
In sheathings of silk,

The sea creeps to pillage,
She leaps on her prey;
A child of the village
Was murdered today.

She came up to greet him
In a smooth golden cloak,
She choked him and beat him
To death, for a joke.

Her bright locks were tangled,
She shouted for joy,

With one hand she strangled
A strong little boy.

Now in silence she lingers
Beside him all night
To wash her long fingers
In silvery light.

ELINOR WYLIE

Here are some suggestions of ways to include personification in your poems:

You can use a verb that shows human actions.

Rain danced on the deserted street.

You can use personal pronouns to refer to objects.

The stream glides on her way through the forest.

You can refer to human body parts on inanimate objects.

The oak lifted its mighty arms to the summer sun.

Try This . . . Choose an object, such as a river or a car or an ice cube, and practice the different ways you can use personification to make that thing come alive. Use a fresh page in your journal so you have plenty of space to try out different possibilities. Here are two examples:

The floor seemed to remember Uncle Waldo because it groaned when he walked across the room.

The creek slid swiftly between her rocky banks.

◆　◆　◆

Figurative language is crucial to poetry. It connects large abstract ideas such as love, friendship, war, and peace to the physical world of the reader. Through figurative language the writer reveals and clarifies her ideas by evoking the senses and creating pictures in the reader's mind. Original use of figurative language offers the reader a unique view of the poem's subject, transforms an idea or experience into something memorable, allows language to work on more than one level, and helps distinguish poetry from other genres. So, collect objects, save old keys, broken calculators, seashells and driftwood, observe your environment carefully and explore how these physical "things" can stand for something beyond themselves.

Judith Steinbergh

PERSONA POEMS

In a sense, the persona poem is the opposite of a poem of address. In a persona poem you *become* another person or object and write a poem from that point of view. Here is a persona poem written by Siv Cedering:

MITTEN DREAMS
In the summer
we sleep

in the attic,
dreaming the mothballs
into snowballs,

dreaming the air cold
so your hands will want to hide
inside the soft white clouds
of mittens,
that would make your hands

feel
like paws of snow
leopards, paws of white
tigers, paws of polar
bears.

SIV CEDERING

I can imagine that a pair of mittens caught Cedering's eye one day, and she began wondering what the mittens might have to say if they could speak. I wouldn't be surprised if she then took some time to observe the mittens and think of them put away for the winter, jotting notes along the way when something struck her fancy. But, since she had no idea what mittens would think, she let her imagination kick into high gear and imagined herself to be the mittens. The result, after numerous revisions, I suspect, was "Mitten Dreams."

The persona poem is another chance for you to let your

observations and your imagination work hand in hand. Let yourself wonder about what you see around you, then let your imagination in on the fun. What might it be like to be your baby brother crawling along on the floor? Get down on all fours and check it out. The world looks quite different from down there! And while you're at it, observe him crying to get out of a playpen, sucking on his fist, or sitting in a high chair getting fed. What might he say at those times? What might he be thinking and feeling? Can you make such thoughts and feelings part of your poem?

You can write a persona poem that reflects your personality or your own feelings. If you feel unwanted and left out, for example, you might want to write a poem as a stray dog. If you feel unattractive or unappreciated, you can write a poem as an animal or a plant that is not considered appealing to the eye, like an ostrich or a dandelion. Here's a persona poem in which the young writer is a crocodile:

CROCODILE
I glide through the greeny depths
Like a slow log
An old moss covered log
I spot my prey
with just my keen eyes showing
I dive silently underwater
Swimming closer
I can see it through the water

I wait a few moments
For the perfect time to strike
Then I leap through the air
With the glare of blood in my eyes
I sink my teeth into my prey
And drag it down, down into the water
And twist it, turn it
Until it has drowned
And then I chomp on it
And swallow it down
Then I feel like it's time for a nap.

WILL CLAXTON

Try This . . . You can also write a persona poem from the point of view of a character in a fairy tale or a nursery rhyme. It's fun to pick a character that is not the main character. For instance, you could write a poem as one of Cinderella's stepsisters or as the Prince. Or, what was life like for the dish and the spoon after they ran away together? Or, what might Old King Cole have to say for himself?

◆ ◆ ◆

When you look for a subject, you might want to consider things that are near enough for you to easily observe. For example, you might want to consider writing a persona poem as wind chimes, a taillight, a tennis ball, a kitten, or a dented trash can. Before you can write a good persona poem, you need to understand your subject. What makes it what it is? For example, what makes a cat what it is? What makes it different as a pet from, say, a dog or a ferret? What might a cat think, want, fear? How can you put it all into words? That's your job as a poet. Here's what a young writer wrote after observing a pond near his home:

CALM POND

I am free to move
In summer, spring, and fall
The wind moving about me
The tiniest ripples
Moving end to end
People come to me
For their thinking place
It is calm and
I hear the slightest sound
A bird from the tallest tree
A frog swims swiftly
Through my black water
Then nestles in the soft mud
At the bottom
Tadpoles waiting for their big day

The days are getting colder
And colder each day
Now I am frozen
And I can't move
Like I used to

Now I wait patiently
For spring to come.

IAN PULLEN

When you've written some persona poems that you are satisfied with, you might try writing a dialogue poem or a poem that gives two sides of a story. What would Jack and Jill have to say about what went on while they were going up the hill? (Or about what went on after all the excitement died down?) What might your locker say to the locker next to it when nobody's around? Would it complain about the mess or the smell or the noise?

The more you look around and observe, the more subjects you will find for your persona poems. After you've written a few persona poems, your imagination will take over and let you see and hear things that will astound you. But you must be ready. Be alert. Keep your eyes and ears open. And keep a notebook handy to capture all the surprising ideas that come your way.

WRITING TIP FROM A POET

Get in the habit of quietly observing and experiencing the world around you. Trust your five senses to lead you to ideas, which are everywhere, just waiting for you to connect with them—and make them your own.

Bobbi Katz

Something to Read

Advice for a Frog (Lothrop, Lee and Shepard Books, 1995) by Alice Schertle is a dazzling collection in which the poet introduces us to a menagerie of remarkable creatures.

Narrative Poems

A narrative poem is one that tells a story. You are probably familiar with some of the long narrative poems that tell stories of fictional characters, poems such as "The Cremation of Sam McGee" by Robert Service, or "Casey at the Bat" by Ernest Thayer. You might even recall the opening lines of "The Highwayman":

> The wind was a torrent of darkness among the gusty trees.
> The moon was a ghostly galleon tossed upon cloudy seas.
> The road was a ribbon of moonlight over the purple moor,
> And the highwayman came riding—
> > Riding—riding—
> The highwayman came riding, up to the old inn-door.
>
> Alfred Noyes

When you write a narrative poem, most likely the story will be about something that happened to you. The first place you can look for a subject for your story poem is in your journal. If you've been keeping a journal, you may have a rich treasure chest of memories to consider for your poem. And, if you are attentive to what is happening around you every day, you will notice new experiences that will be worth writing about. Just make sure that you save them in your journal. Writing a narrative poem gives you the chance to capture in words the significant incidents of your life as well as the feelings that go along with them. (Of course, you might want to invent a character and write a narrative poem about him or her, or continue the story of a character that already exists, like Casey after he made the final out in "Casey at the Bat.")

Since many of our memories are connected to objects, you might find a good subject if you look through that shoe box or the bottom drawer where you keep the souvenirs of your life. That seashell might recall last summer's visit to the ocean with your family. That woven bracelet was given to you by a new friend you met at camp. A brass doorknob reminds you of the apartment you used to live in. While you can certainly write a poem describing these objects, look beyond the object to the memory or story it brings to mind.

Bear in mind that not all your memories or stories will be pleasant. Some of our most vivid memories are unhappy ones. Family members die. Neighbors move away. Friendships end. We fail at things that are important to us. Those sorts of things happen to everyone. It's a good idea to write about these memories as well as the happy ones because it might help us understand these memories or learn how better to deal with them. Also, a reader may take comfort in your poem when she recalls that the same thing happened to her. In this way, poetry can connect us to one another and offer consolation.

When you write about memories it is important to keep one thing in mind: You do not need to stick to the facts. You are writing poetry, not history, so it is all right to change some details to make your poem more dramatic or more entertaining. When we read "Cottontail" by George Bogin, we have no idea if this memory is factually accurate. That doesn't matter. The important thing is that the poem rings true when we read it.

COTTONTAIL

A couple of kids,
we went hunting for woodchucks
fifty years ago
in a farmer's field.
No woodchucks
but we cornered
a terrified
little cottontail rabbit
in the angle
of two stone fences.
He was sitting up,
front paws together,
supplicating,
trembling
while we were deciding
whether to shoot him
or spare him.
I shot first
but missed,
thank god.
Then my friend fired

and killed him
and burst into tears.
I did too.
A little cottontail.
A haunter.

GEORGE BOGIN

Suppose, for example, you want to write about the day your family pet of many years died. The incident is very vivid to you because it was such a sad day. You remember that the day was bright and sunny. However, it doesn't have to be a bright, sunny day in the poem you write about that event. You can have the day be cloudy or stormy because that adds to the mood or shows how you were feeling at the time. On the other hand, you might want to keep it a bright and sunny day because it makes a strong contrast to what you were going through. In either case, make sure you describe the day vividly. The point is worth remembering: You do not need to stick to the facts when you write your poems. Writing honestly has little to do with the facts, unless, of course, you are writing a poem that requires historical or scientific accuracy.

Try This . . . If you have trouble starting your narrative poem, you can always draft it as a prose story. Put in all the specific details, all the vivid language, all the honest feelings that will make the incident come alive. When you are satisfied that you've included what's important, read through your draft and draw a circle around every word and phrase that is absolutely essential to your story. (No fair drawing a big circle around the whole story!) It might be a word here, a phrase there. When you have drawn all your circles, copy all those words on a new sheet of paper, writing whatever was in a circle on a new line. In other words, if you circled a single word, it goes on one line of your next draft. If your next circle included several words, they go on the next line. And so on. When you have finished recopying all the encircled words, your draft will look like a poem. It isn't a poem, not yet, but it is beginning to resemble one. Now you are ready for the real work of writing: revising.

Read over what you have written. Does it make sense? Not completely. You will need to add some connecting words—but be careful to add only what's absolutely essential. You will need to cut out and change other words. Slowly, as you repeat this process, your poem will emerge. It will take time and focus, of course, but from your original mass of words will come a poem that tells your story as only you can tell it.

◆ ◆ ◆

Since setting, or place, might be important in your narrative poem, be sure to include details that appeal to your senses: sight, sound, smell, taste, and touch. I don't mean that every scene must include every sense, but make sure you include the senses that are especially important to the scene you are describing. For example, if your poem is set in your grandmother's house, you might want to include details that appeal to the sense of smell. But don't be satisfied with saying, "I recall how wonderful my grandmother's house smelled." That's vague. It doesn't create a word picture. Instead write something like, "When I think of my grandmother's house, I remember the smell of baking bread and frying chicken." Can you see how these details would give your reader a better sense of what it was like in your grandmother's house?

A good way to describe something is to use figurative language and to make comparisons. Metaphors, similes, and personification are a few ways a writer can make a scene or feeling come alive. If you're not sure how these types of figurative language work, the POETCRAFT: FIGURATIVE LANGUAGE (page 63) should help you.

WRITING TIP FROM A POET

If you are troubled or sad or lonely, pick up your pencil and tell the page about how you feel. Don't think. Just do it. Poems are made from what life gives us, good or bad. You will be surprised by what happens. You will probably have written a poem. Try it. Be a poet.

Julia Cunningham

SOMETHING TO READ

The exciting story of the world's most famous women pirates comes alive in Jane Yolen's narrative poem, *The Ballad of the Pirate Queens* (Harcourt Brace, 1995).

POETCRAFT: LINE BREAKS

There are no rules about where a line ends in free verse. But that is no reason to panic, or to simply write a poem without giving any thought to where the lines break. Keep in mind that line break is often as important a part of a free verse poem as end rhyme is to a poem written in couplets.

Basically, when you write a free verse poem, you want to keep the words that belong together on the same line. This will mean that sometimes your line will end with punctuation, but more often it will probably run over onto the next line. There are a number of reasons—too many to list here—for breaking up lines in a particular way, but consider the reasons on this checklist:

✓ You may want to emphasize a word or phrase, so you would put it at the end of a line or on a line by itself.

✓ Carrying a word or phrase to the next line may add suspense or surprise to your poem.

✓ You might want to arrange your poem so the alignment of the lines creates a desired visual effect.

✓ Sometimes it just feels right to break lines in a certain way. Don't be afraid to follow your intuition in this way.

As I've said, when you draft a poem it's okay if you write it to look like a paragraph or a chunk of prose. After you do some tinkering with sharpening the images and the language, you can simply draw slash marks where you think the line breaks should come. Then copy your poem onto a new sheet of paper, making sure that you put in your line breaks. Your poem will not be finished at this point, of course, but it's starting to look like a poem, and you can now revise it further, perhaps even changing some of the line breaks.

Try This . . . I've taken one of my poems from *Brickyard Summer* and rewritten it as a prose passage. Read through it and see if you can get a sense of which words belong together on each line of the poem. On the next page I'll show you the poem as it appeared in the book. No peeking! Try this exercise *then* look at the poem.

"Raymond"

Hair the color of pencil shavings, eyes as dark as a night river, best friend since fifth grade when he seemed to stop growing. Large enough to blacken Danny Webb's eye when he said, "Hiya, pipsqueak," the first day of eighth grade, small enough to get into the movies as a kid. At the Top Hat Cafe, gave me one play on his juke box quarters. For three nights, trusted me with the false teeth (uppers only) he found on a park bench. In The Tattoo Emporium, let me help him pick out the eagle-holding-thunderbolt he'd claim for his chest the day he turned eighteen.

RAYMOND

Hair the color of pencil shavings,
eyes as dark as a night river,
best friend
since fifth grade
when he seemed to stop
growing.

Large enough
to blacken Danny Webb's eye
when he said,
"Hiya, pipsqueak,"
the first day of eighth grade,

small enough
to get into the movies as a kid.

At the Top Hat Cafe,
gave me one play
on his juke box quarters.

For three nights,
trusted me
with the false teeth
(uppers only)
he found on a park bench.

In The Tattoo Emporium,
let me help him
pick out the
eagle-holding-thunderbolt
he'd claim for his chest
the day he turned eighteen.

Chances are you came pretty close to breaking the lines the way I did. Probably not exactly, but that's okay. We have all read poems in which the line breaks seem arbitrary. In fact, if I were to tinker with "Raymond," I could find a few line breaks that I would change. For example, in the last stanza, I would leave "pick out" on that line and move "the" to the next line to go with "eagle-holding-thunderbolt." The important thing to keep in mind is that as a poet you must have your reasons for putting certain words on certain lines in your poem. So, make sure when you revise, you pay attention to line breaks. One good way to do that is to read the poem carefully aloud because you will hear things you might miss when you read the poem silently.

◆ ◆ ◆

Finally, let me offer one more checklist you might want to use when you write a poem:

✓ Choose a topic for your poem that interests you. If you are not interested in it, there's no way you can expect your reader to be interested in it.

✓ Take the time to brainstorm freely some ideas related to the topic. See what happens.

✓ Don't settle for using "good" words in your poem. Work until you get the *right* word.

✓ Read your poem aloud, to yourself or to someone else.

✓ Find someone who will read your poem carefully and offer suggestions.

✓ Let your poem rest out of sight for a while before you look at it again.

✓ Remember: Revision means to see again. Revise with care.

Learning to write a good poem is like learning to play the piano or turn a double play. It takes practice and patience. Don't be discouraged if your early poems don't say exactly what you want them to say. The more you work at the craft of writing a poem, the more your poems will shine like diamonds. Look and listen to life with care. Practice your writing. Give yourself time to be a better poet. You will be pleased with what writing poetry can bring to your life.

CHAPTER FIVE
WHEN YOUR POEM IS FINISHED

YOU SHOULD WRITE POEMS FOR YOURSELF. BECAUSE YOU want to. Or, better, because you *have* to write poems to express the emotions you're feeling or to examine the way you see things. If you truly write for yourself, you'll be happy saving your poems in a fat folder or binder as you work harder to make better poems. You will know the satisfaction of shaping words into an engaging poem.

MAKING BOOKS

On the other hand, you might feel that you want other people to read your poems. If you have a number of poems ready to publish, you can consider putting them into a book. When you think of a book of poems, you probably think of the traditional kinds of books we are all used to reading. And that certainly is one way to publish your poems. But there are easy ways to make less formal books. The easiest way to make a book is to fold sheets of paper down the center and staple them together along the center fold. You can then print your poems or, if you have the talent, write them in calligraphy on the blank pages.

For a more professional-looking book, you can use a word-processing program to print your poems. Check the computers at your school. There is probably a word-processing or desktop publishing program installed on the hard drives. These programs allow you to select a type face and printing arrangement which will work best for your poems.

To dress up your book you might want to use a sheet of colored paper for the cover. For a firmer cover, you could use poster board or a file folder.

While a stapled booklet works quite well, a booklet that is stitched together looks even better. You will need some basic equipment and patience to create a nicely sewn book, but there are a number of helpful books that you might find in your library. For starters, you can look for these:

Book Craft, Henry Pluckrose, Franklin Watts, 1992.

Making Cards, Charlotte Stowell, Larousse Kingfisher Chambers, 1995.

Making Shaped Books, Gillian Chapman and Pam Robson, The Millbrook Press, 1997.

Making Shaped Books with Patterns, Gillian Chapman and Pam Robson, The Millbrook Press, 1995.

The Young Author's Do-It-Yourself Book: How to Write, Illustrate, & Produce Your Own Book, Donna Guthrie, Nancy Bentley, and Katy Keck Arnsteen, The Millbrook Press, 1994.

Another type of book that you can make is a concertina or accordion book, which looks just like its name implies. If you have ever folded a piece of paper so it looks like an accordion, you have the basic idea of this type of book. One of the good things about it is that it requires no equipment or supplies to hold it together. Check *Making Shaped Books* for more help with the concertina book. You can have a lot of fun with it.

MAKING CARDS AND POSTERS

One of my favorite ways of sharing new poems is to print them on bright-colored cards and mail them to friends and family. Nothing fancy, just the black letters on an orange or yellow postcard. If you feel more adventuresome — and have more talent for drawing than I do! — you can include your poem in a folded card that opens like a regular greeting card. Paint a picture on the front, and you have a thoughtful gift to send to someone special. (If you put your artwork on the inside of the card facing the poem, you can tape the card shut and write the address on one of the blank sides.) Another possibility is to use a photograph instead of artwork. Or, you can make a pop-up card, something I learned recently with my daughter. A few cuts and a fold or two, and your card will come alive in the reader's hands. *Making Cards* will be very helpful if you want to take a crack at a pop-up card.

What if your poem is too long to fit on one card? You could divide the poem into parts and send "installments," say, once a week until you've sent the whole poem. Or, you could make a poster that can be rolled up or folded for presentation.

And don't forget that you can put your poem on a poster and jazz it up with a painting or a drawing or pictures cut from a magazine. A poster can be simply a sheet of typing paper, or it can be larger, like a piece of oak tag. The bigger the poster, the more room you have for your art and the larger you can write your poem. On the other hand, sometimes bigger isn't better, especially if your poem is short.

If you've ever received a handmade gift, you probably remember the thrill of being blessed with a gift that someone special worked on just for you. Well, when you write a terrific poem and present it to someone on a card or poster, you are giving that person a gift he or she will cherish for a long time.

SUBMITTING POEMS TO A PUBLISHER

Finally, let me say a few words about submitting your poems to a magazine or a contest. Most writers will admit that they like seeing their poems in a magazine or book because it means that many people have a chance to read their work. There are a number of magazines that publish poems written by students, and you might be interested in submitting some of your work to them. But, be warned: Lots of young writers are trying to do the very same thing with their poems, so it is very competitive. You must decide to submit nothing but your very best efforts.

Where should you submit your poems? First of all, check the magazines you like to see if they accept poetry submissions. If they do, you might want to start with those magazines. If they do not, then you need to do some research. Start in the periodicals room of your local library. Find the magazines for young readers and see if they accept poetry. Read some back issues to make sure that the kind of poems you write would be appropriate for a particular magazine. For examples, some magazines consider only free verse poems. Others may only publish poems about religious themes or nature or astronomy. Don't waste your time—and the editor's time—by submitting material that a magazine would not possibly publish.

If you want a wider selection of magazines for young readers, visit a good bookstore and see what they have on their racks. If you find some promising magazines, check to see if they will send you a sample copy and a set of their writers' guidelines. Most magazines will send both, although usually for a small fee. Build a file of magazines that publish the kind of poetry that you write. And submit your poems to those magazines.

Get a copy of *Market Guide for Young Writers* by Kathy Henderson (Writer's Digest Books, 1996). It's a terrific resource if you want to submit poems for publication. A good library will have a copy, although if you are serious about submitting poems, you might want to invest in your own copy.

Once you decide where you want to submit your poems, you need to make sure that you improve your chances of having a poem accepted by following the rules for submitting poems. As I said earlier, you should send only your best poems. Make sure that you correct all grammar, punctuation, and spelling mistakes in your poem before you mail it to a magazine.

There are some special considerations if you plan to submit your poems to a contest. Each contest has its own specific guidelines and rules that you must follow. So, when you learn of a contest, send for the guidelines and make sure you follow them. Some contests may require you to pay a small fee, so make sure you are prepared to do that. A number of contests publish the winning poems in a magazine or book. If possible, you should read the winning entries to see what kinds of poems have won in the past.

Many, many writers have poems rejected by magazines and contests. But I'd suggest that you not judge the quality of your work by the opinion of a magazine editor or contest judge. Your poem is as good as you've made it, regardless of what someone else thinks about it. I know young writers who wanted so badly to have their poem published that they began to write for magazines and contests instead of writing for themselves. Don't let that happen to you. Write your poems for you. Share them with family and friends, if you like. Submit them to contests and magazines, if you like. But always remember that *you* are the one who has to be satisfied with your poems. True, you need to work to make your poems better, but if you like a poem, then the poem is successful. You have every right to be pleased and proud of your work.

A CHECKLIST OF GOOD POETRY BOOKS

Advice for a Frog. Alice Schertle. Lothrop, Lee, and Shepard, 1995.

All the Small Poems and Fourteen More. Valerie Worth. Farrar, Straus & Giroux, 1994.

American Sports Poems. Compiled by R.R. Knudson and May Swenson. Orchard Books, 1988.

The Ballad of the Pirate Queens. Jane Yolen. Harcourt Brace, 1995.

Been to Yesterdays: Poems of a Life. Lee Bennett Hopkins. Boyds Mills Press, 1994.

Brats. X.J. Kennedy. McElderry Books, 1986.

Brown Angels: An Album of Pictures and Verse. Walter Dean Myers. HarperCollins, 1993.

Canto Familiar. Gary Soto. Harcourt Brace, 1995.

Caribbean Dozen: Poems From Caribbean Poets. Edited by John Agard and Grace Nichols. Candlewick, 1994.

Celebrate America: In Poetry and Art. Edited by Nora Panzer, illustrated with works of art from the National Museum of American Art, Smithsonian Institution. Hyperion, 1994.

Classic Poems to Read Aloud. Compiled by James Berry. Kingfisher, 1995.

Cool Salsa: Bilingual Poems on Growing Up Latino in the United States. Edited by Lori M. Carlson. Holt, 1994.

Could We Be Friends?: and Other Poems for Pals. Bobbi Katz. Mondo, 1996.

Dance With Me. Barbara Juster Esbensen. HarperCollins, 1995.

The Dragons Are Singing Tonight. Jack Prelutsky. Greenwillow, 1993.

The Dream Keeper: and Other Poems. Langston Hughes. Knopf, 1994.

The Earth Under Sky Bear's Feet: Native American Poems of the Land. Joseph Bruchac. Philomel, 1995.

I Feel a Little Jumpy Around You: A Book of Her and His Poems Collected in Pairs. Edited by Naomi Shihab Nye and Paul B. Janeczko. Simon & Schuster, 1996.

The Inner City Mother Goose. Eve Merriam. Simon & Schuster, 1996.

The Invisible Ladder: A Young Readers' Anthology of Contemporary Poetry. Selected by Liz Rosenberg. Holt, 1996.

Joyful Noise: Poems for Two Voices. Paul Fleischman. Harper-Collins, 1988.

Life Doesn't Frighten Me. Maya Angelou, illustrated by Jean-Michel Basquiat. Stewart, Tabori & Chang, 1993.

Mummy Took Cooking Lessons and Other Poems. John Ciardi. Houghton Mifflin, 1990.

Near the Window Tree: Poems & Notes. Karla Kuskin. Harper & Row, 1975.

One at a Time. David McCord. Little, Brown, 1977.

The Place My Words are Looking For: What Poets Say About & Through Their Work. Edited by Paul B. Janeczko. Bradbury Press, 1990.

Poetspeak: In Their Work, About Their Work. Selected by Paul B. Janeczko. Bradbury Press, 1983.

Random House Book of Poetry for Children. Selected by Jack Prelutsky. Random House, 1983.

The Rattle Bag: An Anthology of Poetry. Edited by Seamus Heaney and Ted Hughes. Faber & Faber, 1985.

Reflections on a Gift of Watermelon Pickle…And Other Modern Verse. Compiled by Stephen Dunning, Edward Lueders, Naomi Shihab Nye, Keith Gilyard, and Demetrice A. Worley. ScottForesman, 1995.

Rich Lizard: And Other Poems. Deborah Chandra. Farrar, Straus & Giroux, 1996

Riddle•icious. J. Patrick Lewis. Knopf, 1996.

Sing a Song of Popcorn: Every Child's Book of Poems. Selected by Beatrice Schenk de Regniers, Eva Moore, Mary Michaels White, and Jan Carr. Scholastic, 1988.

Sing to the Sun. Ashley Bryan. HarperCollins, 1992.

The Space Between Our Footsteps: Poems and Paintings from the Middle East. Naomi Shihab Nye. Simon & Schuster, 1998.

A Suitcase of Seaweed and Other Poems. Janet S. Wong. McElderry Books, 1996.

Sweet Corn. James Stevenson. Greenwillow, 1995.

That Sweet Diamond: Baseball Poems. Paul B. Janeczko. Atheneum, 1998.

This Same Sky: A Collection of Poems From Around the World. Selected by Naomi Shihab Nye. Simon & Schuster, 1992.

A Time to Talk: Poems of Friendship. Selected by Myra Cohn Livingston. McElderry Books, 1992.

Turtle in July. Marilyn Singer. Macmillan, 1989.

Two-Legged, Four-Legged, No-Legged Rhymes. J. Patrick Lewis. Knopf, 1991.

Under All Silences: Shades of Love. Selected by Ruth Gordon. Harper & Row, 1987.

A Visit to William Blake's Inn: Poems for Innocent and Experienced Travelers. Nancy Willard. Harcourt Brace, 1981.

Waiting to Waltz: A Childhood. Cynthia Rylant. Bradbury, 1984.

Where the Sidewalk Ends: Poems and Drawings. Shel Silverstein. HarperCollins, 1974.

GLOSSARY

*(Terms marked with * are discussed in more detail in the text of this book. Terms in **bold** appear else-where in the glossary.)*

*ACROSTIC POEM: **free verse** poem in which the first letter of each line, when read downward, forms a word, usually the title and/or subject of the poem. For example:

> Harry
> **H**appy
> **A**nd
> **R**arely
> **R**eady to
> **Y**ell.

*ALLITERATION: repetition of the initial consonants of words. For example, *Peter Pan.*

*ASSONANCE: repetition of the vowel sounds in words. For example, the *ee* sound in *meet me.*

*BALLAD: a **narrative**, rhyming poem or song characterized by short **stanzas** and simple words and usually telling a heroic and/or tragic story. Here are the first two stanzas of "John Henry," a traditional American ballad in ten stanzas:

> When John Henry was a little tiny baby
> Sitting on his mama's knee,

He picked up a hammer and a little piece of steel
Saying, "Hammer's going to be the death of me, Lord, Lord,
   Hammer's going to be the death of me."

John Henry was a man just six feet high,
Nearly two feet and a half across his breast.
He'd hammer with a nine-pound hammer all day
And never get tired and want to rest, Lord, Lord,
   And never get tired and want to rest.

And here are the opening stanzas from "Bonnie Barbara Allan," a traditional Scottish ballad:

It was in and about the Martinmas time,
   When the green leaves were afalling,
That Sir John Graeme, in the West Country,
   Fell in love with Barbara Allan.

He sent his men down through the town,
   To the place where she was dwelling;
"O hast and come to my master dear,
   If you be Barbara Allan."

[Martinmas is St. Martin's Day, November 11.]

BLANK VERSE: poetry written in unrhymed iambic pentameter (five iambic feet per line). Shakespeare's best plays are noted for their fine blank verse. Here's an example from *Romeo and Juliet*:

Give me my Romeo, and when he shall die,
Take him and cut him out in little stars,
And he will make the Face of Heav'n so fine
That all the World will be in love with Night
And pay no Worship to the garish Sun.

CATALOG POEM: another name for a **list poem**

CINQUAIN: a five-line poem of one or two sentences of twenty-two syllables divided in this way:

line 1: 2 syllables
line 2: 4 syllables
line 3: 6 syllables
line 4: 8 syllables
line 5: 2 syllables

Here is a cinquain by Adelaide Crapsey, who is believed to have "invented" this form in the early 1900s:

> NIAGRA
> How frail
> Above the bulk
> Of crashing water hangs,
> Autumnal, evanescent, wan,
> The moon.
>
> ADELAIDE CRAPSEY

*CLERIHEW: a short rhyming poem written of two **couplets** that pokes gentle fun at a celebrity

*COUPLET: two lines of poetry that rhyme. For example:

> Listen, my children, and you shall hear
> Of the midnight ride of Paul Revere

ELEGY: a lament, a poem of grief or mourning

EPIC: a very long, heroic **narrative poem** about a great and serious subject. Examples of epic poems include the *Iliad* and the *Odyssey*, as well as *Beowulf*, a long Old English poem.

FEMININE RHYME: a rhyme of two syllables, one stressed, one unstressed, e.g., *smother/another*

***FIGURATIVE LANGUAGE:** nonliteral expressions to get across certain ideas or things more vividly. **Metaphor**, **simile**, and **personification** are examples of figurative language.

***FREE VERSE:** a poem without predictable **rhyme**, **rhythm**, or length of line or **stanza.**

HAIKU: a form of poetry that developed in Japan. A haiku usually has seventeen syllables in three lines of five, seven, and five syllables. The poet tries to capture a simple scene from nature and to convey his/her strong feeling about it. The haiku should contain a seasonal word or suggest a season. Here are two classic Japanese haiku:

> An old silent pond . . .
> A frog jumps into the pond,
> splash! Silence again.
> > > BASHŌ (1644–1694)

> Over the wintry
> forest, winds howl in a rage
> with no leaves to blow.
> > > SOSEKI (1275–1351)

***HISTORY POEM:** a **list poem** that illustrates some sort of theme that runs through at least part of a poet's life

***HOW-TO POEM:** a **list poem** that gives directions or instructions

HYPERBOLE: excessive exaggeration to make a point in a poem. For example, Lady Macbeth uses hyperbole in Shakespeare's play, *Macbeth*, when she laments,

Here's the smell of blood still: all the
perfumes of Arabia will not sweeten this little hand.

*IMAGE: a picture the poet creates with vivid words that appeal to the reader's senses of sight, smell, sound, taste, and touch

LIMERICK: a type of light, humorous poem, generally nonsensical in nature, of five lines, in which lines 1, 2, and 5 rhyme, as do lines 3 and 4. The rhythm of a limerick is equally important. The lines that rhyme also have the same rhythm, as well as the same number of syllables. For example,

A bridge engineer, Mister Crumpett,
Built a bridge for the good River Bumpett.
A mistake in the plan
Left a gap in the span,
But he said, "Well, they'll just have to jump it."

*LINE BREAK: where lines of poetry end

*LIST POEM: a poem that is based on a list or catalog of some sort created by the poet

LYRIC POEM: a poem that expresses the poet's observations and feelings and often tells of the poet's personal experiences

MASCULINE RHYME: a rhyme of one syllable, as in *click/stick*

*METAPHOR: a comparison of two dissimilar things that implies some sort of equality between the things, e.g., *My love is a blossoming flower.*

METER: the measured rhythm of a line of poetry, made of poetic units called feet, which are determined by the stressed and unstressed syllables in a word or phrase. (In the word *follow,* for example, the first syllable is stressed, the second is unstressed.) Four basic types of poetic feet are used: iamb, trochee, anapest, and dactyl. The chart below illustrates the stressed (ˊ) and unstressed (˘) syllables in each kind of foot and gives some examples:

˘ ˊ	iamb	surprise, today, apart, amaze, arrange
ˊ ˘	trochee	pretty, sunny, quarrel, water, buyer
˘ ˘ ˊ	anapest	understand, disagree, introduce, intercede
ˊ ˘ ˘	dactyl	elephant, syllable, carelessly, happily

The number of feet in a line of poetry will determine how that line is described. A line with five feet of any kind in it, for example, is called pentameter. If those feet are iambs, the line is called iambic pentameter. Here are the names of the lines:

FEET PER LINE	NAME
1	monometer
2	dimeter
3	trimeter
4	tetrameter
5	pentameter
6	hexameter
7	heptameter
8	octameter

*NARRATIVE POEM: a poem that tells a story

ODE: generally speaking, a poem that uses exalted language to celebrate a subject. Although classic odes followed a specific form and were written about formal subjects, such as solitude and a decorative Grecian urn, modern writers have written odes about more everyday subjects, such as watermelon and sneakers.

*ONOMATOPOEIA: a word that makes the sound of the action it describes. For example, *bang*.

OPPOSITE: a short poem made up of *couplets* that describes something by describing its opposite

PARODY: an exaggerated, usually humorous, imitation. My "Ten Little Aliens" is a parody of the nursery rhyme "Ten Little Indians."

PERSONA POEM: a poem in which the poet writes from the point of view of another person or thing

PERSONIFICATION: a comparison that gives human qualities to inanimate objects, e.g., *The old house groaned in the fierce storm.*

POEM OF ADDRESS: a poem that is written *to* someone or *to* something

POETIC LICENSE: the imaginative freedom of poets to break some of the rules of standard English. For example, in writing a line in an acrostic poem that begins with *x*, you might use *xciting*, *xcellent*, or *xactly.*

QUATRAIN: a poem or **stanza** of four lines

REFRAIN: a line or lines repeated throughout a poem

RHYME: the repetition of sounds at the ends of words

RHYME SCHEME: the pattern of end rhymes in a poem, described with lowercase letters to indicate which lines rhyme. A limerick, for example, has a rhyme scheme of *aabba*, which means that the first, second, and fifth lines have the same rhyme, and the third and fourth lines have the same rhyme.

RHYTHM: the basic beat in a line of poetry, the sound pattern created by stressed and unstressed syllables (see METER)

SENRYU: a poem that follows the form of a haiku, but with a humorous slant. For example:

> O, unlucky man
> while eating shiny apple
> you find half a worm
>
> PAUL B. JANECZKO

*SIMILE: a comparison that uses "like" or "as," e.g., *He is as graceful as a coatrack*.

SONNET: a fourteen-line poem written in iambic pentameter that follows a particular rhyme scheme. The English, or Shakespearean, sonnet (three quatrains and a final couplet) has a rhyme scheme of *abab cdcd efef gg* while the Italian, or Petrarchan, sonnet (an eight-line octave of two quatrains, followed by a sestet) has a rhyme scheme of *abba cddc cfgefg*.

SPEAKER: a character telling a poem

*STANZA: a group of lines of poetry, usually similar in length and pattern. Among the most common stanza lengths are:

couplet: a two-line stanza
tercet: a three-line stanza
quatrain: a four-line stanza
quintet: a five-line stanza
sestet: a six-line stanza
septet: a seven-line stanza
octave: an eight-line stanza

SYMBOL: something in a poem, e.g., a person or an object, that stands for something larger than itself. For example, a poet might use an American flag as a symbol for freedom or patriotism, or a ring as a symbol of undying love.

*SYNONYM POEM: a two-line rhyming descriptive poem with a first line composed of three or four synonyms

THEME: the underlying meaning of a poem, the idea it presents about people or about life. Although sometimes stated directly, the theme of a poem is more often suggested by the content of the poem. The theme reflects the poet's concerns or feelings about the subject.

BIOGRAPHICAL NOTES

E(DMUND) C(LERIHEW) BENTLEY (1875–1956) is best known throughout the English-speaking world for his classic locked-room mystery novel, *Trent's Last Case* (Carroll and Graft, 1991). Bentley studied to become a lawyer, but chose a career as a journalist and, for many years, wrote for London newspapers. He published a few collections of light verse. *(p. 38)*

GEORGE BOGIN (1920–1988) spent much of his life in the retail furniture business and did not begin to write until he was in his late fifties. His poems appeared in a number of magazines. A generous selection of his poems can be found in his book, *In a Surf of Strangers* (University Presses of Florida, 1971). *(p. 77)*

SIV CEDERING lived the first 14 years of her life by the Arctic Circle in Sweden before she moved to America. She is the author of 17 books, including novels, children's books, and collections of poetry. She currently lives near the ocean on Long Island, New York, where she spends much of her time painting. *(pp. 37, 69)*

WILL CLAXTON was born in Dallas, Texas, but now lives in Maine, where he enjoys soccer, drawing, running track, and skiing with his family. He was a fifth grader when he wrote "Crocodile." *(p. 71)*

JARED CONRAD-BRADSHAW wrote "How to Get Out of Homework" when he was a seventh grader at the American School of London. He and his family have returned to the United States, and Jared now goes to school in Massachusetts. *(p. 49)*

ADELAIDE CRAPSEY (1878–1914) is remembered as the person who created the cinquain. Toward the end of her life and in failing health, she wrote a volume of poems, *Verse*. After her death, Adelaide Crapsey became an inspiration for young poets. *(p. 99)*

JULIA CUNNINGHAM has spent most of her life traveling and writing but she didn't publish her first piece of fiction until 1960, when she was forty-four years old. The *Vision of François the Fox* was inspired by a visit to France. Perhaps her most popular novel is *Dorp Dead* (Pantheon, 1965). *(p. 80)*

JIM DANIELS was born in Detroit in 1956. He is the author of ten collections of poetry, including, most recently, *Blessing the House* (University of Pittsburgh Press, 1997). He has also written a screenplay and a one-act play. He lives with his wife and their two children in Pittsburgh, where he teaches at Carnegie Mellon University. He is an avid cyclist and "a mediocre but enthusiastic" softball player. *(p. 4)*

OLLIE DODGE was a seventh grader in the Shenandoah Valley of Virginia when she wrote her list poem, "When I'm Alone I . . ." *(p. 52)*

AMANDA GRANUM was a seventh grader at the American School of London when she wrote "A History of the Faulty Shoes." She still lives in London and attends ASL. *(p. 48)*

CHRISTINE HEMP lives and writes on an old adobe ranch in Taos, New Mexico. She teaches poetry and writing workshops at schools, pueblos, colleges, science laboratories, and artist colonies across the United States and as far away as Britain and Tobago. A flute and guitar player, Christine believes that music colors her poems, as do her paintings. *(p. 12)*

DAVID HUDDLE has published poems, short stories, reviews, and essays. A professor of English at the University of Vermont and at the Bread Loaf School of English, Huddle believes that naps are "an essential part of a writing life." *(p. 47)*

BOBBI KATZ has written poetry, picture books, and articles for teachers and librarians. She has worked as a freelance writer, a social worker, executive director of a weekly radio program, and editor of environmental materials. Until her retirement a few years ago, she worked as an editor and in-house writer for a major publisher. *(p. 74)*

X.J. KENNEDY began his writing career when he was nine years old and published homemade comic books to sell to his friends for a nickel. Since then he has published poems for adults as well as poems for young readers. You might want to look for *Uncle Switch* (McElderry Books, 1997), a book of limericks. Kennedy, who has five grown children, lives with his wife in Massachusetts next to a busy bicycle path and a one-cow farm. *(p. 30)*

KARLA KUSKIN, a native New Yorker, began writing early in her childhood and received much encouragement from her parents. "As far back as I can remember," she says, "poetry has had a special place in my life." She has published many books of poetry, some of which—like *Dogs and Dragons, Trees and Dreams,* and *Soap Soup and Other Verses* (Demco, 1994)—she illustrated herself. *(p. 44)*

MYRA COHN LIVINGSTON (1926–1996) began writing poetry when she was a first-year college student, and published her first poem in 1946. She went on to create an enormous body of work that includes poetry anthologies and books of her own poems for children. She said that writing was hard work, a process of "growing, discarding, and keeping only the best." *(p. 10)*

GEORGE ELLA LYON was born in the mountains of Kentucky, the daughter of a dry-cleaner and a community worker. Her first ambition was to be a neon sign maker. In addition to poetry in magazines and anthologies, Lyon has published 3 novels and 17 picture books. She lives in Kentucky with her husband and two sons. *(p. 2)*

KATE MANTHOS was born in London where she still lives. She attends the American School of London. A seventh grader when she wrote "Grandmother" *(p. 60)*, Kate enjoys writing, listening to music, and traveling.

ALFRED NOYES (1880–1958) is best known in his native England, as well as in the United States, for his ballads and romantic narrative poems. However, he also published fiction and drama in his lifetime. Although he is perhaps best remembered for "The Highwayman," his historic imagination is also apparent in his earlier books of poems, such as *Tales of the Mermaid Tavern*. *(p. 75)*

JENNIFER NUSSINOW loves dancing, skiing, and playing soccer and softball. She was in the fifth grade when she wrote "Hiccups." She lives in Maine. *(p. 62)*

EDGAR ALLAN POE (1809–1849) had a worldwide influence on literature as the creator of the detective story and other forms of storytelling, like his highly musical poems and narratives. The list of his famous poems is long, but must include "The Raven," "Annabel Lee," and "The Bells." *(p. 24)*

IAN PULLEN was in fifth grade when he wrote "Calm Pond," which is based on his exciting experiences on the 10 acres of woods and fields that surround his home in Maine. His favorite sports are basketball and base-ball, and he enjoys playing the drums. *(p. 73)*

LIZ ROSENBERG was born and raised on Long Island, New York. She has published many books for children and adults. Her most recent anthologies of poems for young people are *Earth-Shattering Poems* (Henry Holt, 1998) and *The Invisible Ladder* (Henry Holt, 1996). She works as a visiting poet and teaches English and creative writing at the State University of New York at Binghamton. *(p. 59)*

JUDITH STEINBERGH is a poet, lyricist, and teacher of poetry. She has been working with student writers of all ages for more than 25 years. Judith's books include *Reading and Writing Poetry: A Professional Guide for Teachers, K–4* (Scholastic, 1994). She co-produced the award-winning *Where I Come From, Songs and Poems from Many Cultures* (Talking Stone Press). *(p. 69)*

MARK VINZ was born in Rugby, North Dakota, but grew up in Minneapolis and in the Kansas City area. Since 1968 he has taught in the English department of Moorhead State University in western Minnesota. He lives in Moorhead with his wife; they have two grown daughters. Vinz's poems have appeared in many magazines and anthologies. His two books of poetry are *Climbing the Stairs* (Spoon River Poetry Press, 1983) and *Mixed Blessings* (New Rivers Press). *(p. 54)*

ANNE WALDMAN was drawn to poetry at an early age, and today is known as an energetic performance poet. She published her first book of poems, *On The Wing*, in 1966, two years after graduating from college. In 1974 she helped establish the Naropa Institute in Boulder, Colorado, and has been a teacher there ever since. *(p. 45)*

WALT WHITMAN (1819–1892) is best known for *Leaves of Grass*, his monumental work of free verse. The "good gray poet" was deeply affected by the Civil War, particularly by his experiences as a volunteer nurse to wounded soldiers from both sides. He lived his last 19 years in Camden, New Jersey, revising *Leaves of Grass*. *(p. 46)*

ELINOR WYLIE (1885–1928) was born in New Jersey but published her first collection of poems anonymously in England in 1912. Although her literary career was brief, it is notable for two well-received volumes of poetry, *Nets to Catch the Wind* and *Black Armour*. Her *Collected Poems* (Knopf) was published four years after her death. *(p. 67)*

INDEX

ABOUT THE AUTHOR

N.V. Edris

I DIDN'T START OUT TO BE A POET. I started out as a kid in New Jersey who had two major goals in life: to survive one more year of delivering newspapers without being attacked by Ike, the one-eyed, slobbering, crazed mutt that lurked in the forsythia bushes at the top of the hill, and to become more than a weak-hitting, third-string catcher on our sorry Little League team. I failed at both.

At that point in my life, poetry meant no more to me than George Washington's wooden teeth or the chief exports of the Belgian Congo. I was "gifted" only on my birthday and Christmas. But, by some strange twist of fate, I was lucky enough to become a writer of poetry. I wish I could name the teacher or poet who turned me around, but I can't. I suspect, however, that it was poetry itself that showed me what poetry could be. Poetry changed my life by changing the way I looked at the world. I discovered what Phillip Booth meant when he wrote that poetry "changes the world slightly in favor of being alive and being human." Poetry has become my constant companion. I can't imagine my life without it.

BOOKS BY PAUL B. JANECZKO

POETRY ANTHOLOGIES

The Crystal Image, Dell, 1977

Postcard Poems, Bradbury Press, 1979

Don't Forget to Fly, Bradbury Press, 1981

Poetspeak: In Their Work, About Their Work, Bradbury Press, 1983 (also available in trade paperback from Collier Books/Macmillan)

Strings: A Gathering of Family Poems, Bradbury Press, 1984

Pocket Poems, Bradbury Press, 1985

Going Over to Your Place, Bradbury Press, 1986

This Delicious Day, Orchard Books, 1987

The Music of What Happens, Orchard Books, 1988

The Place My Words are Looking For, Bradbury Press, 1990

Preposterous: Poems of Youth, Orchard Books, 1991

Looking for Your Name, Orchard Books, 1993

Wherever Home Begins, Orchard Books, 1995

I Feel a Little Jumpy Around You (with Naomi Shihab Nye), Simon & Schuster, 1996

Home on the Range: Cowboy Poems, Dial, 1997

Very Best (Almost) Friends, Candlewick Press, 1998

POETRY

Brickyard Summer, Orchard Books, 1989

Stardust Otel, Orchard Books, 1993

That Sweet Diamond: Baseball Poems, Atheneum, 1998

FICTION

Bridges to Cross, Macmillan, 1986

Young Indiana Jones and the Pirates' Loot (written as J.N. Fox), Random House, 1994

NONFICTION

Loads of Codes and Secret Ciphers, Macmillan, 1984

Poetry from A to Z: A Guide for Young Writers, Bradbury Press, 1994

A Scholastic Guide: How to Write Poetry, Scholastic, 1999

BOOKS FOR TEACHERS

Favorite Poetry Lessons, Scholastic, 1998

CREDITS

"What's In a Word" used by permission of the author.

"Edgar Allan Poe" by E.C. Bentley reproduced with permission of Curtis Brown Ltd., London, on behalf of the Estate of E.C. Bentley. Copyright E.C. Bentley.

"Things That Go Away and Come Back Again" used by permission of the author. Copyright 1970 by Anne Waldman.

"A History of Pets" from *Stopping by Home*. Copyright 1988 by David Huddle. Used by permission of the author.

"A History of the Faulty Shoes" used by permission of the author.

"How to Get Out of Homework" used by permission of the author.

"When I'm Alone I . . ." used by permission of the author.

"Grandmother" used by permission of the author.

"Hiccups" used by permission of the author.

"Sea Lullaby" from *Collected Poems* by Elinor Wylie. Copyright 1921 by Alfred A. Knopf Inc. and renewed 1949 by William Rose Benet. Reprinted by permission of the publisher.

"Mitten Dreams" used by permission of the author.

"Crocodile" used by permission of the author.

"Calm Pond" used by permission of the author.

"Cottontail" by George Bogin. Used by permission of the Estate of George Bogin.

"Niagra" from *Verse* by Adelaide Crapsey. Copyright 1922 by Algernon S. Crapsey and renewed 1950 by The Adelaide Crapsey Foundation. Reprinted by permission of Alfred A. Knopf Inc.

Poems by Paul B. Janeczko are used with the author's permission.

Writing tips are used with authors' permission.